DIMINISHED CAPACITY

DIMINISHED CAPACITY

A Novel

Leighton H. Rockafellow

iUniverse, Inc.

New York Bloomington Shanghai

Diminished Capacity
A Novel

iUniverse books may be ordered through booksellers or by contacting:

iUniverse
1663 Liberty Drive
Bloomington, IN 47403
www.iuniverse.com
1-800-Authors (1-800-288-4677)

Because of the dynamic nature of the Internet, any Web addresses
or links contained in this book may have changed
since publication and may no longer be valid.

This is a work of fiction. All of the characters, names, incidents, organizations, and
dialogue in this novel are either the products of the author's imagination or are used
fictitiously.

ISBN: 978-0-595-50385-8 (pbk)
ISBN: 978-0-595-49800-0 (cloth)
ISBN: 978-0-595-61484-4 (ebk)

Printed in the United States of America

Prologue

Art couldn't believe his bad luck. He had gone into business with a wimpy little shithead with a college degree. Art knew how to run a bar! Tom didn't know shit!

In six months the bar had been nothing but a money pit. It was a black hole, and Art was tired of pouring good money after bad. It was time to bring this partnership to an end.

It was early Sunday morning. The month of May had been another financial disaster. Art picked up the phone and called Tom.

"Hello."

"Tom, this is Art. We need to talk. I got the accounting from last month and I lost my ass again. I'm tired of this shit. I want to come over right now!"

Tom hesitated before he answered. "I don't think that's a good idea, Art. It's Sunday morning. I have some things to do today. This can wait until tomorrow."

Art was fuming. "Now, Tom! We talk now! I'm coming right over." Art slammed the phone down, grabbed his keys, a box of bar records, and went out to his car.

In the 20 minutes it took to drive out to Tom's house, Art turned everything over in his mind. He decided that the bar's failure was all Tom's fault. He would demand Tom's set of keys, lock him out, and have his lawyer dissolve the partnership. He would have to find someone else to qualify for the liquor license, but he was sure he could find someone with a clean record to do that for him.

Tom was looking out the living room window when Art's Lincoln pulled into the driveway. Shit! What a mistake to go into business with an illiterate, obnoxious, loudmouth drunk! There was no way the Odyssey could ever survive if Art kept coming in every day. His loud mouth, dirty jokes, and come-ons to every woman in the place drove customers away faster than Tom could get them in the door.

Tom decided that today was the day. Tom held the liquor license and Art didn't. The bar couldn't stay open without Tom, but it sure as hell could without Art. It was time to give Art the boot. Tom could see Art was headed for the kitchen door at the rear of the house. He met him on the porch.

Art was carrying a box of papers. He didn't look happy. As soon as he saw Tom he lit into him. "Do you know how much money I've lost because of you?" was his greeting.

Tom could see Art was mad. He knew Art had a temper, and he had seen him explode before. He didn't want a confrontation here at the house.

"Art, you're upset. I know things aren't going well. Why don't we both take a day to think about it, and let's meet at your lawyer's office tomorrow to discuss where we go from here?"

Art's response was predictable. "Fuck you Tom. I don't need a lawyer to tell me what to do. Give me your fucking keys. We're done. I don't want to see you at the Odyssey again!" Art stood there, glaring at Tom, his hand held out for the keys while still trying to balance the box of papers in his arms.

Tom wasn't about to give Art his keys. "I think you should leave, Art. You're upset. I'm not giving you my keys. I hold the liquor license and I'm the one responsible to the Liquor Control Board if anything goes wrong."

Tom could almost see the steam coming out of Art's ears. Art stood there glaring at Tom for what seemed like an eternity, but in reality was only about thirty seconds.

Art turned abruptly and walked back to his car. Tom went back inside the house. He watched out the window to make sure Art was leaving. He didn't leave. He didn't even get into the car. He was bending down as if he was getting something from under the front seat.

Art stood back up, turned, and started walking back to the house. Tom couldn't believe it, but Art had a gun in his right hand.

Shit! Was Art crazy enough to demand the keys at gunpoint? Laura was in the bedroom. What if the crazy bastard was going to kill them both?

Self-protection was all Tom could think about. He had an old .44 Bulldog his friend Gary had given him a while back. He had never shot it, but it was loaded, and it was in the kitchen. Tom headed for the kitchen, grabbed the Bulldog from the drawer, and met Art on the steps of the back porch. As Art came into view at the end of the porch, Tom called out to him. "Put the gun down, Art. We can talk about this tomorrow when you aren't so upset."

Art scowled back at Tom. "Give me your fucking keys you little shithead!" Art raised his right hand and began firing. Tom reacted by firing back. Tom could hear bullets whizzing over and beside his head. He kept firing until the gun would fire no more.

When the gunfire stopped, Tom was still standing. He checked his body and saw no blood. He looked out on the porch and saw Art lying on the porch, blood oozing from the back of his T-shirt. Art wasn't moving.

Just then Laura came out of the kitchen screaming. "Tom! I heard gunfire! What happened?"

Tom turned to meet her.

> She saw the smoking gun still in his hand. "Tom! What happened? Are you okay?"

Tom stepped aside and pointed to Art lying crumpled on the porch.

"Oh my god! Tom! What have you done? Is Art dead?"

"I don't know Laura. He came at me like a crazy man! I asked him to put his gun down, but he just started firing at me. What should we do?"

Laura wasn't listening. She ran back to the bedroom, crying hysterically.

Tom called his best friend Gary. Gary was a forest ranger, carried a gun for work, and in Tom's mind was sort of a cop.

Gary answered on the third ring. "Hello."

"Gary, it's Tom. You've got to come over here! I think Art's dead!"

"Tom, slow down. What happened? Where are you?"

"Gary, I'm at home. Laura is hysterical. I think Art's dead. You've got to come over here. He shot at me Gary! He was crazy! I shot back and I hit him. He's bleeding real bad, Gary. I think he's dead!"

"Tom, listen to me. Hang up now and call 9-1-1. Call 9-1-1 Tom. I'll be over as fast as I can get there."

CHAPTER 1

▼

June 3rd

Tom had never been in jail before. It wasn't a very nice place, and all he could think of was how to get out—and fast. He soon learned that the one-phone-call rule he had heard so much about on TV was meaningless; at least it was at the Pima County Jail. There was a pay phone for the prisoners to use whenever and as often as they wanted to use it. The only problem was prisoners weren't allowed to have money, so all of the calls, even local ones, had to go through the operator as collect calls. It was Sunday afternoon and Tom had waited in line for over an hour to get his turn at the phone. There were plenty of others behind him.

He was also having trouble thinking of someone who would be at home and willing to take a collect call from the jail.

Karen was the only person he could think of. He was usually able to reach her on Sundays and she would probably accept the call without question. He punched in the number from memory and held his breath as he heard the phone ring for the fourth time and prayed he wouldn't get the answering machine. Just before what would have been the fifth ring he heard Karen's voice on the line.

"Hello?"

The operator answered for Tom: "Will you accept a collect call from Tom Rogers?"

Karen was confused. She had seen Tom just yesterday when he had dropped off some receipts from his business so she could finish the bookkeeping for the month of May. He hadn't mentioned anything about going out of town, and Karen knew that Sundays were one of the busiest days at the Odyssey, Tom's sports bar. She knew that Tom and his partner, Art Mendoza liked to be at the bar on Sundays for several reasons.

They were both sports addicts and enjoyed watching the games on the big screen TVs just like the customers. They also liked to mingle with the customers, get to know them better, and keep an eye on the cash register to make sure that the college kids didn't help themselves to the receipts to supplement their minimum-wage-plus-tip income.

It was also NBA playoff season, and Karen knew that Tom and Art were hoping for good receipts, as they surely needed it. The bar had never made a profit in the six months of its existence.

"I guess so," Karen heard herself say. "Where is he calling from?"

Tom felt a knot form in his stomach when he heard Karen ask that perfectly logical, innocent question. He wanted to shout over the operator and say, Karen, it's Tom! Take the call! I'll explain! While he wanted to, he didn't. He waited for the operator who said, "The Pima County Jail."

More confused than ever, Karen responded, "OK."

The operator told them to go ahead and for the first time in six hours Tom had the attention of someone who would listen to him.

"Tom, where are you?" asked Karen.

"The Pima County Jail," answered Tom. "I need a lawyer. Can you help me find one? This phone is hard to get to, and I need to talk to someone today. Will you make some calls for me?"

"Why are you in jail? Why do you need a lawyer? What have you done?" asked Karen.

Tom thought for a second before he answered. While the prisoner phone was supposed to be secure and not monitored, Tom didn't trust it, and also didn't know who might be listening in the adjoining cells, or standing in line behind him to use the phone.

"Listen Karen. I can't say much but I'm in big trouble and I need a lawyer today. I can't stay on the line much longer because other guys are waiting to use it. I know you do books for some lawyers, do any of them do criminal law?"

"Well, yes," said Karen, "but what's this all about? What do you want me to tell them? How can they call you? It's Sunday afternoon, Tom, I probably won't be able to find anybody."

Tom was starting to get an angry look from the next guy in line. Most of the prisoners waiting for the phone wanted it to call family. They weren't at all concerned about Tom Rogers and his immediate problem of finding a lawyer.

Tom heard the prisoner behind him say: "Wait until tomorrow. They got to appoint you a lawyer at your IA and then you'll get one for free from the PD's office. Now, get off the phone so I can call my old lady!"

Tom knew he didn't have much time left to impress the urgency of the situation on Karen. He really didn't know her that well, but she was a nice person, she knew a lot of local lawyers from her work as a freelance bookkeeper, he couldn't think of anyone else to call, and he knew that in about thirty seconds the burly prisoner behind him would either reach over and press down the receiver to end this call, or push Tom out of the way and take the handset away from him. What the hell were an IA and a PD anyway? In jail for less than three hours and already he had to learn prisoner lingo!

"Tom, are you there?" asked Karen, "Tom?"

Tom was thinking as fast as he could and he knew his time on the phone with Karen had precious few moments left.

The prisoner behind him shuffled his feet, looked at Tom and said, "Get off the fucking phone asshole! I told you I got to call my old lady!"

Tom could see that mister nice guy behind him was about out of patience. He mustered up his best-polished salesman's delivery and said to Karen, "Listen, Karen, Art's dead and I've been arrested for murder. I've got to get off the phone now and I can't call back. Please call one of your lawyer friends and have him come to the jail today!"

Just as he was ending the word "today", the handset was torn away as he was shoved out of line. Now all he could do was wait and hope that Karen would come through for him.

CHAPTER 2

▼

The Odyssey wasn't much as far as sports bars go. Located on Grant Road in an old auto parts store, it was ugly from the street. The sign was crude and didn't even light up at night. The parking was in the back and the biggest TV in the place measured a scant thirty-five inches. The neighborhood was mostly low-budget apartments, gas stations, used car lots and car repair shops.

The bar had been Tom's idea. Art Mendoza had supplied most of the money to get it started. Older than Tom by thirty years, Art had led a rough life with several felony convictions to his name including marijuana smuggling. Because of his felony convictions Art couldn't qualify for a liquor license. Still involved in drug trafficking, Art needed a business for a front so the cops wouldn't wonder how he supported himself.

Art also liked young women, and a bar gave him plenty of opportunity to look at the young women customers and flirt with, as well as demand favors from the young cocktail waitresses that worked for him.

Tom and Art had met through Art's daughter Angie. Angie and Tom's wife, Laura had taken an art class together at the University of Arizona, and had developed a friendship.

It was a strained partnership from the beginning. While Art was basically a smalltime criminal, and uneducated except in the ways of the street, Tom had worked most of his life since college as a salesman. Originally from Ohio, Tom and Laura had moved to Tucson three years ago. Tom had a degree in Business Administration from Ohio State University. Like most Tucson transplants, Tom and Laura were tired of the winters and were looking for better opportunities. In their late twenties, they also wanted to get away from their parents, start a family, and have a life of their own.

Tucson looked like the perfect place. Tom was very interested in solar energy, and thought the year 'round sunny weather would make it easy to find a job selling solar energy products.

Laura was still a few credits short of her Art History degree, and the University of Arizona would be a perfect place to finish her education.

Tom found a job selling solar products and things were going just fine until Uncle Sam pulled the plug on solar tax credits. Without the tax credits as a sales tool, Tom could no longer convince his customers to buy solar just to reduce their tax bill and screw Uncle Sam by placing solar panels on their roofs. Now he had to rely on convincing them how much money they would save on their gas and electric bills.

The end of the tax credits cut deeply into Tom's sales volume. It didn't take too long for it to become abundantly clear that he was going to have to find another way to earn a living. Fortunately, while times were good, Tom and Laura had purchased a house, acquired a horse, and managed to save almost twenty five thousand dollars. Always on the lookout for an opportunity, Tom spotted the "For Lease" sign in the window of the old auto parts store on his way home from work one night. He jotted down the number and talked to Laura about it that night.

It wouldn't cost much to fix up the old store as a bar as the parts counter could work as the bar and by tearing out the shelves that had previously held parts, approximately 2500 square feet would be available for tables, a dart throwing area, and even a pool table and a video machine or two. The sports bar concept was popular, and Tom felt it would be easy to hang TV sets all over the place to promote the Sports bar theme.

The location was near the University of Arizona campus, and Tom thought that low drink prices would surely lure the college crowd. He also planned to draw on the college population for low cost employees. He would offer flexible hours and with all the apartment complexes within two miles of the old store housing mostly college students, Tom felt he had a built in customer and employee base.

The kids wouldn't mind if it wasn't the nicest place in town. As long as the TVs worked, the beer was cheap, and it was close to home, Tom was sure the place would be filled whenever the Arizona Wildcats played at home or on the road as all of the football and basketball games were broadcast locally on cable television.

The next day after art class, Laura mentioned Tom's idea to her friend, Angie. She knew Angie had worked in several bars during her college days and Laura thought she might have some ideas. To Laura's surprise Angie was not only interested, she mentioned that she and her father had been talking about opening up a bar but hadn't gotten any further than the talking about it stage. Angie mentioned that Art had some extra money that he needed to invest.

While Laura had never met Angie's father, she had often heard Angie speak of him in the glowing terms that most daughters reserve for their fathers. Laura pictured him as handsome, in his late forties or early fifties, polished, successful, and generous. Angie promised Laura that Art would call Tom just as soon as possible.

Laura could hardly wait to tell Tom the news that night. As she was in the middle of the story, the phone rang. Laura answered and a man with a very heavy Spanish accent asked for Tom.

Tom took the phone and Art Mendoza identified himself. "I hear you have an idea for a sports bar near the UofA," said Art. "I also hear you need a partner with some money."

"Yeah," said Tom, "I do have an idea. I have a place in mind and I could use someone with business experience and some money to invest. Would you like to meet so we can discuss it further?"

"Sure," said Art. "Why don't we meet tomorrow at the place you have in mind and we can look it over?"

They talked for a while longer. A time was agreed upon, Tom gave Art the address, and it was agreed that Tom would call the real estate agent and try to get him to meet them so they could enter the building for an inspection. So far, so good. This business idea was coming together nicely for Tom.

The real estate rental agent was reached that night, and he agreed to meet Tom and Art the next day at noon for an inspection. It was beginning to look like Tom's days as a solar energy salesman was coming to an end.

Tom and the real estate agent, Sam Niles, arrived at the Grant Road location at the same time, five minutes before noon. They decided to wait for Art before entering the building. Thirty minutes later they were tired of waiting, and entered.

The building was just as Tom had imagined it. It was just the right size, and not too difficult to remodel. As they were poking around inside a man walked through the back door.

"Sorry I'm late; I got held up at another meeting. I'm Art Mendoza."

Tom was a little surprised at what he saw. He too was expecting what Laura had envisioned. Art wasn't even close. He stood about five-foot, seven-inches tall and weighed at least two hundred twenty five pounds, with a huge stomach that hung over his pants. His Polo shirt had a pocket filled with a package of Lucky Strikes. The hair was black, the face was old, weathered from the sun, and bore ancient evidence of acne scars.

Tom could also see a large scar that started on the left side of Art's jaw and traveled in a jagged line under his chin and halfway down his throat. It looked to be of fairly recent vintage. He was sipping from a bottle of Corona. This was not the man that Tom thought he would meet today, and certainly didn't look like someone who had twenty five to thirty thousand dollars to invest in a business venture.

Sam Niles was similarly unimpressed. Not only did Mendoza look bad, he had a bad mouth. Every other word out of his mouth was what the Nixon Administration referred to as an "Expletive Deleted." What the hell, thought Niles, this won't be the first time I've wasted my time showing property to someone who can't even afford to buy lunch.

Niles decided to ignore Art's appearance and just show the property. As the minutes went by, both Niles and Tom realized that while crude and vulgar, Art was no dummy. He had a charming demeanor, and spoke of his successful business ventures, many of which Tom and Sam were aware of, but had no idea Mendoza was behind them as the money person.

He asked intelligent questions, said he had a lawyer on "retainer" and asked Niles to fax the listing agreement to his lawyer's office. Niles agreed to do so, shook hands with Tom and Art and left them to discuss their plans together.

Art invited Tom to lunch at the Twin Peaks bar, a country western Honky-tonk just around the corner. Art began walking towards the street and it was then that Tom noticed that Art was headed for a brand new Lincoln that was parked at the curb. Surely this beautiful new car couldn't belong to Mendoza!

"Come on," yelled Art, "let's go. You can ride with me. I just got this new Lincoln last week. It's got voice activated satellite radio, and the air will freeze your ass off."

Tom glanced at his old Mazda and was sure the Lincoln would be a better ride. As they pulled away from the curb, Art gleefully announced, "Hang on, Tom! I don't have no fucking driver's license and I can't see for shit."

By the time they arrived at the Twin Peaks two minutes later, Tom needed the bathroom a lot more than he needed a menu.

Over lunch, Art bragged about his successful businesses, and explained that the scar on his chin was from a fight in a bar that had occurred a year or so ago.

When Tom asked what had happened to the other guy Art bragged, "You don't want to know, but you ain't gonna find him to tell you about it."

If Art was to be believed, he had done everything there was to do, had been everywhere there was to be, had owned every luxury car ever made, and knew everyone that was anyone of importance in Tucson. Art's favorite subject was Art. Even so, there was a certain charm about him, and Tom found himself liking this foul-mouthed ugly man. Besides, Angie was so nice. Art had at least raised a nice daughter. He might be a blowhard, but he had cash, and he had a successful track record.

Art said he had twenty five thousand dollars that he could invest in the venture. He thought a stripper bar would be a better idea than a sports bar, but when Tom suggested that the waitresses would all be college girls, and would all wear halter tops and short shorts Art warmed up to the sports bar concept.

Besides, people liked to bet on sporting events, and there was always the possibility of some behind the scenes betting action. He would keep that to himself and not share this source of income with his new partner.

Tom didn't know it, but Art liked the thought of having numerous college age girls around him on a daily basis. He was sure he would get lucky with at least one of them. Money and power were the ultimate aphrodisiacs, and Art had both.

They decided to meet at Art's lawyer's office the next day to look over the listing, and talk about the terms of a partnership agreement.

Art was treated like Royalty at his lawyer's office. He knew everyone there by his or her first names. His lawyer had a respectable office near the courthouse, and assured Tom that getting into business with Art Mendoza was a sure ticket to success. Tom convinced himself that opening a Sports Bar with Art was the right thing to do. Besides, he didn't have any other options at the moment.

In record time, the partnership agreement was signed, the lease was signed, and Tom secured a liquor license from the Arizona Department of Liquor Control. Art never revealed his felony convictions. He told Tom he preferred to be a silent partner. Tom felt secure, knowing that it was he who held the liquor license. Art would put up the money, Tom would get the license and be responsible for the day-to-day operation of the bar, and he and Art would split the profits.

Before they were done with the remodel, Art had spent over fifty thousand dollars. This was twice what Art had planned on, but he was sure the bar would make money. Besides, Tom's wife had a cute ass, and he was planning on making a move on her when Tom wasn't looking. He was sure that Laura would find him irresistible. Art regarded this as just another benefit of partnership.

CHAPTER 3

▼

Karen wasn't sure what she was going to say but she dialed Larry's number from memory and hoped he would pick up. June Sundays in Tucson were reserved for the air-conditioned shopping malls and movie theaters or the backyard swimming pool. Larry was mowing the lawn.

The little patch of green over in the corner of the back yard served as a place for the kids to play, and a reminder of the green grass of his Indiana childhood. It was hard to make grass grow in Tucson, but Larry felt it was worth the effort.

The weather had not yet reached one hundred degrees, and everyone was waiting for the day when the "ice" would break on the Santa Cruz River. The Santa Cruz was classified as a navigable waterway, but was dry as a bone most of the year. In the winter when it rained, it would fill up, and even overrun its banks from time to time.

One of the local TV stations ran a contest every year. If you were the lucky one to guess the day hour and minute that the temperature first reached on hundred degrees, you were the winner of the official "Ice Break Contest," and a fabulous cruise plus other gifts were yours.

Karen had sent in her postcard early, as the earliest postmark was the winner in case of a tie. She was trying to remember if the date she had chosen had already passed when Larry answered the phone.

"Hello."

"Larry?"

"Yes."

"Larry, this is Karen Hargrave, I need a favor."

"Hi Karen, what do you need?"

Karen explained the strange phone call she had received a few minutes earlier.

"I heard about it on the news about an hour ago, Karen. How well do you know this guy?"

"Not too well. I do the books for his business. He's always polite, and he seems real nice, and he sounded pretty desperate. Can you go see him at the jail today?"

"How well did you know the dead guy?" asked Larry. Karen said she had never met him but thought he was Tom's partner in the bar.

Larry looked at his watch. It was already three forty five. By the time he put on some decent clothes and drove all the way over to the jail, it would be five o'clock and seven o'clock or after before he got back home. Larry had just finished a trial Friday afternoon and he was looking forward to a weekend away from the office with no clients to bug him. "Does this guy have any money?"

"I don't know," Karen lied. She knew damn well Tom didn't have any money. Karen added, "Why don't you go talk to him and find out for yourself?"

Larry considered that option. It was a murder case. It had already been on the news. Publicity never hurt any lawyer's career, and if this guy had family, maybe they could come up with the money.

Larry had already figured out that Karen was lying about Tom's ability to pay. She had volunteered that she did the books for Tom's business. If anyone would know if he had money for a lawyer it would be Karen. She also knew Larry was a pushover for a sob story. Larry almost had an out of body experience as he heard himself promise Karen he would get right over to the jail.

As he hung up the phone, he realized his wife, Maggie, wouldn't be too thrilled with the news that another Sunday afternoon had been interrupted by a phone call from the jail, and that her husband had agreed to make another jail call. He was right. She wasn't too happy about it, but she agreed he should go. Why did the major crimes always happen on the weekends? Criminals just had no respect for Larry's office hours or time with his family.

It was well after four o'clock by the time Larry showered, changed and reassured his children Larry Jr., six, and Leann, four, that daddy would be back soon and, yes he really did have to leave. The kids hadn't seen much of their father during the last two weeks because of the trial he had just finished.

Finished. Well, not really. The case of "State vs. Robert Vance" seemed like it would never be over. Vance was a pathetic kid in his early twenties hopelessly addicted to heroin. Like most junkies, he had turned to robbery to support his drug habit.

The trial had resulted in a hung jury. It was the second hung jury in the same armed-robbery case Larry had been living with for almost a year. Unfortunately, the flat fee that Vance's parents had paid that seemed so large a year ago had long ago been spent. Larry wasn't counting on two full-blown trials, and now the prospect of a third loomed large. There was no backing out now.

The rules of ethics required him to stay on the case. Christ! When he went to law school he was never told that he would have to be a slave and work for free. And here he was driving over to the jail on Sunday afternoon to see some guy who was accused of murdering someone and probably didn't have any money for legal fees. He would be full of promises to be sure, but short on cash.

Larry promised himself that this time, it would be different. No money, no lawyer. He owed that much to Maggie and the kids. He already had his share of cases appointed by the court where the fees were pitifully small. He didn't need another freebie.

He was wishing he had just said no when Karen had called as he crossed the bridge over the Santa Cruz headed west toward the jail. He looked to his right. No Ice. No water. Just a dry riverbed littered with trash looked back at him. Some lucky housewife would soon be winning a luxurious cruise, as the temperature would probably crack the century mark within the week.

He parked his Toyota Camry in the parking lot and approached the lawyer's entrance with his driver's license and Arizona State Bar Card in hand.

Pima County made it easy for lawyers to visit their clients at the jail. The lawyer's entrance could be used twenty-four hours a day, seven days a week. With picture ID, and a current State Bar Card, any lawyer could visit any prisoner at any time. Of course the jail kept a record of who came and went including time of arrival and time of departure.

He presented his State Bar Card and Arizona driver's license, and his business card to the deputy working the desk. The deputy was absorbed in the Lakers and Spurs playoff game he was watching on a portable TV set on his desk. "Law Offices of Larry H. Ross" read the card. He only had one office but somehow the plural "offices" sounded better.

The deputy handed him the paperwork to fill out and went back to watching the Lakers and the Spurs battle in the final of the playoff games. The deputy took a break from the game to look over the paper work, handed Larry a plastic tub to dump his wallet, car keys and other personal items into and then picked up a microphone on the desk and intoned, "Take Rogers, number 5771 to interview room two; his lawyer's here to see him. Hey," said the deputy, "you a Lakers fan?"

Larry looked around and realized the comments were directed at him. "Yeah, Kobe's the greatest."

The deputy smiled. He liked anyone that professed to be a Lakers fan, even if he was a lawyer.

"Come on, Rogers," barked the corrections officer, "let's go. Your lawyer's here to see you."

Tom was filled with a sense of relief. He had called Karen at about three thirty and it was now after five o'clock. While that wasn't a long time, sitting in a jail cell had a way of making time pass very slowly. He knew he could count on Karen. Now he had someone to talk to—someone to get his messages to the outside world without relying on the overused prisoner telephone. As Tom entered interview room two, he liked what he saw.

Larry stood to greet him. "Hi Tom, I'm Larry Ross."

Tom had heard Karen speak of Larry and had remembered reading about a case Larry had won. Larry was about five foot eleven inches tall, one hundred eighty pounds, and Tom guessed him to be about thirty-five years old. He had a full head of brown hair, a pleasant smile and confident mannerisms.

Larry was doing his own assessment of Tom. Larry judged Tom to be about thirty, five foot eight inches tall, about one hundred eighty-five pounds, dirty blonde hair with a receding hairline, and big brown eyes that gave him the look of a cuddly puppy dog. This was certainly not what one would expect a murderer to look like, Larry thought to himself.

As Tom sat down on one of the two chairs in the room, Larry handed him a business card. "Karen Hargrave asked me to come and see you. Why are you in here?"

Tom was surprised by Larry's direct approach. Before he said too much he thought he should cover some preliminaries. "Thanks for coming Mr. Ross," said Tom. "Are you going to be my lawyer?"

"I don't know," said Larry, "how much money do you have?"

There! He'd said it! Get the money thing out of the way first! The money thing was what made Larry's job so difficult. There was no end to the people that needed his help. However, Larry had an office to run, and a wife and two kids to support. He didn't work for legal aid or the public defender's office, and no one would pay his bills for him.

Then he remembered a wisecrack he'd heard at a legal seminar a few months ago. He decided to use it on Tom to show he was serious about the money issue. "I can only worry about one thing at a time. Now which would you rather I worry about, your case, or my fee?"

Tom looked surprised by the blunt approach. "I've never been in trouble before. I don't know how these things work. Aren't we supposed to talk about the case?"

Larry replied, "Tom, if you can't pay me, there's not much else to talk about. When's your IA? Has the PD called?"

There were those initials again. Tom didn't want to sound stupid, but he felt he had to ask. "What's a PD? What's an IA?"

Larry realized he was using legal shorthand in his discussion with Tom. He decided to give Tom a thumbnail sketch of the Rules of Criminal Procedure and how the criminal law process worked in Pima County.

He explained that a PD was a Public Defender, a lawyer on the county payroll appointed by the court to represent Tom if he couldn't afford his own lawyer. Larry went on to explain that the Public Defender's office handled eighty-five to ninety percent of the criminal cases in Pima County. Private lawyers, like Larry, that were either privately retained by the client, or appointed by the court if the PD's office had a conflict of interest, handled the remainder.

An IA was the Initial Appearance, the equivalent of an arraignment where the charges were read, a plea of not guilty was entered, and information was obtained from the defendant regarding his finances to see if he qualified for a Public Defender. A PD was always present at the Initial Appearances and was always appointed subject to the paper work being reviewed; a defendant could always get his own lawyer later. Few defendants had private lawyers appear for them at the IA's, as they had to be held within twenty-four hours of an arrest. That didn't give much time to find a lawyer, especially since most defendants were in custody.

IA's were held seven days a week, three hundred sixty-five days a year at nine A.M. at the Pima County Courthouse in a room specially equipped with video monitors as the prisoners appeared from the jail via monitor. The issue of bail was also decided at the IA's. Bail was rarely granted in murder cases. By law, preliminary hearings had to be held within ten days of the IA for prisoners in custody.

Following the preliminary hearing, the magistrate determined if there was probable cause to bind the defendant over for trial. It was a loose standard, and the magistrate could even rely on hearsay evidence as long as it was reliable hearsay. After being bound over, the defendant would have a formal arraignment where conditions of release would again be considered and a trial date would be set.

Trials for defendants in custody had to be held within one hundred twenty days of the initial appearance, or within ninety days of the arraignment, whichever was less. While this was to give the defendant the right to a speedy trial, it also meant that the lawyer didn't have much time to mount a defense.

"Does that mean I'll have to stay in jail until the trial?' asked Tom.

"Tom, I'll do what I can to have you released, but I already told you that bail is rarely granted in murder cases," said Larry. "I'll request a bail hearing, call your friends as witnesses, and inform the court that this is your first involvement with the criminal justice system. If you put your house up as collateral on the bond, there is at least a chance that the judge will decide you're not a flight risk and may release you.

"I would prefer to have you out, so I don't have to come over here every time I want to talk to you. Having you on the outside will also help me as you can go with me to witness interviews. I'm not hopeful I can get you released pending trial, but I'll do everything I can."

"Okay", said Tom, "I would like you to appear for me tomorrow morning. What do you think this is going to cost?"

A reasonable question, to be sure, and one that was difficult to answer, as the cost depended primarily on the number of hours it would take to complete the case. This was also difficult to estimate, as Larry wasn't yet aware of any of the facts. There was also the issue of expert witnesses. Most criminal cases required the use of an expert in some field. Experts didn't come cheap. Larry was also acutely aware of the armed robbery case that had already been tried twice and probably would be tried a third time. He thought long and hard before he answered the question.

"Tom, the county attorney will probably charge you with first degree murder. If there are aggravating circumstances, they could ask for the death penalty. All I know is that someone is dead, and you were arrested, so I have to assume the worst. Before you tell me anything about this case you need to be aware that your life may be at stake. Do you understand that?"

Tom nodded and Larry continued. "My hourly rate for major felonies is two hundred dollars per hour, plus expenses, plus the cost of any expert witnesses that may have to be hired. To do a good job, I estimate at least two hundred fifty hours will be needed, and I would guess ten to fifteen thousand dollars will be spent for expert witnesses."

Tom did the math in his head. That was sixty-five thousand dollars! Where would he get that kind of money? He didn't have it. He and Laura had been living on savings for the last six months and were down to their last ten thousand dollars. They had some equity in their house, but that wasn't anything he could get to fast. He could ask his dad for the money, but Ralph Rogers was anything but wealthy. Laura's parents were comfortable, but they had never been generous.

"Mr. Ross, I have ten thousand dollars in a savings account that my wife can get to you tomorrow. We can put our house up for sale. I can ask my dad and Laura's parents for some help but I don't think I can come up with sixty-five thousand. Will you appear for me?"

Larry's role as tough guy was over. It was the 3rd of June, and he had office rent to pay, and car payments and a mortgage payment to make next week. He also was broke. He always had his share of cases, but criminal clients were notoriously bad about paying their bills. The thought of ten thousand dollars being deposited into the general checking account of the Law Offices of Larry H. Ross suddenly seemed quite appealing. Besides, Larry had never let money get in the way of taking a case that sounded like a challenge. Why should he start now? He convinced himself that the money thing would work its way out. While he had vowed to be tough on the money issue this time around, Larry liked Tom, and wanted to help him. Larry smiled at Tom, and stuck out his hand.

"That's a good start, Tom, Give me your home phone number so I can call your wife after I leave here, and let's talk about what happened today."

Tom was relieved. For the next two hours he told Larry of his relationship with Art Mendoza, and the events that led to Art's death that morning in Tom's driveway.

It was an amazing story. Larry knew he had taken on a tough one. If Tom had been truthful, it might even be a winner. Tom could also be facing the death penalty. Larry had never handled a potential death penalty case before. It was almost 8 p.m. when Larry got home. Maggie was getting the kids ready for bed. Larry was relieved that she wasn't upset that he was later than expected. Every trial lawyer needs an understanding wife. Larry had one of the best.

"Are you going to take the case?" asked Maggie.

"Yep," was Larry's short answer.

"Does he have any money?" was her next question.

Larry frowned. "Come on Maggie, you know I always take care of that. I'm going to call his wife right now, and I should have the first ten thousand in the bank by noon tomorrow."

That was good news. It was also the same amount Larry had been paid for the armed robbery case, but she was sure this one couldn't possibly turn out to be as drawn out as that one.

Larry went to the master bedroom where he kept a desk, a reading lamp, telephone, fax machine and a computer. He didn't like to work at home, but sometimes it was necessary. He punched in the number Tom had given him, and got the answering machine on the fifth ring. Larry frowned. He was hoping to reach Laura and reassure her that Tom was all right. He also wanted to tell her about the IA tomorrow morning. He was going to ask her to bring her bankbook so she could make the first ten thousand dollar payment.

He wondered where she could be when it dawned on him that the Rogers' home was the scene of a murder. The Sheriff's Office probably had yellow tape all around the perimeter by now with Sheriff's deputies on duty, and forensic examiners combing the grounds for physical evidence. Laura had probably been forced to leave her own home.

There wasn't any point in going over there tonight. It was already past dark, and the deputies would never let him past the yellow tape without proof that he represented Tom and that wouldn't happen until tomorrow morning at the IA when the magistrate filled out all the carbon forms and gave Larry his yellow copy.

There was nothing more he could do tonight. He hung up without leaving a message on the machine. He hoped that Laura would be advised by the police of the hearing tomorrow morning and that she would be there.

CHAPTER 4

▼

Tom and Laura's house was nestled in the foothills of the Tucson Mountains on the Northwest side of town. Built in 1977, it was a low ranch style house with three bedrooms, two baths, a living room, kitchen, breakfast nook, and a two car detached garage.

Back in the seventies, developments outside the city limits required lot sizes of one acre or more as the county had no central sewage system, and every home required its own septic tank and leaching field. The rocky ground required space for the leaching field to work properly.

The developer had platted two-acre lots promoting a mini-ranch atmosphere with wide-open spaces. Most of the residents had horses. Until recently the streets were still gravel. Mailboxes stood at the side of the road so the mail carriers could deliver directly from the mail jeep.

The Rogers' home was situated on the lot so that the house was cocked in a Southeastern direction to take advantage of the City light views from the living room and master bedroom. The garage sat off to the North side and behind the house itself.

Tom and Laura had been in the house since February of the previous year. A horse pen, shade for the horse, a small shed for tools, tack, feed and supplies, and a training arena had been built behind the garage for Laura's horse.

They had also put in a pool; complete with solar heat, the collector panels standing proud on the roof of the garage with a southern exposure to maximize solar collection capabilities.

A covered porch ran the length of the rear of the house. Oleander bushes had been planted by the previous owner at the edge of the porch to shield the house from the afternoon sun coming out of the western sky. Oleanders were easy to grow. They were thick, bushy, and required little water or maintenance. They were as high as the roofline of the house when Tom and Laura moved in. Tom had pulled out a few to make a sidewalk from the back porch to the pool. He left the others in place.

The house was on a corner lot. Avenida Grande ran east and west to the north side of the property. Avenida Aguilar ran north and south to the east side of the property. A gravel circular driveway connected the two streets and ample parking in front of the house and garage was also covered with gravel.

Tom and Laura rarely used the front door, usually exiting from the kitchen out to the porch, and then walking north along the Oleander lined walkway to the garage. They would enter the house along the some path.

An evaporative cooler or "swamp box" provided cool air in the summer. Hot water was solar.

The house was still in the county, about five miles outside the city limits. Planes were rarely heard as the house was far removed from the Tucson Airport and Davis Monthan Air Force Base. The obnoxious City Police Helicopter rarely left the city limits, and with no major streets nearby, sirens could only be heard from a distance.

Nights were peaceful. The stars were bright, and the city lights of Tucson twinkled. Coyotes would howl, owls would hoot, and occasionally the smell of skunk would be faintly present.

Javalinas would roam at night and eat the flowers from the pots, so Laura had learned to use large pots the Javalinas couldn't reach into, and put chicken wire around her small garden to keep out the pigs and the rabbits.

The two-acre lots gave a feeling of spaciousness, but also prevented neighbors from getting to know one another. Tom and Laura didn't know anyone in the neighborhood other than by sight.

James Weber lived across the street and a little to the West of Tom and Laura on the North side of Avenida Grande. He had built a two-story house to maximize the city light views from his second story that peeked over the roofline of Tom and Laura's house. From the sun porch outside his master bedroom, Weber had a full view of the North side of the Rogers' house, including the driveway and garage.

Weber had never met Tom and Laura, but he recognized them by sight, and by the cars they drove. He had watched them move in, and had seen them come and go since. He saw the name "Rogers" on the large mailbox by the street. He knew they had an Avenida Grande address even though the front of the house faced Avenida Aguilar. Their address was 6178 W. Avenida Grande. His was 6183.

He knew Tom drove a brown Mazda 626 and Laura had a yellow V.W. Rabbit. They had a horse and two Old English Sheep Dogs that barked way too much to Weber's liking, but he had never complained about it to anyone other than his wife, Glenda.

On Sunday, June 3rdrd, Weber picked up his Sunday newspaper from his driveway about seven A.M., made some coffee, and went upstairs to the sun porch to enjoy the morning, his coffee, and his newspaper. It was about seven thirty when he saw a Lincoln arrive and park on the north side of the house. He saw a short, fat, Mexican man exit the car and walk towards the back porch carrying what looked like a file box.

Weber wasn't spying, he was just being observant. At about eight o'clock, Weber was in his kitchen re-filling his coffee cup and talking to Glenda when they both heard what sounded like muffled firecrackers, a dozen or so, going off. A few seconds later, they thought they heard a woman screaming. They both looked out the front window and saw nothing.

About ten minutes later, Weber was back on his sun porch with his newspaper and his coffee. As he put one section of the newspaper down to pick up another, something from the Rogers' driveway caught his eye.

The Mexican man he had seen earlier carrying the box was now on his hands and knees crawling towards Avenida Grande. Weber stood to get a better look. The man was wearing jeans and a white T-shirt. The T-shirt had a big red blotch on the back near the right shoulder blade area. The man looked like he was hurt. As Weber was deciding what to do, he saw Tom Rogers emerge from the South East corner of the garage carrying an ax.

He saw Rogers cautiously approach the man, who by now, was almost at the edge of the street. As Rogers came up behind him, the man attempted to stand up. He turned to his right as he did so. He saw Rogers lift the ax and deliver not one, not two, but three blows to the man's head just as he would if he were splitting firewood. He continued to watch as Rogers dropped the ax, and walked back to the house.

Within seconds, Weber was on the phone dialing 9-1-1. He took his cordless phone from the bedroom and walked back out to the sun porch to watch the Rogers' driveway as he continued to give information to the 9-1-1 Operator.

He reported what he had seen, and gave the address of the Rogers' home to the operator. He was aware the call was being recorded so he tried to remain calm and not get hysterical. He watched *Cops* and *Rescue 911*on TV and he always thought the real 9-1-1 callers sounded stupid. He wasn't going to sound stupid when this tape got played back in court!

The operator wanted him to stay on the line and assured him that help was on the way. She asked if the man in the driveway was moving. He told her that he wasn't.

A few minutes later, the sheep dogs ran up to the man as he lay in the driveway and began sniffing at him. He heard Rogers call to the dogs. He watched Rogers walk up to the man, pause and look around as if to see if he was being watched. Weber ducked down behind the railing a bit, as he didn't want to be seen. Rogers was holding a blanket.

Rogers placed the blanket on the gravel driveway and spread it out flat. He then rolled the man onto the blanket, folded the blanket around the man and began dragging the man towards the garage. Just as Rogers disappeared around the corner of the garage he saw a Nissan pickup pull into the driveway and park in front of the garage. A man got out. He recognized the pickup and the man. He had seen him come and go from the Rogers' house many times before over the past year or so.

Weber felt like he was in a dream state as he watched these events unfold in front of him. He kept talking to the 9-1-1 Operator, reporting everything that he saw as he saw it. She asked him for the license plate number on the Nissan but he was too far away to read it. She asked him for the license plate number on the Lincoln but again, he was too far away and the car was parked so that he couldn't see the rear bumper, he could only see the side and the top of the car.

About fifteen minutes after he placed the 9-1-1 call, he saw the first of three sheriff's cars approaching north on Avenida Aguilar, lights flashing, sirens blaring. An ambulance appeared a short time later. Weber said goodbye to the 9-1-1 Operator, and went downstairs to tell Glenda what he had seen.

Glenda was in the driveway, as she had heard the sirens coming up the street. She had gone out to look, thinking that someone's house might be on fire as sirens were rarely heard in this neighborhood and she didn't even think police. She was surprised when she saw the sheriff's cars pull into the Rogers' driveway across the street from where she was standing. She and James watched as Rogers and the man who had arrived in the Nissan pick-up approached the Sheriff's deputies. The Deputies had guns drawn, and were barking orders at Rogers and his friend. They watched as both men put their hands up, and leaned against the patrol cars as they were ordered. In all the years of peaceful living on Avenida Grande, Sunday morning had never been as exciting at this.

CHAPTER 5

▼

Sunrise comes early in Tucson in June, and Larry didn't have to set his alarm clock from the middle of May to the middle of September. As soon as the sun came over the Rincon Mountains, the roof of the house would start to creak from the temperature warming the roof, and Larry would be wide-awake.

He woke up at five A.M. on Monday, June 4th. He slipped on his running shorts and a T-shirt, laced up his Nikes, and hit the street for his usual three-mile jog. He was usually back home by five thirty, and the newspaper would be waiting for him in the driveway. The morning jog gave him time to think, and plan his day.

He had an important one today. He had the Rogers IA at nine o'clock. He had two motions in two different courtrooms at ten o'clock, and a new client for a personal injury case coming in at one thirty. He also had a stack of mail left over from last week that he hadn't had time to look at while the armed robbery trial was in session. When he left the office Friday night there were at least twenty-five phone messages in his e-mail box.

He had meant to come in on Saturday, but he didn't. Larry, Jr. had a T-ball game that morning, and he decided that was more important than the office. The office would always be there, and he could work seven days a week if he wanted to. He didn't want to work that Saturday. He did want to see his son play T-ball.

The game was well worth the effort. Larry Jr. hit the ball well off the tee, and was never thrown out at first. Playing at second base, Larry Jr. had also fielded well, and made a successful throw to first that the first baseman even managed to hold on to. He and Larry Jr. celebrated with a strawberry Sundae at McDonald's on the way home.

Then for some insane reason, he decided to wash and wax Maggie's Suburban. That took most of the rest of the day. Larry Jr. "helped," as did Leann. He put the kids in charge of the great "french-fry find." The interior of a Suburban frequented by small children was a magnet for french-fries and other fast-food debris. By the time they were finished they had found thirteen old french-fries, six plastic straws, twelve straw wrappers, five plastic cup lids, two packages of ketchup, one twelve-ounce cup, and two empty bags.

Larry had forgotten how many square feet of paint there were on a Suburban, but once it was finished, it looked great.

The boat was next. It had been sitting in the garage all winter. He usually had been out on the lake by now, as the weather was warm enough. He'd just been busy, and decided this was the weekend to get the boat and the Suburban all slicked up so he could show them off next weekend at Lake Roosevelt.

A new wax product recommended by a friend cut right through all the old water spots on the boat and made the diamond gloss fiberglass finish shine like new. He had ordered some new pull toys to pull the kids around the lake on behind the boat and he was looking forward to using them.

In reality, the T-ball game, the Suburban, and the boat were therapies. The physical exercise felt good, and he could at least step back and see what he had accomplished. It was a good feeling, and he decided he would stay away from the office on Sunday too. He made it all the way to Sunday afternoon before being interrupted, and he was thankful for that. Now it was time to get back to business.

He walked through the back door of the office at seven thirty, started the coffee, and turned on his computer. He went to the form file and pulled up the fee agreement for criminal cases. Criminals had a nasty habit of forgetting the terms of their agreements with their lawyers and were very good at filing bar complaints against the lawyers who were trying to help them. A written fee agreement left no room for argument, and clearly set forth that Larry made no guarantees regarding the outcome of the case. It also set forth the range of sentence, and possible fines for the charge against the client.

He had to get out the criminal code to look up the range of sentence for first-degree murder, and winced when he entered: "life imprisonment, possible death penalty if aggravating circumstances present."

After scanning the monitor to make sure everything was entered properly on the form, he hit the print command, and waited while the laser printer printed out a crisp new fee agreement, personalized for Tom Rogers. He planned to take this with him to the courthouse and after his motions, visit Tom at the jail to collect his signature.

While Larry lived on the East side of town in the Tanque Verde Valley, he kept his office downtown. He was renting an old house about three blocks from the Superior courthouse and directly behind the City Court Building. Federal Court was about four blocks away, and the jail was just a ten-minute drive. All of the major banks kept branches downtown, and the majority of the time Larry could walk to just about anywhere he needed to go during the day.

The old house was only about twelve hundred square feet, but it was just perfect for his practice. He had covered parking in the back for himself and his secretary, and the house was air-conditioned. He had a private office, a reception area that doubled as his secretary's office, a bathroom, a small conference room that also doubled as a library, a kitchen, and an extra office that was often used by a part-time law clerk or secretary, depending on the need. He had it nicely furnished, the carpeting was new, and the paint was fresh. He was very proud to call it his.

Larry's secretary, Cindy Morrow, had been with him for about a year. She was thirty-one, blonde, leggy, busty, and commanded the attention of men wherever she went. Twice divorced, she had three girls ages seven, eight, and nine. Her redeeming quality was her ability to type one hundred ten words per minute and make it perfect on the first try. She was also a whiz with computers, and could make them work almost at will.

She had an annoying habit of being late for work, and going home early, especially when Larry was in trial. As far as she was concerned, if she didn't have anything to type, she didn't have anything to do. It was so easy to put the phone on the answering service and pick up the messages in the morning. She failed to realize that having someone to answer the phone during business hours was actually important.

Maggie had been telling Larry to get rid of Cindy for the last several months, but the thought of getting someone else with another set of problems wasn't very appealing. When it came right down to it, Larry was willing to put up with her bad habits because she could type better than anyone in town, she never complained if her check was a day or two late, and the clients liked her. He liked her, too.

He knew Maggie was a little jealous of Cindy's good looks, but she had nothing to fear. Cindy was an employee only. Larry and Maggie had taken an oath to be true to each other until death, and they had two wonderful kids. Larry wasn't about to jeopardize his stable loving marriage for a meaningless dalliance with a good-looking woman.

Karen Hargrave came in on Wednesdays to do the books. She also did payroll on the 15th and the 30th. Larry didn't let Cindy touch the checkbook, or make any deposits. Larry made most of the deposits, and Karen wrote most of the checks. It was a nice arrangement for Larry. It kept his overhead low, but provided the professional service that he needed.

Cindy was supposed to be at work by eight thirty, but never made it before nine o'clock. Larry had thought about moving the start time to nine, but then realized that would mean she would show up at nine thirty. It was eight thirty-five, and Larry was typing an e-mail message for Cindy when he heard the back door open, and a woman's footsteps walk across the tile in the kitchen. Could it be Cindy was turning over a new leaf and starting the week right by coming to work on time?

"Larry?"

He recognized the voice. It was Karen. It wasn't Wednesday, the 15th, or the 30th. He wasn't expecting her. "In here Karen," he called.

The footsteps came closer and soon Karen was in the doorway. "I talked to Laura last night, and I thought I'd better tell you what she told me before you go to the IA," said Karen.

Larry was glad to hear that Laura had been in touch with Karen. That meant she would be at the IA. "Make it quick, Karen. I need to finish this e-mail message to Cindy and it takes a few minutes to get over to the courthouse. I don't want to be late."

"Tom's dad flew in late last night. He and Laura are going to meet you at the courthouse. His dad's really worried about him, and he wants to talk to you."

Larry finished the e-mail message as Karen was speaking. He pushed the mouse arrow to send, clicked, got confirmation that the message had been sent, stood up from his desk and said,

"Let's go. Why don't you come along?"

Karen agreed.

Larry was thrilled that not only Laura, but Tom's dad, as well, would be at the IA.

It was eight forty-five as Larry and Karen left through the back door, locked up, and left. Cindy was going to have to find another Monday for her new leaf. She was already fifteen minutes late.

As they walked through El Presidio Park towards the courthouse, Larry thanked Karen for thinking of him when Tom needed help. He also thanked her for coming down this morning. He told her he had not been able to reach Laura last night.

She wanted to know if Tom had really killed someone. Larry told her that he had. But, he had a good self-defense argument and Larry was hopeful the County Attorney would eventually accept a plea to manslaughter with no recommendation as to sentence. With some luck, Tom might not spend too much time in jail. On the other hand, if the case went to trial, anything could happen, and Tom might even be facing the death penalty.

Karen couldn't believe what she was hearing. The Tom Rogers she knew was a kind, gentle man with boyish charm. He couldn't possibly be a murderer. They climbed the steps from the park to the bridge over Pennington Street, and entered the courthouse. They went directly to the video arraignment room on the first floor.

Larry spotted a young woman and a man in his sixties standing in the hallway. It had to be Laura, and Tom's dad. Larry approached: "Excuse me, are you Laura Rogers?"

Laura responded, "Yes."

"Hi, I'm Larry Ross. I'm an attorney. This is Karen Hargrave. Karen got a call from Tom yesterday afternoon from the jail and Karen asked me to go see Tom. Karen said she talked to you last night. Thanks for being here."

Laura had never met Karen, but she knew who she was. They had spoken on the phone numerous times. She also knew that Karen did bookkeeping for many lawyers and she, too, had called Karen for a recommendation for a lawyer for Tom. Right now all Laura could think about was Tom.

"Mr. Ross. I'm so worried about Tom. Did you see him yesterday? Is he alright?"

Larry chose his words carefully. Laura looked traumatized. He didn't want to add to her misery.

"He's shaken up, and he's worried about you, but he's fine." Larry then looked at the older man. "Are you Tom's father?" he asked.

"Yes, I am. Ralph Rogers. Thank you for helping my son."

Larry looked at his watch. It was one minute after nine. The proceedings would be starting soon, and he needed to fill out some forms. "We'd better get inside," said Larry. "They'll be starting soon, and they let the private lawyers go first if they get the paperwork filled out."

He smiled at Laura and Ralph, turned, pulled open the door and held it for them as they entered the video courtroom. He helped them find a seat and then walked up to the clerk, told her whom he would be representing, and she handed him the paperwork and a clipboard.

"Oohhh, a murder case! How exciting!" she said as Larry took the clipboard from her.

Larry held his index finger against his lips and quietly said, "Sshhh, his wife and father are sitting back there."

The clerk giggled a little, shrugged her shoulders and whispered, "Sorry!"

Larry was just finishing the forms when the door opened and Magistrate Andrew Dorgan walked into the courtroom.

"Please rise," said the clerk.

Before anyone could even react and stand up, Dorgan was on the bench telling everyone to be seated. He was not a pretentious man. He had been doing Initial Appearances and arraignments for so long they were routine, and he wasted no time on formalities.

Larry stood and walked the paperwork over to the clerk, who handed it to Dorgan.

He looked at it for a moment and then said: "Good morning Mr. Ross. I see you're making an appearance for Mr. Rogers."

"Yes sir!" said Larry.

"OK," said Dorgan, "the monitor is on. Mr. Deputy, please bring Mr. Rogers to the camera," Dorgan said to the video camera hanging from the ceiling and pointed in his face. It took about a minute before Tom appeared on screen.

"Mr. Rogers, can you hear me and see me on your monitor?" asked Dorgan.

"Yes," Tom answered.

"Good. Now listen carefully. This is not the time for you to say anything other than to answer yes or no to my questions and I'll not ask you anything of an incriminating nature. Do you understand?"

"Yes," answered Tom.

The video recorder was running. These proceedings were video recorded and not taken down by a court reporter with a stenograph machine. While important, they were routine, and nothing of any consequence ever happened. If it did, the video recorder was there as a memorial of what had taken place.

"I have Mr. Ross here. He says you want him to be your lawyer. Is that true?"

"Yes," Tom said again.

"Good. He's a fine man. You've made a good choice."

Larry smiled. It was nice to get a compliment from a judge, especially when your client, his wife, and his father were listening.

Dorgan continued. "Mr. Rogers, the charge is first degree murder with special aggravating circumstances. The death penalty is a possibility here. Do you understand this?"

"Yes," Tom said weakly.

"Set the preliminary hearing for June 14 at nine thirty, before Judge Easton. Does the county attorney have a recommendation on release?"

Deputy County Attorney Bill Riggs stood. "Yes, Your Honor. This is a special circumstances case. The victim was bludgeoned to death with an ax. We recommend no release under any circumstances."

Dorgan raised his eyebrows and looked at Larry. "Counselor, what's your position?"

Larry felt sick to his stomach, and his knees were beginning to buckle. Bludgeoned to death with an ax! Shit! This isn't what Tom had told him yesterday. He could hear Laura gasp in the background. The seconds ticked on.

"Mr. Ross! Your position?"

Larry finally spoke. "Mr. Rogers has no criminal record. He has close ties to the community. His wife and his father are in the courtroom. He is not a flight risk. He and his wife own a home that they are willing to pledge to the court for bond. He owns a business. We would request that he be released on ten thousand dollars bond, the house to be used as collateral on the bond. If I am going to be able to adequately defend Mr. Rogers, I need him out of jail so that he can assist me with his defense."

Dorgan looked at Riggs. "Mr. Riggs, your reply?"

Riggs stood and buttoned his jacket nervously. "We object to a release under any terms, Your Honor. This is a special circumstances case."

Dorgan looked over Larry's shoulder towards Laura and Ralph Rogers. Larry couldn't believe it when he heard Dorgan say: "Bond will be set at twenty five thousand dollars cash, or collateral with proof of the collateral's value by appraisal. Upon posting of bond, the prisoner is to be released from custody forthwith."

Riggs began to object.

"Mr. Riggs, sit down. I've ruled, and you're not going to change my mind! Mr. Ross?"

Larry looked up. "Thank you, Your Honor." There wasn't any else he could say. Dorgan had just handed down a miracle.

"Mr. Rogers? Can you still hear me?"

"Yes sir!" said Tom in a clear voice.

"Good. I just set your bond at twenty five thousand dollars. As soon as it's posted, we'll let you out."

"Thank you," was Tom's reply.

Riggs couldn't believe what had just happened. What was Dorgan thinking?

Dorgan was thinking that Tom Rogers didn't look like the typical dirtball prisoner that came before him everyday. He had already retained private counsel. He had a support system in the courtroom in the presence of his wife, and father, both of whom were well dressed, and looked to be upstanding citizens. Ross was probably right. He wasn't a flight risk, and in this day and age of computers, anyone who tried to get away never stayed free for very long.

Bond was supposed to be some assurance that the prisoner would appear for trial. Even persons charged with first-degree murder were entitled to the presumption of innocence. Defendants in custody had a hard time meeting with their lawyers and assisting with their defense, just as Ross had said.

He also recognized the victim's name on the information sheet. Dorgan had been on the bench for over twenty years, and Mendoza had appeared before him numerous times on various charges. Aggravated assault was Mendoza's stock in trade. He was always getting into a fight with someone over something. Maybe this time he had met his match.

Tucson was still a small town in many respects. The criminal legal community was especially small. Everyone knew everything about everyone else. Dorgan knew that Mendoza was a mean, nasty S.O.B. and he had probably provoked the situation that had led to his death. Just a year or so ago, Mendoza had appeared on an aggravated assault charge. Dorgan remembered that when he appeared on the video screen, his face had been cut badly. He had heard later that the victim in that case had subsequently been beaten senseless by unknown persons, had left town, and had refused to testify against Mendoza. The county attorney had no choice but to dismiss those charges.

Everyone, including Dorgan, suspected that Mendoza had arranged for the second beating and had made it clear to the victim that if he wanted to live, he had better not testify. Of course there was no proof that Mendoza had been involved in the second beating.

He also knew of Mendoza's drug-trafficking conviction—Once a trafficker, always a trafficker. The money was just too good to pass up, and criminals never thought they would get caught, even when they had been caught before.

Finally, Dorgan knew that Larry Ross was persistent and sooner or later would probably get Tom released. He decided to give them both a break by setting bond now at a reasonable amount and saving Larry the trouble of filing a motion, and calling witnesses. Rogers would show up for trial. Dorgan was sure of that. Larry's time would be better spent in preparation of Tom's defense and there was no need to chew up valuable billable hours in a bond hearing. Besides, setting bond was within his discretion, and there wasn't anything Riggs or even the County Attorney himself, Mr. Steve McNair, could do about it. He had ruled, and that was that! He called the next case.

Larry left the courtroom in a hurry before Dorgan had a chance to change his mind. He stayed just long enough to get his yellow copy of the paperwork proving that he was Tom's lawyer and setting the conditions of Tom's release. He had not expected it to be this easy.

Laura, Karen, and Ralph Rogers followed him out of the courtroom. As far as they were concerned, Larry Ross was the greatest lawyer in the world. He had just accomplished the impossible with just one sentence. Imagine the magic he could work at a trial!

Larry looked at his watch. It wasn't even twenty minutes after nine, and he had already moved a giant step forward in having Tom released from jail.

"WOW," said Larry to his captive audience, "I didn't expect that. Now, where do we get twenty-five thousand dollars?"

Ralph volunteered that while he wasn't rich, he had saved the proceeds from his deceased wife's life insurance policy when she had died seven years ago. He thought the original fifty thousand dollars was probably close to seventy-five thousand, or more by now. He said he would call the bank, and have them send the funds. He liked this young lawyer, and wanted him to represent his son. Even the judge had said Larry was a good choice.

The banks opened at ten o'clock. By then it would be past noon in Ohio. Larry looked at Ralph and said: "I have two hearings upstairs that I have to get to so I can't go to the bank with you. There's a Bank of America Branch just across the street. I think you and Laura should go over there as soon as the bank opens. Offer to transfer the funds from your Ohio Bank to The Bank of America. If they'll do it this morning, ask them for a cashier's check in the sum of twenty-five thousand made payable to the Clerk of the Superior Court, and have them note on the check: 'Bond CR 345723,' then meet me right here at about eleven. We'll walk right across the hall to that room over there and give the clerk the check and the release papers. The clerk will give us a receipt for the bond money and will prepare an order with the official court seal on it ordering the sheriff to release Tom from custody. Once I have that, I'll drive over to the jail and get him out. If you can get that cashier's check this morning, I'll have him on the street in time for lunch."

Karen volunteered to take them to the bank.

Larry gave them the yellow copy of the terms of release to make sure the right CR (criminal) case number would be printed on the check. Ralph was impressed with this young lawyer. He certainly knew his business, and he didn't waste any time.

"What about you, Mr. Ross, don't you need a check too?"

Larry was about to tell Ralph that could wait until later but then decided to go for the gold. "I told Tom yesterday that I estimated this case would burn up forty to fifty thousand dollars in legal fees plus ten to fifteen thousand in expert witness fees. The most important thing right now is to get Tom out of jail. Why don't you see how much is in your Ohio account, and if there's enough left after posting the bond get another check payable to me for fifty thousand." Fifty thousand dollars! He had never gotten a retainer anywhere close to that. He sounded so important to himself. He had asked for the money just like it was no big deal. He waited for Ralph's response.

"I'll do better than that, Mr. Ross. I'll transfer the funds, pull out the bail money, leave one thousand dollars in the new account to keep the bank happy, and have a cashier's check made payable to you for the balance."

Larry couldn't believe his ears. Yesterday, he wasn't sure how he was going to pay the rent, and today it was beginning to look like he might deposit the biggest legal fee in his career into his anemic bank account. He decided to be bold and push it one step further. "Thanks Ralph, I really appreciate that. Karen is my bookkeeper. My office account is maintained at the same Bank of America branch you're going to. Karen can call my secretary from the bank to get my account number and they can just do a direct deposit from your new account to my existing account. You don't mind helping out on this, do you, Karen?"

Karen smiled and answered: "Not at all. I think that's a really good idea. It will save Ralph the fee for the cashier's check, and it doesn't make much sense to give you a check just so it can be deposited right back into the same bank. Is it okay with you Mr. Rogers?"

"Makes sense to me," said Ralph, "let's get over to the bank and quit wasting time, I want my son out of that jail today, and I want Mr. Ross to know he's going to get paid for all of his work."

Larry looked at Ralph and said: "Thanks Ralph, and please, call me Larry. And Ralph. It's only nine twenty-five, and the bank doesn't open until ten. It's getting hot out there. The bank isn't going to open early just for you. You might as well have a seat right here in the hall and wait until just before ten and then go across the street."

They shook hands. Larry turned to catch the elevator to the fifth floor for his ten o'clock motion and Karen, Ralph, and Laura sat down to watch the clock.

The elevators in the courthouse were always crowded on Monday mornings. This morning was no exception. Larry squeezed his way in. Just as the doors were closing, a hand from the outside reached in the door and tapped the bumpers that told the door to open again. It was Ray Martin, the prosecutor from the Vance armed robbery trial.

"Good morning Larry," said Martin, "Good win last Friday."

Larry was annoyed. "I wouldn't call a hung jury a win. Why don't you guys just give up and leave my poor innocent client alone?"

The other lawyers in the elevator chuckled to themselves. Martin was County Attorney McNair's Chief Criminal Deputy. He wasn't known for walking away from a prosecution just because two juries couldn't come to a unanimous decision.

Martin gave Ross a long hard look. Just then the elevator stopped at the fourth floor. "Come on Larry, take a walk with me."

Larry looked at his watch. It wasn't quite nine thirty, and he didn't have another appearance until ten. What the hell! Maybe it was good news. He got out on the fourth floor with Martin. Martin spoke first.

"McNair and I had a little meeting this morning at eight about your boy Vance. McNair doesn't want to spend any more tax dollars on this one. We're going to move for a dismissal of the charges. I assume you won't be objecting."

Larry looked down at his feet for a moment, and then looked Martin right in the eye and said, "And deprive my client of the right to have his good name cleared by a jury of his peers? Of course I'll object!"

Martin knew Larry was joking. "Yeah right. Vance is a convicted felon with a nasty heroin habit. He's got a name all right. Dumb shit! That's his name. You tell that little puke that when he gets out on his current probation violation for dropping dirty urine, he'd better find an honest job, because we'll be watching his ass. He got lucky this time. Next time he won't, and there will be a next time. There always a next time with these assholes."

Asshole was a term of art in criminal law. It was preserved for the not-so-beloved criminals that forever came through the system. Pathetic assholes would be more accurate, but that would sound too sympathetic.

"Thanks Ray," said Larry. "I'll be sure to tell him that. I won't leave out a word, especially your carefully selected terms of art."

Ray turned and said as he was leaving, "We'll file the motion today and fax a copy to your office. We'll get you next time!"

Yeah, Larry thought. Next time. Ray would probably be assigned to the Rogers' case. At least he knew his style: Tough, and always prepared. Larry let Ray get on the elevator by himself and decided to take the next one. He didn't feel like staring at elevator walls with Ray and they didn't have anything else to talk about at the moment.

Larry wondered if Ralph would be able to get the money transferred this morning. He was going to have to do something real nice for Karen and her husband Mark. He couldn't pay a referral fee. That was against the rules of ethics. However, as a part-time employee, he could ethically pay a small bonus. She was overdue for one. He hadn't given her a bonus of any kind in the three years she had been doing his books, and she had never raised her rates.

Another dilemma. How much was enough to properly say 'thank you' and not enough to feel like he was running up against an ethics problem? He would have to worry about that one later. Right now, he had to get up to the fifth floor, check the calendars to see where his cases were on the lineup, and decide which courtroom to go to first.

He was first on the list in Judge Donner's courtroom and fifth on the list across the hall in Judge Anderson's courtroom. He told Anderson's bailiff that he would be across the hall in Donner's courtroom, as he was first on the list over there. The bailiff assured him it would be okay as Anderson had some sticky motions on the docket in front of Larry's. It would be ten thirty, at least before his case was called. Larry went back over to Donner's courtroom, and waited for His Honor to take the bench.

Robert Donner was young for a judge. A classmate of Larry's at the UofA College of Law, Donner had worked in the County Attorney's Office for eight years before his appointment to the bench by the governor. He had played all of his cards right, connecting with the right Political Party, and influential people within the Party. He was also quite capable, and was one of the lead criminal deputies at the time of his appointment.

On the bench for less than two years, he had asked for and received permanent assignment to the criminal bench. During that time, he had been assigned some high-profile cases, and had handled them well.

He ran a tight courtroom, and treated both sides fairly. He knew the law, so there was no bullshitting the judge. On the other hand, if you were right on a legal issue, he would rule in your favor, even if it meant cutting a defendant loose on a technicality and being called soft on crime by the newspaper the next day. He didn't care what the newspaper said. What was right was right. He was the judge.

He didn't have to run for election against anyone but himself. Every four years, the voters in Pima County would vote "yes" or "no" for the judges up for retention that year. No one had ever been non-retained in Pima County since the appointment system had been voted in by referendum in 1975. It gave the judges a real sense of security to know they could make unpopular decisions and not risk losing their jobs over it. Once appointed, a judge could pretty much stay as long as he wanted, at least until the mandatory retirement age of seventy. Judges were paid just under one hundred thirty thousand dollars per year, and were fully vested in the State Retirement System after twelve years. It was a good job, and Donner enjoyed the job, as well as the prestige.

As usual, Donner entered the courtroom at ten o'clock straight up. "Please rise," intoned George, his bailiff, as George ceremoniously rapped the gavel three times. All in the courtroom stood and waited for Donner to make his way to the bench.

"Be seated please," intoned George again as Donner took his seat. Donner picked up a file. "State vs. Grant. Mr. Ross, this is your motion to take the deposition of witness Gloria Santa Cruz. What's your position?"

Larry stood, buttoned his jacket and addressed the court.

"Your Honor, Miss Santa Cruz is an eyewitness to the crime my client is accused of committing. She gave a statement to the police that is filled with inconsistencies. She refuses to speak to me. The county attorney has offered to allow me to informally interview her in their office, but I want her under oath so I can have a transcript of what she says, and have that transcript to use at trial in case she tries to change her story again."

"I understand that the Rules of Criminal Procedure only allow for depositions in circumstances where the defendant cannot obtain the information any other way. I also understand that this motion is solely within the court's discretion. I would ask that you exercise that discretion and order that I be allowed to take her deposition under oath before a court reporter as soon as possible. Trial is scheduled in four weeks, and I need time to test the validity of her alleged "eyewitness account." State vs. Bowie is authority for my position. Thank you, Your Honor."

Funny as it might seem, depositions under oath could be taken in civil cases by merely sending out a notice of deposition to the opposing side, and subpoenaing the witness to appear. Failure to appear as ordered was considered civil contempt of court, and an arrest warrant could be issued for the person who failed to appear. Civil cases usually involved matters of money only. Criminal cases involved issues of life, death, and restriction of civil liberties; yet a court order was necessary before a deposition could be taken.

The Rules of Criminal Procedure required the lawyer to attempt an interview, and if that failed, had to request that the county attorney assist in setting up the interview. Witnesses were never anxious to talk to defense counsel. The defendant's lawyer was usually viewed as contemptuously as the defendant himself. "I've said everything I have to say to the police, go talk to them," was the usual reply Larry got for an interview request.

To make it worse, the interview couldn't even be tape recorded without the permission of the court. This turned the lawyer into a witness as to what was said, or not said. It was a terrible system, and Larry hated it. He liked his witnesses under oath and "on the record", especially if they were squirrels like Santa Cruz. She was a South Sixth Avenue hooker, and Larry doubted the reliability of her "eyewitness" account.

Deputy County Attorney Linda Jenson appeared for the state.

"Miss Jenson, what's your position on this?" asked Donner.

Jenson stood. "Your Honor. We have offered Miss Santa Cruz for interview in our presence. We don't think that circumstances exist warranting the expense of a deposition. Perhaps we can tape record the interview, and have a notary in the office put her under oath. That would accomplish the purpose of memorialized testimony that can be relied on at trial, and will avoid the expense of a court reporter."

Donner looked at Larry. "Mr. Ross, Miss Jenson's suggestion seems like a logical one. You'll have your witness under oath, and you'll have a tape recording of the interview. Depositions are common in civil cases, but not in criminal cases. Unless you can give me a real good reason why you need that court reporter, I'm inclined to enter an order in line with Miss Jenson's suggestion. Do you want to be heard further?"

Larry wasn't stupid. The judge had just told him what he was going to do and it was a good compromise position for the county attorney to take. Having won, it was time to be gracious and thank the county attorney for her cooperation.

"Your Honor, I agree that Miss Jenson's suggestion will accomplish my purpose. I would ask that you so order, and include in that order that the interview take place this week. Friday morning at nine A.M. at Miss Jenson's office would be perfect with me."

"Miss Jenson," Donner said, "is Friday at nine all right with you?"

"Yes, Your Honor." was her reply.

"Very well," said Donner as he turned to his courtroom clerk. "So ordered. Betty, get that typed up today for my signature so Mr. Ross and Miss Jenson will have a formal order they can rely on. Is there anything else?"

"No, Your Honor." was the simultaneous reply from Jenson and Ross.

"You're excused," said Donner. He was calling the next case as Larry and Jenson left the courtroom.

"Thanks Linda," Larry said in the hallway. "What made you change your mind?"

"Good sense." Said Linda. "We know that Donner is inclined to grant these motions, and we just don't have any budget for depositions. We were more concerned about the expense of the deposition than the process itself. Tuck that into your brain for next time. Ask nicely, and you won't even have to file a motion."

"Fair enough," said Larry. "Thanks for the tip. See you Friday at nine. I'll bring doughnuts."

Linda Jenson smiled, said goodbye and rushed off to her next motion. Larry walked across the hall to Judge Anderson's courtroom.

Anderson must have had some no-shows that morning as he was just calling Larry's case as he walked into the room. It wasn't quite ten fifteen. It was a garbage motion, but Larry had to be there. One of the detectives in State vs. Porter was going to be on vacation during the week set for trial. Porter was out of custody so it was no big deal. Detectives had lives too. The State needed a short continuance. It would be included in allowable time between arraignment and trial if Larry objected, but he didn't plan to object.

Vance was over—FINALLY! A good compromise had been achieved in State vs. Grant, and this motion was a no-brainer in State vs. Porter. Now if he could collect his fee in Rogers, and get Tom out of jail, the morning would be a complete success.

He rode down the elevator alone humming "Celebrate" by Kool And The Gang in his head.

It was only ten twenty five when he got off the elevator on the first floor. As he turned the corner to go to the benches to wait for Laura, Ralph, and Karen, they were already coming through the metal detector. As they walked toward him he could tell they didn't look happy.

"Hi," Larry said cheerily. "How did it go at the bank?"

"Not too good." was Ralph's reply. "They require a forty-eight hour wait until they will let me draw funds on the new account. I talked to the bank manager in Columbus, and authorized transfer of the entire account to the Bank of America branch across the street. The local bank manager says they require a forty-eight hour wait."

"How much did you transfer?" asked Larry.

"All of it," said Ralph.

"Okay. How much was that, Ralph?" Larry asked again.

"Seventy eight thousand, two hundred fifty six dollars and seventy three cents," was Ralph's reply.

"Okay," said Larry. "I guess we'll have to wait until Wednesday or Thursday to get Tom out of jail. If the bank says you have to wait forty-eight hours, then you have to wait forty-eight hours."

Ralph looked at Laura, and then looked back at Larry. "Isn't there something you can do, Mr. Ross? I can't stand the thought of my son spending another night in that jail. Bad things happen in jails. What if he gets raped or beaten?"

Larry wasn't happy about this either. He was counting on making a deposit to his account today so he could pay the first of the month bills. He didn't want to appear desperate, and wasn't about to ask Laura for the ten thousand dollars she and Tom had left in their savings account. He wanted to play the part of the successful, confident lawyer. He certainly didn't want to send a signal to Ralph or Laura that his fee was the most important thing in his life.

The bills could wait a day or two. Tom was expecting to get out of jail soon, and would want to hear from him today. Visiting hours were in the evening on Tuesday from five to seven thirty and in the afternoons on the weekends from one to three thirty. Larry could go see Tom at any time. Larry decided he should drive to the jail and let Tom know what was happening.

"Look, Ralph. I know you're disappointed. We made great progress today. I never expected bond to be set today at a level that was within reach of anyone's ability to pay. We'll get Tom out of jail this week. It just isn't going to happen today. He'll be all right. I've never had a client raped or beaten in the jail. I'll drive over there right now and tell him what's going on. We're a lot farther along than I had ever hoped for."

"You're sure there's nothing else you can do today?" Ralph asked again.

"I'm sure," Larry said. "What hotel are you staying at?"

"Why?"

"I'll call you after I see Tom at the jail, and let you know how he is. You had a long trip last night, and I'm sure you're tired. Go back to the hotel, take a nap, and I'll let Tom know what's happening. You can see him tomorrow during visiting hours between five and seven thirty. On Wednesday, the funds will be available, and we'll get him released. It's okay."

"I'm at the Holiday Inn, right across from the community center. Room 235. I'll wait for your call."

"Okay, Ralph. I'll need that yellow sheet back for the jail," said Larry. Ralph handed it back to Larry.

They shook hands. Larry assured Laura he would call her too. She gave him a friend's phone number, as she still couldn't go back to the house. Karen said she would go back to the office, and let Cindy know Larry was going to visit Tom at the jail.

"That's okay, Karen. I've got to go back to the office to get the car," said Larry. "We might as well walk back together. Your car's there too."

"Sure thing," said Karen.

Laura and Ralph left the courthouse to go to the Holiday Inn, and Larry and Karen walked back to the office. It was just eleven A.M., and already the temperature reading on the display on the Tucson Federal Tower was ninety-four degrees. Larry loosened his tie, and took off his jacket. Some kids were skateboarding in El Presidio Park, even though there was a City Ordinance against it. Today just might be the day that the ice would break on the Santa Cruz River.

CHAPTER 6

─────────────── ▼ ───────────────

When Larry and Karen got back to the office, the air conditioning felt cold and refreshing. Just a ten-minute walk in the heat had made them sticky and uncomfortable.

The weather was going to get a lot worse before it was going to get better. Cindy reminded Larry of his one thirty appointment with the new Personal Injury client. She had called the client that morning to reconfirm the appointment she had made for Larry last week while he was in trial.

It sounded like a good case, and Larry could always use a good case. The client said she would keep the appointment. Cindy had also made a three thirty appointment for a new divorce case. Larry hated divorce work, but it helped pay the bills, and it wasn't terribly difficult. It was just terribly aggravating and emotional. The clients were always carrying a lot of baggage, and looking for someone to unload it on. They looked at Larry as a shrink, priest, and lawyer, all wrapped in one package. Cindy also had some good news.

Jack Bailey had sent a check to pay for his last drunk driving case: Thirty-five hundred dollars, and no cents, it said on the check. Bailey was a fairly successful real estate agent who had a bit of a drinking problem. This was the third time Larry had handled a DUI for Bailey in seven years. So far, Larry was batting a thousand. Three arrests, three trials, no convictions. He probably wasn't doing Bailey any favors by getting him off, and the public was not being served by leaving Bailey behind the wheel of his Cadillac. But then Larry was a lawyer. He wasn't a social worker.

The settlement check on the Morris case had also come in: Twenty-five thousand dollars plus costs of one thousand five hundred dollars would help a lot.

Larry had been expecting the check for two weeks. The insurance company was headquartered in Illinois, and supposedly the check had been misrouted and had to be re-issued. The Morris's were beginning to think Larry had taken the money for himself. Clients were like that. Larry had asked for a letter from the insurance company to confirm that the delay was their fault. Larry's fee was on third of the twenty five thousand, plus one thousand five hundred in costs reimbursement he had advanced while the case was being processed. Cindy had made a five o'clock appointment for the Morris's to come in and sign the settlement papers, and pick up their check. He didn't have the Rogers' money, but he did have a pretty good start on the month.

Since she was there anyway, Karen agreed to stay and fill out the deposit slips, prepare the settlement ledger for the Morris case, and pay the bills today instead of Wednesday. Larry decided he had better get to the jail and talk to Tom, since he had to be back in the office for his on thirty appointment.

As he drove to the jail, he called Maggie on his cell phone to give her the good news about the Bailey check and the Morris settlement check finally arriving. He also told her he was real close to getting the largest legal fee he had ever earned in his ten-year career. They agreed to go to San Diego for a week in July. Larry said he would bring his trial calendar home that night so they could pick out a week. They also agreed to try to make it to Lake Roosevelt for the weekend. Maggie said she would call the Roosevelt Lake Resort to see if she could get a room for Saturday night.

As Larry pulled into the jail parking lot, he noticed Alan Gimble's car. It wasn't hard to notice. It was a bright-red bathtub-Porsche kit car resting on a Volkswagen chassis—flashy, but without substance. Just like its owner. Gimble and Larry had been partners for a short while. They had met while handling a case where Larry had one defendant and Gimble had the other. They had won over unlikely odds. They had also had fun doing it.

Practicing law alone can take its toll. It's hard to get away for a vacation. Motions get filed, and have to be responded to while you're gone. Sometimes, you are required to be in two places at once, an impossible task even for the most accomplished trial lawyer. It's also nice to have someone to bounce things off of once in awhile. Two heads were often better than one.

The partnership had ended at Larry's insistence five years ago. Gimble thought he was a real hot shit criminal lawyer. He managed to get his share of high profile cases, but most of his clients ended up in prison. Gimble's win-loss record was abysmal. He was a supreme egotist. He thought he was smarter, and better looking than everyone else. He wasn't.

Gimble was also a liar. During the life of the partnership, Gimble was always taking money from the partnership account without telling Larry. He would do it by taking a check from the back of the checkbook, cashing it, and then making up some cock and bull story at the end of the month.

One time, Alan even had the balls to buy his brother a car, and wrote the check from the partnership account. He said his brother was going to get a loan from his credit union, but being the deadbeat that he was, of course he never did. It wasn't like the partnership was swimming in money. Did Gimble really think that the firm had an extra eight thousand dollars just lying around that wouldn't be missed?

Finally, Larry had enough of his crap, closed the account, gave half of the remaining money to Gimble, and announced it was over. Ever the sore loser, Gimble refused to leave the office they shared together. Larry wasn't about to leave.

Both of them had signed the lease, and he knew Gimble would never pay the rent. There were still three years left on the lease. They stayed under the same roof together for a year after the partnership dissolved. True to form, Gimble was always late with his share of the rent. Also true to form, Gimble went out of his way to be a pain in the ass.

Larry finally paid him five thousand dollars just to have him leave. The day Gimble moved out was like liberation day. Larry swore he would never have another partner. It was a struggle to pay the rent all by himself on an office that was twice as big as it needed to be, but it was worth it to be rid of Gimble.

Gimble was also nosy, and a gossip. He just had to know everyone else's business. He was a world-renowned authority on just about any topic, or at least he thought he was. He really did know something about just about everything. He was also full of bullshit. His mouth was just as big as his balls, and they were huge. Gimble would say anything, and do anything to be the center of attention. Larry hoped they wouldn't see each other at the jail. Gimble would be full of questions about why Larry was there, and whom he was there to see.

It wasn't meant to be. As Larry approached the lawyer's entrance, Gimble was just coming out to the parking lot. Gimble stuck out his hand.

"Hi Larry! How 'ya been? How's Maggie, and the kids?"

Larry looked at Gimble in wonderment. How could this little prick act like he was Larry's best friend?

"Hi Alan. They're fine. Excuse me. I'm in a hurry. I have a client to see, and I have to be back at the office by one thirty."

Gimble didn't take the hint. He wanted to talk.

"If you're here to see Tom Rogers, I think you'll be disappointed."

"Why is that, Alan?" Larry couldn't figure out what Gimble was talking about. How did he even know Rogers was his client? What did Gimble know that Larry didn't?

"Because he just hired me!"

Larry couldn't believe what he had just heard. Surely Alan was playing head games with him. He loved to do that to people. Besides, Larry had entered a formal appearance for Rogers just a couple of hours ago. He had persuaded Dorgan to set bail at a reasonable amount. What the hell was Alan talking about?

"That's right!" said Gimble as he stood there grinning at Larry, "I just had him sign a fee agreement. Would you like to see it?" Alan reached into his jacket pocket and pulled out a wrinkled fee agreement. He handed it to Larry. Larry looked at it. He read the words, but couldn't comprehend them. Gimble had agreed to represent Tom all the way through trial for a flat fee of ten thousand dollars.

Larry wanted to grab Alan by the throat and strangle the life out of him. Away from Gimble for five years, and still getting fucked by the little turd! How could this have happened? There was no way Gimble could do a good job for ten thousand dollars! Expert witnesses would cost at least that. He wanted to tear up the agreement, and shove it down Alan's throat. He didn't do either. He calmly handed the fee agreement back to Gimble.

"Where do you get off meeting with my client behind my back you little shit?"

Gimble recoiled. "Whoa there partner. He's not your client until you get him to sign a fee agreement. I have one. Do you?"

"Don't call me partner you lying sack of shit. Who asked you to come and see him, or did you just read about it in the newspaper and decide to solicit him yourself?"

"Larry! Would I do that?"

"Yes, Alan, you would."

"Well, not that it's any of your business, but his old boss at Sunshine Solar is a client of mine, and he asked me to come out here this morning to visit him. He was worried about him. I came prepared with a fee agreement. You should have thought about that yesterday—perfectly ethical and on the up-and-up, Larry. I hope you haven't spent that huge legal fee you quoted him."

Larry felt sick. It was almost noon. The sun was high in the sky and it was probably close to one hundred degrees. He wanted to get inside where it was cool. "I think I'll go inside and tell Tom what a lying little prick he has for a lawyer. He won't stay with you for long once I tell him how many of your clients are in prison. It's a wonder you're not in prison with them."

"I wouldn't do that if I were you, Larry." Before Larry could respond Gimble added. "He's my client now. I have a signed fee agreement. You don't have shit. You talk to him without my consent, and I'll file an ethics complaint with the State Bar if you even try to talk to him. This one's mine, now, Larry."

How ironic. The most dishonest lawyer in Tucson was threatening to file an ethics complaint against someone he had just stolen a client from. This couldn't be happening! But it was happening all right—big as life. Larry decided he would stop the conversation with Gimble and go back to the office to think it over. Standing out in the hot sun arguing with Gimble wasn't getting him anywhere. This battle was far from over, but there was no point in continuing the argument with Gimble. Short of grabbing the fee agreement back from him and ripping it to pieces, which he had already decided against, he had lost for now.

"You haven't heard the last of this one, Alan. You think you're pretty smart. I just think you're a smart-ass. It might take awhile, but this one will catch up to you."

"Don't give me any of that moral crap, Larry. I've done nothing wrong. There's nothing you can do about it. Go back to your office and forget about it. You can read about this one in the newspapers."

There was only one reply that Larry could think of and it wasn't very original. "Fuck you, Alan!"

"I don't think so, Larry. I think you're the one who just got fucked! See ya!"

Larry stood and watched as Gimble walked out to his plastic Porsche with the Volkswagen engine. What an asshole to even drive a car like that. It didn't have a top, it had no heater in the winter, and it had no air conditioner in the summer. When it rained, Gimble wore a "slicker" and a rain hat. Larry hoped the sun would bake the brain right out of his head. But the stupid little car commanded attention. Attention was everything to Gimble.

Larry walked inside to get a drink of water from the water fountain before going to his car. He decided to check the log to see what time Gimble had checked in to see Rogers. The log said nine fifty. Larry asked the deputy to make a copy of the page. He was glad to oblige. Larry had an idea. Gimble might have a signed fee agreement, but Larry was attorney of record in the court file before Gimble had even signed in at the jail, and he had his yellow copy of the proceedings from this morning to prove it.

He tried to call Cindy from the lobby phone to tell her he might be a few minutes late for his one thirty appointment. Of course, she was at lunch, and he had to leave a message with the answering service. He signed the log, showed his State Bar Card, and his driver's license, and entered the jail to see Tom.

Tom looked ashamed and sheepish when he entered the interview room to see Larry. "Hi, Mr. Ross. Thanks for coming to see me again."

Larry decided to cut to the chase. "So, who's it going to be, Tom? Me or Alan Gimble?"

Tom broke eye contact with Larry and began inspecting the tops of his jail-issued shower thongs. "I'm real sorry about that, Mr. Ross. He's a friend of Phil Drummond's. He said Phil sent him to see me. He said he's done six murder cases and you haven't done any. He said he would do my whole case for ten thousand. He said you two used to be partners, and he broke it off because you lost too many cases."

Larry contemplated his response. "Listen, Tom. Who came over here yesterday on a moment's notice? Who showed up for you this morning and got bail set in a first-degree murder case at twenty-five thousand dollars? Who then came right over here to see you?"

"You did, Mr. Ross."

"That's right, Tom. I did. Did Gimble tell you how many of those murder cases he won?"

"No, he didn't."

"Well, he didn't win any of them. Did he tell you he used to steal money from the partnership, and that he's lucky I didn't turn him in to the county attorney?"

"No."

"Do you know that your dad's in town and that we've already made arrangements to post your bond and we'll have you out of here in forty-eight hours?"

"Dad's in town?'

"Yes, he is."

"How did he get here so soon?"

"Laura called him, and he caught the red eye through Chicago. He's real worried about you, Tom. He's made arrangements to pay your legal fees, too. He went to the bank this morning and transferred funds from his bank in Columbus to a new account here. The Bank here requires a forty-eight hour wait before he can draw on the account."

Tom looked relieved and stunned at the same time. "Thanks, Mr. Ross. I guess I panicked. I didn't know how I was going to pay you, and I didn't know how I was going to come up with the bond. Alan said he really wanted the case. He said he'd do the whole thing for ten grand"

"Come on, Tom. You might be scared, but you're not stupid. Do you really think he can do a good job in a murder case for ten thousand? I told you yesterday that the expert witnesses would cost that."

"But he said you've never done a murder case."

"That's the only thing he said that wasn't a lie. He's right. I haven't. But that doesn't mean I don't know how to do one or won't do a good job. A murder case is just like any other case. Do it right, and the client foes free. Screw it up, and the client could die. I've got a much better win/loss record than Gimble does. I don't like to lose, Tom, and short of doing things that are illegal or unethical, I'll stop at nothing to win for you."

"Okay. How's Laura?"

"She's worried sick about you, Tom. She can't even stay at the house. The Sheriff's Office has the house taped off right now as a crime scene. I think it's great that she and your dad have each other to lean on. Tom, there are a lot of things to do today. Am I your lawyer, or not."

"Do you still want to be my lawyer?" asked Tom.

"Yes, Tom, I do. Now, sign this fee agreement I brought with me, and I'll prepare a disengagement letter for Gimble. I've got to get back to the office, so I can't stay much longer."

"Okay," said Tom. "I'm real sorry about the confusion this morning."

"That's okay, Tom. I know you're scared. Now, sign this fee agreement while I write up Gimble's walking papers. And Tom, keep your mouth shut in here. Don't talk to anybody about anything. You'll be out in two days. Don't give the county attorney anything to work with. Self-defense is our only hope on this one. I don't want some jailhouse snitch making a deal for himself by going to the county attorney with a story about you. Keep your mouth shut and don't even talk about the weather! Do you understand me?"

"Yes, sir," was Tom's reply.

It took five minutes or so for Larry to write the disengagement letter. Tom signed it and Larry couldn't wait to fax it to Gimble as soon as he got back to the office. Larry had to leave. It was already after one o'clock.

Larry stood to leave. "Gotta go, Tom. Your dad and Laura will be out tomorrow during visiting hours. We'll have you out by noon, Wednesday. Stay out of trouble, and please don't talk to anyone. ANYONE! Got it? That means your dad too. I'll brief him and Laura. If you talk about the case with them, your dad can be called as a witness. Laura has spouse privilege. No one can make her testify against you. Your dad has no statutory privilege. Keep the conversation light. Don't talk about the case."

"What about Mr. Gimble? I talked to him about the case."

"I know. But the attorney-client privilege will apply to that conversation. Even Gimble isn't unethical enough to repeat your conversation with him. It would be bad for him if he did. There's no reason for him to do that. He gains nothing by it. Don't worry about it. He's a jerk, but you get a pass on that conversation."

Larry turned and left. "I'll see you Wednesday, Tom."

Larry was pleased with himself as he left the jail. One more battle with Gimble fought, one more battle with Gimble won. He wished he had a fax machine in the car. He wished he could see Alan's face when he got the disengagement letter. More like an "up-your-ass" letter. It was one fifteen, and he would just make it back to the office for his one thirty appointment. There would be no time for lunch today.

As he crossed the bridge over the Santa Cruz River, the temperature sign on the Tucson Federal Tower downtown flashed one hundred degrees. The "Ice" had officially broken on the Santa Cruz River. Karen Hargrave would learn later on in the day that she was the winner of the "Ice Break Contest," and she and her husband Mark would soon be going on a cruise and enjoying many other prizes.

CHAPTER 7

▼

May 5th (Cinco de Mayo)

May 5h, (Cinco de Mayo in Spanish) was always a good day for bar business in Tucson. Cinco de Mayo marked a victory against the French in the struggle for Mexican Independence. It was a good excuse to drink and act stupid. Bar owners had discovered this long ago, and the bars in the college campus area were particularly anxious to offer specials on Corona Mexican Beer and Tequila Shooters in celebration of Cinco de Mayo.

As if the college crowd really cared about this 18th century Mexican victory over the French. Most of them had no idea what they were celebrating. They did know that Corona for two dollars a bottle, and shooters for two dollars a shot was a good deal. You could get pretty fucked up on as little as twenty bucks. Who could pass up such a good deal?

Tom Rogers and Art Mendoza had decided to join in the traditional celebration in a big way. They had purchased radio time on one of the popular radio stations in Tucson that catered to the younger market. The ads for the Cinco de Mayo blowout had been running all week. They had even arranged for a live "remote" broadcast.

A popular Mexican Mariachi band had been hired to begin playing at two, and a rock n' roll band would take over at eight o'clock to carry the revelers to closing time at two A.M. The afternoon drive-time DJ would broadcast live from the Odyssey and create hype for the good time being had by all. The noise in the background would be a testament to rowdiness. By six o'clock Tom and Art figured the party would be going strong enough that it would carry through to two A.M. without continuing the live remote.

One of the local TV stations had agreed to send a news crew to do a "comprehensive" one minute thirty second piece on the celebration taking place at the Odyssey. Celebration of Cinco de Mayo by getting drunk and acting stupid had become a newsworthy event, especially when the broadcast came from one of the college area bars. The TV cameras would undoubtedly pick up images of bare-chested guys, and halter-topped girls groping each other and yelling "HI MOM," into the camera as they hoisted their Coronas, and threw back their shooters chased by a lick of salt and a suck on a slice of lime.

By two P.M. the Odyssey was at capacity, and Tom was afraid the Fire Marshal might show up, count heads, and order people to leave, as the occupancy limit had been reached and exceeded. Tents and tables had been set up in the parking lot to accommodate the overflow, which meant the patrons were parking on the street, and in the parking lots of neighboring businesses.

Tom and Art had scheduled every waitress and bartender they had to work this day. Tom had cautioned the staff to check ID for age. He didn't want any trouble from liquor control

He was a little worried about the crowd in the parking lot as liquor was not to be consumed outside the premises and he had applied for and received a limited use permit to allow alcohol consumption in a roped off area of the parking lot that acted as an extension of the bar on this special day.

So far, everything was going smoothly. With any luck, this party would establish the Odyssey as the place to be for the college crowd. Memorial Day wasn't far off. This would be another excuse for another big party. This would be another opportunity for the Odyssey to become THE COLLEGE BAR.

The TV crew was scheduled for three o'clock so they could get their videotape back to the studio and edited in time for the five o'clock news. Ed Carlson, the DJ, had set up in the bar over by the band riser where the Mariachi Band blared its trumpets and strummed its brand of Mexican Mariachi Music.

The Odyssey was in full swing, and the money flowing into the cash register. When the news crew showed up, the partygoers were ready to whoop it up for the cameras. Someone had brought a homemade sign that had been hastily placed over the back door to the parking lot. "PARTY 'TIL YOU PUKE," was the sage advice. The crowd roared as two muscular surfer types stood on chairs and taped it to the wall. The sign was definitely fodder for the TV camera.

Art was celebrating with the crowd. After all, he was Mexican, and Cinco de Mayo was an important milestone in the liberation of his country. He was also an alcoholic, and it didn't take much to find an excuse to drink.

By three o'clock, Art had consumed at least three Coronas, and six shooters, and was beginning to feel no pain. As the Mariachi Group began its rendition of "El Rancho Viejo" (The old Ranch), Art climbed onto the stage and began singing with the group. He wasn't too bad, either, having played in a Mariachi Group years before. The TV crew took some footage of this for the newscast and then moved around the bar and out into the parking lot asking questions of patrons hoping for the particularly witty comment that could be used in the clip for the five o'clock newscast. Five o'clock co-anchor Sandy Rathman was doing the announcing, and reporting for the piece. She was genuinely having a good time.

Tom was working the bar with two other bartenders and trying to keep a close eye on the cash register. It wasn't easy, but he was doing the best he could. The money was flowing, and he had already tucked one thousand dollars into the safe. If they could clear a thousand bucks an hour between now and closing, the advertising and extra staffing would turn out to be a good investment.

As the news crew was finishing up, but while the cameras were still rolling, Art approached Sandy. Holding out his arms, offering her a hug, he approached with a boozy stagger. "Sandy, thanks for coming. Come back after the last newscast tonight. Drinks are on the house for you and your crew."

As he got closer, Sandy could smell his beer/tequila breath. She had no desire to be hugged by this drunk, fat, ugly man. Ever aware of the cameras, Sandy put on her best TV smile and put out her hands to deflect the oncoming drunk.

Art mistook her movement and big smile for an invitation. He grabbed her, gave her a bear hug, and planted a big kiss right on her mouth, inserting his tongue for good measure.

Understandably, Sandy began struggling, trying to push Art away, and trying to make noise, although it was difficult with Art's mouth glued onto hers.

Art liked women that put up a fight. The more Sandy struggled, the harder he hugged her. Soon he had his hands on her ass, and was pulling her into his crotch. Sandy felt his erection, and was horrified. She was practically being raped right on camera. Wasn't anyone going to help her?

The camera crew knew a good story when they saw one unfolding in front of them. They kept the cameras rolling, recording every movement and sound. They waited for some Good Samaritan to come to the rescue.

Tom Rogers was behind the bar when he heard the struggle and looked up to see Sandy trying to get away from Art. He couldn't believe what he was seeing. Sandy's newscast was the most watched in the city. This was not the image Tom was looking for on the news when he had persuaded Sandy and her news crew to cover the Odyssey's Cinco de Mayo celebration.

Ed Carlson noticed the action too. He was in the middle of his remote broadcast when the action began. He started commenting on it live: "Whoa everybody. Hold On! News anchor Sandy Rathman is being given a very friendly goodbye kiss by Art Mendoza, co-owner of the Odyssey. It doesn't look like she's too happy about this. Maybe Art's had a little too much tequila this afternoon! Hey! This isn't funny anymore. Somebody help her. Art! Let her go! It looks like Tom Rogers is stepping in to help. Oh No! Tom just got knocked on his butt! I can't believe what I'm witnessing here. There's a pile of people with Sandy Rathman and Art Mendoza on the bottom of the pile! What a fight. Elbows are flying!" Every word was being broadcast live to the entire City.

Tom had jumped over the bar to rush to Sandy's aid. He grabbed Art by the shoulders and screamed, "Let her go Art, let her go!" Art's response was an elbow to Tom's gut, which knocked the wind out of him and sent him to the floor, landing on his butt.

By now, the entire bar crowd was aware of what was going on. Several male patrons grabbed at Art to pull him off of Sandy, but he resisted with all his might. The liquor and the adrenalin were giving him almost superhuman strength. Finally, he crashed to the floor, still holding on to Sandy's ass. The cameras rolled on.

As Sandy wriggled free of Art's grasp, one of the bartenders picked up the phone and called 9-1-1. By now, three large football players from the UofA front line were restraining Art. Finally, Art gave up the struggle, and the football players let him up. No sooner had he stood up than he lunged at all three of them, and the fight broke out again. As the fight continued, sirens could be heard in the background.

Realizing the police were on their way, and not wanting to be questioned, the patrons began leaving faster than a cannonball leaving the barrel of a cannon. By the time the police arrived, the only ones left in the bar itself were Sandy, her camera crew, Art, Tom, Carlson, the two bartenders, the band, and the waitresses.

The Football players had split out the side door. They weren't about to jeopardize their football scholarships by being involved in a melee, and having to explain to the world, and their coach about their fake ID's. Art was brushing himself off as the police entered through the back door. Sandy was collecting herself, and running her fingers through her hair to smooth it out.

Seeing the police, Sandy was thinking fast about how to handle this situation. She was mad—to be sure—but she had escaped unharmed. She was a high profile person in the Tucson community. She wasn't anxious for a news story making her the focus of the story, especially one about being manhandled in a bar. It wouldn't be good for her image, or the image of the station. It was her job to report the news, not *be* the news. Besides, she knew Art was drunk. He probably didn't mean anything by his improper behavior. It was just the tequila acting out. She rationalized that Art was more or less an innocent bystander.

Sandy decided to play it cool, as if nothing had happened. If this became news, it would haunt her all summer. She would have to testify in court against Mendoza. That would be humiliating, and would create more news stories featuring her as the *story*, not the *storyteller*. That option was just unacceptable. It would be different if she had been hurt, but she wasn't. She had a newscast to do at five. She didn't want to have to hang around forever answering a bunch of questions about something that took less than a minute to occur.

Officer Tanner spoke first: "Okay, what happened here? We have a report of a fight."

Art looked at Tom. Tom looked at Sandy. Sandy looked back at Tom and shook her head slowly from side to side. The cameras continued to roll.

Sandy cleared her throat, straightened her jacket and said, "Just a misunderstanding, officer. We were here doing a news story when one of the customers got a little friendly with me, and Mr. Mendoza here tried to help me out. It got a little crazy for a minute, but I'm okay."

Tanner recognized Mendoza. This was not the first time he had been summoned to a fight that Mendoza had been involved in. "Is that right, Mendoza?" asked Tanner.

"Yeah! That's right!" was Mendoza's surly reply.

Tanner looked around the room. "I don't suppose anyone saw who started this?"

Everyone looked to Mendoza. He glared at Tanner. Tom was about to speak up, but decided to remain silent. The camera crew decided to follow Sandy's lead. The band could care less and really hadn't seen anything anyway. The bartenders and waitresses weren't going to rat on Art if Sandy was willing to pass it off. That left Carlson, the DJ. Also being a public figure, he sympathized with Sandy's plight.

Tanner asked again: "Well, did anybody see anything, or not?"

Carlson began to walk over from the stage area and Art threw him an unmistakable glance that had "keep your mouth shut" written all over it. Carlson decided to follow Tom's lead and remain speechless. Silence hung in the air for what seemed like forever, but in reality was only about thirty seconds.

Finally, Tanner spoke: "Are you all right, Ma'am?"

Sandy replied, "Yes, thank you, I'm fine. There really wasn't any need for you to come. Will you be filing a report on this?"

Tanner looked around the room. He rocked back and forth on his heels and finally said: "So far, the only thing I have to report is that I responded to the scene. Nothing was happening when I got here, and no one has any complaint to file against anyone. I'll take your names and addresses for the report and be on my way."

Everyone gave his or her name and address to Tanner's partner, Officer Bell. Tanner sat down and called dispatch on his portable radio to let them know the scene would be clear in the next fifteen minutes or so. "Cinco de Mayo," he thought to himself. "Always good for at least one call of a fight in progress, and usually no one around to file a complaint once the police arrive."

Carlson was stuck with a live remote that didn't end until six o'clock. He couldn't leave, and he didn't have much to say about the Odyssey's Cinco de Mayo celebration after the cops left. He kept it pretty low key, doing his best to be professional, reporting the drink specials and making it sound like the afternoon at the Odyssey was a rollicking good time. A few more customers straggled in and by six; the place was half full again. The party had definitely lost its momentum.

The band played, Carlson talked, and Mendoza drank another beer. Tom went back behind the bar and began filling the waitresses' drink orders again. He knew he had to get out of this partnership, but he didn't know how he was going to do it. Art had showed his temper enough times for Tom to know that he wouldn't like it when Tom said he wanted out. Besides, Tom had the liquor license. No license, no bar. Tom felt he held the advantage on that one.

On the way back to the studio, Sandy decided to run the piece as originally planned. A good time held by all at the Odyssey Sports Bar. The extra footage would end up on the cutting room floor and then in the trash dumpster. She didn't want any memorial of what had happened being preserved on film. God! What a crazy business!

Back at the Odyssey, Art told Tom that if he ever interfered in his business again, he would kill him. After that threat, Tom decided he should wait for another time to tell Art he wanted to end the partnership.

This was the second time Tom had witnessed Art in a fight. The first one had involved a man who had come to the bar asking for Art. Polite conversation at one of the tables near the back door had turned ugly. Soon, the two were headed for the parking lot. Art pulled a scrap of two by four from the dumpster and attacked the man with it. The man managed to get his own piece of two by four from the dumpster, and soon, Art was being struck as well. Tom and two of the waitresses stood and watched as the two men beat each other bloody with two-by-fours.

Finally, the fight was over, and the stranger limped to his car and left. Tom offered to take Art to the hospital, but he declined. The hospital would mean an accident report, and a report would mean a visit from the police. Art didn't want anything to do with the police. He told Tom to mind his own business. One of the waitresses put hydrogen peroxide and bandages on his cuts from the first aid kit kept at the bar.

The next day, Art acted as if nothing had happened. When Tom asked if he was okay, his reply was, "I told you to mind your own fucking business. Now what do you think that means? MIND YOUR OWN FUCKING BUSINESS! THAT'S WHAT IT MEANS."

Tom got the message. He also developed a healthy fear of Art Mendoza.

CHAPTER 8

▼

Homicide Detective Jeff Cotter was a twelve-year veteran. He had been on homicide six years and had seen his share of grisly crime scenes. He hated being called out on weekends, but that was part of being on the homicide detail.

Pima County had about eighty homicides a year. Half of them remained unsolved. Being only sixty miles from the Mexican border, there was a lot of drug trade in Pima County and drug deals gone bad were common scenarios for drug dealers shooting one another and leaving the bodies in the desert to be found days or weeks later by hikers or vultures.

Working in the desert wasn't much fun. Animals would get to the body and scatter evidence all over the desert floor. The drug dealers often didn't carry ID, or if they did, it was fake ID. It wasn't very often that anyone reported them to be missing, as most of them were illegal aliens to begin with. These circumstances made being a Pima County Homicide Detective very frustrating.

Then there were the children. Pima County had far too many crimes against children—boys as well as girls. Society was becoming perverted. Several years ago, two boys had been abducted from a local hotel during a chess tournament. They were found dead in the desert. They had been molested and tortured. They were only twelve years old. Leads were few.

Finally, a schoolteacher had been arrested a year later on an indecent exposure charge and had become a suspect. It was learned he had been in attendance at the chess tournament the year prior. During his interrogation on the indecent exposure charge, he confessed to the abduction and murder of the two young chess players. He pled guilty to second-degree murder and had received a twenty-five year sentence without possibility of parole.

He never got to serve his sentence. He was killed in prison only a few days following confinement. There is honor among thieves, and the prison population scorns child molesters. They rarely come out of prison alive.

Cotter had worked that case, and it had taken an emotional toll on him. Dealing with the death of a scumbag drug dealer was easy. Notifying the families of two innocent twelve year olds was devastating. The year between the deaths and the arrest had been particularly hard. He kept in constant contact with the families, advising them of every lead and reassuring them that the perpetrator would be apprehended, charged, and convicted. He still recalled the sense of relief and closure he witnessed the families experience at the sentencing. He also called them the day the newspaper reported the death of Craig Milton, the schoolteacher turned child molester/murderer. He was dead now, and could never hurt anyone again. That was permanent closure. Cotter was glad Milton was dead. He would never have to investigate another one of his crimes. Ever.

On Sunday, June 3rd, Cotter got a call from dispatch to report to a homicide scene at 6178 W. Avenida Grande, on the northwest side of town. It was about nine thirty when the call came in. He and his wife were getting dressed for Church. There would be no time for Church today. He changed into blue jeans and a Pima County Sheriff's Office T-shirt, grabbed a Sheriff's Office baseball cap, his ID, badge, and gun, and was out of the house in less than fifteen minutes. He was allowed to keep an unmarked car at home as detectives were often called out at odd times. Having the car at home sped up the process of responding to the call.

Cotter lived midtown. Being Sunday morning, the traffic was light, and he was on the scene in less than twenty minutes. When he arrived, the yellow tape was already around the perimeter of the property. Three patrol cars were still in the driveway. He approached Deputy Carl Mahoney first. "Good morning Carl. What have we got?"

Mahoney pointed to the south side of the garage. "We've got a body over by the garage. Mexican male. Arthur Mendoza according to ID we found on the body. MVD confirms that Lincoln over there is registered in his name. The body shows evidence of multiple gunshot wounds, and multiple blows to the head by a blunt object, which we believe to be an ax we found near the body with blood and hair on it. We've already bagged the ax for the crime lab.

"We found a .38 special snub-nosed revolver in those bushes over there. Brick on the garage shows evidence of bullets hitting it and glancing off. There are several bullet holes through the roof of the porch and through the door to the kitchen and the kitchen window. The .38 has six spent shells in the cylinder. We bagged that, too."

Cotter considered what he had just heard. "Is this the victim's house?"

Mahoney continued, "No, the house is owned by Tom and Laura Rogers. Rogers and Mendoza were business partners in a bar on Grant Road called the Odyssey. Rogers admits he shot Mendoza, but says it was self-defense. From the looks of the porch, he could be right. It's pretty obvious that bullets were flying from two different directions: toward the house, and away from the house. Rogers says the .38 belongs to Mendoza. We also have a .44 Bulldog that Rogers says is his. It also has six spent shells in the cylinder. Rogers admits he fired it, but he doesn't remember how many times. His wife didn't see anything. She just heard the gunshots and freaked out. She's still pretty shaky. We have them separated."

Cotter was thinking that this would be an easy one. The victim and the perp were already identified and the perp was in custody. At least this one wouldn't go down as another unsolved shooting in the desert. Then he had a thought. "Carl. This can't be that easy. What does Rogers have to say about the ax?"

Mahoney chuckled. "You're right. It isn't that easy. Rogers admits the ax belongs to him. Says he kept it by the woodpile over by the garage and used it to split firewood. He also says he doesn't remember touching it today.

"There's also evidence that the body was moved from the end of the driveway over there to where it is now. You can see the drag marks in the gravel. The body is wrapped in a blanket. The blanket was dragged across the gravel with the body lying on top of the blanket.

"We've also got an eyewitness. A guy who lives across the street named Weber says he saw Rogers hit Mendoza over the head with the ax three times. He also watched him drag the body away in the blanket."

Cotter thought about the information he had just been given. He should be on his way soon. Now there was an eyewitness to go with ID of the victim and the perp—a homicide detective's dream. There wasn't much to investigate. It was all there for him. He decided to take a look at the body. Mahoney led him over to the south side of the garage.

There, beside the woodpile, lay the lifeless body of Art Mendoza. He was face down. His jeans hung low around his hips, exposing the crack in his butt.

There was a nasty gash in the back of his head. The black hair was matted with blood and drying blood. On the left temple area was what appeared to be a bullet wound. There was also a large blotch of blood over the right shoulder blade area.

The ID tech was busy shooting photos. When he had finished with the back of Mendoza's body, Cotter, the tech and Mahoney rolled him over onto his back.

Lifeless eyes stared back at them. There was a bullet hole in the upper right chest area. The T-shirt Art was wearing was slipped up over his huge belly. The tech took more photos as Cotter began dictating into his portable tape recorder.

The Medical Examiner was on his way, so they needed to finish with the body first. Two Old English Sheep Dogs barked at the deputies from the kennel about ten feet away. Cotter was wishing they could talk, as they were probably eyewitnesses. Then he remembered that had been done in the movies. "Turner and Hooch" with Tom Hanks before Hanks got famous by winning two Oscars in two years.

The blanket Mendoza was on was a ratty old pea green army surplus blanket that had probably come from the garage. It was soaked in blood from the upper torso area. Cotter bagged Mendoza's hands so the M.E. could do a paraffin test to determine if he had gunpowder residue on his hands. If he did, that would be a good indication that he had in fact fired one of the two weapons found at the scene.

The M.E. would also take fingernail scrapings to see if there was any skin or fiber under the fingernails that could be linked to Rogers or anyone else. Cotter decided that he had better impound the Lincoln, and have it towed to the storage yard where its contents would be inventoried. He called dispatch on his radio to have them send a tow truck.

Next, he witnessed the ID tech photograph the driveway and the obvious pathway that had been left by the blanket with the body on it being dragged across the gravel. At the end of the driveway, about eight feet from the pavement of Avenida Grande, was a large pool of blood. Samples were taken for testing in the lab, and the blood was photographed as well.

He then talked to Jim Weber who confirmed what he had seen and heard. He recorded the interview with Weber's permission. Glenda Weber was able to confirm the time when she heard what she thought were firecrackers. It was obvious now that the firecrackers were in fact gunshots.

Next he talked to Laura Rogers. She was pretty shaken. He found her in the kitchen drinking a Diet Coke from a can. She told him that Mendoza and Rogers were indeed partners in the Odyssey. Art had called early that morning and wanted to come over to talk to Tom about splitting up the partnership. Laura was in favor of the meeting, as things had not been going well. Mendoza was an uncontrollable partner, and she and Tom wanted to get away from him.

She told Cotter that Mendoza had arrived about seven thirty A.M. Laura busied herself in the bedroom leaving the men alone to talk. Soon after Art arrived, she heard what she thought were gunshots. She raced from the bedroom to the kitchen. She had seen Tom coming into the kitchen from the back porch with a gun in his hand. When she asked him what had happened, Tom had told her that Art had tried to kill him. When she asked where he was, Tom told her he had shot him and he was lying on the back porch.

Laura remembered screaming. First she ran out the front door, but realized there was no place to run to. Then she ran back into the house, and into the bedroom. She tried to call 9-1-1 but Tom was on the line with Gary Miller, Tom's best buddy. She didn't know how long Tom and Gary were on the phone. She never came out of the bedroom again until the deputies arrived. She wanted to know if Tom was going to be arrested. She had already been told that Art was dead.

The conversation was not recorded.

Cotter tried to calm Laura as much as he could, but she was really shaky. He asked if she could find a place to stay and told her the house would be off limits to everyone except the Sheriff's Department for the next several days. She told him she could stay with friends and asked if she could use the phone. Cotter told her it was her phone and she could use it all she wanted to. Cotter decided to talk to Tom next.

CHAPTER 9

It was one thirty on the nose when Larry pulled the Camry into his covered parking space. Cindy's ancient and very unreliable Mustang was there. Larry also noticed a newer model Buick in the parking lot respectfully parked off to the side and away from the covered parking that was labeled as reserved. On a hot day like today, Larry wouldn't have blamed anyone for taking Alan's old covered spot that sat vacant most of the time.

As he entered the office, he noticed an anxious looking couple sitting in the waiting area. Larry correctly guessed these were the clients with the new PI case.

"Hi, I'm Larry Ross. I hope you haven't been waiting long."

The man stood. "I'm Mike Newman, this is my wife Margaret. We just got here about five minutes ago. Thanks for seeing us today."

Mike and Margaret, thought Larry. I wonder if she goes by Maggie like my wife does. He decided not to ask, and instead asked Cindy to get all of them a cold glass of water, and ushered them into his office. Larry couldn't help but notice that Mike and Margaret looked very worried.

"Thanks for coming to my office today," said Larry. "What can I do for you?"

Mike cleared his throat, looked at Margaret and said, "We need a good lawyer, and a friend of ours that you represented says you are good at what you do."

"Thanks, who is your friend?"

"Jim Jenson, do you remember him?" asked Mike nervously.

Remember him, how could he forget him? Jim had been horribly injured in a motorcycle accident five years earlier. Two broken legs, and lots of road rash. He was a victim of a left turning car that just didn't see him even though he was there in plain sight with his headlight burning and motoring through a green light at the speed limit.

Jim's landscaping business had barely survived while he recovered from his injuries. Larry had gotten him all of the insurance there was available for this accident; one hundred thousand dollars from the left turner, ten thousand dollars in medical payments from Jim's medical payments policy on the motorcycle, and another one hundred thousand dollars from Jim's underinsured policy. It came piecemeal, but added up to a whopping fee for a small law office like Larry's. Larry and Maggie had used some of the money to pay off some debt, and put a down payment on the house they now lived in. Oh Yes! He remembered Jim Jenson!

"How is Jim?" asked Larry.

Mike answered, "Doing well. Still bothered by a nasty limp but uses it as an excuse to supervise his crews and not work behind the mowers and the hedge trimmers anymore. He wanted us to say "hi" and hopes you and your family are well."

"Please tell him we are doing great. I have a new little girl since I last saw him. It was nice of him to remember me. Now, how can I help you?"

Margaret started crying.

Mike immediately touched her hand to comfort her. He then looked at Larry and said, "We lost both of our children in a car accident last weekend. We are still in shock and disbelief."

Mike continued: "Maybe you read about it in the paper. Their soccer team was headed up to Phoenix for a camp and the van rolled over for some unknown reason. No one else was even injured that seriously, but both of our children were killed. We need to find out what happened. This is killing us."

This was as bad as it gets. Larry had only done one other death of a child case before, and it was gut wrenching. The parents had blamed themselves; then they blamed each other. They went into a deep depression, and ended up getting divorced.

The money the case finally brought was not much comfort to them, and as far as they were concerned, still didn't answer the questions they had about what had happened and why.

They didn't even want to sign the release, as it had the standard language about not admitting any liability and entering into the settlement was done so in an effort to buy peace and was not to be considered an admission of liability.

Larry remembered it took them almost a week to finally come around and sign the release and accept the money, which represented the policy limits that were available to the person that had run down their precious child while he was on his bicycle. He looked at Mike and Margaret, immediately thought of his own children, and really didn't know what to say next. He took the safe route.

"I did read about that in the paper. What a tragedy. I'm so sorry for your loss. How old were your children?"

After a glance at Margaret, Mike volunteered: "They were fourteen year old twin boys. They had just finished their freshman year at St. James Academy. They loved soccer, and were going to soccer camp for a week to hone their skills in the hopes they might make the varsity team as sophomores. Soccer has been their life since third grade."

"We are devastated, and no one is giving us any answers. The school is mum, the police keep telling us the investigation is open, our babies have been buried, and we want some answers.

"Vans just don't roll over without a reason. Something happened. Maybe the driver was drunk; maybe the road was bad. We have to know what happened out there and why. Can you help us Mr. Ross?"

Larry didn't want to sound too much like a lawyer right now. Mike and Margaret needed a sympathetic ear. They also needed some sound legal advice. He decided to approach it gently, one fact at a time.

"Who owned the van?" asked Larry.

Mike took the lead again. "The school. It was one of those fourteen-passenger Galaxy Transporters that everyone uses to haul kids around to sporting events. The school has a fleet of them. They look pretty new. We thought they were safe, or we never would have let Timmy and Tommy ride in them. Why does it matter who owns the van?"

Larry contemplated his answer very carefully. What he wanted to know was how much insurance was behind this catastrophe. A van owned by Joe Schmoe parent probably didn't have a very big policy on it. A van owned by the school had a better chance of being properly insured, especially since the school used them for student transportation. Rather than answer Mike's question directly, Larry decided to ask another question.

"Was this a school sponsored event?"

Mike answered again while Margaret bravely used a tissue that had appeared out of her purse to wipe tears away from her eyes. "Yes, it was. In fact the assistant soccer coach was driving. He dislocated his shoulder. We thought he was a friend, but he says the school has forbidden him to talk to any of the parents about this. Father Frank called to offer condolences, and the school is planning a memorial mass in honor of Tim and Tom next weekend, but that isn't going to bring them back. We are going crazy with grief. Margaret's a wreck. I can't work. This is consuming us. Can you help us?"

It was hard for Larry not to think about the fact that this was potentially the largest case that had ever come to him. He felt guilty thinking about it, but this was no nickel and dime rear-ender that would go to mandatory arbitration. This was major league. This was a personal injury lawyer's dream case. It had huge damages, nice claimants, and a wealthy private school behind it. It had it all.

He also knew that it would be more complicated than the Newmans could ever imagine. Grieving parents wanted answers. Larry wanted to give them the answers. He wanted this case for many reasons. He felt confident he could do a good job for the Newmans. He knew the responsibility of handling such a large case would be great.

"Mr. and Mrs. Newman, I have children. I can only imagine what you are going through. I can help you. I have a very good engineer who does accident reconstruction. This accident is so fresh, there is still probably evidence out on the roadway that can be helpful in reconstructing what happened. I can get him on it today.

"The school probably has a big insurance policy on the van, so there should be plenty of insurance to go around to pay everyone who was injured. That is important. The insurance company will want to settle all of the claims within the limits of the policy, and I'm sure the parents of every child who was injured even slightly in this crash is seeking legal advice. This is going to be a hard case that will take many months to sort out, if not longer. I'm flattered that you would choose me to represent you in this tragedy.

"I can't tell you what happened right now, but I can tell you that I will do everything that I can to find out, and if there is a person or a company responsible for it, I will pursue it for you. Would you like to discuss fees and costs?"

Suddenly, Margaret spoke up. "Mr. Ross, Jim already told us how good you are and how much you care about your clients. We just met, but I think I speak for Mike too when I say this. We like you. If you will give us the same fee agreement you gave Jim, that is good enough for us. We want you to get started on this right away. Do you need any money from us for costs?"

Mike quickly agreed. "We had insurance policies on the boys that will pay off in about the next thirty days—one hundred thousand dollars each. We are willing to help out with the costs. We want you to be our lawyer. Will you help us?"

It didn't take Larry very long to answer. In ten years of practicing law, he had never had a client volunteer to pay for costs in a personal injury case. PI clients always expected to have the lawyer pay for everything, and also take the chance that the case would work out. Most of the time, they did. Sometimes they didn't, and when they didn't, it was a disaster. Not only did a loss mean no fee, it usually meant eating the costs, as the clients never had the ability to pay them.

He really liked the Newmans. They had come in as a referral from a satisfied client. He wanted to give them a good deal. Money was not the overwhelming issue for Larry wanting this case. It would be a legal and professional challenge. It would be something exciting and new from the humdrum rear-enders, DUI's, divorces, and armed robberies that paid the bills but didn't make life very exciting.

"I'll tell you what. Generally I charge 33 $1/3$ percent for cases that settle, and 40 percent if they have to go to trial. Costs are always additional. I usually advance those costs for the clients. This case could be expensive. It might even turn out to be a products case against Galaxy. We just won't know until Paul does the reconstruction.

"If you will advance twenty-five thousand for costs, which I will deposit in my trust account, and only use for your case, I will do the case for thirty percent if it settles, and thirty-five percent if it goes to trial. Any money left over will be refunded.

"If the costs go over twenty-five thousand, you won't have to advance anymore than that. I'll take care of the rest. You do have to understand there is a small risk that the case might be lost, and if it is, while you won't owe any legal fees, you will owe the balance for costs if there is a balance. How does that sound?"

Mike looked at Margaret. Margaret nodded. Mike answered for both of them.

"That sounds more than fair to us. Draw up the paperwork and we'll sign. We want you to get started on this right away."

Just like that. Ten years of waiting for a really good case to come in, and now Larry had two in one day. A really challenging criminal case with a good fee behind it, and now a potentially huge wrongful death case that could be worth millions.

Larry picked up the phone, paged Cindy, and asked her to come in with a blank fee agreement and some releases for the Newmans to sign. Larry filled in all the blanks, explained the agreement in detail, had them sign, and promised them he would call Paul Lattimore, the engineer, that very afternoon.

Cindy made copies of everything for them. The Newmans said their goodbyes, and Larry watched them walk out to their Buick. Two grieving people. Two dead kids. And Larry had the awesome responsibility of helping them out. There was no room for error on this one. This one had to be done right. He hoped he was up to the challenge. He was determined not to let Mike and Margaret down. He would do his very best times two in this one.

He wasted no time in calling Paul. Cindy ordered the police report. Paul said he would do a fly over the next morning to photograph the freeway location where the accident occurred to preserve the landscape. Larry told Paul where the van was, and asked him to photograph it, and inspect it, as well as he could. Then he dictated a letter of representation directed to St. James Academy asking them to forward his letter on to their liability carrier and to have the adjuster assigned to the claim call him.

Adjuster. What a funny word to give a person who worked claims and whose only interest was getting the file closed by paying as little as possible. They can adjust this one all they want, Larry thought. He was going to go for the gold in this one. He wasn't going to let them off the hook easy. Money wouldn't bring Tim and Tom Newman back, but it could make Mike and Margaret's life easier, and it would act as a deterrent to whoever had to pay it to shape up and be more careful in the future.

It wasn't long before the three P.M. potential divorce client showed up. It wasn't too much later before she left the office with an appointment to see another lawyer tomorrow. Larry just didn't want to load himself up with a divorce case right now. His plate was pretty full. He would have to give his full attention to Tom Rogers and Mike and Margaret Newman for the next several weeks and months. There was no time to be squabbling over support payments and child visitation issues.

Larry called his good friend Bill Wilson and referred the divorce client over to him. Bill would do a good job, the client would get a lawyer who wasn't distracted by a big murder case and a double wrongful death case, and Bill would be happy to earn a decent fee. It was a good compromise for all involved.

Larry Ross, the referral lawyer. What a change! Usually he was the one receiving referrals of overflow-cases that busier lawyers couldn't get to, or thought were dogs. Now, he was the one making the referral. That felt pretty good.

Friday night he had gone home dead tired. He had experienced a second hung jury. There would be another trial looming ahead, with no fee. The rent was due. He had no money in the operating account.

Monday, two decent fees came in, and got deposited. The rent got paid. He signed up a major criminal case and was looking at being paid a huge fee in two more days. He had a new double wrongful death case that could be worth millions. The third trial had disappeared like magic.

What a difference a weekend makes. He had never imagined in Law School that the life of a lawyer could be this volatile. It was never wise to get too exuberant. Tomorrow might bring a ruling in the mail that could be disastrous to some case and client. Larry took it all in stride. Just another day at the office, doing the best he could to serve his clients and hopefully earn a living at the same time.

Just before leaving for the day, Larry got out a fax cover sheet and a black felt tip pen. He carefully wrote these words on the page:

"You're Fired!" borrowing from Donald Trump's trademark phrase. He then faxed Tom's handwritten disengagement letter accompanied with the fax cover sheet over to Alan Gimble's office.

Alan always left the office early, so he wouldn't see this after-five fax until the next morning.

Billie Joe McAllister might have jumped off the Tallahatchie Bridge on the 3rd of June, but Larry Ross would always remember the 3rd of June as one of the best days of his professional life. It was the day he met Tom Rogers. It would be the day that would define his career from this point forward.

He called Maggie on the cell phone on his way home and told her he was taking her and the kids out to Trail Dust Town for dinner. He was going to wear a tie just so the waitress would cut it off, ring the cowbell, make a big fuss, and delight the kids. They always loved it when daddy did that. They were definitely going to hit the lake this weekend.

CHAPTER 10

▼

June 5th

Tuesday was pretty uneventful. Most of the day was spent catching up on phone calls that had come in the week before, and catching up on the mail as well. How did lawyers ever practice law without telephones, fax machines, e-mail, computers, and copy machines? It was just mind boggling to think of Abraham Lincoln sitting in his Springfield office hand writing a contract, and then turning it over to a scrivener to make copies to have everyone sign.

Scrivener. There was another funny word that no one used anymore. Then again Xerox didn't command much of the copy market anymore, but everyone still referred to "Xeroxing" a document rather than copying it. The noun, "Xerox" had become a verb. Words. They were the backbone of every successful lawyer's practice. Larry liked to think about words. They fascinated him.

Ralph Rogers called. Larry went to the jail to see Tom. Paul called and said he got the fly over photos and that the storage yard where the van was had made arrangements to let him photograph it Wednesday. Paul suggested he bring an automotive engineer along to look for possible manufacturing defects that might have contributed to the roll over. Larry agreed. Paul said he knew a good one, and Larry trusted Paul's judgment.

Laura Rogers called. Larry wanted to get out to the Rogers' home but he just didn't have the time on Tuesday.

He did call the County Attorney's Office. He found out that Rick Bay had been appointed to Tom's case. Rick was next in command after Ray Martin. Larry knew him well. He was a good prosecutor. He was someone that Larry could work with.

Larry decided to subpoena the Cinco de Mayo tape from the TV station that had been at the Odyssey with Sandy Rathman.

Tom had told Larry about Art's behavior that day. He told Larry of Art's threat to kill him if he ever interfered in his business again. Larry also subpoenaed the tape from the radio station live remote broadcast just to hear what might be there as Tom told him Ed Carlson was reporting the melee over the radio. Evidence like that could be invaluable to Tom's defense, and it would be wise to get it before it got misplaced or destroyed in the ordinary course of business.

He also got the name of the witnesses from Tom regarding the two-by-four brawl that Art had in the parking lot a few weeks earlier.

Next, Larry called his private investigator David Norton, and asked David to contact the witnesses to see if he could take statements from them. Self-defense was going to be Tom's primary defense. He needed to show that Tom not only feared Art, but also had good reason to fear him. He also told David to get over to Superior Court and run a search on Mendoza's criminal files to see how many there were, and if any of them were active at the time of Art's death.

Finally he called his favorite psychologist, Doug Ball. Doug and Larry had become friends over the years. Doug would do Rule 11 evaluations for Larry when Larry suspected a criminal client might have a mental disorder that might be used as a defense. Doug was no whore. He would always tell it like it was. If the defect were there, he would support it with psychiatric testimony. If there was no defect, Doug would give Larry the news and that would be the end of it.

Larry wanted Doug to interview Tom about Sunday's events to see if there was something that might be helpful. Doug often used hypnosis to get people to remember repressed thoughts. Larry wanted Doug to do that in this case as Tom insisted he never hit Art with the ax, yet the physical evidence was pretty clear that he had. Christ, there was even an eyewitness that saw him do it! It was pretty hard to overcome that one. Maybe Doug could get Tom to remember something helpful while under hypnosis.

He also called the morgue, and found out that Bruce Parchman, the Chief ME was doing Art's autopsy. Larry knew from experience that Bruce never missed anything. He made Quincy look like a quack. Maybe he would get lucky, and find that Art had illegal drugs in his system or was legally drunk. It would be weeks before all the tox screens were in, and the preliminary hearing was in nine days.

He did some more research on murder one, aggravating and mitigating circumstances, and wondered what judge would be assigned to the case. Not that it really mattered. Thanks to the U.S. Supreme Court, Arizona juries now handed out the death penalty, not judges. Larry felt pretty confident it would be hard to convince twelve people that Tom Rogers should get the death penalty. Bay was good but not that good.

There was so much to do, and so little time. Larry felt he was truly on the verge of breaking out from the pack and becoming one of Tucson's best-known trial lawyers. But first, as the saying goes, he had to win these two cases, and at the same time juggle his other case load and pay attention to everything else that would have kept him busy if these two cases had not come in. He even thought of hiring a law student to help out with research for the summer, but then remembered his last bad experience with a law student, and decided to shelve that idea for the time being.

There was so much he wanted to know, and he wanted to know it today. He would have to wait, but the suspense was killing him.

Before he knew it, the day was over, and Wednesday was next up. Would Ralph really have seventy seven thousand dollars transferred to his bank account? If he did, Larry had his overhead in the bank for the summer, and then some. Usually Larry had to think ahead just to get the rent paid. If everything went right tomorrow, he wouldn't have that worry again any time soon. He could focus on Tom's case, and the Newman case, and not worry about the money thing for a while. What a welcome relief that would be!

As he left for the day, he noticed an old Monte Carlo cruise down the street behind his parking lot. The music was blaring Rap music from the CD. The car was a classic low-rider. Skinny tires, flashy chrome-spoke wheels, and lowered, so the car rode only a few inches above the street. The two punks inside fit the definition of gang bangers. Young, Hispanic, shaved heads, white "wife beater" T-shirts, lots of gold hung around their necks, and their arms and necks were heavily tattooed.

Larry imagined that if they got out of the car they would be wearing the rest of the uniform that consisted of huge denim pants cinched up by a belt just above the pubic bone, and the crotch hanging down to their knees. They thought they looked cool. Larry thought they looked stupid. How could you even keep your pants on like that? They all waddled like Penguins just to keep their pants from falling down.

It was also an easy make for the police. They fit the profile of small time drug dealers, and drew attention to themselves with the uniform garb, haircut, and car. Larry wondered what they were doing in this quiet neighborhood tucked in by the courthouses and office buildings that made up the "Snob Hollow" area of downtown Tucson. They were probably up to no good. He was glad his office had an alarm system. If they tried to break into his office, the audible alarm would probably scare them off, and if it didn't, the police would respond quickly, as the police headquarters was only a few blocks away on Stone Ave.

He didn't give it much more thought as he pulled out of the parking lot and headed for home. He did wonder how anyone grew up to be that way. Certainly, their parents must have been absent, or abusive. The gang culture was something Larry just didn't understand, even though he had represented numerous gang members. From what he could see, the gang life was a dead-end street that led to prison or death. Larry imagined it wouldn't be long before these two were behind bars.

CHAPTER 11

▼

June 6th

Today was the day. If the bank came through, the money would be deposited to Larry's account today. What a thrill! Even better, bail would be posted, and Tom would be out so Larry could talk to him without having to go to the jail.

As Larry drove into town from the Tanque Verde Valley, he tuned in to the oldies station hoping to find "Celebrate" by Kool and the Gang. Not today. Instead he got "I got you Babe!" by Sonny and Cher. The parking lot was only a block away and the eight A.M. newscast was just beginning. Of course Cindy's Mustang was nowhere to be seen. If it had been there, Larry would have thought something was wrong.

He parked the Camry, got out, and walked up to the parking lot entrance to the office. As he got to the door, he noticed a dead pigeon on the doorstep. That was odd. The door wasn't glass, so birds usually didn't fly into it confusing the reflection for open space. Then he noticed a note taped to the door. Bold, printed block letters proclaimed "BACK OFF!!"

Larry looked down at the pigeon. Its neck was obviously broken. Larry's first thought was this was a note from Alan Gimble. The little shithead probably saw the fax first thing this morning, and decided to respond in kind. Well he wasn't going to give him the satisfaction of even a call.

He got a broom and dustpan from the office closet, scooped up the pigeon, and walked it out to the dumpster near the end of the parking lot. When you run a one-man office, you do it all. It's for sure Cindy wouldn't do it, and he didn't want a dead pigeon stinking up the doorstep all day.

He crumpled the note and tossed it in the dumpster with the dead bird. This was not the greatest way to start a day that he had hoped would be so grand and glorious.

Eight-thirty came and went, no Cindy. The phone was ringing, and the answer light was blinking, so he decided to answer this one himself and pull the messages off the recorder later.

"This is Larry"

"Larry?"

God that was so annoying! Didn't he just announce himself when he answered? The only thing more annoying was "Hi, it's me," the caller assuming anyone could identify the "me" on the other end of the phone.

"Yes, this is Larry, how can I help you?"

"This is Laura Rogers. Is Tom getting out today?"

"That's a good question Laura. Karen will be in today and plans to call the bank at about Ten Thirty. If the money is in the bank, I'll have Tom out by noon. I plan to go to the jail myself to bring him back here for an interview. I can call you back as soon as I know. Where can I reach you?"

Laura said she was still at the Millers' and also left her cell phone number.

"Laura, can you have Gary call me today or tomorrow? I need to interview him about the call Tom made to him before he called 9-1-1. Will you pass that message on for me?"

"I'll be glad to. Please call me as soon as you know if Tom is getting out today. I've been so worried about him in that awful place."

"I'll do that, Laura. Here comes Karen now. I'll remind her to call the bank promptly at ten thirty."

"Thanks, Larry. I'll call Ralph and let him know too. I'll ask Gary to call you. I'll have the cell phone with me all day. That is probably the best way to reach me."

"Okay, Laura. Karen or I will call just as soon as we know."

"Hi Larry," said Karen as she walked by his office and headed for the kitchen to make the coffee. "Is today the day Tom gets out?"

"That was Laura on the phone. She wanted to know the same thing. Please call the bank at ten thirty sharp. If the transfer has been made, let me know immediately. I don't care if I'm on the phone with the President of the United States, interrupt me and let me know. Write the bond check to the Clerk of the Court so I can go over to the courthouse, post the bond, and get the release papers. Then I'll go to the jail and get Tom. I'm sure he'll be looking for me."

"Should I take a message if the President calls or should I ask him to call back?"

That was Karen, always the smart ass, always quick with a comeback. It was hard to stay ahead of her. "Just have him call back later, when I'm not so busy."

"Okay. I'll let you know when the coffee is ready."

Nothing else had to be said. Larry knew Karen would do what he asked her to do, and he didn't have to worry about that in the slightest. Larry thought about telling Karen about the pigeon, but decided against it. He saw no need to concern her with the stupid little prank of a stupid little man. Karen hated Alan almost as much as he did, but there was no proof it was Alan. The paper had already run a story about Tom's case, and the article mentioned Larry Ross represented him. Anyone could have dropped a dead pigeon on the doorstep. It was nothing.

He decided not to tell Maggie about it either. She was already uncomfortable about the publicity in the paper over such a high-profile case. He didn't want to concern her any further. One of the reasons he chose to live on the far-east side was to keep his wife and family as far away from the crime-ridden downtown and south-side area of town as possible. Criminals tended to operate in their own neighborhoods, and not look for out-of-the-way places to commit their crimes.

Larry busied himself with checking e-mail; going through more unanswered mail, and finally heard Cindy come in about ten after nine. He was going to have to talk to her, and make her realize she couldn't always be late, always take a long lunch, and yet expect to be out the door promptly at five. He could do that another day. There was no need to ruffle any feathers today.

At ten thirty, Karen called the bank. She calmly went to the bank and was back in the office a few minutes later. She walked into Larry's office with a check in her hand, and a smile on her face.

"Don't you have something to do this morning?" she asked as she handed Larry a check for twenty-five thousand dollars made out to the Clerk of the Court for Tom's bond.

Larry just looked at the check. It had really happened!

Karen was speaking again. "What do you want me to do with the rest of the money?"

"Transfer it to the trust account, mark the client ledger to keep at least ten thousand for costs. I'll keep track of my time, and we can bill the case at the end of every month, and pay my fee from the trust account every month until the case is over. Hopefully there will be some left over. Isn't this fun?"

Karen replied, "Yes it is. Now get going, I'll order in some sandwiches for lunch, and it will be here waiting for you and Tom when you get back. I'll call Laura and Ralph and have them here about two P.M. I'm sure you are going to want to have some time alone with Tom before he sees Laura or his dad. Now go, and don't come home alone!"

Larry left his sport coat in the office for the trek over to the courthouse. He had the bond posted and the paperwork in hand in record time and went back to the office to pick up his car and head to the jail. It was days like today that made him thankful for covered parking and air-conditioned cars. He was sweating profusely by the time he made it back to the office parking lot.

It didn't take long to get to the jail and collect Tom. He came down the hall dressed in the clothes he was wearing Sunday morning when he had been arrested. He had that hangdog puppy dog grin and stuck out his hand for Larry to shake.

"I don't think I have ever been so glad to see anyone in my whole life. I waited all morning for the call to tell me you were here. When it finally came, I almost thought I was dreaming. It's good to see you! Get me out of here as fast as you can!"

Larry smiled. "Will do. My chauffeured limo awaits yonder. The champagne and caviar are on ice."

Tom looked at him with one of those "You've got to be kidding me" looks. Larry let him off the hook.

"What? A Camry, a Subway sandwich, and a Coke aren't good enough for you?"

"Nothing has ever sounded better to me," said Tom as they fell into step with one another and walked out into the sunshine and over to Larry's car.

Larry decided not to get into any deep discussion with Tom until they were back at the office. He told him Laura and Ralph would come by at two and that would give them some time to talk about Sunday's events and the history of the Odyssey bar. He asked if Tom had spoken to anyone at the jail about the case and Tom assured him he had not.

As Larry was pulling into the office parking lot he noticed what looked like the same Monte Carlo he had seen the night before coming down the street from the opposite direction. It drove on by as Larry parked. He made a mental note to get the plate number the next time he saw this car. It didn't belong in this neighborhood, and he didn't like it cruising by his office. Whoever they were, they were probably up to no good. Low-riders weren't known for doing charity work.

Tom made eye contact with Cindy as soon as he entered the reception room. He gave her curvaceous body full attention. He smiled as Karen came in from the conference room with a Subway bag in her hand.

"Want to join me for lunch?" she said.

"You bet," he said, as he followed her back into the conference room. He stopped and looked over his shoulder back at Cindy. "Aren't you going to introduce me?" he asked Karen.

Cindy took the hint. "Hi. I'm Cindy Morrow, Larry's secretary. It's nice to meet you." Then she flashed one of her patented man-killer smiles, got up from her desk, and walked towards Tom with her arm outstretched. Tom's attention was quickly drawn to her thin waist and long legs. It was easy to see that Tom was taken with Cindy's looks. No surprise there. Most men were. Larry decided to give him a break. He had been in jail for the last three days. Most men couldn't help but look at Cindy, and Tom was no exception.

"Come on Tom. Let's get to work. We have a lot of ground to cover before two P.M., so let's get started."

Tom followed Larry and Karen into the conference room. Larry decided to let Karen stay and take notes. The attorney-client privilege extended to Larry's employees as well, and Karen fit the definition. Besides, he wanted Tom to focus on the facts, not on Cindy's body. He reminded Karen of the attorney client privilege, she said she understood, and they got started.

Larry started by getting the history on how Tom and Art had met, how well they knew each other, and how it had come to be that they were business partners. Tom told Larry of Art's felony convictions that kept him from getting a liquor license. He also told him about Art's temper, his numerous threats to kill Tom, and his penchant for putting the moves on the female help, most of whom were college girls.

When Tom got to the finances of the bar, Larry realized this wasn't going to look very good in court. Art had put up all the money. Tom and Laura were living off of savings from his prior success at Sunshine Solar. Art would come to the bar, drink like a fish, get loud and obnoxious, manhandle the help, and the customers, and basically do his best to make sure no one would want to be a regular as the Odyssey was the home of a fat ugly man who had a foul mouth, and liked to play grab-ass.

At the end of every week, Art would blame Tom for receipts being less than expected, and wouldn't take the hint that maybe he really should be a "silent" partner, just like they had agreed in the beginning. It was Art's mouth and behavior that were keeping customers out of the bar. In little more than a month, Tom had regretted ever meeting Art Mendoza, and certainly regretted going into business with him.

Tom recounted the Cinco de Mayo disaster, followed by the Memorial Day disaster that led to the Sunday morning meeting at Tom's house that ended with Art on a slab in the morgue, and Tom wearing an orange short sleeved jumpsuit with "PIMA COUNTY JAIL" stenciled on the back for the next three days.

Larry also learned that Art had severe cataracts in both eyes, was probably legally blind or close to it, and did not have a driver's license because he couldn't pass the vision test, but continued to drive anyway. There wasn't much good to say about Art. The only good thing in his life was Angie, Laura's friend from art class at the UofA. Tom also informed Larry that Art let it be known he carried and always had a gun with him or nearby, and wasn't afraid to use it. Tom had never seen him with a gun until Sunday at the house. He saw it big as life that day, and recalled the shoot-out on the back porch.

Larry inquired where Tom had gotten his gun and why he even had it. Tom told him that Gary Miller had given it to him when they moved out to the desert "for protection" Tom said he had never fired it, and it only had the six bullets it had come with when Gary gave it to him. Tom said he had never fired a handgun, and had only fired a shotgun a few times back when he lived in Ohio, and that had been during pheasant season.

According to Tom, the pheasants were safe when Tom was in the field with his shotgun. At Gary's urging, the .44 Bulldog had been kept loaded in one of the kitchen drawers. Tom and Laura didn't have children; none of their friends had children, and according to Gary, an unloaded gun was as useless as a rock.

Gary was familiar with guns, as his job as a forest preserves officer required that he carry one while on duty. He had offered to take Tom to the shooting range on several occasions so that Tom could become familiar with the Bulldog, but Tom always declined. He settled for five or ten minutes of instruction out in the driveway on how to load, unload, use the safety, aim, and shoot although no shooting had ever occurred. Art had run out of bullets firing at Tom, and had never come close to hitting him. This was probably because he couldn't see well enough to hit anything. But here was Tom, facing a first-degree murder charge because a friend had given him a gun, and he had decided to use it.

Larry asked how the argument started that morning. Tom explained that Art was very upset that the bar had finished another month in the red. He wanted to go over the books with Tom, and he wanted to do it that Sunday morning.

Tom had reluctantly agreed to meet Art at Tom's house. Art arrived with a file box full of documents, and immediately started accusing Tom of being a bad manager, and a poor businessman. Tired of being yelled at, Tom told Art that if he would stay out of the bar, and quit scaring the customers away, maybe he would have a chance of making the Odyssey work.

Art blew up, turned and stormed off of the porch, and Tom watched from the kitchen window thinking Art was leaving. Instead, he saw him reach in the front seat of the Lincoln, and start walking back to the house with a gun in his hand.

Tom quickly got the Bulldog out of the kitchen drawer, and went out to the back porch to meet him. He wasn't going to let Art in the house carrying a gun. Laura was there. He called to Art to put the gun down. Art's response was to raise his right arm and start firing.

Tom fired back as he backed into the house. Art kept coming. Tom thought he shot Art once or twice with some of the last shots he fired, as Art was pretty close by then. Tom entered the kitchen badly shaken, and not knowing what was going to happen next. Just then Laura came out of the bedroom asking what happened. He told her. She looked out on the porch and saw Art lying there, bleeding, and went into hysterics.

Now Larry decided to ask about the ax. If it weren't for the ax to explain away, Tom would have a great case of self-defense.

Tom explained that there was an ax that he kept by the wood pile on the side of the garage to split wood with in the winter for the fireplace. He said he hadn't used it in months. He insisted he had no recollection of touching it on Sunday, and thought Jim Weber must have been seeing things if he thought Tom had hit Art over the head three times with the ax.

Larry decided to let him tell the story. Part of being a good defense lawyer was being a good listener. He wanted to listen carefully to see if he thought Tom was telling the truth, or just bullshitting him like so many criminal clients do. He was also testing what he heard this time against what Tom had told him the first day in Jail. The stories were remarkably similar but now Larry knew a little more about the facts, and was able to dig deeper into the details.

Tom recalled how he tried to calm Laura down after the shooting was over which took some considerable doing. He then decided he should check on Art to see if he was alive or dead. To his horror, when he went back out to the porch, Art was gone! Where the hell could he have gone? He knew he had shot him. He remembered seeing blood on Art's tee shirt. This couldn't be happening!

Tom recounted how everything went into slow motion at that time. It was almost like he was having an out of body experience. He remembered being very frightened that Art was hiding in the oleander bushes, and was going to ambush him.

He couldn't find Art's gun on the porch either, which meant he still had it. He watched himself as if in a dream searching for Art, worried about Laura, and worrying that Art was going to find a way to shoot at him again. He was sure it was all a bad dream and he would wake up. It wasn't. This was a real as it gets.

Tom couldn't remember going back to the house, but his next recollection was calling Gary.

Gary was his best friend. He was sort of a cop. He would know what to do. Tom couldn't think. Laura was screaming again. The dogs were barking, and Tom couldn't think. What to do? What to do?

Gary answered. It took Tom a few minutes to tell Gary what had happened. Laura was still screaming. He couldn't think with her screaming like that. God, he wished she would stop screaming so he could think!

He remembered Gary said he would come right over. He remembered Gary said to call 9-1-1 just as soon as they hung up. Laura was still screaming. Would she ever shut up? He hung up with Gary.

He spent a few more minutes trying to calm Laura down, assuring her that he was all right, she was all right, and everything would be okay. He looked out, and saw the dogs barking incessantly. He went out to the porch, whistled for them, and put them in the kennel by the side of the garage.

Shit! Gary said to call 9-1-1. He'd better do that! He did. He told the operator what had happened.

She wanted him to stay on the line, but it was taking forever.

His next memory was seeing Gary's pickup pull into the driveway and walking towards him. Just about then, he heard the sirens in the distance. He and Gary had decided to wait in the shade on the back porch and walked out with their hands up when the police arrived, as Gary told him that was what he should do unless he wanted to get shot by the police. Gary told him this would be a Priority One call, and the cops would exit their vehicles with guns drawn. They weren't going to take any chances with their own lives with some unknown shooter who already told the 9-1-1 Operator he had shot someone.

Then he gave his statement to the detective. The detective made a phone call, and then told Tom he was placing him under arrest. Tom willingly complied; said goodbye to Laura, and that was about it. He again denied touching the ax, or hitting Art with it. He couldn't believe anyone would think he could do something like that.

That was when Larry heard the door to the conference room open. Laura poked her head in, then ran in and gave her husband a big hug. Ralph followed her into the room. They never did get to the Subway sandwiches. Larry vowed he was going to develop better eating habits. This was the second time this week he had missed lunch because of Tom.

CHAPTER 12

▼

After Tom, Laura, and Ralph left the office, Larry was exhausted. He asked Karen to type up her notes and save them in Tom's file that had already been opened. Larry was hungry, and decided to run over to El Charro, a landmark Tucson Mexican Food Restaurant that was only a block away, for a quick lunch. At this time of day it wouldn't be busy, and he needed a break. On the way over his cell phone rang. It was Paul Lattimore.

"Larry, it's Paul. I've finished my scene investigation, and we look at the van this afternoon. I think you will like the fly over pictures I got. You can see the scuffmarks on the pavement the van left when it went out of control. It follows a path out to the right edge of the roadway where it finally came to rest. It looks like the driver was driving at or below the 75 mph speed limit. From the scuff-marks, it also looks like the right front wheel locked up, and left skid marks before the other tires did. I'm taking Don Hastings with me to look at the van. He's an SAE certified automotive engineer. He used to work for Galaxy. He should know what to look for. I'll call back when we're done. Is there anything else you want us to do?"

Not being an engineer, or an accident re-constructionist Larry replied, "Paul, I'll leave it up to you and Don. Take plenty of pictures. If you see a part that needs to be examined later, photograph it well. Mike and Margaret need some answers and if this case is going to fly, I need proof of why that van rolled.

"Get interior shots of the van too, and check all of the seatbelts. If this is a seatbelt failure case I need to know that.

"Check the tires and photograph them. Measure the tread depth. Pull the wheels and check the brake pads and rotors. Anything you can think of. I don't think we will get a second shot at seeing this van.

"I'm going to file a motion with the court to have it preserved as evidence, but I need an affidavit from you first to tell the court what I think I'm going to find, so do everything you can today. This is an important one Paul, don't let me down."

Paul replied, "I won't. Don and I have worked together for years. We are a good team. What I don't see, he will, and vice versa. I'll call you tomorrow with our findings."

"Thanks, Paul. I'll talk to you tomorrow." Larry ended the call, and ordered the El Charro combination plate for lunch. This was much more food than he needed, but it let him have a little of everything. It was good to have a break. He turned off his cell phone. He needed peace and quiet if only for a few minutes.

The rest of the day was uneventful. Just the usual phone calls and mail that had to be dealt with. Cindy wanted to leave at Four Thirty because she needed to do something with one of her kids. He let her go. He just had to quit doing that. One thing at a time. The Cindy problem hadn't reached critical mass yet, and it could be dealt with later.

He called the Newmans to let them know about Paul's preliminary findings. They were glad to hear from him. Larry had learned a long time ago that most of keeping a client happy was just keeping in touch, and letting them know what he was doing for them and what he was learning about the case. He had told them he would get right on this, and he wanted them to know he was true to his word. He assured them he would call them again tomorrow.

Mike still wasn't back at work. His employer had given him three weeks off with pay. He was grateful for that, but even so, didn't really know how he would return and be even semi-productive when the leave of absence was used up. Mike assured Larry the insurance check was expected soon and confirmed that Larry would get the cost advance as soon as the check arrived. Larry told him thanks and hoped it would be soon, as Paul and Don were sure to submit a whopper of a bill.

If this was going to turn into a products case against Galaxy the twenty-five thousand dollars would evaporate before no time, and he would be left to finance the rest of the case on his own. A deal with a client, while always subject to later negotiation, was pretty much cast in stone. He didn't want to send the wrong signal to the Newmans by asking them for more money before he even got the first costs check.

Clients always expected the lawyer to do everything he said he would do, and more, expense be damned. He was glad the Newmans had agreed to help out at least a little. Larry remembered reading somewhere that Galaxy had a recall on brakes on their vans for caliper springs that would break, causing the brake pads to clamp down on the rotors, and lock up a wheel. This sounded like a logical reason why the right front tire might have locked up. If that is what it ultimately turned out to be, the school was no longer a potential defendant.

Later, back at the office, he did an internet search on automobile recalls and learned that in fact Galaxy had a current recall going on brake calipers that could produce sudden, unexpected braking if the failure occurred. Larry printed the information for the file.

He then checked the news services and found a number of stories on Galaxy van accidents because of sudden, unexpected front wheel braking, usually occurring at highway speeds, and often resulting in a rollover accident. Ten deaths had been reported, and Galaxy was deep into the blame game pointing the finger at its supplier of calipers. Several lawsuits were well underway.

Larry printed those articles as well, and decided he would contact the lawyers who were handling those cases from other states. There was no need to reinvent the wheel when he could go to school on someone else's litigation discovery and documents already received from Galaxy on the issue of the front brake calipers. He would also check with the school to see if it ever got the recall notice. If it did, and didn't bring the van in within a reasonable time, it was still a potential defendant.

On the way home that night, Larry opened the sunroof on the Camry and reflected on the last three days. He again turned to the Oldies station hoping to hear "Celebration." Instead he heard "Satisfaction" by the Stones. This wasn't a bad second choice considering the whirlwind of activity he had been through this week. He had a good fee safely tucked away in the bank, a criminal client out on bail, and a great PI case well on the way. He wished every week could be so productive. He decided to call Laura's cell phone just to see if Tom had any questions.

Laura answered on the first ring. They were fine, but she wanted to get over to the house. She had left enough food and water out for the dogs and the horse when she left on Sunday, but she wanted to get over there tomorrow to check on them, and take the dogs over to Gary's. The horse would have to stay put for the time being.

He asked to speak to Tom, and reminded him not to talk about the case even with Gary as anything he said to anyone other than Larry, Larry's employees or

Laura could be subject to being used against him at trial. It was certain Gary was going to be called as a witness, so it would be best if they just did not discuss anything about the case until the trial was over. Tom said he understood, and would tell Gary they were forbidden to communicate about the case.

Larry promised to call the detective to see if the scene had been cleared. Larry wanted to get over there himself to view the lay of the land with his own eyes, and take David Norton with him to take photos. Having something described to you is one thing. Seeing it is another.

That evening, Larry and the kids and Maggie all enjoyed their backyard pool and each other's company. The kids were growing up way too fast. The summer would go quickly. Once September arrived, Tom's trial would be right around the corner, and following that, the Newman case would be heating up. He decided he had better enjoy Larry Jr. and Leann while he could. They would only be little once.

He was looking forward to hitting the lake this weekend, and towing the kids behind the boat on the new big inner tube he had recently purchased. He was hoping he might even start to teach Larry Jr. how to water ski on his new set of children's skis. The way the summer was shaping up, it might be the only chance to get to the lake all summer.

Life was good, and he had a lot to be thankful for. Maybe "Celebration" would play on the radio during his drive time to work tomorrow. He hoped so. If it didn't, he decided he would stop at Circuit City, and buy the old CD by Kool and the Gang so he could listen to it whenever he wanted to. It was a corny old disco dance song, but it was fun to listen to and sing along with. It also accurately reflected his current mood. Larry had never felt so confident about his future.

CHAPTER 13

▼

June 7th

The alarm went off at five o'clock. The morning guys were just signing on, and telling the Tucson area that today was going to be another hot one. No surprise there.

Larry rolled out of bed, put on his jogging shorts, and hit the street for his three-mile morning run. It was so hard to get motivated to run with so much going on at work, but once he had the first half-mile under his feet, it got easier.

The morning was beautiful. The sun was low in the sky just over the Rincon Mountains to the east. The longest day of the year was just a few weeks away, and then daylight hours would start to shorten by a few minutes every day. Larry felt so energized; he literally decided to go the extra mile and headed up towards Soldier Trail Road rather than take his usual route around Longhorn Drive.

He had some time to collect his thoughts. With nothing on the calendar today, he decided he would call Detective Cotter first thing and get clearance to go to the Rogers' home to look at the crime scene. It was always helpful to see with your own eyes what had been described to you. It always looked so different. He would bring his digital camera and Dave Norton along to preserve the vision and have an independent witness to testify about the photos that were taken.

He also needed to call Rick Bay and find out when the Preliminary Hearing would be held so he could get it on the calendar and start planning who to call as witnesses, if any. A PH was really more of a time to listen and learn about what the prosecution really had in the way of evidence. He held no hope that Tom wouldn't be bound over for trial. It was rare that anyone got cut loose at a PH, but there was always a chance. Visiting the scene was a must before the PH. He wanted a diagram of the home laid out on the lot so the Judge hearing the case could also get the lay of the land so to speak.

He decided to call Copper State Aerial to see if they had any aerial views of Tom's neighborhood. Copper State routinely surveyed the city for different private interests, and sometimes he would get lucky, and find just what he needed from their archives. If not, he could always call Paul Lattimore and have it done privately. It would be more expensive, but he would get exactly what he wanted. For once, he had some money to spend on investigation and case development. He wasn't going to waste Tom's money, but it was nice to know it was there if he needed to use it. The aerial photo would also be a good exhibit at trial so the jury could see exactly what was being described in words. Most people weren't that visual, and needed help in understanding word descriptions.

As he approached the end of his run with the house in sight, he remembered Laura also needed to go to the house to care for the horse and the dogs. It would be a good idea to have her and Tom there too.

He entered the house as quietly as he could. Maggie and the kids would still be asleep. It was only five forty-seven. School had finished for the year in mid-May, and there was no need for the whole house to be up this time of the morning.

He made it back into the house without waking the kids. Maggie got up and joined him for a cup of coffee and a glass of juice out by the pool. He shared his plans for the day with her and told her he would try to be home in time for another quick swim with the kids before dinner.

She knew he meant it, but held little hope it would happen. She had come to realize years ago that Larry was driven by work. It was what defined him as a man. It was why she had been so attracted to him in the first place. Always thinking ahead. Always planning. Never wasting a waking moment. She kissed him good-bye, and told him to have a great day. He said he would.

It was just a few minutes past eight when Larry pulled into the office parking lot. Cindy's Mustang was already there. What a shock! Maybe today was the day she would turn over a new leaf. He hoped so. He had enough on his plate already. He didn't want to have to deal with personnel issues right now. Cindy might be a pain in the ass, but she was a typing wizard. She could do more work in an hour than a lot of others could do in a day.

As he entered the office, he could smell the coffee brewing. He could also smell Krispy Kreme doughnuts. Not only was Cindy at work early, she had made the coffee and brought disgustingly delightful delicious doughnuts too. This was definitely going to be a good day.

His first call was to Norton. He was available to go out to Tom's. He would wait for the call. His second call was to Copper State. They would pull the aerials they had of Tom's neighborhood to see if there was anything useful. The photos were only three years old, so they should work. Tom's house had been there for over thirty years, so there wasn't much that was going to change other than a mesquite tree growing a little more. He made an appointment to stop by at two P.M. to look at what they had.

His next call was to Cotter. Cotter said the scene would be released back to Tom and Laura today. The Sheriff's Office was done gathering evidence and photographing the bullet holes and taking the measurements they felt were necessary. He gave Larry a green light to go out to the scene and take anyone he wanted with him.

Rick Bay was next. Rick said the PH was set for Wednesday, June 12 in front of Justice of the Peace Jerry Easton. The hearing was set for one thirty and would go until finished. Bay said he planned to call Cotter, Parchman, the M.E. and a criminalist from the Sheriff's Office who had conducted the paraffin tests on Tom and Art. The same criminalist would be called to testify about bullet trajectory, and the other physical evidence that he had gathered at the scene. Larry told him of his plans to get an aerial photo of Tom's house. Bay said he would have no objection to it, and told Larry he was sorry he hadn't thought of it first.

Laura was next. She agreed to meet Larry and Norton out at the house at ten A.M. Tom would come with her. He then called Norton back. Norton would meet Larry at the office at nine thirty, and they would go out together to meet Tom and Laura and see for themselves what real bullet holes looked like.

As Norton and Larry were driving out to the scene Larry's cell phone rang. It was Laura.

"Larry, it's Laura. Tom and I just got to the house, and something terrible has happened. The house has been ransacked, and horrible things have been written all over the walls in spray paint. What should we do?"

Larry didn't have to think very hard before giving an answer. "Don't touch anything. Stay out of the house. I'll call Detective Cotter and report this. Maybe he can come right out to take a report. I'm sorry Laura. Are the horse and the dogs okay?"

"Yes, thank God," was the answer. "Whoever did this left a mess, and the language is horrible. I'm scared, Larry. I think some of Art's friends did this."

"Why do you think that?"

"Because of what the awful words say. Hurry and see for yourself."

Larry assured her he was on the way and would be there in a few minutes.

He called Cotter and to his surprise actually got him on the phone. He was so used to leaving voice mail messages these days it was a surprise when someone actually picked up the phone. Cotter told Larry he would send a forensic unit out right away, and would also come out himself. Larry told him that Laura thought some of Art's friends might be behind this. Cotter wasn't surprised. He knew Art Mendoza was a bad apple and most of his friends were just as bad. Retaliation and revenge were a lot more understandable to Mendoza and his ilk than was justice and orderly court proceedings. At least no one was hurt. Intimidation was one thing. Physical violence was much worse.

Larry and Norton arrived at the home a few minutes later. Laura was hysterical as she and Tom met them in the driveway. Tom looked really shaken. He was doing his best to console his twenty-eight year-old wife who had been through so much trauma in the last five days. He wasn't sure how much more she could take. He wasn't sure how much more he could take. He wished he had never heard of Art Mendoza, and certainly wished he hadn't gone into business with him. God, he wished they had never met!

Larry asked Tom and Laura to wait out on the back porch while he and Norton went into the house. Norton had his camera in hand. He preferred his own, and had told Larry to leave his at the office.

It was an unforgettable sight. As they entered the kitchen through the back door, the first thing Larry saw was the refrigerator lying on its side. The door was open, and all of the food was spilled out and dumped all over the floor.

The same mess applied to the cupboards. Every dish, every glass, and every box of food had been pulled out and thrown on the floor. Broken glass was everywhere. The kitchen table and chairs had been broken like matchsticks. The tile counters had been smashed with hammers. A big pile of horseshit had been left in the sink. This was no robbery. This was vandalism at its worst.

Norton busied himself taking photos of the kitchen while Larry went into the dining room/living room area. Then he saw the message scrawled in spray paint across the living room wall.

"Arts ded. Yur bich is nex"

There was no room for doubt in that message. Laura was a target. Her safety was in danger. This was a threat that had to be taken seriously. He called to Norton to come in and photograph this message.

The living room wasn't any different than the kitchen. Chainsaws had been used to cut up the furniture. Quarts of motor oil had been dumped on the carpet, the empty bottles left behind. Horseshit had been smeared on the walls. The front window was broken out.

Larry made his way down the hallway. The hall bathroom had been trashed as well. Hammers did a good job of destroying ceramic tile counters and bathtub enclosures. More horseshit was in the sink, and the bathtub. Whoever did this wasn't afraid to get their hands dirty. The smell was overpowering

As Larry entered the master bedroom he saw the message written in lipstick on Laura's mirror over the dresser.

"Yur ded Bich!"

Again, no room for doubt—Laura was a target.

Norton photographed everything. He and Larry touched nothing although they were pretty sure whoever did this wouldn't be dumb enough to leave any fingerprints behind.

Larry and Norton met Tom and Laura on the porch. It was then that Larry noticed the bullet holes through the roof of the porch and through the window from the porch to the dining room. He could also see bloodstains on the cement porch floor.

Larry addressed Tom: "Do you have any idea who might have done this?"

Tom shook his head. "No. Art had a lot of unsavory friends but I didn't even know most of them by name. They would come by the bar and Art pretty much kept me away from them. Larry. We're scared. Laura is in danger. We need some police protection."

Larry agreed. "Laura, I think you should consider going back to Ohio to be with your family for awhile. Tom can't leave, as his conditions of release won't let him leave the State and he has to be here to help me with the case and make court appearances. I just don't think you should rely on the police to protect you. They can't give you twenty four-seven protection, and the best thing is for you to leave town. I think you should leave today."

Laura looked at him. "I can't leave Tom, he needs me. Why is this happening to us? Am I really in danger?"

Larry replied, "I think you are. I think we have to take this seriously. Whoever did this is probably capable of violence. Criminals don't think like rational people. Art's people want revenge, and the best way to get revenge is to hurt someone close to Tom. That would be you. I really think you should leave town today."

Laura resisted. "But don't you need me for the trial?"

Larry thought about that one. "Probably, but that is a ways off. Trial won't be until September, or later. Tempers can cool off between now and then. We can always bring you back for the trial. I don't want to have to worry about your safety all summer while we get ready for trial.

"Tom needs to focus on the case. I can't have him distracted by worrying about whether some thug is going to kill you. Right now, I think you and Tom should get back to the Millers and you should call the airlines and get a flight out today. I'm dead serious about this Laura. You need to do this."

She wouldn't give up. "What about the dogs? What about the horse? Who will take care of them?"

Tom spoke up, "Laura, I think Larry is right. I'll take care of the dogs and the horse. I can find a stable for the horse, and the dogs can stay at the Millers with me. They'll be fine. It's you I'm worried about. I just don't know what I'd do if something happened to you. I love you! Let's go call your mom and make a plane reservation. I'll be okay. Larry needs me here, and I can't leave anyway. You can. I think you should leave today."

Laura knew she had lost this fight. She also knew that Tom and Larry were right. She was so sorry she had introduced Tom to Art Mendoza. This terrible man had ruined their life. In a few short months everything had fallen apart. Now her husband was accused of first-degree murder, and she was in danger. She agreed to make the arrangements to leave today.

Tom and Laura left for the Millers. Tom told Larry he would keep Laura's cell phone in case he needed to call him.

What a mess!! Larry had hoped for a nice scene investigation and now he had another problem on his hands.

Cotter showed up with the forensic team shortly after Laura and Tom left for the Millers. Larry walked him through the house, showing him the destruction, and the vivid messages that had been left behind.

Cotter agreed that Laura was indeed in danger, and the best thing was for her to leave town. She couldn't be hurt if she wasn't here, and Art's friends probably weren't energetic enough to try to find out where she went. If they did, they wouldn't bother to follow her all the way to Ohio to carry out their threats. This was a problem that could best be solved by taking the intended victim out of harm's way.

Cotter then walked Larry and Norton through the scene pointing out all of the bullet holes in the porch and against the garage brick wall. He showed them the pool of blood at the end of the driveway where Art had crawled. Larry was amazed at the distance between the porch and the end of the driveway. It had to be one hundred fifty feet or more.

Cotter also showed them the woodpile by the side of the garage and the place where Art's body had been dragged to on the blanket. Again, Larry was amazed at the distance Tom had dragged Art's body. He must have been very strong or very determined. Tom was not a big guy; probably one hundred eighty-five pounds at most, and only about 5'8". How could he have dragged Art's fat ass that far?

Norton took photos. Cotter assured Larry that a full disclosure would be made of everything the Sheriff's Office had done, but Larry wanted his own photos just in case the forensic team might have missed something. This was a big case. A man's life was at stake, and he wanted to make sure he took the time to do as good a job as he could.

Cotter also pointed out where Art's car had been parked. Just as Tom, had said, there was a clear view from the house window to the area in the driveway where Art had parked. Tom would definitely have been able to see Art coming back to the house with a gun in his hand.

Cotter even shared with Larry that he was reluctant to arrest Tom, and had done so only because McNair had insisted. Cotter's personal belief was that Mendoza had this one coming, and had gotten what he asked for and deserved. Without the ax, Tom would have taken a walk on this one.

Larry told Cotter that Tom admitted the shootout, but denied ever touching the ax.

"Yeah right," was Cotter's reply, "his fingerprints are all over it. Art's hair and blood are all over it, and we have an eyewitness that saw him hit Art with it three times. How can he not remember that? He should just own up to it, and cop a plea for manslaughter. Nice guy like Tom will probably get probation."

"Yes, but he would be a convicted felon, and that would stay with him for the rest of his life," was Larry's reply.

Cotter looked at him. "That's better than being dead, or in prison for twenty-five to life."

Larry decided on the way back to the office that he had to question Tom more carefully about the ax. He also put in a call to Doug Ball to get an exam date set up. He would need Doug's opinion on this one whether he called him as a witness or not. Ball's secretary set up an appointment for Friday at one P.M. Larry assured her Tom would be there.

Larry got lucky that afternoon. Copper State Aerial had a good shot of Tom's street. By cropping the photo and enlarging it, Larry had a great aerial shot of the Rogers' house, the Weber house, and how the Rogers' driveway connected to Avenida Grande and Avenida Aquilar. The garage could be seen off to the back of the house, just off the covered back porch and the woodpile next to the garage could even be seen.

The pool wasn't in the photo as that was added after Tom and Laura had bought the house, but the pool was of no consequence. It didn't play a part in this so it didn't matter it wasn't in the photo. There was even a car parked in the driveway very near where Art's car had been parked. For seventy-five bucks, Larry had secured an excellent visual tool to use at the PH and the trial. The same thing would have cost five hundred, or more if Lattimore had done it fresh. Copper State would have it ready for pickup the following day.

He went back to the office and called Tom on Laura's cell phone. He told Tom to be at Dr. Ball's the next day at one o'clock, and explained Doug's role in this. Tom agreed to be there. Tom also told Larry that Laura had reservations to leave for Ohio at six P.M. He wasn't happy about it, but he knew Larry was right. Laura probably was in danger, and he wanted her where she would be safe.

It was now a little after three. He made a few more phone calls, dictated some letters for Cindy to work on, and decided to leave early. It had been a full day, and he wanted to get home early to see the kids. Maggie was surprised when he called and said he was on his way home. She told him they would be in the pool waiting for him.

CHAPTER 14

▼

Julio and Oscar Mendoza pulled into Maria's Auto Salvage about noon. Julio was driving his prized '74 Monte Carlo low-rider. The trunk was filled with batteries, and the undercarriage was a complex array of hydraulics that could make the car ride high, ride low, or even "dance" by jumping the front end up and down on the skinny tires that were framed by fancy chrome-spoke-wheels. This was early for them. They were brothers, only one year apart in age. They were the bastard sons of Maria Mendoza and two different boyfriends. Neither of them had ever met their father, and didn't want to.

Their mother Maria was the worthless alcoholic baby sister of Art Mendoza. Never married, always drunk, and completely dependent on her big brother to take care of her. And take care of her he did.

The auto salvage business was in Maria's name. Being a female, and from a minority group, it was a shoe in to get the City contract for towing. Art supplied the money, his lawyer took care of all the proper licensing, and a very odd book-keeper who asked very few questions would show up once a week and spend an afternoon going over the ledgers and preparing the financial reports necessary to keep the motor vehicle department happy. A computer geek kept the inventory up to date. With the push of a button, he could tell you every make, model and year car that was in the yard, why it was there, where it came from, and if it was damaged, where, and what parts were available for salvage.

Most people didn't realize it, but the auto salvage business was a gold mine. Parts were worth more than a whole car. Towed cars were often later abandoned by the owners. A title service would apply for and receive abandoned titles on cars left over sixty days without being claimed. Title in hand, the yard could part out the cars to body shops and garages that always needed used parts.

Insurance companies always insisted on using LKQ (like kind and quality, or used) parts to repair any car five years old or more. A hood and a door could bring hundreds of dollars. A set of wheels and tires would easily go for a hundred bucks. Air bags and dashboards would go for five hundred each, and it was all found money. The salvage yard's investment consisted of a tow, and sixty days of storage, plus a few bucks to the title service to handle the paperwork.

Sometimes they got lucky, and a really nice car would be abandoned. It then made its way to the auto auction in Phoenix, and would fetch several thousand dollars.

Overhead was low. Four tow trucks were always on call to respond to accident scenes, and tow the disabled cars to the yard. They also responded to tows requested by private businesses for parking violations. They would charge the hapless dumb-ass that couldn't read a sign up to two hundred bucks to get his car back, depending on how many miles the car was towed. They demanded cash. No credit cards, no checks. No cash, no car.

They also did repo work for the banks. Repo work was easy and fun. Find the car, have a key made from the vehicle identification number (VIN) the bank was glad to supply, and snatch it in the middle of the night or during the day right out from under the deadbeat owner's nose.

The key was used to enter the car, and unlock the steering column, and the car would be towed to the yard. Five hundred bucks a pop for very little work. The banks were glad to pay, and the boys were glad to take their money.

Julio and Oscar loved nothing more than grabbing a new Lexus or Mercedes out of an office parking lot and towing it back to the yard. This was legal car theft that paid well, and carried very little risk. What could be better? People were always in over their heads on fancy cars. The banks never seemed to learn. They kept lending money for fancy cars to people who couldn't afford them. Hey, what did they care? Business was business.

Tows from private businesses were even more fun. Reading the VIN from the driver's corner of the windshield, they could have a key made in an instant from the mobile key service van they always had on call. Or they could use a Slim-Jim to pop the door lock, enter the car and ready it for towing. More than once, they would watch the rear view mirror as a bewildered deadbeat behind in his payments, exited a store or office to watch his car being hauled away on a flatbed tow truck. Once in while, someone would show up while the car was being readied for towing. Once in awhile, someone would try to resist. The boys loved that.

They chose to work together, and between their heavily tattooed arms, bulging muscles, and menacing demeanor, people backed off pretty quick. Those who didn't found a stiletto knife in their face.

As soon as the car was on the truck, the police would be called, and the snatch would be reported as a legitimate repo or tow. That way, if the owner would call the car in as stolen, the police would already know the car was in fact not stolen, but repoed or towed because of a parking violation. They were on a first name basis with most of the patrol deputies on the Tucson Police Department and the Pima County Sheriff's Office.

The tow trucks had no name on the side and were identified only by a business license number, which the police had on file to verify if an owner called it in. They didn't want owners to know where the cars were being taken, and they made it difficult for them to find out. That avoided a lot of reverse snatches where the owner finds the car, and drives it away using his own keys to do so.

Maria's was way out by the airport, an out-of-the-way place that was hard to find, and took a long time to drive to. The land was leased from the State for next to nothing. A Police sanctioned chop shop is what it amounted to.

Maria's Auto Salvage was legitimate in every way. Art had made sure of that. It was a great source of income for the whole family, and gave him a source of income he could claim on his tax returns so the cops wouldn't wonder where he got his money. He couldn't hold any of the licenses because of his felony convictions, but he was carried on the payroll as a consultant. He rarely went to the yard, but he knew its finances well.

On a good month two hundred thousand dollars could roll through the yard. Overhead for everything was less than forty thousand a month, including all the drivers and yard guys it took to run the place. The rest got divided up among Art, Julio, Oscar, Maria and Angie. Because so much of it was cash, a lot of it didn't get reported. There was no need to pay taxes if you didn't have to!

The yard was also a good cover for Art's marijuana business, and Julio and Oscar's cocaine business. It was so vast, and gave so many places to hide a few pounds of grass or coke, that no one could ever find it, even if they did have a search warrant.

The car crusher also came in handy from time to time to get rid of a hot car that the police were looking for, or a weapon that had been used in a hit or a heist.

In business for ten years now, Maria's was known to law enforcement as the tow yard of choice. Despite Art's past record, no one suspected that tons of marijuana and kilos of cocaine went through the place every month. Maria's was incorporated. None of the corporate officers had any criminal background and a lot of the police didn't even know it was Art's baby. On paper it was clean as a whistle.

Julio and Oscar were thugs. They carried stilettos with them at all times. They loved to use them. Julio cut the nose off a dealer who owed him money once. That son of a bitch never snorted coke again, and the word got out quick not to fuck around with Julio.

Oscar stuck his stiletto into the left eye of some "Chollo" who had been giving his girl the eye. Well, now he only had one eye to look at women with, and he damned sure wouldn't be looking at Oscar's woman anymore. Oscar had long since moved on to another girl. So what! The prick deserved what he got!

The dealer knew he would be killed if he reported the maiming. The "Chollo" knew the same. "Don't mess with the Mendoza boys" was the mantra of the barrio that covered the south side of Tucson.

The previous night had been a blast for them. Rather than repoing cars, they drove a nondescript old Chevy van out to the Rogers' house, and waited for cover of darkness to strike.

Rogers had really screwed up their business by killing Art. Art had all the contacts. Dumb as he was, he was a lot smarter than Julio and Oscar put together. Their livelihood was being threatened. They couldn't believe this wimpy little white boy had taken out their big bad Uncle Art.

It was thrilling to wreck the Rogers' home and write graffiti on the walls. The horseshit was Oscar's idea. Julio thought it was a lot of work to bring the shit in from the horse arena to the house but a wheelbarrow and a couple of shovels they found out by the arena had made it a lot easier. It left a powerful message of intimidation and a helluva mess as well.

It was Julio's idea to threaten Tom's skinny assed little wife. They had seen her once or twice at the bar. They talked of making her suffer for her husband's misdeeds.

Julio would make sure she suffered. They hadn't yet decided who would get the pleasure of slitting her throat after they had tortured her and made her beg for her life. First they wanted to make her afraid. Then, when she least expected it, they would pounce on her and she would be theirs. Julio and Oscar enjoyed watching people suffer while they tortured them. The Chevy van would make a perfect kidnap vehicle. The tool shed at the yard would be a perfect torture chamber. When they were done, her body could go in the trunk of a car headed for the crusher, and no one would ever know what happened to her. She would be gone without a trace.

They also wanted to take care of the preppy lawyer who was defending Tom. They saw him once or twice as he was coming and going from the office. They could take him, easy. They had to be more careful with him. Lawyers were high profile, and would be missed a lot more than some Gringo skinny bitch. They left him a note and a dead pigeon on his doorstep, but the dumb fuck must not have appreciated the threat, as he was still on the case. They decided they would leave him alone for now. Tom would just get another lawyer if they took him out. Tucson was filled with lawyers. Someone would take his case. They could always take Mr. Preppy out later.

There would be no acquittal for Tom. They would get his wife. If he was convicted and sent to prison, they would make sure their contacts on the inside would spread the word. Tom would be someone's bitch within a week of entering The Joint. He fucked them by killing their Uncle. He would get fucked over and over for years to come.

If he got lucky, and Mr. Preppy got him off, well then Tom and Mr. Preppy could kiss each other's asses goodbye. It might take awhile, but the Mendoza's would strike, and Tom and Larry would die a tortuous death.

Making people suffer was sport for Julio and Oscar. They hoped Tom would be acquitted. That would give them the personal pleasure of seeing the little wimp suffer at their hands at the end of their stilettos.

Mr. Preppy didn't know it, but he was going to get it one way or the other when the trial was over. Win or lose, it made no difference to them. He was a dead man. Julio and Oscar dreamed how they would torture Larry before killing him. Cutting his tongue out, and gouging out his eyes would be a good start.

They were bad to the bone, and they weren't going to let Art's death go unpunished.

The rest of the day they spent conducting legitimate business. The police helped them out all day long by taking their reports of snatched cars. What a wonderful world they lived in!

CHAPTER 15

▼

Larry got to the office about eight thirty-five on Friday morning. It was late for him, but early for Cindy. To his surprise, the Mustang was there, and he could smell the coffee as he entered the office. Cindy was even at her desk typing on the computer keyboard. Larry decided he had to ask a question.

"Turning over a new leaf?"

Her reply was predictable, "What do you mean?"

"I couldn't help but notice that you were early yesterday, and it looks like you were early again today. What's up? Usually you can't get here any earlier than nine o'clock, even though you know I like you here by eight thirty."

She pouted like Larry had spoken an untruth. "Billy picked up the girls Wednesday night for his six weeks of summer visitation. He took them back to Tennessee with him. With just myself to get ready in the morning, and no one to take to daycare, it seems like I have oodles of time in the morning. Would you prefer I come in later?"

Nice try Cindy, Larry thought as he formed a reply. "No. I like you here when I get in. I like the phone to be answered by eight thirty. I'm going to look forward to the next six weeks. I've got some phone calls to make. Did you bring any doughnuts?"

"Do you smell any doughnuts?"

He didn't. Stupid question. He decided to let it be and went to his office.

His first call was to Paul Lattimore. Paul had good news. He and Don had confirmed a broken caliper spring in the right front brake rotor on the van. It was Don's opinion that was why the right front wheel locked up and caused the van to go out of control and flip. They had carefully photographed everything. Measurements had also been taken. They wanted to take the spring, but the insurance storage yard wouldn't let them.

The school's insurance company had also hired a team of experts to go over the van. Anticipating a series of lawsuits, they wanted to determine for themselves if the van had a defect.

This sounded exciting. Larry and the school might be on the same page, and would take a united front against Galaxy, and Southfield Spring, the manufacturer of the caliper spring. From the beginning, Larry didn't like the thought of suing a Catholic High School. He asked Paul and Don to put an affidavit together to document their findings, and include the photos and measurements as exhibits. He decided to call King and Branch in Dallas Texas next.

King and Branch was a huge PI firm headquartered in Dallas. They were mentioned in many of the news articles Larry had pulled up about the Galaxy caliper spring problem. Brad King was truly the king of medical malpractice. He had a string of victories and was invincible in the courtroom.

Mitchell Branch was the king of product liability. Auto manufacturers quivered when they heard his name. It sounded like King & Branch already had the goods on Galaxy and Southfield. Larry wanted to see if they might be interested in associating on this case as well.

Of course he would have to split the fee with them, but these were experienced Product Liability lawyers. They even had their own model division that made mock ups of products to demonstrate the defect to juries. They had engineers on staff. They were Big League. Larry was smart enough to know he needed some help with this one. A big company like Galaxy could bury him in discovery costs.

He told the receptionist who answered that he had a potential wrongful death case against Galaxy, and he thought it was a caliper spring case. She wasted no time in putting him through to Mitchell Branch himself.

Branch was a legend in Product Liability Law. Larry had heard him speak at legal seminars over the years, and had read many of his articles in *Trial* magazine, the voice of the American Association For Justice. (AAJ). He couldn't believe that Branch himself was actually going to speak to him. Speak to him he did.

"Good morning, this is Mitch Branch, how can I help you?" intoned the resonant baritone voice that Larry recognized from the seminar circuit.

"Good morning, Mr. Branch, this is Larry Ross from Tucson. I'm calling you this morning because I have a wrongful death case, and I think it was caused by one of Galaxy's faulty caliper springs. A Galaxy van filled with high school kids went out of control on Interstate 10 and rolled. My clients lost their fourteen-year old twin boys in the wreck. Would you be interested in helping me with the case?"

There! He had gotten it out and managed to sound like he knew what he was talking about. He hoped that Branch had been impressed.

Branch replied, "Please, Larry, call me Mitch. Everybody does. What makes you think this is a caliper spring case? If it is, we are interested, and we can help. We have about five of these going right now, and our engineers have it all figured out. We have Galaxy by the balls on this one."

This was earthy language for a man of stature, but vintage Branch. He was known as a pull-no-punches, spread-no-frosting kind of guy. The guy talk was meant to convey to Larry that he was just one the boys—just another "country lawyer" seeking justice.

Larry decided to take the bait and respond in kind. "I've already had a reconstructionist do a fly over. It shows the right front wheel locked up first, and caused the van to flip. He and a former engineer from Galaxy have looked at the van, and they found a broken caliper spring on the right front. We have photos and measurements. Is that enough to squeeze their balls for some money?"

Branch chuckled at Larry's brashness, and willingness to return an earthy comment with another. He could tell he would like this guy from Tucson. Branch could tell in an instant if someone was okay, or not okay. It was a trial lawyer's instinct, honed by years of interviewing witnesses, taking depositions, selecting juries, and trying cases. This guy Larry Ross was okay. "Larry, it sounds like it. Can you come to Dallas to meet me this weekend?"

Come to Dallas! This weekend! There goes the lake trip! Maggie would be pissed, and the kids would be disappointed. He had promised, and the kids remembered when he promised them anything. Think fast, Larry. You're on the phone with Mitchell Branch. He asked you to come to Dallas. He wants to help out with this case. Better come up with a good one.

"Mitch, I was hoping you or someone else could come out here next week. That way you can meet the clients, and you can look at the evidence my engineers have already gathered. If you bring one of your engineers, the van may still be at the storage yard in Phoenix, and he can look at it there. The school's insurance company has already figured out that this one probably belongs to Galaxy. They are having the van inspected today, and I can probably call their house counsel and have him put a hold on the van so it doesn't get parted out too soon."

There. He said it. He had told the great Mitch Branch to come to him. He was stunned by Branch's reply.

"Larry, that sounds like a great idea. What day next week is good for you and your clients and the engineers? Thursday looks good for me. Will that work?"

Not knowing if it would or wouldn't, he decided to make sure it would work and just insist that everyone make themselves available next Thursday.

"Let me check. Yes. I'll have to move a few things around, but I can make that work." His calendar was clear for next Thursday, but Branch didn't need to know that. Mitch Branch himself was coming out to see Larry Ross! What a thrill. "I'll clear the day. Give me a call when you have the plane reservations so we can decide when to meet. I would suggest you come in Wednesday night, and stay at the downtown Radisson, which is just two blocks from my office. Phoenix is a two-hour drive up the freeway, so we will need to get started early. Should I start setting this up?"

"Sounds good to me," was the reply. "Book two rooms at the Radisson for Wednesday night. Here, I'll give you my credit card number. I'll have Robert Burns with me. He is the chief engineer we have working on this one.

"Give me your office address and phone number. We'll find it, and we don't need a ride from the airport. We'll rent a car. Let's meet at seven sharp on Thursday in the hotel coffee shop. Have your clients and the engineers meet us later at the office. Say about eight? We can get acquainted, and then head to Phoenix to look at the van. Bob and I can fly back to Dallas from Phoenix. You won't mind driving the rental car back and turning it in for me will you? Will that work?"

Larry couldn't believe how easy this was. In less than ten minutes, he had set up one of the most important meetings his career had ever experienced. This was huge. This was colossal. This was going to make all the difference in the outcome of the case. The Great Mitch Branch, helping little Larry Ross from Tucson! He was so excited he could hardly stand it. He collected his thoughts and said, "That will work Mitch. I'll have everything arranged. I'm looking forward to meeting you and Mr. Burns."

He then gave Branch the necessary addresses and phone numbers to his office and the hotel. He got the nicest rooms the Radisson had to offer; suites on the tenth floor that gave a good view of the city.

He called Lattimore and told him that he and Don had to be at his office next Thursday morning at eight thirty. He wanted a half hour with Mitch, Mike and Margaret before getting into the technical engineering discussion. Paul was as excited as Larry was to meet Mitch Branch. He said he and Don would be there.

Then he called Mike and Margaret. He explained to them that the Branch law firm had a great head start on this, and that Mitch Branch was one of the best-known lawyers in the United States. They offered no resistance, and promised to be there.

He called Bruce Masters, chief counsel for Unity Insurance, the school's insurance company. Bruce already knew that Larry was on the case, as the storage yard had called to report whomever had requested access to the van. Bruce promised the van would be there, and would not be looked at again until Branch and Burns had a chance to look at it. He told Larry that his team of engineers was going to inspect it today and wondered where Larry thought this was headed.

"Right into the Galaxy Motor Company Board Room," was his reply.

Bruce liked that answer. Unity had a two million dollar policy on the van, and he was hoping Unity wouldn't have to reserve it. What had originally looked like a potential huge loss for Unity was starting to look like a ninth-inning save.

Bruce said he wanted to be present for the inspection. Larry had no objection to that. Bruce didn't really need to be there. He just wanted to meet Mitch Branch too. Bruce said they could all meet at the storage yard at eleven o'clock. He was going to have them move the van inside the air cooled garage so they would have a hard surface floor to work off of, and not have to cook their brains out in the hot afternoon sun.

Larry's next call was to Maggie. He shared the good news with her. She was quite impressed with the courage Larry had shown by asking Branch to come to him. Of course it made sense. The clients and the van were in Arizona, not Dallas.

The lake trip was saved. Mitch Branch was coming to Tucson, and would partner up with Larry Ross on the Newman case. This was going to be fun. Whatever he was doing, he was doing it right. Everything was lining up perfectly.

He celebrated by going out to Krispy Kreme and picking up some doughnuts. It was almost ten o'clock—time for a morning break.

The morning didn't have much left by the time Larry returned from Krispy Kreme. By lunchtime he wasn't very hungry, as the Krispy Kremes were still sitting at the bottom of his stomach like the lump of lard that they were. How could something that tasted so good going down make you feel so lousy an hour later? When would he learn to remember that before sticking another one in his mouth?

He remembered his vow of just a few days ago to change his eating habits. They had changed, but not for the better. He swore off Krispy Kremes for the rest of the summer, or until Tom's case was over, whichever was longer.

He stayed in over the noon hour, and caught up on correspondence and phone calls. That gave Cindy a few things to do that afternoon. He had a one thirty appointment with Gary Miller that Cindy had set up for him. He was looking forward to talking with Gary, and learning a little more about Tom Rogers.

Gary showed up on time. He assured Larry that he and Tom had not been discussing the case. After sharing concern over Laura's safety and the terrible things that had been done to the Rogers' home they got down to business.

Gary had met Tom at Ohio State. They were in the same dorm as freshmen. Gary majored in Forestry; Tom was a Business major. Tom had an entrepreneurial spirit. He had started a sandwich business in the dorm the first semester. He would go to the grocery store, buy the ingredients, make Hogie Sandwiches on Sunday afternoon, and sell them at the dorms from a pushcart on Sunday nights.

He had a captive, hungry audience. The cafeterias were closed on Sunday nights and the students had to fend for themselves. The dorms didn't allow hot plates or microwave ovens in the rooms, so the options were starve or go out for dinner. Tom had given everyone a third low-cost and satisfying option.

It wasn't long before Tom had two or three other guys helping him make the sandwiches and sell them off the carts. The business became so successful it pretty much paid Tom's way through Ohio State.

Tom and Gary rented a small house together, and had been roommates their junior, and senior years. After graduation, Gary took a job with the U.S. Forest Service and got stationed in Montana. It was beautiful country but very cold in the winter.

Gary had been the Best Man at Tom and Laura's wedding four years ago and Tom had been Gary's Best Man at he and Julie's wedding a year later. Julie and Laura were friends.

When Tom and Laura moved to Tucson, they called Gary and Julie to come for a visit. Gary and Julie liked the weather a lot better than Montana. They had decided one hot summer was better than a cold fall, winter, and spring. Gary asked for and received a transfer to the Tucson area, and was pleased to be assigned to Catalina State Park, which was on the Northwest side, and close to Tom and Laura's home. Gary and Julie bought a home nearby, and the friendship continued.

Gary recalled how he had insisted that Tom and Laura keep a gun in the house. They lived in the unincorporated area of Tucson, and had to rely on the Sheriff's Office for protection. The Sheriff's Office was spread thin. Pima County covered thousands of square miles, and response time in the County was a lot longer than it was in the city.

Gary offered his old .44 Bulldog. It was reliable. It was easy to use, and packed a punch. Tom resisted, but finally agreed. He never would go out to the range with Gary.

According to Gary, Tom was one of the gentlest souls on earth. If he had a flaw, it was that he trusted people too much. Gary never liked Art Mendoza, and told Tom not to go into business with him. Tom said it would be okay. Art was only putting up the money. Tom would run the business, and had been successful at everything he had ever done from the college sandwich cart to Sunshine Solar.

Gary had seen guys like Art operate before. They put up the money, and then controlled your life. Gary also wondered where a fat, ugly man like Art got his money. Something didn't add up.

As the months went by, the unlikely alliance grew strained. Art would park his fat butt in the bar everyday and scare the customers away. Every time Tom would plan a promotion, Art would get drunk, start a fight with someone, and the police would show up. This was not too good for business.

Cinco de Mayo had been a disaster. Memorial Day wasn't any better. Tom had worked really hard to promote Memorial Day. The semester had ended the week prior, and business would be slowing down soon. He wanted another blow-out before all the students left town for the summer, and before the summer sessions began. Art had promised Tom he would stay away from the Odyssey on Memorial Day. He didn't.

He showed up as the party was in full swing. An hour or so later he was drunk on his ass, and mouthing off to a couple of football players who weren't in the mood to take his crap. Soon, the inevitable fight started, and the police showed up again. The customers cleared out, and another opportunity to promote the bar had been wasted.

Tom was worried. The bar was losing money every month. He couldn't keep a cocktail waitress longer than two weeks. Art would be all over them, and they would quit. Tom was worried about a sexual harassment lawsuit.

The State Liquor Board had issued a letter of concern because of all the police calls reported at that location. Two more would mean a hearing to determine if the license should be pulled. The police reported every call to a bar to the Liquor Board.

Tom and Laura were living off of savings. Tom hadn't taken a paycheck since the bar had opened. He asked Art for an advance, and Art had told him: "no fucking way am I giving you any money until this place starts making money. Be a manager, not a fucking crybaby!"

Tom was afraid of Art. He had told Gary about the two-by-four fight in the parking lot. He told Gary how Art had threatened to kill him if he ever interfered in his business. He told Gary that Art would brag about carrying a gun. He told Gary about his gangbanger nephews who would stop by almost daily to pay homage to their uncle. Tom was desperate, and didn't know where to turn.

Then he recalled Sunday, June 3rd. The phone rang about eight o'clock. It was Tom. He was incoherent. He wanted Gary to come right over. Gary calmed him down and Tom told him about the gunfight on the porch. He wanted Gary to come over right away.

Gary told Tom to hang up and call 9-1-1 right away, and to check on Art and give him first aid if he was still alive. He got in his pickup and went straight to Tom's, about a ten-minute drive. He had spent a few minutes explaining to Julie where he was going, and why, and told her she had better stay home.

Tom met Gary in the driveway as he pulled up. He walked him over to Art's body by the woodpile. Gary could see the drag marks in the gravel and asked Tom why he had moved the body. Tom didn't have an answer.

Gary noticed that the back of Art's head looked like it had been bashed in. He asked Tom how that happened, and Tom said he didn't know. They waited for the sheriff in the shade of the porch, and had walked out with their hands up when the first deputy had arrived.

After that, the deputies separated Tom and Gary. Gary didn't have much else to say. He watched as Tom was taken off in handcuffs, and couldn't believe what he was seeing. His best friend was under arrest for murder, and he had never even seen him get into an argument with anyone in the twelve years they had known one another. This was a nightmare. He thanked Larry for getting Tom out on bail so quickly, and assured him he could stay with he and Julie as long as necessary.

Larry digested what he had heard. It was remarkably similar to Tom's version. It still didn't explain that damned ax. Maybe Dr. Ball would have some insight on that. Tom should be at Doug's at this moment taking the standardized tests, and having his psyche examined by a trained forensic psychologist. This was interesting and challenging.

Could Tom have just blocked out the ax from his memory? It sure sounded like it, but how could he convince a jury that Tom just forgot about hitting a man three times with an ax? That would be a tough one. He couldn't do anymore for Tom today. He decided to go home early, and get the boat all squared away for the trip to Roosevelt tomorrow morning. It had been a heck of a week, and he was looking forward to some playtime.

He was sure Cindy locked up and left within a few minutes of when he left the parking lot. He didn't care. She was coming in on time, and all of the work was done for the day. He was going to enjoy the weekend, and not think about his law practice until Monday morning. The next forty-eight hours would be devoted to the pursuit of happiness, and the enjoyment of his wife and children.

CHAPTER 16

▼

Wednesday, June 12th

Today was the PH in front of Judge Easton. Larry was nervous, but there wasn't anything he could do to prepare for the hearing that he hadn't already done. He had his aerial exhibit ready. He had Norton's photos developed and organized. He even had an artist do a floor plan of the house with the dimensions of the rooms written in and all the windows noted by size. He wanted the Judge to be able to visualize the layout so there would be no confusion. He had his notebook ready on the different elements of first degree, second degree, and various degrees of manslaughter.

He had on his best suit, and had shined his shoes the night before. Tom would meet him at the office at one o'clock. Tom would not testify today. Today was to decide if there was probable cause to bind Tom over for trial and on what charge. Larry was sure he would be bound over, and was hoping it would only be for second-degree murder, not first. That would be a victory today.

He had Dr. Ball's preliminary findings. They were interesting, and something Larry needed to read up on. Again, this was not a time to be calling Dr. Ball to the witness stand. He would save that for the trial.

He had spent Monday and most of Tuesday researching Arizona law on products liability. It was favorable. Arizona was one of only a few states that had a constitutional provision that prohibited a cap on damages that could be awarded at trial. Many states had succumbed to the "Tort Reform Drum" that the Republican Party had been beating for years, and had passed laws that put a cap on non-economic damages.

That meant out-of-pocket losses could be recovered, but damages for emotional upset and pain and suffering, were limited by law, usually by about a two hundred fifty thousand dollar ceiling. In the Newman case, that would have been bad, as the case was really one of emotional damages, not out-of-pocket losses. The Newmans were not dependent on Tim and Tom for support. Their actual out-of-pocket losses for funeral expenses were small. Larry was glad that he didn't have to tell them that the law limited their recovery to two hundred fifty thousand for each child.

Because of the constitutional provision, a constitutional amendment was necessary before the law could be changed in Arizona. Twice, the forces of evil, (the insurance companies) had spent millions of dollars on a media blitz to convince Arizona voters that lawsuits were ruining the economy, were keeping businesses out of Arizona, and if Arizona wanted to thrive with the rest of the nation, it had better amend its Constitution.

Twice, the Arizona voters had said no. Arizona continued to grow and thrive.

Arizona also had favorable case law on punitive damages. Many states had also passed prohibitions on punitive damages. Punitive damages were meant to punish the wrongdoer, not compensate the victim of the wrong. They were meant to act as a deterrent to the wrongdoer to send a message, so that similar conduct would not repeat itself.

The U.S. Supreme Court and the Republican Party absolutely hated punitive damages, and railed against them every chance that came along to do so.

Punitive damages were alive and well in Arizona. All that was required was a showing of advance knowledge that a tragedy could occur, an opportunity to correct the problem, and a blind eye to the problem in the hopes that the tragedy wouldn't occur, or if it did, no one would find out about the advance knowledge.

This was one of the reasons auto manufacturers had recall campaigns. Once they found out about a safety problem, they had a duty to correct it, and notify everyone who owned one of the affected cars to bring it in for repair. If the owner ignored the warning, and tragedy struck, the company would have a defense of contributory negligence against the lazy owner who never bothered to bring his car in for repair. With the problem fixed, the manufacturer eliminated the risk of suit.

The problem was the cost of recalls. They were incredibly expensive, and the manufacturers resisted them. Not only were they expensive, they reduced consumer confidence in the product specifically, and the manufacturer in general. No one wanted to get a notice in the mail that his new thirty thousand dollar van might suddenly have a wheel lock up and spin out of control. Ah—but there was another sneaky way the manufacturers could get around a full-blown recall.

Instead of notifying the consumer to bring the car in for repairs, the manufacturer would send out Technical Service Bulletins to the dealers telling the dealers to check for a specific defect every time a certain model came in for routine work. As most cars now came with a standard three-year thirty-six thousand mile warranty, most customers would bring the car back to the dealer for routine maintenance like oil changes and other warranty work. Some manufacturers were even including oil changes and other regular service during the standard thirty-six thousand mile warranties. It wasn't because they were benevolent or generous. It was because they knew the customer would regularly bring the car in. The dealers would check the VIN on the car and bingo, the problem was fixed. The consumer and the unsuspecting public would never know about the problem. Everybody wins.

However, once in awhile the TSBs didn't get the job done. Once in awhile a problem was so specific that failures could occur rapidly, and many accidents could happen in a short period of time. That would get the attention of the Department of Transportation (DOT) and they would investigate. If the problem presented a safety risk, DOT would force the manufacturer to do a complete recall.

This is what had happened with the Galaxy vans. Southfield Spring had notified Galaxy that a certain batch of caliper springs were defective because improper cooling during the manufacturing process had made them brittle, and subject to failure.

Because the notice came so soon after the springs went into the vans, Galaxy decided to handle the problem with TSBs, rather than a formal recall. They made good progress for a few months. Then all of sudden, Galaxy vans were spinning out of control all over the country. Galaxy started investigating and found that all of the vans had between thirty and forty thousand miles on them when the crashes occurred. Obviously, the failure point on the brittle springs arrived at that mileage interval.

The oldest vans in question were approaching two years old. Most still had less than the critical-failure-point mileage showing on the odometer; some probably had a lot more as these fourteen-passenger vans were routinely used by shuttle services and schools. That tended to pile on the miles pretty quickly.

It presented another problem for Galaxy. When these vans crashed, they were usually filled with people; which meant multiple claims—not just one or two claims per occurrence.

Well, Galaxy hid the ball again. Instead of doing a full recall, they sent out a second TSB to the dealers requesting that the dealers step up their efforts to get the vans in for a fix. The dealers were encouraged to send coupons to known owners of these vans offering a free "multi-point inspection, oil change and tire rotation," just so the owner would bring in the van. While it was there, the dealer would change out the caliper springs. Some did. Many did not. After all, it is a hassle to bring your car in for service, and a lot of people put it off until it just *has* to be done.

Finally the word got out, and DOT leaned on Galaxy to do a full recall. They didn't have much choice by this time. The notices went out the first part of May. It was conceivable that the school hadn't even gotten their notice yet, or if they did, had not had time to act on it.

The point was, Galaxy had advance knowledge of the problem. They hid the problem from the unsuspecting public not once, but twice. Only after DOT leaned on them did they reluctantly do a full recall. That was the classic set up for punitive damages. Protecting corporate profits at the expense of the public safety.

Once a threshold showing was made, the Court would allow evidence on the inner workings of Galaxy. The jury would get the true bottom line including the net worth of the company, the compensation to the highest paid executives, the cost of the recall, and the number of lives lost while Galaxy fiddled and sent out TSBs instead of recall notices. Now that packed a punch!

Even one percent of Galaxy's net worth would be tens of millions of dollars. Recalls often cost hundreds of millions of dollars. There was potential here for damages that Larry could hardly even imagine. Mitch not only imagined scenarios like this, he experienced them. He had recovered over a billion dollars from Galaxy lawsuits in his career, and Galaxy was only one of many manufacturers he routinely went after for defective products.

Larry had learned all of this in the last few days from Mitch Branch. Mitch had been on Galaxy's trail for years starting back with the exploding Neptune gas tanks, through the Park-to-Reverse problem, the Gentry tire/Starflight SUV debacle and the exploding Constellation gas tanks.

Police officers were being killed or horribly burned all over the country, as the Constellation was the car of choice for law enforcement agencies. A heavy rear end collision to the Constellation would turn it into a flaming coffin. Galaxy had denied the problem for a while, and only reluctantly did a full recall and offered to install re-designed gas tanks.

In the meantime, police officers became reluctant to work out of the Constellations, and law enforcement starting using other cars instead of the preferred rear wheel drive Galaxy Constellation. Galaxy's delay on the recall cut deeply into the sales volume of the Constellation

Every time he read a story in the newspaper about a crash involving a car that seemed to happen for reasons unknown, Mitch would get his private investigator on the case and start sorting it out. He knew how to find the TSBs. He had his sources.

He had found the TSBs on the caliper springs, and had pounced soon thereafter with a small case that wasn't worth all that much money, but was valuable as a tool to take depositions of Galaxy engineers and subpoena internal Galaxy documents. He had already learned that Galaxy had calculated the cost of the recall at four hundred fifty million. By the time he got Larry's call, he was ready to go with a big case. The Newman case had all the right elements, and would be located in a jurisdiction that had no damage limits, and favorable case law on products liability.

Galaxy hated Mitch, but they also feared him. Galaxy already knew he had the goods on them on the caliper spring issue. They were well into lawsuit damage control, and making suggestions about having a Settlement Master appointed to review claims, and settle cases out of court.

Mitch would have nothing to do with it. He wasn't going to let Galaxy sweep this under the rug a third time. He wanted a public forum, and the public awareness that would go with it.

Mitch had been excited to learn that Arizona law had no cap on actual or punitive damages and that the product liability law in general was favorable to the consumer rather than the manufacturer. He asked Larry to think about running ads in the *Pima County Bar Newsletter* and *Summation,* the voice of the Arizona Trial Lawyers Association advising members that he and Larry were available for association on these Galaxy caliper spring cases.

Mitch and Larry couldn't approach victims directly, but victims went to lawyers, lawyers read those publications, and the lawyers all knew who Mitch Branch was. Soon, they would know who Larry Ross was, too. Mitch was hopeful that would identify a few more cases. As long as they were doing the work, it wasn't much harder to represent ten people instead of two. There was no conflict of interest as everyone had the same interest: "Make Galaxy Pay For Hiding The Problem and Killing People in the Process!"

The Newmans had the perfect case to present to a jury. A married couple that had lost their only children at the hands of a greedy mega corporation that wanted to save a few bucks by not doing a recall. It didn't get any better than that. If a few more injured people wanted to tag along for the ride, all the better. They would probably all benefit by being tacked on to the Newman case.

Cindy had arranged for Larry, Mitch, and Bob Burns to meet for breakfast at the Radisson coffee shop on Thursday morning at seven A.M. They had all agreed to wear Levi's, and pullover cotton shirts, as they were going to be going up to Phoenix to see the van and crawl around it. There was no need to wear a coat and tie. The weatherman was predicting one hundred seven degrees for Phoenix for Thursday, so it would be plenty hot. The garage where the van was located was cooled by a swamp cooler that pulled air over damp straw-like pads. It wasn't air-conditioned. It would probably be close to ninety degrees in the garage.

Larry had faxed over his research on Arizona Law and had also prepared a notebook carefully tabbed and organized just in case Mitch forgot to bring the material Larry had faxed. Mike and Margaret would be at Larry's office at eight. Paul and Don would arrive at eight thirty. They hoped to be on the road to Phoenix by nine.

He had also faxed over the fee agreement with the Newmans. Mitch wasn't too happy about the thirty/thirty-five percent fee, but said he would honor it as the case was potentially huge, and there should be enough to go around. He offered to split the attorney fee fifty-fifty with Larry, which Larry thought sounded more than fair. They signed their own agreement on that.

Mitch was going to tell the Newmans to keep their cost advance money. His firm always advanced all costs, for clients, and this would be no exception. Mitch encouraged Larry to sign up any future cases at forty percent if it settled or forty-five percent if it went to trial. This was the customary fee in a products case. Larry agreed.

In the midst of doing all the work on the Newman case on Monday and Tuesday, Larry had also managed to settle another PI case for fifty thousand dollars. This would be a handsome fee that should be in the bank by the end of the month, or before.

The money side of the business had rarely looked better. His caseload was filling with quality cases. Now he had to pay attention to Tom's PH and not get too disappointed if Tom got bound over on first-degree murder.

The next day and a half was going to be quite exciting. He liked it that way. It was a whole lot better than sitting in the office answering mail and making phone calls. Being in the courtroom, and out in the field doing the investigation was where the excitement was.

The office was necessary to keep everything together. He wished he had a clone that could sit in the office, do the boring work, and let Larry go to court every day to fight one battle after another. He didn't have a clone. He had to do it all.

Larry went over to Chuy's for lunch. He ordered his usual chicken, rice, and beans. He met Tom at the office at one. He spent a few minutes reminding Tom that today was not the day to put on any evidence. It was a day to listen, learn, and hope for the best.

Larry had ordered a court stenographer privately so he would have a reliable transcript of the proceedings. It was too hard to listen and take notes too. The stenographer would get every word, and it would be transcribed for him to read and digest within the week. They started over to the courthouse about one fifteen, and arrived a few minutes later. It was hard not to feel tense, but he was trying not to.

The calendar showed the case had been re-assigned to Judge Andrew Dorgan, the same judge who had set Tom's bail. Larry felt that was a good sign.

Rick Bay, Bruce Parchman, the ME, and Jeff Cotter, the homicide detective, showed up about one twenty-five. The show was about to begin.

Dorgan took the bench precisely at one thirty, and the proceedings began; Bay called Cotter to the stand first.

There were no surprises with Cotter's testimony. He laid the foundation for how he got the call, what he found when he got to the scene, and his conversation with Tom. The twelve minutes between the calls to Gary Miller and 9-1-1 were also discussed. Larry challenged none of it.

On cross examination, Larry got Cotter to admit that Tom had denied touching the ax, that Tom had told Cotter he was afraid of Art, and that Art had bragged about not being afraid to use a gun—hearsay to be sure; but fair game at a PH since "reliable" hearsay is admissible at this level. He also got Cotter to admit that six bullets had been fired from Art's gun in Tom's direction. He then walked Cotter through the aerial photograph, and the house diagram and dimensions.

Cotter agreed with everything Larry asked him, and agreed that Tom had been very cooperative during the questioning. There was now no question that Tom had fired his gun in self-defense.

Next up was Dr. Parchman. It got real interesting when Bay got to this series of questions:

"Dr. Parchman, did you examine Mr. Mendoza's body to determine the cause of death?"

"I did."

"And did you determine the cause of death?"

"I did."

"And what was the cause of death?"

Larry: "Objection, lack of foundation."

Dorgan: "Sustained. Mr. Bay, please lay some foundation for this. I assume the body showed some evidence of trauma."

Bay: "Yes, Your Honor. Dr. Parchman, did you find evidence of trauma to Mr. Mendoza's body?"

"I did."

"And what did you find?"

"I found two bullet wounds. One had entered the right chest just above the nipple, and had exited out the scapula area of the back. The right lung was punctured."

"And did you determine if this was the cause of death?"

"I did."

"Was it?"

"No, it was not."

"Where was the other bullet wound?"

"To Mr. Mendoza's left temple area."

Now we're getting somewhere, thought Larry. The head wound would have to be fatal. He eagerly anticipated the next question.

"Did the bullet enter Mr. Mendoza's brain?"

"It did not."

What? How could that be? Tom was firing a .44—a large caliber gun. How could the bullet not have entered the brain? Larry didn't think the next series of questions were going to be very good for Tom. They weren't.

Bay puffed out his chest and continued: "Please tell us, Dr. Parchman where the bullet entered Mr. Mendoza's skull and where it exited."

Parchman frowned, looked at his notes and began describing the wound: "It appears Mr. Mendoza was hit by the bullet to the chest first. As he was struck by that bullet, the force propelled him backwards and to the right. It is my opinion that the second bullet struck at an angle to the skull, rather than straight on. The human skull is very hard and durable. Its purpose is to protect the brain, which is what it did in this case. Rather than penetrate the skull, the bullet just glanced off the bone, leaving a crease in the skull, but making no penetration. There was no clear entry or exit wound as there was no penetration of the bone."

Larry knew what was coming next. He braced himself for the worst. It came.

"And was this bullet wound to Mr. Mendoza's skull the cause of death?"

"No. It would have left him with a bad headache, but nothing worse than that."

"Did you find evidence of other trauma to Mr. Mendoza's body?"

"I did."

"What did you find?"

Larry reached out and touched Tom's arm to brace him for what he was about to hear. It wasn't pretty.

"I found evidence that Mr. Mendoza's skull had been penetrated three times by a blunt object."

"And did you determine what that blunt object was?"

"I did."

"And what was it?"

"It was an ax found at the scene. The blunt end of the ax had hair and blood all over it. We took the ax to the lab, and matched the hair and blood on the ax to Mr. Mendoza's hair and blood. The skull indentations matched the width and length of the blunt end of the ax. It is my opinion that the ax found at the scene is the blunt object that penetrated Mr. Mendoza's skull three times."

Here came the sixty-four thousand dollar question:

"And was the penetration of Mr. Mendoza's skull by the ax found at the scene the cause of death?"

"It was."

Bay turned and looked at Larry: "Your witness, counselor," he said with a smirk.

This was bad. Larry had to think fast. Remember this is only a PH; there will be another day; but then again, get what you can now—this is free discovery. Larry cautiously rose and began asking Dr. Parchman questions. It didn't go well. "Dr. Parchman, wouldn't you agree that the chest wound that collapsed the right lung was a potentially fatal wound?"

"Potentially fatal—yes. Fatal—no. Mr. Mendoza would have survived if medical care had been received within forty-five minutes to an hour, if that were his only wound. The bullet wound to the head was really nothing to speak of. It was the skull penetration from the ax that was fatal, and almost instantly so."

Larry wobbled on his feet. This was not going well. He decided he might as well find out how bad it really was. "And why do you say almost instantly so?"

"Because the penetration was so deep. The bone from the skull was driven into the brain almost like a spike being driven into a railroad tie. The force exerted on Mr. Mendoza's skull by those three blows was enormous. I've never seen anything like it. He could not have lived more than a minute, or two at the most, after those blows were struck."

Great. Two questions, and two strikes—should he go for a third and have a complete strike out?

Parchman leaned back and waited for the next question.

Larry took a deep breath and said, "Thank you doctor, I have no further questions."

Bay stood, and asked the bailiff to check the hallway to see if Jim Weber had arrived. As if he hadn't heard enough, now Larry was going to hear from Tom's neighbor how he watched Tom beat Art to death with an ax. This was a nightmare! It was barely two thirty, and it seemed like the PH had been going on for an eternity. Larry looked at Tom. He looked ashen.

Weber entered the room, took the oath, took the stand, and after being asked the preliminary questions of who he was, and where he lived in proximity to Tom, Bay got right to the point. Walking over to the aerial photo, Bay pointed to Weber's house; which could clearly be seen in the photo. "Is this your house?"

"Yes, it is."

"And from your balcony, do you have a clear view of Mr. Rogers' driveway as it exits the street side of your home?"

"Yes, I do."

"Please tell the court what you saw the morning of June 3rd."

Weber gulped, looked at Tom, looked at the judge, gulped again, and said in a quiet voice: "I saw a man laying in the driveway near the street. He looked hurt. He was moving, so I knew he was alive."

"Did you also see Mr. Rogers in the driveway that morning?"

"Yes, sir."

"Where was he in relationship to the man you saw that you thought was hurt?"

"He walked up to him very cautiously. He was carrying an ax. The man tried to stand. He almost got to his feet. He started to turn toward Mr. Rogers. I watched Mr. Rogers raise the ax, and strike the man with it three times. I couldn't believe what I was seeing."

"And what did you see Mr. Rogers do next?"

"I saw him walk back towards the house. I called to my wife to call 9-1-1. I continued to watch the driveway. I saw Mr. Rogers come out to the man again. The man wasn't moving any more. I thought he was dead. I saw Mr. Rogers roll him onto a blanket, and drag him over by the garage out of my line of sight. A few minutes later, a pickup truck that I had seen at the Rogers' house before, pulled into the driveway, a man got out, and Mr. Rogers walked over to talk to him. They walked back towards the house. It wasn't very long before the police arrived, and I saw Mr. Rogers and his friend in the pickup walk towards the police with their hands up, as if they were surrendering."

Well, there it was. The ax, and a crushed skull were the cause of death. The murder weapon belonged to Tom. An eyewitness had seen him strike the fatal blows. Art would have survived had he gotten immediate medical attention. Instead of calling 9-1-1 right away, Tom had wasted valuable minutes trying to calm Laura down, and then more valuable minutes by calling Gary first.

This was a disaster. If it had ended with the bullets being fired, and Tom calling 9-1-1 right away, this PH wouldn't even be happening. It would have been a classic case of self-defense. Now it was a classic case of first-degree murder.

Larry hoped Bay wouldn't be calling any more witnesses. He was relieved when he heard Bay tell the judge:

"The state rests, Your Honor. We believe we have shown more than probable cause to bind the defendant over on the charge of first-degree murder and the lesser-included offenses of second-degree murder and manslaughter. We also ask that the defendant's bond be revoked, and that he be held in the Pima County Jail until trial."

Dorgan looked troubled. He looked at Larry. "Mr. Ross, do you have any witnesses?"

"No Your Honor," was Larry's reply. He had already done enough damage with the attempted cross-examination of Dr. Parchman. There was no need to make it any worse.

Dorgan intoned, "And what is your position on what charge the defendant should be bound over for trial, and whether or not bond should be revoked?"

Larry decided to take the easy one first. "As to bond, the defendant has clearly demonstrated that he is not a flight risk. He is here today. If he were going to skip, he would have done it by now. I request that bond remain at twenty-five thousand dollars. I need ready access to Mr. Rogers to adequately prepare his defense. Having him in jail between now and trial will make it very difficult for me to have conferences with him, and have him assist me in his defense.

"As to the charge, the State has failed to prove any motive Mr. Rogers would have had to kill Mr. Mendoza other than in self-defense. There is no evidence that Mr. Rogers planned the events that unfolded at his home on June 3rd. This is a manslaughter case at the very worst. I would request that Mr. Rogers be bound over for trial on the charge of manslaughter only."

Dorgan looked at Tom, looked at Bay, and looked back at Larry. "Bond will remain at twenty-five thousand. I will add a condition of bond that Mr. Rogers shall not leave Pima County without prior court approval.

"I am troubled by the eyewitness account. Mr. Ross, I think I'll let you try to convince a jury otherwise, but I am binding the defendant over for trial on the charge of first-degree murder. I find the State has made a prima facie showing of motive. Malice aforethought can be quick. It doesn't have to be something Mr. Rogers planned out for months, or weeks, or days. Malice aforethought can be as quick as successive thoughts of the mind. Mr. Rogers had plenty of time to think about what to do. The record shows he had enough time to call his friend Mr. Miller before he called 9-1-1. Twelve minutes went by between those calls; valuable minutes that could have been used to save Mr. Mendoza's life. It was more than enough time for Mr. Rogers to decide he would finish what was started on the back porch.

"That is my ruling. Mr. Rogers, I suggest you stay real close to home. I won't hesitate to revoke your bond if I hear you have left or are even thinking about leaving the county.

"Trial is set for one hundred twenty days from today, unless that falls on a Saturday, Sunday or legal holiday. The clerk will send out a notice of the actual trial date."

Dorgan looked at a list he kept on his desk. He pondered as he made his decision for trial assignment. "The trial will be assigned to Judge Donner. That is all, gentlemen." Dorgan got up and left the bench.

It was barely three fifteen. In the last hour and a half, overwhelming evidence had put Tom well on his way to life in prison or maybe even subject to the death penalty. They walked slowly back to Larry's office. Barely a word was spoken between them.

The reality of the situation had hit Tom harder than a Mike Tyson punch.

Larry kept thinking about the awesome responsibility he had taken on. Tom's life was on the line, and Larry was hoping he was up to the task of adequately defending him. The only good thing that happened today was having the trial assigned to Larry's law school chum, Judge Donner. Lawyer and client didn't share their thoughts with each other as they walked back to Larry's office.

CHAPTER 17

▼

With the Rogers' PH behind him, Larry was looking forward to his breakfast meeting with Branch and his engineer. He got to the Radisson coffee shop at six forty-five, and ordered coffee only.

Branch and Bob Burns appeared promptly at seven. Larry recognized Mitch from various AAJ meetings where Mitch had been a featured speaker. Now sixty, Mitch was still a good-looking man. About six feet even, trim waist, about two hundred pounds, thick head of gray hair, quick smile, and a friendly demeanor.

Burns also looked the part of a seasoned engineer. Mid-fifties, receding hairline, gray hair, glasses, a little on the heavy side, but certainly not grossly overweight. He looked professorial.

They got right down to business after the obligatory introductions and handshakes. Mitch and Bob told Larry all about the discovery they had done so far in the small case in Texas that Mitch was basically using as a discovery tool to get the goods on Galaxy. They had the TSBs. They had the projected cost of the recall.

They even had the projected savings to Galaxy by doing it through TSBs rather than a recall—about three hundred million. Mitch had already decided that this would be the punitive damage award he would seek in the Newman case. If Galaxy wanted to save three hundred million, and at the same time take a chance with people's lives, then they would pay three hundred million for taking the lives of the Newman twins and others.

This would be a deterrent to Galaxy in the future, or so the argument would go. Mitch knew it probably would not be a deterrent. The only thing Galaxy feared was getting caught. He knew they would be back with more TSBs instead

of recalls. It was his personal mission in life to keep Galaxy and other auto manufacturers honest. It was a daunting task.

They arrived at Larry's office at eight. Cindy was there with her bright smile,
and had the coffee ready. The Newmans were in the reception area. Larry introduced Mitch and Bob to the Newmans, and they went to the conference room to
discuss business.

As expected, the Newmans were pleased to meet Mitch. He assured them that
their tragedy would become an example to Galaxy, and other manufacturers to
shape up and not put lives ahead of profits. He made them believe that their case
would make a statement to the country. He assured them that King and Branch
would advance all costs.

Larry had made arrangements with Unity Insurance, and Bruce Masters, to
meet at the yard where the van was being stored. If they were all in agreement
that this was a caliper spring issue, Unity and the school would be off the hook,
and would cooperate in letting Mitch have the van for salvage value and remove
it anywhere he wanted to. Thinking ahead, Mitch had already made arrangements for a flatbed tow-truck to transport the van to Dallas the following day to a
storage facility Mitch used in all of his auto cases.

Don and Paul arrived about eight thirty. Larry made all of the introductions.
They briefed Bob and Mitch on their preliminary findings, and showed them the
photos. It was a familiar sight to them. This was a typical caliper spring failure.
The van had about thirty seven thousand miles on it at the time of the crash. The
Newmans were again reassured that everything was looking good.

By nine A.M., Larry, Mitch, Bob, Don, and Paul were on Interstate 10 to
Phoenix to do the inspection. Masters would meet them up there.

Mitch had rented a huge Galaxy Constellation for the trip. It was comfortable,
but a bit ironic that Galaxy had built the car that was taking them to the van that
they also built and had killed two innocent teenagers. They got to the storage
yard about ten forty-five A.M.

Larry was shocked by the amount of damage to the van. The right front corner
of the roof was squashed down from the roll, and had grass and weeds wedged in
the metal and the crevices from its contact with the desert during the roll. There
were personal items belonging to children strewn all over the interior. It was
mainly backpacks and soccer equipment. Masters was waiting for them.

The engineers went to work with their cameras and measurements. Mitch,
Masters, and Larry watched for a while, and then went to the office area to talk.

Mitch assured Masters he had no intention of suing the school or the driver.
He could not assure him that Galaxy would not try to bring them into the mix.

Masters agreed to sell the van to Mitch's law firm for the high salvage bid of four hundred fifty dollars.

Mitch then called the tow company to confirm the tow that had been set up for the following morning. Larry, Mitch, and Bruce decided to go to lunch and let the engineers finish their work.

The stage was set. At lunch, it was discussed that suit would be filed fairly soon against Galaxy, and Southfield Spring. Masters wanted Mitch and Larry to represent the van driver as well. His injuries were fairly serious. A ruptured spleen, a torn rotator cuff to the right shoulder, and a broken femur on the left. They wanted to but couldn't. While there was no actual conflict of interest, there would be the appearance of one, and a suspicion of collusion that some defense lawyer from Galaxy would try to exploit. Ed Allison, the teacher, Soccer Coach, van driver, would have to find his own lawyer. Nothing was discussed about the other injured children.

By two thirty, the engineers were finished. Larry dropped Mitch and Bob off at Phoenix Sky Harbor for the flight back to Dallas at six ten P.M. He, Paul and Don drove the Constellation back to Tucson. He and Maggie would take it back to the airport and turn it in the next day.

On the way back to Tucson, Paul and Don told him how impressed they were with Bob Burns and how much he knew about the caliper spring issue. The Newman case was in good control. He wished he could say the same about the Rogers' case.

CHAPTER 18

▼

The weekend flew by. While Larry was still reeling from the testimony about the brutality of the way Tom had bludgeoned Art to death with an ax, he was buoyed by the good news Friday had brought in the Newman case.

It was almost too good to be true. Here he was, thirty-five years old, and working as co-counsel with the great Mitch Branch from Dallas on a case that he never thought he would ever have a chance at seeing in his whole career. He resolved to keep focused and not let it go to his head.

There was no such thing as a slam-dunk case, and the Newman case was no exception. The money that Mitch talked about so casually was so astronomical that it really didn't have any meaning to Larry. They were just numbers. He would leave the money to Mitch, and just focus on getting the job done, and doing what Mitch asked of him.

He had a meeting set up with Dr. Ball for Monday morning at Ball's east-side office. It was on the way in to work for Larry. He was hoping for good news. He had read Doug's preliminary report, but he wanted to talk to him in person about it. He needed something to defend Tom with, and maybe psychiatric testimony would do it.

Larry started the meeting by telling Doug about the testimony from Dr. Parchman at the PH. Doug didn't seem phased by the brutal description.

"So, how do I defend this mess?" Larry asked.

Doug's reply was thoughtful and measured: "Tom was in a Dissociative State when he killed Mendoza. He is amnesiac of the event because that is his brain's way of blocking out the horror of what happened to him. Tom has never been faced with danger like he was faced with that morning. He has never been in the military. He has never had any experience of being threatened or shot at. This was a first experience for him. You have heard of Post Traumatic Stress Disorder?"

Ball answered his own question: "Well, this is the acute phase of PTSD. A true Dissociative State is always preceded by an emotional, or physically threatening crisis. What happened to Tom the morning of June 3rdrd doesn't get any more emotional or physically threatening. The threat increased dramatically when Tom went back to the porch, and Art was gone. His brain went into an automatic protective state of survival. Art was a threat. The threat was still there, but no longer visible.

"Tom's brain was telling him to find the threat and eliminate it, which he did. However, the way in which it was done was so horrible, and so foreign to Tom's personality, that he has no memory of the event. He was protecting his life, and his wife's life. He was in a survival mode, and more or less on automatic pilot.

"This happens to soldiers in combat all the time. They do things that are called heroic, yet they have no memory of it. They are on automatic cruise control, protecting themselves and those around them. This is very well known in psychiatric circles, and explains why Tom acted as he did, and professes to have no memory of it. He in fact has no memory of it."

Larry let this sink in for a minute. "Does this mean he would meet the test of temporary insanity; not knowing right from wrong at the time the act was committed?"

Doug thought for a moment and replied, "I know the law likes to talk about temporary insanity. I don't like that term, but yes, it meets that definition. The only thing Tom knew at the time was that Art was a threat to his life, and it was kill or be killed. He would not know the difference between right and wrong at that time.

"This is best likened to a combat situation in war. I have counseled numerous Viet Nam and Gulf War Vets on this issue. The ones I counsel have gone on to develop PTSD because they get flashbacks of the horrible events. Tom does not have PTSD. He has no flashbacks, and probably never will. His brain has permanently blocked the event with the ax from his mind.

"If intent and motive are an issue, Tom is innocent. His only intent was to protect himself. His motive was to protect his life. It makes no difference to me that Art was essentially helpless at the time the fatal blows were struck. Tom didn't perceive him that way. Dissociative means detached from reality. Tom was detached from reality, and himself, during those moments. If the jury believes this, he will be acquitted."

If the jury believes it. That was a big if. Larry was having a hard time believing it, and he wanted desperately to believe it. "Have you ever offered an opinion like this before in a criminal case?" was his question. He didn't like the answer.

"No. It has never come up before. However, I have authored an article on Dissociative State, which was published in a respected psychology journal, and presented at the annual psychiatric convention a few years back. I made you a copy. I am a recognized expert on this issue. Tom fits the criteria like your shoe fits your foot. This is solid, Larry. It is a legitimate psychiatric diagnosis. I will support it. The State is going to have a hard time finding a psychiatrist who will refute this. It fits the definition perfectly."

Larry knew better. The State would indeed find someone. That someone would probably be more respected, renowned, and published than Doug Ball, and would be willing to say so under oath. This would turn into a battle of the experts. It would come down to whom the jury believed. A man was dead. He had been bludgeoned to death with an ax. Tom's life was at stake. This was as serious as it could get.

"Doug, you know the State will find someone to rebut your opinion. Who is the most published psychologist on Dissociative State?"

"Mark Jamison," was the reply. "He wrote the diagnostic criteria for Dissociative State that is used in the DSM IV manual which is used by all psychologists and psychiatrists to make diagnosis from. He won't disagree with me."

"And how do you know that?" asked Larry.

"Because I have heard him speak at different conferences. He is a true believer. He teaches at USC. I've had lunch and dinner with him several times. He won't disagree."

Larry knew then and there that Jamison would be the State's expert witness on Dissociative State. He also knew that he would disagree that this psychiatric disorder had taken over Tom's persona for a few moments and had prevented him from knowing right from wrong at the time Art was being bludgeoned to death, and then not remembering the event.

"Doug, can you really hold up under cross examination on this? A man's life is at stake here. If you have even the slightest doubt in the quality of your diagnosis, tell me now. Once I disclose this to the State, we are committed, and there will be no turning back."

"Disclose it. I'll be your witness. I will not waiver. Tom Rogers was not responsible in a criminal manner for killing Art Mendoza. I will not give an inch on this. You can count on it."

Larry considered that. Doug was a good witness. He was experienced. He was published on the topic. He was local. This might work. He sure as hell didn't have anything else to explain Tom's actions that morning. "Okay Doug. You're on board. I hope you don't have any plans to take a long vacation this summer. I'll need you to be around for consultation while I develop this defense. You do realize that Tom's life is riding on your opinion?"

"Larry, I know that. I'll be here all summer. I'll make this a priority. I believe in this very strongly. Tom is an innocent man."

They shook hands, and Larry went on to work for the day. Doug agreed to work on the case at one hundred fifty dollars per hour, a reasonable rate for a psychologist of Doug's stature and experience. Larry agreed to send him a twenty-five hundred dollar retainer to cover the work already done, and work that would be done soon. Larry and Doug had been friends for years. Doug had never let him down. Larry was hoping this would not be the first time.

CHAPTER 19

▼

Thursday, June 20th

Larry popped in the videotape from the TV station he had subpoenaed for a review. It started with the "PARTY 'TIL YOU PUKE" sign that had been hung over the Odyssey entrance and continued on inside. It included footage of Art Mendoza singing with the Mariachi Band. He was obviously drunk. He was also big, ugly, and scary looking.

Then the tug of war over Sandy Rathman came into view. It was graphic. Art was all over her. They fell to the floor together. Tom tried to come to her rescue, but Art elbowed him in the gut, and sent him flying like a rag doll.

Then a couple of big guys that looked like football players tried to help. Art succumbed, and they backed off only to watch as Art charged them as soon as he got up from the floor. Once the sound of sirens could be heard in the background, Art stopped fighting, and tried his best to look presentable.

Shortly after the cops came into the bar the filming stopped. The whole thing only took a couple of minutes, but it was enough to convince Larry that Art was a dangerous man, and Tom had good reason to be afraid of him.

He then turned his attention to the report from Dave Norton on what he had found over at the courthouse on Art's criminal history. There were a lot of low-level felonies for aggravated assault, theft, bad checks, and one transporting-marijuana-for-sale charge that had landed him in the State Prison in Florence for three to five years. He was out in less than two, and finished his parole without incident. All of this was more proof that Art was prone to violence.

Norton had also pulled up the Arizona Corporation Commission reports on Maria's Auto Salvage. Art was not listed anywhere as an officer or director, yet it was well known that the salvage yard was his, and his sister was only a front. The reports did list a local CPA as a director. Larry dictated a subpoena directed to the CPA's office to get the financials and the tax returns on Maria's Auto Salvage for the last three years.

Norton had also canvassed the Barrio where Art was well known. Even though he was now dead, no one would offer up much, as they knew Julio and Oscar were still very much alive, and would not hesitate to take revenge on a snitch.

Larry logged onto the Internet and did some research on Psychological Autopsies. He had heard about this in a legal publication he had read last year and wanted to learn more. After he finished his research he put in a call to Doug Ball's office. He knew Doug saw patients on the hour and used a fifty-minute hour so he would have ten minutes between patients to make notes, use the bathroom, or return phone calls. As expected, Doug returned the phone call at about seven minutes before the hour.

"Hi, Doug, thanks for returning my call so promptly. I wanted to ask you what you know about Psychological Autopsies."

"What would you like to know?"

"Are they recognized as valid? Have you ever done one? What kind of information do you need to do one?"

"They are valid. I have only done one, and that was a few years back. I need as much information as I can get on the deceased to come up with a psychological profile of the personality. Who do you want me to profile?"

"Art Mendoza. I have his criminal record; I have a videotape of a fight he was in at the Odyssey on Cinco de Mayo, and I have witnesses who can confirm that he attacked a man with a two-by-four in Tom's presence. What else do you need?"

"What does the criminal record show?"

"Lots of convictions for aggravated assault—five to be specific."

"Larry, I think I can help. I have to get to a patient. Drop all this stuff off for me to review today, and I'll get back to you tomorrow."

"Okay, I'll drop it by on the way home through your mail slot. Please look at it first thing tomorrow and give me a call."

"I'll do that. I assume you are taking the angle that Art was prone to violence, and that Tom reacted reasonably by perceiving him as a lethal threat to his life."

"You are a genius, Doug. You should think about becoming a mind reader instead of a psychologist."

"I learned how to read minds in psychology school. I just read yours, didn't I?"

"Yes, you did. I'll talk to you tomorrow."

Larry hung up the phone, and hoped that Doug would come to the same conclusion he had about Art. He was mean, he was violent, and Tom had every reason to be afraid of him. He had Cindy make a copy of the criminal history, and dub a tape on the dual deck recorder he kept in the office just for this purpose. He shoved the envelope through Doug's mail slot on the way home that night.

CHAPTER 20

─────────────── ▼ ───────────────

Monday, July 1st

Cindy rang on the intercom and let Larry know that Alan Gimble was on the line.

"Tell him I'm busy. I've got nothing to say to him!"

"Larry, he says he represents Ed Allison, the van driver. He wants to talk to you about associating on the case."

Oh Crap! Here he was again. Would this little cockroach never die? "Okay, put him through."

Larry decided to play the professional route. "Hi, Alan, thanks for calling. What's on your mind today?"

"Hi Larry. I saw your ad in *Summation* about associating in on Galaxy caliper spring cases. I signed up Ed Allison last week. I understand you and Mitch Branch have already filed in Federal Court against Galaxy and Southfield Spring. I would like to tag along for the ride."

And tag along he would, thought Larry. Alan was a moocher. He would do nothing, be in the way all the time, never do anything assigned to him, and would beat the door down as soon as the check arrived for settlement. Besides, he had already told Allison through Bruce Masters that he and Mitch could not represent him. He was on his own. "No can do, Alan. I already told Bruce Masters that we couldn't represent Allison. It would look like collusion, and Galaxy would exploit it. He is on his own. You'll have to go it alone."

"I kind of thought that's what you would say. What's to stop me from filing my own case on Ed's behalf, and then moving the court for an order to consolidate the two cases? The issues are the same, and in the interest of judicial economy, I'm sure the motion will be granted."

Larry pondered that for a moment. Alan might be lazy. He was most certainly dishonest. He wasn't stupid. "I guess that's what the rule is there for. I'll oppose the motion, but who knows what the judge will do? Whatever happens, we absolutely, positively cannot associate as counsel for Allison."

"You know I'll get all of your discovery and disclosures once the cases are consolidated. Once I'm in the case, I get everything."

He was right again. Alan would get a free ride. Larry and Mitch would do all the work, and spend all the money. Even so, there wasn't anything Larry could do about it.

"Then file your motion. I can't stop you. I have to keep my distance. Galaxy has already named Allison as a non-party at fault claiming that it was his negligence that caused the van to leave the roadway and roll. His deposition will be taken anyway. He might as well be a party as a non-party. He is in the mix. Do what you have to do Alan, but don't call me, don't come over here to look at files, and don't try to talk to me on the street about this. Everything that you and I do on this case will be by the book, and on the record. There will be no secret sharing. Do we understand each other?"

"Loud and clear ol' buddy. I'll send you a copy of my Complaint and the Motion to consolidate the cases. See you in court."

Well. That was enough to ruin any day. Larry called Mitch to give him the bad news. Mitch agreed there was nothing either of them could do about it. The rules were the rules, and the judge would probably consolidate the cases. Mitch told Larry he was going to Detroit in three weeks to depose the head of consumer product safety for Galaxy. Larry wanted to go, but there was no need to have two lawyers at the deposition. Mitch had deposed this man several times in the past, and knew what he was doing. Larry would stay in Tucson and enjoy the heat.

So far, Alan was the only one who had called in response to the ads placed in *The Writ*, and *Summation*. Either the other families had not yet gone to lawyers, or the injuries to the other kids weren't serious enough to justify an expensive case against Galaxy.

Then again, maybe everyone was taking a wait-and-see attitude. The statute of limitations didn't even begin to run on kids until their eighteenth birthday. Most of the injured kids were only fourteen or fifteen. The statute wouldn't run out until their twentieth birthday. Maybe the lawyers were waiting to see the outcome of some of the cases that were pending against Galaxy, hoping that a big verdict or two might bring Galaxy to the bargaining table without spending a lot of money. Why share a fee with Larry Ross and Mitch Branch if they didn't have to? Let them do the work and then reap the benefits of it.

Allison was another story. He was an adult and only had two years to bring his claim. Galaxy had named him as the person responsible for causing the crash. Like it or not, Allison was in this and didn't have much choice other than to join in. His choice of lawyers was poor, but it was his choice. Larry and Mitch would just have to live with Alan's annoying presence, and hope that he didn't screw things up too badly just by being there. It was never easy.

Even with a seasoned warrior like Mitch Branch at his side, Larry still felt overwhelmed with the responsibility of representing the Newmans. He wasn't going to let a little piss-ant like Alan Gimble interfere with his focus and concentration.

CHAPTER 21

▼

Mid-July

By now, it seemed like the summer was here to stay forever. It hadn't rained in Tucson since March. The weathermen kept assuring the public that the summer monsoon rains were on the way, but so far nothing but dust and non-productive clouds followed by day after day of temperatures over one hundred degrees was all the city got. It had to rain soon. It just had to. Tucson's annual rainfall averaged about twelve inches. So far, less than three inches had been recorded for the year.

Tom was sinking into depression. His house was being repaired by his homeowners insurance for the vandalism done to it in June. He couldn't work because the whole town knew he was charged with murder, and no one would hire a man who might be in prison in a few months.

His savings was just about depleted, and he felt guilty for continuing to impose on the Millers for a place to stay. He decided to list the house for sale, thinking that he would lose it to a foreclosure sale if he didn't sell it.

Laura was still in Ohio, and the last time he talked to her, she was sounding distant and detached. She couldn't come back to Tucson for safety reasons, and he couldn't go to Ohio because of his conditions of release.

Phone calls and e-mails were a poor substitute for communication between a husband and wife. Tom and Laura had enjoyed a very active sex life and he missed that too. Life was not very enjoyable for Tom at the moment.

He sold the horse, which gave him a little money to spend, and at the same time cut out the expense of boarding it, and calling the vet and the horseshoer every couple of weeks. Horses always needed something, and he just didn't have the money to afford that luxury any longer.

His car needed tires, the brakes were squeaking, an oil change was way overdue, and he just felt desperate. Just one year ago, everything had been great. Now he was losing everything, even his wife. Daytime TV was boring, and he had read every novel that interested him in the last several weeks. The days just dragged.

Dr. Ball had issued a positive finding on the psychological autopsy done on Art. Everything pointed to the conclusion that violence, threats, and intimidation were Art's dominant personality traits. His convictions for aggravated assault, coupled with the eyewitness accounts of other fights that didn't result in an arrest, were proof of that.

If allowed to give his opinions in court, Ball was prepared to state that Tom Rogers had very good reason to fear Art Mendoza, and that Mendoza was fully capable of carrying out the threat to kill Tom.

His clinical diagnosis was Impulse Control Disorder: specifically, Intermittent Explosive Disorder coded as 312.4 in the DSM IV manual. The video tape of the Cinco de Mayo party at the Odyssey was proof positive that Art could become enraged at the slightest provocation, yet could calm down, and act rationally only a few moments later.

Trial had been set for October 8. It seemed to Tom that date was too far off in the distance. It seemed to Larry like it was tomorrow.

Larry had disclosed Dr. Ball's opinions to Rick Bay on July 9, the day the court had set for exchange of disclosure. Bay was amused by the disclosure. He called Larry the afternoon he got it in the mail to pull his chain a little. He also told Larry he was going to ask for an independent Rule 11 examination by a court-appointed psychologist to see if Ball's opinions were valid.

Once again, the Rules of Criminal Procedure provided for it, and Larry had to tell Tom that once again, he would have to subject himself to a psychological examination. The exam was set for July 31.

There was nothing Tom could do to ready himself for this exam. The appointed examiner was well known to be "conservative," which meant skeptical of any diminished capacity defense. Tom was not looking forward to taking the standardized tests again, and telling his story one more time.

Depression can also lead to other problems. In Tom's case, he had found a sympathetic ear in Cindy Morrow, Larry's secretary. She was always ready to listen. She was also willing to take her clothes off for Tom.

Tom missed Laura, and loved her. He didn't look at his tryst with Cindy as cheating or being unfaithful. It was a physical outlet. Cindy had a beautiful body, and was a sensuous lover.

Her kids were gone for a few more weeks, she was between boyfriends, and Tom decided to take advantage of her willingness to lend a sympathetic ear, and share her bed with him. It was becoming almost a nightly ritual. It was getting hard to act cordial to one another when Tom was in the office, and not let on that sparks were flying between them.

Tom and Cindy both knew this had to stop before her kids came home from summer visitation with Billy, and certainly before Larry got wind of it. The problem was, they genuinely liked each other and were compatible.

To Cindy, Tom was an educated and sensitive man who treated her like a lady and was polite to a fault. She had no fear that he would knock her around like Billy and other men had done as soon as she said no to any of their sexual demands. Tom's requests were straightforward, not perverted or rough. She was enjoying his company, and even thought there might be a future for them if Larry could get Tom acquitted.

When Billy called and wanted to extend the visitation for three more weeks, Cindy readily agreed. She missed the girls, but they only got to see their father in the summer, and she was enjoying her time with Tom. She didn't even have to feel guilty about making the call. Billy had initiated it, and the girls had all confirmed they were having a great time, and wanted to stay until just a few days before school started. School start date was August 17, and Billy agreed to have them home on the 15th.

As the weeks went by, Tom missed Laura less and less, and wanted to be with Cindy more and more. She had come up rough, married too young, had too many kids too soon, and would be a low level earner for all of her life as she didn't have any way to better her situation. He felt sorry for her, and felt almost paternalistic towards her. At least he did until they got into bed together. He also thought that maybe they had a future together if Larry could get him off.

Tom felt he should be doing more than counting the days to October 8, but there really wasn't anything for him to do except park his butt in Pima County somewhere, as he couldn't leave, and look forward to getting into bed with Cindy every night.

Even sex was getting to be monotonous. They couldn't go out anywhere for fear it would get back to Larry. Even if they could, Tom didn't have any money to spend. So stay at Cindy's apartment is what they did. Watching TV and then climbing into bed together. Here he was, screwing a beautiful woman almost every night, and being bored with it. Life could sure throw some curve balls.

He decided he would make the best of it, and just live one day at a time, and count his blessings that he at least had Cindy to talk to and share time with. It could be worse. It can always be worse.

Tom presented himself to Dr. Richard Llewellan's office on July 31 as planned. Llewellan interviewed him for about an hour, and then gave him the standardized tests. The whole thing took more than four hours, and Tom was mentally exhausted when it was over.

Llewellan told him he would have his report to Rick Bay within ten days, and that Bay would have to share it with Larry Ross. He left no indication of what his conclusions would be.

Tom took comfort in Cindy's body again that evening. Gary and Julie were beginning to wonder where he was spending his time every night, but so far they had not been too nosy. It never occurred to them that Tom would be seeing another woman. That was just out of character for him. Then again, it seemed like the phone calls between Tom and Laura were getting less frequent, and when Julie would call Laura, she either got the answering machine or Laura didn't seem very interested in talking. Julie chalked it up to stress, or depression, or both. Gary and Julie thought October 8 was a lifetime away as well.

The summer was taking its toll on everyone. Searing heat, coupled with stress and uncertainty made the days seem longer than twenty-four hours.

Larry kept himself busy in July working on the Newman case and other cases that were pending so October could be devoted to Tom's trial. Mitch had Newman under control. He would keep in touch with Larry weekly, and send transcripts of every deposition taken of every Galaxy employee who knew anything about the caliper spring issue. Larry was impressed with how thorough and professional Mitch was. He took no bullshit answers. He got an answer to even the hardest questions.

Galaxy's knowledge of the defective springs was extensive. They were looking pretty bad, and had no real excuse other than the desire to save money for not doing a full recall on the vans in question when Southfield had notified them of the problem.

Southfield, wanting to shift the blame to Galaxy, was forthcoming with all the documents that proved they identified the problem early on, and had notified Galaxy immediately. They were responsible for making a batch of bad springs, but they had done all they could do to pull them off the market.

Mitch was beginning to think this would be the next big one against Galaxy as every deposition taken seemed to tighten the noose around Galaxy's corporate neck. Galaxy was talking about holding a settlement conference. Mitch wasn't ready. He wanted everything, so he could deal from a position of strength, and let Galaxy know they had no choice but to pay up. Galaxy would not weasel its way out of this one.

The costs were over twenty-five thousand dollars, and the case was barely six weeks old. Mitch was used to spending money to develop big cases, and had not hesitated in getting his model division ready to work on a courtroom size mock up so the jury could see what everyone was talking about.

Trips from Dallas to Detroit and back were expensive too. Mitch didn't stay in budget motels. He liked the best. He delivered the best, and the clients never complained about Mitch's travel expenses.

Larry had Norton chasing down a few more leads on Mendoza and his violent propensities. He had pretty much all he needed to try the case. He just needed October 8 to get here.

Larry, Maggie, and the kids even found a week to go to La Jolla for a family vacation. For a glorious week, Larry pushed everything but beach, bed, and family out of his mind. He came back refreshed and ready to go.

Then, the wheels fell off.

CHAPTER 22

▼

August 13th

The day started out just fine. When the mail came it wasn't good news.

The first thing on the stack was an Amended Disclosure Statement from Rick Bay naming Dr. Llewellan as a trial witness and attaching his report of psychological examination. Larry wanted to turn to the last page and read the conclusions first, but he forced himself to start on page one and read to the end. It was twelve pages long, so it took awhile.

According to Dr. Llewellan, the Minnesota Multi Phasic Personality Inventory, (MMPI), found Tom to be manipulative, aggressive, and "wanting to look good," by providing "look good" rather than honest answers.

Tom's IQ was judged to be about 120, or twenty points above what is considered average. Not genius level, but a lot smarter than average.

Then the hammer came down. Llewellan could find no evidence to support Dr. Ball's finding that Tom suffered from a Dissociative State at the time Art was hit with the ax. Even worse, it was Llewellan's opinion that Tom was trying to cover up the crime by dragging Art's body over to the garage, and that the call to Gary was made first as Tom knew he had committed a crime, and wanted advice from a police officer who also happened to be a friend before reporting it.

According to Dr. Llewellan, Tom had been in full control of himself at all times. He was feigning amnesia. His denial of having any recall of the event with the ax was a ruse. In short, Tom was trying to cover his ass.

He also concluded that Tom was desperate to end the partnership with Mendoza, and thought that Tom planned the meeting the morning of June 3rd as an opportunity to kill Mendoza and claim self-defense.

Of course all of these opinions were backed up by Llewellan's thirty years of clinical experience, and his interpretation of Tom's standardized tests.

Larry couldn't help but wonder how two forensic psychologists could come to such divergent opinions concerning the same man. He would argue that Llewellan was biased in favor of the state. Bay would argue that Ball was biased in favor of the defendant, and had been hired to save his butt.

Twelve strangers who knew nothing about psychology or the law would make the decision of guilt or innocence.

The only good thing about Llewellan's report is that it was from a local guy. Larry had really been expecting Bay to haul out the big guns and consult with Mark Jamison, the USC professor and author of the DSM IV diagnostic criteria for Dissociative State as a separate and distinct psychological condition.

At least the county budget woes were producing some positive results. Jamison was probably way too expensive, and travel would triple the expense.

Larry asked Cindy to fax Llewellan's report over to Ball's office with a note to read it and then give him a call.

He then turned his attention to the rest of the mail. There was a pleading from the Legal Aid office with a caption that read: Laura Rogers, petitioner, vs. Thomas Rogers, respondent. Laura had filed for divorce through the Pima County Legal Aid office.

The pleading was accompanied by a letter from the Legal Aid staff attorney requesting that Larry have Tom sign an acceptance of service form to save the costs of having a process server serve him with the paper.

The only thing Laura asked for in the petition was dissolution of the marriage, and restoration of her former name. She wanted nothing else, not even a piece of the equity in the house.

Arizona was a "no fault" divorce state. There was nothing Tom could do to stop this snowball. If Laura wanted a divorce, all she had to do was allege that the marriage was "irretrievably broken with no reasonable prospect of reconciliation." Her petition contained those magic words.

This could present a problem. It meant Laura's marriage to Tom would be ending just at the time the trial was starting. This would distract Tom. Larry needed him to be focused.

Once the Decree of Dissolution was entered, Bay could also call Laura as a witness, as there would be no more spousal privilege to assert. Decrees became final sixty days after filing. This one had been filed August 9. That meant the decree date and the criminal trial date would be one and the same. This was definitely not good.

Larry wondered if Bay knew about this. There was no requirement that Larry tell him. However, the petition was a public record, and before trial Larry was sure Bay would have one of his investigators do a public record search to see what came up on Tom Rogers. Bay would find out whether Larry told him or not.

It got worse. Tom called wanting to borrow six hundred dollars to catch up on his car payments. He was two months behind, and was getting warning notices from the bank almost every day. Larry had to say no. First of all, it was against the rules of ethics to loan money to a client. Secondly, it would be stupid. Tom might be in prison in a few months. He would have no way to pay back the loan.

While he had him on the phone, Larry told him of the divorce petition that had come in the mail. He asked Tom to come over to pick up a copy and sign the acceptance of service.

Tom didn't take the news very well.

Then he told him about the report from Dr. Llewellan. Tom didn't take that very well either. Even so, Tom said he would be at the office within the hour. He didn't have anything else to do. At least he could catch a glimpse of Cindy. That was something to look forward to.

Tom got there about two thirty. He looked like shit. He was wearing old sneakers, a ratty pair of shorts, and a crummy T-Shirt. He was way overdue for a haircut. He hadn't shaved in three or four days. Larry decided to overlook the appearances and got right down to business.

"So, Tom. Dr. Llewellan says you are manipulative, aggressive, and you like to look good."

Tom looked out the window to the parking lot. "No big surprise there Larry. I'm a salesman. Those are all good qualities in a salesman. I'm sure Dr. Ball can tell you that."

Larry had to agree with that reply. "And what about his conclusion that you planned the whole thing? You did have a loaded gun in the house ready to go. You told me yourself you had to bring an end to the partnership somehow. Killing Art would certainly do the trick."

Tom looked stunned. His reply was not unexpected. "Whose side are you on, anyway? I thought you were my lawyer. You're working for me. How come all of a sudden you believe anything that gets written on paper? Llewellan is full of crap. He's only known me for a few hours. I barely spent an hour with him face-to-face. I didn't plan this. Art insisted he come over that morning. I didn't know it would lead to this. If I had, I never would have let him come over. This is a nightmare! The only problem is, I never wake up. He tried to kill me Larry! You saw the bullet holes in the porch roof. Lucky for me he couldn't see for shit, or I'd be dead."

Larry considered Tom's comments. "I'm on your side, Tom. I just wanted to hear you deny Llewellan's accusations. I have to decide if you are going on the stand or not. You're beginning to convince me that you might pull it off. I've already faxed Llewellan's report over to Doug. He should call me in the next day or two. You have to admit, I told you to expect something like this. Do you want to see the divorce petition?"

"Why not? I've been expecting it. Laura won't talk to me anymore; and her parents are very protective. I'm sure they are very happy to have her back home. My life is a mess. It's probably the right thing for both of us. She's only twenty-eight. She has her whole life in front of her. As for me, who knows? I really don't blame her."

Larry decided that this was not the time to discuss what it meant to no longer have the spousal privilege of immunity from testifying. That could be covered another time.

Tom signed the acceptance, and Larry dictated a letter back to the Legal Aid lawyer telling him there would be no response filed to the petition. Laura could file a default in twenty days after the acceptance was filed with the court. On October 8 or after, she could appear at a default hearing at one thirty P.M. any day of the week and get her Decree of Dissolution. It was that simple.

Tom left the office feeling pretty down.

Later that night, an unmarked flatbed tow truck driven by Julio and Oscar Mendoza picked up Tom's Mazda while it was parked in Gary Miller's driveway. They had gotten the repo order earlier in the week.

They wanted to do this one themselves. They were hoping Tom Terrific would challenge them, so they could stick him with a knife. They weren't going to kill him, just hurt him bad, and leave a nice scar on his face for the world to see everyday.

They made as much noise as they could while picking up the car, hoping to wake someone up. The dogs didn't even bark. Sometimes you can't catch a break.

They would have to wait for another time to confront Tom face-to-face. His skinny wife might have disappeared, but he was still here. They hoped Mr. Preppy could get him off, so they could take care of him themselves. He would never see it coming. Just when he thought his troubles were over, he would find trouble like he had never imagined.

Revenge often came in small measures. Snatching Tom's Mazda was not only fun, they got paid five hundred bucks to do it, and knew the poor bastard would be a pedestrian in the morning. He just didn't know it yet.

CHAPTER 23

▼

August 17th

It was the first day of school for Cindy's girls. Of course, she was late for work. Larry had gotten spoiled over the last nine weeks. Sure, he knew being a single mom was tough, and getting three kids ready for school in the morning was no easy task. To his surprise, she apologized for being late, and even promised she would try harder to be in on time.

Doug Ball had called Larry on his cell phone about eight ten. He had some good news. "Larry. I've read Llewellan's report and I've discussed it with Mark Jamison."

Larry wasn't sure where this was going so he asked, "Jamison?"

"Yes—the professor who wrote the diagnostic criteria in the DSM IV for Dissociative State. Remember, I said he wouldn't disagree with me? Well, he doesn't! In fact he's willing to testify on Tom's behalf. His qualifications are impeccable. He is a prolific author on the subject. He is the recognized authority on the subject of Dissociative State."

"I don't know if we can afford him Doug. Isn't he over in California teaching at USC?" Just getting him over here is going to cost thousands of dollars. His rates are probably a lot higher than yours too. Besides, I've already disclosed you as our expert on the issue. The deadline to amend expert designation is in four days. I appreciate the thought, Doug, but I don't think it will work."

"Then you don't want to hear that he is in Tucson, that he is a visiting Professor in the Psychology Department at the UofA for the semester that started today, and that he wants to do this pro-bono because he is so pissed that Llewellan wouldn't agree with my opinions, and that Llewellan is a former student, and that Llewellan did his graduate work under Jamison, and that Jamison doesn't think much of Llewellan?"

Larry couldn't believe what he was hearing. It wasn't April 1, and Doug was not one to be a jokester. "Are you pulling my chain, or are you serious?"

"I'm serious Larry ol' pal. He wants to meet with you this afternoon about two, if you are available. He'll even come to your office. I gave him the address. Can you make it?"

"I'm putting it on the calendar as we speak. Should I have Tom here too? Can you make it?"

"I can be there. Tom should be there for sure. This is exciting Larry. You have the world's expert on Dissociative State testifying favorably for your client's case for free, and he is the mentor of the guy who is going to say he doesn't know what he is talking about. It doesn't get any better than that. I'll bring all my test data on Tom. Mark can testify on Dissociative State, and I can give the psychological autopsy on Mendoza and let the jury know what a violent mean S.O.B. he really was. You will overwhelm the jury with psychological testimony. Tom should start planning a vacation. He's going to be free man real soon."

"Hold on Doug. Let's not get ahead of ourselves. I'll meet with you and Jamison this afternoon. We'll take this one step at a time. I'm sure Jamison is wonderful, but I want to see him with my own eyes and decide for myself."

"You won't be disappointed Larry. If you like me, you will love Mark Jamison. He's a lot smarter, and a whole lot better looking than I am. He's the Marcus Welby of psychologists. Mr. Wonderful. He'll have the jury eating out of his hand, and when he tells them he is doing this for free because he believes in the case so strongly, and is so convinced that his diagnosis is correct, Bay won't have anything to impeach him on with accusations of bias, and being a hired gun."

"I'll see you at two, Doug. You have never let me down yet. This just sounds too good to be true, and when that happens I get worried."

"Not to worry, my friend. I'll see you at two."

Larry called Cindy on the intercom and told her to find Tom and get him to the office by two P.M., even if she had to go get him. It wasn't but a minute later that she rang back and said she had talked to him and he would be here.

Cindy hoped Larry would have good news for Tom. He was really down. Losing the Mazda to the repo man was humiliating and inconvenient. He still had Laura's Rabbit to drive, piece of shit that it was. He told Cindy he would coax it to start one more time, and make his way to the office by two.

CHAPTER 24

▼

Tom was thinking about the old adage that when you hit bottom there is no place to go but up. That had always sounded like a load of crap to him. Up until just a short while ago, his life had been the picture of success.

When he woke up on August 14, and noticed the Mazda was missing, he knew it had been repossessed. He confirmed it by calling the Sheriff's Office to report the car as stolen. They called back about thirty minutes later, and told him the car was reported as repossessed, and told him to contact the bank that held the lien to make arrangements to get it back.

There was no use in that. He didn't have any money to catch up the payments with. He needed to conserve what little cash he had just to eat with. He would drive Laura's venerable old Rabbit, and hope that it would hang together until this ordeal was over.

It was hard to imagine that he was down to actually thinking about how he was going to eat. Tom Rogers. Mr. Success. Super Salesman. Broke—about to lose his house if it didn't sell soon—unemployed, and facing life in prison, maybe even the death penalty.

When Cindy called and told him Larry wanted him to come to the office at two he was relieved to know that at least he would have something to do this afternoon. He shaved, put on some decent clothes, and combed his hair the best he could given the fact that he really needed a haircut.

Then the phone rang again. It was Sam Niles, the real estate agent. He had an offer on the house and wanted to present it this afternoon. Tom made the appointment for five P.M., and agreed to meet Sam at his real estate office. He didn't want to interrupt the meeting with Larry and the shrinks.

Sam told him it was a good offer, the buyers were qualified, and they wanted immediate possession. They would pay rent until closing as they had their kids enrolled in school, had just moved to town the week previously, and needed a place to live immediately.

The crew started to assemble in Larry's conference room about one forty-five. Doug arrived first. Tom followed, and shortly thereafter Mark Jamison arrived.

He was as Doug had described. About sixty-five years old, white hair starting to thin in the front and the back, probably six foot two inches tall, and very robust looking. He was even wearing a tweed jacket! Nobody except college professors wore tweed jackets anymore, especially in Tucson in August. This one looked like it had been around since the mid-seventies. It even had patches on the sleeves!

Larry had to take a peek at the parking lot to see what he was driving. It was a new S Type Jaguar. At least Jamison had good taste in cars. When Larry was sure everyone was accounted for, he entered the conference room and introduced himself to Dr. Jamison.

"Dr. Jamison. I'm Larry Ross. You know Dr. Ball. Have you met Tom yet?"

"Larry. Good to meet you. Yes, Doug introduced Tom to me. I'm glad you could meet with me today. This is a very interesting case. How can I help?"

"Doug tells me you and he have discussed the case, and you would like to be Tom's expert witness on Dissociative State. He also says you can rely on the standardized tests he gave Tom and that you just need to interview Tom to see if you can come on board. I'm sure I speak for Tom when I say we are glad to have you with us. I did an Internet search on you earlier today, and you are quite renowned, and well published."

Tom looked nervous. "Doctor, how long will you need with me? I have already been through this twice, and the process is very stressful for me. I'm really glad to hear I don't have to take those standardized tests again."

Jamison gave Tom a knowing look. "Doug did a fine job and gave you all the standardized tests needed for a proper diagnosis. There is no need to repeat those. All I need to do is spend about an hour or two with you to get some background, and discuss your memory of June 3rd with you. Is that too much to ask?"

Looking very relieved, Tom answered, "No. I can do that—the sooner the better. I do need to know how much this is going to cost though. My finances are limited, and from the sounds of things, you could be very expensive."

Tom really liked Jamison's answer. "Tom. I'm nearing the end of my career. I'm doing a visiting professorship at the UofA this semester in the psychology department. I only teach one class, and it only meets three days per week.

"My wife died two years ago. I don't have any significant other. I'm going to be bored to tears if I don't have something exciting to work on while I'm here. I just finished a book. I have seven textbooks in print right now. I'm financially well off. Money is not the motivating factor. I told Doug I would do this for free. Frankly, I'm disappointed in the opinions expressed by my former student, Dr. Llewellan. But then, he was not one of my brighter students. I remember him well—adequate—certainly not outstanding.

"I enjoy doing legal work. It challenges me. It stimulates me. Doug has shared his findings with me. I've never known him to be wrong. I just want to help. Will you let me do that?"

Larry smiled at Tom. "I'm sure Tom will have no objection to that. Will you Tom?"

Tom shook his head no.

"OK then. Dr. Jamison. When can you meet with Tom?"

"Well, I have no class to teach tomorrow. The university has given me free run of the psychology building. Tom, can you meet me about nine thirty tomorrow morning on campus? We should be done before noon, and you can have the rest of the day."

"Sure. I'll be there. Just give me the room number. Do you want me to bring anything?"

"Just get a good nights sleep and bring yourself. I'll review Doug's file tonight so I will be completely familiar with the case. I'll also review his material on the deceased. Doug is prepared to give testimony on the psychological autopsy on Mendoza. If things go as I think they will, I will provide testimony on your defense of Dissociative State. If I don't like what I hear, Larry will just stick with Doug for both issues, and not disclose me. Our meeting will be confidential, and if I can't help you, I won't pollute Doug's opinions with mine by sharing my findings with him. It really is a win-win situation for you. If I can help you, I will. If I can't, I'll stay out of the way."

Larry interrupted: "Doctor, our disclosure deadline is Friday. I need your written report to disclose to the prosecution on my desk by Friday morning so I can amend my Disclosure Statement and get it on the fax machine to Rick Bay before five o'clock on Friday. Can you do that?"

"Yes, I can do that. Give me your fax number and I'll fax it over to you on Thursday just as soon as I finish it. I'm excited to help. This is a most interesting case."

Jamison gave Tom the room number, and reminded him the psychology building was in the center of campus just south of Old Main. Tom assured him he knew where it was, and would be there.

Larry gave Jamison a business card that had the office fax number on it. He also wrote down his home and cell phone numbers on the back of the card, and told Jamison to call if he had any questions or needed any material from the file.

Larry provided Jamison with copies of the police photos, the aerial, and the floor plan of the house so he could get acclimated to the geography of the things being described to him. Jamison was glad for the help. He was used to Southern California homes that were jammed together on small lots. He was surprised to see only one house on a two-acre lot and was amazed at the distance from the back porch where the shootout occurred, to the end of the driveway where Jim Weber had watched Tom beat Art to death with the ax.

Jamison had worked with a lot of lawyers in his time, including the great Melvin Belli, F. Lee Bailey, and Johnny Cochran. He was impressed with the young lawyer from Tucson. He was organized. He was confident. He cared about his client.

He also liked Tom. First impressions are usually lasting impressions. Tom impressed Jamison as a gentle soul who was a stranger to violence, yet someone who would protect his life if it were threatened, which it was.

Yes, this would be fun. He was looking forward to meeting with Tom tomorrow and reading the file tonight. An old man had to look hard for pleasure. He had found it in State v. Rogers.

CHAPTER 25

▼

August 14th

With Art dead and out of the way, Julio and Oscar were getting greedy and sloppy. Art had insisted that Maria's Auto Salvage be completely legitimate. He would not hear of a stolen car running through the yard. All cars had the proper paperwork, and clean titles.

Julio and Oscar thought they were missing out on a golden opportunity. Uncle Art was a stupid old man. They were still going to take revenge for his death, but they were glad he was out of the way so they could run the business the way they wanted to.

They were well aware of the top ten model sellers in the U.S., and the Southwest in particular. Those cars also had a high accident rate, because there were so many of them on the road.

Taking the Toyota Camry and the Honda Accord as an example, both had carried air bags since 1991. Air bag units were a big seller on the used market. There were a ton of Camrys and Accords on the road that were over five years old, and the demand for used parts for those two cars was high. They kept their resale value, and if they were in an accident, the insurance companies always insisted on LKQ or used parts to repair them. It seemed there was no end to the demand for used hoods, doors, fenders, dash panels, and air bag units for those two models alone.

The Ford F 150 was another popular model. A runaway best seller for the last thirty years, they, too, held their resale value and the demand for used parts for the F 150 was even higher than it was for the Camry and Accord as so many people in Tucson chose the popular pick-up over a family sedan.

Not content to scoop Art's share of the monthly take from Maria's for their own without sharing it with their mother, or Angie, they wanted more. They had dreams of amassing millions, and spending the rest of their lives on the beaches in Mexico living the good life with women and servants at their beck and call any time of the day or night.

They were increasing their trips to Nogales, Sonora to stash American Dollars in their Mexican bank accounts. Nogales was only sixty miles away. They would go down for "lunch" and make a nice deposit while they were there.

The word was out on the street that Julio and Oscar would allow a stolen car or two every week to run through the yard. Soon the number increased to five or six, then eight to ten. They were only interested in the top ten sellers, which were also the top ten stolen for the same reason.

The thieves might be dishonest, but they knew the market for car parts. The thieves were also anxious to take advantage of the opportunity to have a new place to run the cars through.

The computer geek looked the other way for an extra five hundred bucks a week. The accountant never knew the difference, as he left it up to the geek to keep track of the cars and the titles. He did notice business was beginning to improve. Julio and Oscar had more cash in their pockets, and felt invincible. They had been operating outside of the law for so long, and getting away with it, they had no conception of ever getting busted.

When the word gets out on the street that there is a new chop shop for stolen cars, it eventually gets back to law enforcement as well. The Tucson Police Department, and the Pima County Sheriff's Office had a Joint Task Force that worked stolen car theft rings. They knew who the players were. They had undercover officers who would infiltrate the rings, and after months of careful surveillance and evidence gathering, would pull out, and let the arrests take place.

By early August, the word was out that Maria's Auto Salvage was running stolen cars through the yard. An undercover officer applied for and was hired on as a tow truck driver for Maria's. He was Hispanic, spoke fluent Spanish, was in his mid twenties, and looked the part of the typical Maria's driver.

Within just a few weeks, he had gathered overwhelming evidence that Maria's was quickly turning into a chop shop and was no longer a legitimate salvage yard. All of this information was dutifully reported in the official police reports he would file every Saturday detailing the prior week's activities.

Scott Munson was the Lieutenant with TPD who was in charge of the Joint Task Force for stolen vehicles. He had suspected Maria's was dirty for some time, but had never had any proof. Now he had it.

He reported his findings to the Chief of Police and the Sheriff. They authorized a raid on Maria's for early September. In the meantime, the undercover officer would continue to work at Maria's, and keep track of the stolen cars that were sitting in the yard, waiting to be parted out.

Munson was particularly interested in making sure Julio and Oscar would be pegged and arrested as the masterminds behind this enterprise. He knew they were also suspected by the Narcotics Division as being drug-runners—yet no charges had ever been brought.

With Art's death, the boys had gotten sloppy on that end of the business as well. The Narcotics division was looking at them very closely and an undercover officer had been planted at Maria's as a yardman as well. So far, he had not reported much, but the rumors were there. He had recently reported that he had heard talk of a big cocaine shipment that was to arrive towards the end of the month.

A lot could happen in three weeks. Criminals usually got bolder, and bolder, as time went on. Julio and Oscar were greedy. The more they had, the more they wanted. Munson, and Jaime Garcia, the head of the Joint Task Force on Narcotics decided they would work this one together. If they could pull off a good bust, they were confident they would reduce the number of car thefts and illegal drug trade in Tucson significantly.

In the meantime, the undercover officers would continue their work and try to buddy-up to Julio and Oscar and try to gain their confidence. The boys were not the brightest bulbs on the shelf. They were going to fall, and they would never see it coming.

CHAPTER 26

▼

August 16th

Mark Jamison had spent two and a half hours with Tom on Tuesday the 14th. He had thoroughly reviewed the standardized test results of the MMPI and others that Ball and Llewellan had administered. The answers Tom had given were consistent, and the profile was valid.

Jamison agreed that Tom showed aggressive tendencies, but not in a bad way. He also agreed he was manipulative, and tended to endorse "look good" answers like "Which would you rather do: a) go swimming; b) read a book; c) go to a movie; or, d) read to a sick person. People who wanted to "look good" would usually choose "d". That was Tom's choice.

However, the choice also fit in with the rest of his personality profile. Tom was a caring person. The profile showed no tendencies to violence. All humans are manipulative to some degree. Tom was a trained salesman. Salesmen usually showed more manipulative tendencies than the rest of the general population.

As for aggressive tendencies, this again was not bad aggression. This was assertiveness. This was another characteristic of salesmen. Jamison could find nothing to support Llewellan's conclusions that Tom had plotted to kill Art the morning of June 3rdrd, and had lured him out to the house to do so.

The more Jamison reviewed the file and considered his interview with Tom, the more convinced he became that Doug Ball was right on the money, and Llewellan had missed it by a mile.

Tom was definitely in a Dissociative State when he struck Art with the ax, and had subsequent Dissociative Amnesia, another separate and distinct diagnosis in the DSM IV manual. The two diagnoses usually went together.

Tom did not remember the event, and probably never would. Physical violence was so out of his personality profile that his mind had erected a barrier that shielded him from any memory of the event. He was not suffering from Post Traumatic Stress Disorder or PTSD as he had no memory of the event, and did not experience flashbacks of the event. This was a textbook example of Dissociative State followed by Dissociative Amnesia.

He dictated his report in the morning, proofread it in the afternoon, and had it faxed over to Larry's office before five o'clock. He had told Larry he would do that, and he always kept his word. He knew how critical time deadlines were for disclosure of witnesses in criminal and civil court cases.

Larry read the report Friday morning, dictated an Amended Disclosure Statement adding Jamison as an expert on the issue of Dissociative State/Dissociative Amnesia; clarified that Ball would only offer testimony on the psychological autopsy of Art Mendoza; attached Jamison's impressive thirty-page CV and equally-impressive report that basically said Llewellan was an idiot; and had Cindy fax it over to Bay's office at four thirty.

He left the office as soon as that was done. He and the family were going to hit Lake Roosevelt again this weekend. Even Tucson summers didn't last forever, and he hadn't had the boat on the water since early June. Things were definitely shaping up.

Karen Hargrave and her husband were on the Alaska cruise they had won in the Ice Break Contest. She would be back in on Wednesday to do the books, and balance the checkbook. He couldn't wait to share the good news with her.

CHAPTER 27

▼

September 5th

Munson and Garcia were in the command post vehicle that had been set up two miles away from Maria's. It was a bus-type motor home specifically designed for police work. It was filled with communications and surveillance gear. It was also air-conditioned, and gave them a comfortable spot to run the show from.

Everything was in place. They were going in at four o'clock. The big cocaine shipment had arrived, and the undercover yardman had found out where it was stashed. A pile of cars would have to be moved to get to it, but he was sure of the location.

The undercover tow truck driver had given them a list of twenty-five cars in the yard that he was sure had been stolen. The driver and the yardman had "quit" the previous day and collected their paychecks.

Just as Munson and Garcia had hoped, the boys had gotten even greedier and more careless as time went on. This was going to be fun, and satisfying.

Julio and Oscar didn't suspect a thing. They were used to their low-life, minimum-wage employees coming and going. These two guys were just two more in a long string of employees who would come and go out of Maria's. They would not be missed at all. There was always another guy looking for work who was glad to have a job.

Julio's prized '74 Monte Carlo sat proudly in front of the yard office gleaming in the sun. It was a testament to his success, and let his people know that he had "arrived." He loved to make it "dance" up and down on the front tires, and show off by raising and lowering it as he drove down the street.

He didn't know it yet, but it would soon be in the TPD impound lot as seized property thought to be illegally gained from drug activity. His Mexican bank accounts weren't going to be any help to him, as he couldn't access the accounts from a jail cell. Life as he and Oscar knew it was going to be over very soon.

At three fifty five, they heard a helicopter hovering over the yard. At three fifty seven, a squad of unmarked SUV's pulled into the yard parking lot, and men dressed in black with POLICE stenciled on the front and back of their T-shirts spilled out like an army. They were heavily armed with shotguns and automatic weapons. Then the SWAT team tank rumbled up, and sat blocking any exit that still existed. They were surrounded. There was no way out, and nowhere to go.

By four ten, Julio and Oscar were in handcuffs, and headed for the Pima County Jail. They weren't stupid enough to resist arrest and risk being shot. Before they were hauled off, Munson and Garcia served them with a search warrant, and the search of the premises began. They knew what they were looking for and they knew where to find it.

A hired crane operator fired up the yard crane, and started moving the pile of cars that sat on top of the cocaine stash. By five P.M., five hundred pounds of pure cocaine had been seized. By five thirty, all of the twenty-five stolen cars had been found and tagged.

By six o'clock, the Monte Carlo was on a flat bed that was part of Maria's fleet, and was on its way to the impound lot. The other tow trucks followed, as they were all seized as illegally gained property. Forfeiture proceeding would be started, and the law enforcement agencies would share the proceeds of what they brought at auction a few months down the road.

By seven o'clock, the gates were padlocked, police tape was strung around the perimeter, and legal notices were posted on the office door advising the public that the entire yard had been seized, and was now under police control. Maria's was out of business.

The case against Julio and Oscar was airtight. They wouldn't get out on bail as they were a flight risk, and were known to frequent Nogales at least twice a week. They would be in prison until they were old men. They could tell their stories of short-term fame and fortune to the other inmates who were willing to listen, but they would never steal another car, or deal any more drugs for years to come. Their street drug-dealing days were over for now.

Munson and Garcia didn't know it, but they had also probably saved the lives of Tom and Laura Rogers, and Larry Ross. Julio and Oscar couldn't hurt them from prison. It was a good day's work for the Joint Task Force on Narcotics and Car Theft. The Chief and the Sheriff would be pleased.

CHAPTER 28

▼

September 6th

With renters in his house until it closed in late September, Tom felt like he had a new lease on life. He used the rent to pay the September mortgage payment, and still had two hundred bucks left over.

After his meeting with Dr. Jamison on August 14th, he got a haircut, and drove over to the Tucson Auto Mall. He stopped in at the Toyota dealership, applied for a job as a salesman, and was hired the next day. He was surprised that no one recognized his face, or his name, as it had been all over the news in June, but this was August. People had a tendency to forget quickly.

He didn't volunteer that he had to quit in October, or take a few weeks off for a trial, or that he might be in prison for the rest of his life. He needed a job. He couldn't just sit around any longer.

He was put into a training program, and was guaranteed five hundred dollars a week against earned commissions for two months. If, after two months, he wasn't cutting it, they would turn him loose. Little did they know he didn't even have two months to work.

Tom sold three cars his first week, five the second and ten the third. He was a superstar. With his paychecks and commission checks, he rented an apartment in the same complex Cindy and the girls lived in.

It was good to get out of the Millers' and be on his own again. The self-confidence boost did wonders for him. He and Cindy continued to see each other, but the bedroom activity had all but stopped with Cindy's girls back in town. They were down to Sundays when the dealership was closed, and Cindy could leave the girls with her mother for a few hours in the afternoon. They were falling in love, and each desperately hoped that Larry could pull this one off. They didn't talk about it much, but it was constantly on their minds.

He and Laura had talked on the phone. She was sorry, but felt she had to move on. He said he understood. She told him she was coming out on the 8th of October to get her Decree of Dissolution of Marriage, and wanted to know if it would be okay if she stayed to watch the trial.

Tom was appreciative of the offer, but told her it was probably not a good idea to stay in town. Besides, he didn't know what the outcome would be, and he didn't want her there if the jury returned a guilty verdict. There was also the issue of her personal safety. The thugs who had wrecked the house and threatened Laura were probably still out there and watching. They would expect her to be at the trial, and there was no sense in taking the chance and giving them an easy target.

She agreed. It all seemed so business-like. The passion was gone. They were wrapping up a business deal. No one would die in this partnership dissolution.

Larry picked up the paper in the morning and read about the police raid on Maria's Auto Salvage. He recalled that the place was one of Mendoza's legitimate businesses, and was glad to hear that his nephews had bitten the dust.

Cindy had been pretty good about getting to work on time. He didn't know that with Tom living in the same complex, he would take the girls to school, and let Cindy get to work. Tom didn't report to the sales floor until ten o'clock. which gave him plenty of time to get the girls all deposited at school. Cindy's mom had agreed to pick them up after school and keep them until Cindy could pick them up after work. Life was back on schedule, and he liked it that way.

The mail came about eleven thirty that morning. Cindy opened it, and couldn't believe what she saw in the envelope from the law firm that was defending Galaxy in the Newman case. It was on pleading paper, and had the formal caption. It was entitled "Offer of Judgment." She read it very carefully.

Defendant Galaxy Motor Company, pursuant to Rule 68 of the Federal Rules of Civil Procedure offers to allow the plaintiffs Newman to take judgment against defendant in the sum of Thirty Million Dollars ($30,000,000).

Failure to accept this offer within thirty days will subject the plaintiffs Newman to the penalties set forth in Rule 68 of the Federal Rules of Civil Procedure. The offer is made inclusive of all costs incurred by the plaintiffs to date.

If not accepted, this offer is deemed withdrawn and evidence concerning the tender of this offer will not be admissible at trial.

The offer is contingent on the terms of the offer remaining confidential between Galaxy Motor Company, and plaintiffs Newman.

An acceptance of this offer is attached, and a form of judgment is enclosed for submission to the court.

Dated this 4th day of September,

S. Connor Peterson,

Chief Counsel,

Galaxy Motor Co.

Two copies of the Offer of Judgment were enclosed. It showed that a copy had been mailed to Mitch Branch. A form of acceptance was a separate document, and a judgment form against Galaxy Motor Co. was enclosed.

It contained all of the proper language, and also contained the confidentiality clause, which meant no announcement could be made to the media, and the deal would be a secret between the Newmans, their lawyers, and Galaxy Motors

All Larry had to do was sign the acceptance form, and present the paperwork to the judge. The judge would sign the Judgment just as soon as he had called Peterson to confirm that the offer had in fact been made, and Galaxy had no objection to entry of the judgment. The form of judgment even contained language that the funds would be delivered within thirty days of the entry of judgment.

Cindy read it over and over. Surely this had to be a mistake. Galaxy had not even deposed the Newmans yet. The depositions were scheduled for next week. Larry was doing preparation for that as she was opening the mail. She looked at the envelope. She looked at the pleading paper. She looked at Peterson's signature, and even pulled out another pleading he had signed, and did her own amateur handwriting analysis. It was real. She picked it up, and walked into Larry's office. "Larry, I think you should look at this right away."

Larry looked up from what he was doing. Cindy looked like she had seen a ghost.

"What is it Cindy, bad news?"

"I don't think you are going to have to spend any more time working on the Newman case."

Larry was becoming annoyed. "Spit it out Cindy, what is it?"

She handed him the paperwork, and stood back to watch him read it. His eyebrows danced up and down. It was five minutes before he looked up again. "I'd better call Mitch, and ask him if he has seen this. Please call the Newmans and see if they can come in late this afternoon. Do you know what this means?"

Cindy's answer was slow and deliberate. "I think it means Galaxy wants to pay the Newmans thirty million dollars to make this go away, and all you have to do is carry the paperwork over to the judge, and he will sign it. The case will be over, and the Newmans will have closure."

Larry let out a sigh. He hadn't yet crossed the bridge of what the offer meant to him. The real key was what it would mean to the Newmans. They were sure to be pissed at the non-disclosure clause. What the Newmans really wanted from Galaxy was an apology, not money. Even so, he had a duty as their lawyer to explain the offer to them and let them know what it meant legally.

He picked up the phone to call Mitch. He was out, and he had to leave a message on his voice mail. Shit! He really needed to talk to Mitch!

Cindy arranged the meeting with the Newmans for four thirty. At Larry's instruction, she didn't tell them why he needed to see them. Larry was hoping he would talk to Mitch before the Newmans came in. The Newmans would want to know what Mitch thought. Larry wanted to know what he thought too. This was a big decision to talk about, and he wanted Mitch to be in on the decision-making.

CHAPTER 29

▼

Sept 6th, 4:30 p.m.

Mitch had called Larry back about two o'clock. He, too, had a copy of the Offer of Judgment. Larry got out the Federal Rule Book, and read the rule. It was different from the Arizona Rule with the same number.

In Arizona, a plaintiff could file an Offer to Accept Judgment, and put the monkey on the defendant's back. In Federal Court, only the defendant could make an offer under the rule.

The penalties under the Arizona Rule were greater than they were under the Federal Rule. In Federal Court, an offer not accepted meant that the plaintiff could not recover compensable court costs as defined by statute if the verdict was less than the offer. The plaintiff also had to pay the jury fees, and had to pay the defendant's costs. This could amount to a hundred thousand dollars, or more, in a products case like this one.

The real kicker was having the courage to say no to thirty million dollars. He and Mitch could make no guarantee on the outcome of the trial. There was no way Larry and Mitch could even guarantee that the jury would find in favor of the Newmans, let alone award thirty million dollars for the death of two children. It was a hefty offer. It was designed to get everyone's attention. It had Larry's attention.

Mitch knew what Galaxy was up to. They wanted to get him out of the discovery loop. There was probably something he hadn't found yet that was the true smoking gun, and Galaxy didn't want him to find it. Galaxy was waving money in front of the Newmans, hoping they would take it, and walk away from their quest for revenge.

Galaxy desperately wanted this one to go away quietly. A big verdict in New-man would mean lots of publicity for the great Mitch Branch, and a lot of bad publicity for Galaxy. The news shows would play it up big. That would bring more cases out, and Galaxy wanted to keep this as quiet as it could.

Galaxy had researched the financial status of Larry Ross and Mike and Marga-ret Newman. The Newmans were solid middle-class. A house, and two cars, had a 401k retirement plan at work, did not have much in the bank, and had no inde-pendent stock portfolio. They did have a two hundred thousand dollar CD, which Galaxy correctly assumed was the proceeds of insurance policies on the deceased Newman children.

The fact that the Newmans had it in a CD was proof to Galaxy that the New-mans considered the money to be special and not to be touched. Galaxy was right. They did consider the money special. They had made a pact between them not to do anything with that money until the case against Galaxy was concluded.

Larry Ross was the same. He didn't even have a 401k. He didn't have any CDs. His net worth was next to nothing. This would be a fortune that the New-mans and Ross would find hard to turn down. Or at least they hoped so.

As for Branch, his net worth was approaching two hundred million dollars. A lot of it was from cases against Galaxy. He wasn't working for the money any longer.

Despite his wealth, Mitch lived relatively modestly. He didn't have any expen-sive hobbies like airplanes or yachts. He was married to the same woman he had started out with thirty-five years ago, so he had lost nothing to a nasty divorce. His children were grown. One was a PhD chemical engineer, the other a derma-tologist. Both of them were successful in their own right, and did not depend on their parents for anything. Both enjoyed successful marriages.

The money wouldn't tempt Mitch Branch, but he had an ethical obligation to his clients. He couldn't be fulfilling his personal vendetta against Galaxy at his client's expense. He would have to tell them what the Offer of Judgment meant to them.

Mitch had his accounting staff do a cost reconciliation, and he faxed a pro-posed settlement ledger over to Larry's office so he would have numbers to present to the clients. It was really their call. He doubted they would be interested in Galaxy's offer. He had concluded that money was not their motivation in going after Galaxy. Mitch was rarely wrong about a client's true motivation, and he didn't think he was wrong this time.

Even holding out a generous one hundred thousand dollars for costs, the led-ger showed a net recovery to the Newmans of well over twenty million dollars.

The payment would be a tax-free event for them as personal injury and wrongful death settlements were exempt from income tax. The fees earned by the lawyers were taxable to the lawyers as income. The IRS gave the personal injury and wrongful death survivors a free ride.

If they invested the money in safe tax-free government bonds at a modest four percent, they would have a lifetime income of about eight hundred thousand dollars annually without ever touching the principal. This would again be exempt from income tax.

Galaxy had already run the calculations on this, and decided this would be too much money for the Newmans to say no to. Mitch expected them to say no.

The Newmans got to the office about four fifteen. Cindy showed them to the conference room and Larry joined them about four twenty-five with a folder in his hands and a smile on his face.

Mike started the conversation. "Cindy said it was important that we meet with you today if we could. Is something wrong?"

That was the usual client response to most calls from their lawyers. They always thought something must be wrong. Larry took a deep breath, laid the Offer of Judgment on the table, and pushed it towards Mike and Margaret. "I thought you should know about this right away. Galaxy has offered to settle your case for thirty million dollars. We have thirty days to think about it. Because they mailed it, the time expires October 8. I start a trial that day, so we need a decision long before then. I've talked to Mitch about this. His accounting department prepared a ledger for you to review, and has made some suggestions on how to invest the money. He is okay with it. The decision is yours to make."

Margaret spoke up. "Are they admitting fault for what happened? Can we go public with this, so the world will know that Galaxy killed our babies?"

Mike chimed in: "I thought Mitch said this case was worth three hundred million. I thought he wanted to teach Galaxy a lesson. This is ten percent of what they should be paying. Are you suggesting we take it?"

Larry didn't expect this reaction from them. He paused before he answered. He didn't want them losing faith in him. "We can't guarantee the outcome of any trial. We think this is a solid case but anything can happen. Trials are always risky. Settlements are a sure thing. You need to think about this. We think it is an offer you should consider carefully. If you accept it, we won't have to go through your depositions next week. I know you have been dreading that experience."

Margaret spoke again. "You still haven't told us if they are admitting fault, or if we can go public with this. Are they? Can we?"

"No. Galaxy will pay thirty million dollars. In return, they want an agreement of confidentiality, which means no media hype. The standard settlement agreement will deny responsibility for what happened."

Larry was having a flashback to the last time he had a conversation with grieving parents who wouldn't sign a settlement agreement that denied responsibility of the defendant for the death of a child. It took those clients awhile to come around to the recognition that they needed to settle the case, and get on with their lives. He decided he had better inform them of the penalties if they declined the offer, and didn't do better at trial. As he was in the middle of that long, legal explanation Mike interrupted him.

"Larry, we still have the insurance money from the kids' policies. That should be enough to cover the costs at trial. I don't think we should take their first offer. We want them to apologize to us. We want them to admit they were wrong. We want them to suffer the bad publicity of a big jury verdict against them. We don't really care about the money. Money isn't going to bring the kids back."

Larry felt sick to his stomach. There it was. The clients didn't care about the money! Great! Should he remind them that he did, and this was a business for him, and he couldn't eat a defense verdict if one were to come down? Not hardly.

They would lose faith in him, and might shop for another lawyer. He had to maintain client control, and not show weakness.

There it was again—the horrible money thing. God he hated it! Why couldn't he just be a lawyer, and not have to deal with the money thing all the time? Larry put his personal feeling aside and focused on the clients in front of him. They were grieving. They had put their trust in him to represent their interests. He had known all along that the Newmans were more interested in an apology and publicity than money. Put the client first Larry! You know it is their call! Quit thinking about the money Larry!

Larry took a moment before he answered. This was a delicate time. He had to say the right words. "Mike, I can't imagine how you and Margaret must be suffering. I don't think Galaxy will ever offer an apology, or agree to publicity. How would you like me to respond to them?"

Mike banged his fist on the table. "We won't settle for a penny less than the three hundred million Mitch told us this was worth. We want Galaxy to admit fault, and we want publicity. We are inflexible on this, aren't we Margaret?"

Margaret nodded her head in agreement.

He knew Mitch should never have mentioned that astronomical number. Now it was imprinted in their minds as if it were carved in stone. Larry never pitched a number to a client in the beginning. Things always looked great in the beginning, and clients had very selective memories. They remembered what they wanted to remember, and forgot the disclaimer of only using that number as an illustration. It was no longer an illustration. It had turned into a client expectation. Mitch was an experienced trial lawyer. What was he thinking?

Then again, the money wasn't really the stumbling block. The Newmans wanted a pound of flesh, and they would measure it by an apology, and publicity, two things Galaxy would never agree to. The Newmans would probably settle the case for nothing if they could get their apology and the right to put Galaxy on a public pedestal of scorn.

He decided they should get Mitch on the phone. He had agreed to take an after-hours call on his cell phone if the Newmans wanted his input.

"Would you like me to call Mitch, so you can talk to him about this?"

Mike hunched his shoulders and leaned forward. "Larry, there is no need to call Mitch. If Galaxy won't accept fault, we won't settle. If Galaxy won't let us talk to the press, we won't settle. I don't care if they offer us a billion dollars. If they offer us three hundred million, accept fault, and let us publicize this, we have a deal. Otherwise, forget it. You've got a job to do. You work for us. We expect you to do your job. Are you with me Margaret?"

Margaret again nodded her head in agreement.

Oh, the joys of working on a contingent fee! When things went well, the clients always wanted an adjustment downward. When you lost, they walked away, and never even thought twice about the hours the lawyer worked for free.

It was easy for the client to be demanding. They weren't paying Larry by the hour to work for them. But that was the way Larry had chosen to work. He had to honor the client's wishes. After ten years of practice, he knew this was the way all clients thought. The Newmans weren't any different from anyone else he had represented on a contingent fee. They had their agenda, and he had known this from the beginning.

Larry decided it was time to stop pushing, and just let this news sink in for a while. Maybe with the passage of a few days, or even a few weeks, they would see things differently. Maybe he should send them home with a copy of the Offer of Judgment. Maybe it was too soon. Maybe they needed to have their depositions taken, so they could feel like they had a chance to get their grief off of their chests.

Maybe. Maybe they were crazy. Maybe they were right. Who knew? He did know they weren't going to say yes today, and prolonging the discussion was only going to make it worse. Besides, being in trial with the great Mitch Branch would be fun, and Mitch wasn't known for losing his cases. The Newmans may have called this one right.

It was after five when he showed them out. To his surprise, Cindy was still at her desk.

"Did they take it?"

Larry looked at her. "No, they want three hundred million, an apology, and publicity. They probably also want a full-page apology from Galaxy on the front page of the Wall Street Journal. I told them to think about it, but I don't think they are going to change their minds."

"Can't you make them take it? That is so much money. What if they lose?"

"They say they don't care about the money. Usually, when I hear that, I know they care about the money. This time, I believe it. I really don't think they care about the money. What they really want is Galaxy to publicly apologize for killing their kids. And no, I can't make them take it. They have the final say. The rules of ethics are crystal clear on this. I guess I better call Mitch, and give him the news."

Cindy gathered up her purse and locked up on her way out, leaving Larry to make the phone call to Mitch. She couldn't imagine the Newmans had said no. She felt sorry for Larry. He worked so hard, and most of the time his clients just took him for granted. They never thought about how their decisions might affect him. She thought the Newmans were being selfish and greedy. But then again, they had lost both of their children at the same time, all because Galaxy wanted to save a few dollars.

Since this was too much for her to think about, she decided to turn her thoughts elsewhere. She called her mom and asked if she could keep the kids for dinner.

Tom wasn't working today and she needed some time alone with him. Since school had started, their time together had been very limited. She was sure Tom wouldn't mind. He didn't. The sexual release was good for both of them, and took their minds off the mounting pressures they were facing.

They picked the girls up from her mother's at about eight, and stopped at Baskin Robbins on the way home for a treat. The girls were in bed by nine. Tomorrow was another day.

CHAPTER 30

▼

September 30th

Maria Mendoza had been in an alcoholic stupor for most of the last ten years. Since her big brother had been killed; and her boys thrown in jail, life as she had known it was over.

The cash flow from Maria's Auto Salvage had dried up in August. Her brother and her boys had only given her what she needed. Her cash reserves ran out fast. She didn't know how to manage money.

In the past, if she needed something, Art or one of the boys would take care of it. Now she was on her own. She had to take a job with her cousin's janitorial service. One of the accounts was the Pima County Courthouse.

She hated being sober, but she had to work to get the money to buy food and liquor, so her drinking had slowed down considerably. She reported for work every night at six, and would finish about two thirty in the morning.

The cleaning crews would enter the courthouse from the underground parking garage through the judge's elevators. The janitorial company had a bond to cover theft.

The court security personnel got off at six, and no one ever checked the janitorial staff through the metal detectors, as by six, the only ones in the courthouse were the janitors themselves. The judges and support staff were gone by five thirty. It was time to ready the building for the next day of business.

Maria was assigned to the courtrooms on the fifth, and sixth floors. That added up to twelve courtrooms, and four public bathrooms, plus the huge hallways and the private offices of the judges, clerks and court reporters. The judges also had private bathrooms and that gave her twelve additional smaller bathrooms to clean every night.

She was part of a crew of four. She had to hustle to get it all done in an eight-hour shift. It was basically empty the wastebaskets, run the vacuum, dust the desks, and clean the sinks and toilets quickly every night.

The men in the crew ran the buffers that cleaned the tile and ceramic tile floors. She hated it. She hated Tom Rogers for killing her brother. She hated the police for arresting her boys. She hated the fact that she was broke. It was a few weeks into the job when the idea came to her.

She had a snub-nosed .38 police revolver at home. She could bring it into the courthouse during one of her shifts. She could tape it to the underneath of one of the chairs in the courtroom where Tom Rogers was going to have his trial. Only she would know which chair it was under. No one would ever think to look under a chair. She would stash it the night before she planned to use it, and only a few hours would pass between the plant and the shootout.

She knew Tom's trial date was October 8. The calendars were always hanging on the bulletin boards every night, announcing what would be heard the following day and in which courtroom. She could enter as a spectator. All trials were open to the public. She would take her seat, and wait for the opportune moment to pull the gun from under the seat and blast the little bastard where he stood.

She had no life anyway. Prison didn't scare her. A grief-stricken sister that struck down the killer of her brother would never get the death penalty. Rogers would get what he deserved, and she would be taken care of for the rest of her life. She wouldn't have to work at this shitty job cleaning shitty toilets. It sounded like a good plan to her alcohol-addled brain.

The trial started one week from tomorrow. That would give her plenty of time to work out the details of her plan. She would plant the gun on Monday night during work hours, show up Tuesday morning for the trial, and right in the middle of jury selection, she would have her very own day in court. She might even take out his lawyer while she was at it.

Her boys had told her of their plans for Rogers and Mr. Preppy, his lawyer. The boys could no longer carry out the plan. Yes. The more she turned it over in her mind, the better it sounded.

She had hollow point bullets for the .38. That would blast a hole in Rogers he wouldn't recover from. At close range, she might even blast him six times. She would make sure he was finished before she turned the gun on Mr. Preppy.

Earlier in the day at Larry's office, Jamison had stood up well under Bay's questioning during his taped interview. Without saying so, it became clear he thought Llewellan was a dope and his opinions were unsupported by any of the evidence in the case.

Following Jamison, Larry had his turn with Llewellan. He stood his ground, but he was defensive, nervous, and had a hard time justifying his opinions.

Larry and Bay had a talk after the two interviews were completed.

"Your man Jamison is impressive. I might be able to talk McNair into a plea of voluntary manslaughter. We would recommend no more than five years."

Bay had Larry's interest. Few criminal trials in Pima County ended in a flat out verdict of acquittal. The juries usually convicted the accused of something. Voluntary manslaughter would be a good compromise. Tom would be out by the time he was thirty-five. He would have a felony conviction attached to his name for the rest of his life, but it was better than facing the prospect of life in prison, or maybe even the death penalty. This was something he would have to talk to Tom about.

"I was thinking more along the lines of involuntary manslaughter. Parole is possible for that. Jamison just told you that what happened was involuntary on Tom's part. You just said he was impressive."

Bay thought about that one. "I don't think McNair will go along with that. I'm even afraid to ask him, but I will. If Tom had just left Mendoza to die in the driveway, this would have been a lot easier for all of us, Larry."

Larry had to agree with that observation. He recalled how Cotter didn't even want to arrest Tom at the scene and only did so because McNair told him to. He decided to remind Bay of that.

"You know, Rick, Detective Cotter was so impressed with Tom at the scene he didn't even want to arrest him. He only did so because he called McNair for advice, and McNair told him to slap the cuffs on him so we could sort it out later. Well, now it's later. We've sorted it out. Tom killed that miserable son of a bitch, that's for sure. But he has a good diminished capacity defense that is backed up by the world's leading expert in the field. I'm thinking I smell an acquittal in the air."

Bay didn't even like the sound of the word acquittal. It had been years since the Pima County Attorneys Office had prosecuted a murder trial that had ended with an all out acquittal. As the chief criminal deputy assigned to the murder one trials, Bay didn't want an acquittal attached to his name and his track record. He had to agree that an acquittal was a possibility, if not a probability.

"You talk to Tom, Larry, and let him know about the voluntary manslaughter offer. He needs to consider it. I'll talk to McNair about involuntary this afternoon. If we are going to plead this out, we need to get an agreement done this week by Friday at the latest so we can let the judge know his division will be free for another trial next week.

"If we do try this, I'm going to object to the psychological autopsy bullshit that your man Ball is supposed to pontificate about. I doubt if you will get that in. You know that character evidence is generally not admissible in trial to prove a pattern of conduct."

"I expected that. However, I'm offering it to prove that Tom had good reason to fear Mendoza, and believe his threats against him were real. I have witnesses who will testify that they heard Mendoza tell Tom he would kill him if he ever interfered in his affairs again. He had witnessed him beat a man bloody with a two-by-four. He had punched him in the gut when he tried to rescue Sandy Rathman. I've got that one on videotape.

"We know Mendoza fired six shots at Tom. Your own forensics team will prove that. The purpose of the psychological autopsy is to show that Mendoza suffered from a Rage Impulse Control Disorder, that Tom had witnessed it, and acted reasonably by considering Mendoza to be a threat even after he had been shot.

"I think I will get it in. You know Dr. Ball is well respected by all of the judges. He's not known to go out on a limb just for a paycheck. I'll bet you a steak dinner that it comes in."

"I only eat steak at McMahon's, Larry. You can't afford it. No bets. I'll get back to you as soon as I talk to McNair. I would like to do something to make this one go away. I don't think Tom is a dangerous criminal who will strike again. In some ways, he is more of a victim than Mendoza is. Talk to Tom. Five years or less isn't a bad way to go when the death penalty is a possibility."

Larry had a lot of thinking to do. Until a short time ago, the judges decided the penalty phase in first-degree murder cases. If that were still the case, Larry was reasonably certain that no judge would give Tom Rogers the death penalty.

However, because of a recent United Stated Supreme Court Decision, juries now handed out the death penalty in a separate penalty phase of the trial after a verdict of guilty was entered. It could happen that Tom's jury would be filled with a bunch of ultra conservative Republican Rush Limbaugh listeners who would actually decide that death is what Tom had coming. He had to tell Tom to carefully consider Bay's offer.

The Newmans weren't considering the thirty million dollar offer from Galaxy any longer. Not that they ever had. They made it clear that without an admission of wrongdoing from Galaxy, an apology from Thomas Galaxy himself, and unrestricted publicity on the settlement, there was no amount of money that would settle the case.

Galaxy was of course not going to do that. They would probably pay more money. They would never admit fault, issue an apology, or agree to unrestricted publicity. The battle lines were drawn. Newman v. Galaxy was going to trial.

The Newmans did well at their depositions. They had impressed Connor Peterson, Chief Counsel on the case. He had reported to Galaxy that the Newmans weren't in this case for the money. That was what Peterson called a dangerous Plaintiff. They couldn't be tempted with money.

Allison had also done well at his deposition. Peterson didn't like his cocky little lawyer, but Allison did a good job of explaining that he was just driving along at the speed limit when all of a sudden, he felt the right front wheel lock up, and the van started to skid out of control. He had done his best to correct its path of travel, but at seventy-five miles per hour, things happened very quickly.

The Reconstructionists had proven that he gave it a gallant effort, but once the van had started to tip, it was over. There was nothing he could do to right it again.

Conner realized that trying to blame Allison for the crash would not work. He withdrew that defense. He didn't want to piss off the jury.

Allison would be a good witness for himself, and for the Newmans. As Gimble had predicted, the judge had consolidated the two cases. The best way out for Galaxy was to divide and conquer. Settle with the Newmans, which was the better case with the better lawyers, and let Allison go to trial alone with his cocky and annoying lawyer.

Without Ross and Branch along beside him to foot the bill for the experts and present the case the way it should be presented, Gimble wouldn't have a chance in hell. Once the Newmans were out, Allison would follow for a small amount.

Galaxy had also researched the financial status of Allison and Gimble. Allison was better off in the net worth department than his lawyer was. Gimble probably had a negative net worth. He lived in an apartment, owned no real estate, and had a ton of credit card debt. Oh yes. Allison and Gimble would grab for the bone Galaxy would toss their way once the Newmans were out of the equation.

The Newman and the Allison cases were now joined at the hip, just like conjoined twins. The cases would walk the same path to victory, or defeat. There would be no in between.

Galaxy's hope to divide and conquer was another one of its money saving schemes. It was all part of the strategy. Peterson had successfully used the tactic in the past. Pick on the weak by settling with the strong who supported them.

Right after Bay left the office, Larry called Tom to tell him that Bay had offered a plea to voluntary manslaughter with a recommendation of five years or less. Tom's response was what Larry feared.

"What do you think I should do? I thought the case was going well. I thought we could win? Why should I spend five years in prison and live the rest of my life as a convicted felon if I can walk away a free man?"

"The case is going well. I do think we can win. However, I can't guarantee an outcome. If convicted on the murder one charge, you could be facing life in prison without parole, and maybe even the death penalty. That is a huge risk to take. With a plea, you know what the outside limit of the penalty will be. You will probably get a lot less than five years, but I can't guarantee that either. This is something you need to consider, Tom. We need to know by Thursday at the very latest as trial starts next Tuesday. I'm sorry the time line is so short, but the offer was just made to me a few minutes ago. It was made in response to how well Jamison did on his taped interview."

"Okay. I'll think about it. I need to call my dad. I need to talk to Gary and Julie about it. This is pretty overwhelming. Five years is a long time to be in prison."

Larry's reply brought it all into perspective: "The rest of your life is also a long time to spend in prison. The choice is yours. Call me as soon as you make a decision. In the meantime, I will continue to prepare for trial."

Late that morning, Tom went to Pima Title to close on his house sale. He went over the closing documents with Sam Niles and the escrow officer. He signed the paperwork, and walked out of the title company with a check for $48,763.72, the net equity in his house after payment of all commissions, fees, expenses and satisfaction of the outstanding mortgage. Not a fortune, but a good day for Tom Rogers. He reported for his shift at work at one P.M.

Despite his thoughts being elsewhere, he sold a Sequoia Limited and an Avalon sedan that day before his shift was over. The two sales he completed today would make him salesman of the month. He would get a bonus, and a preferred parking spot in the shade for the next month. He decided he had to tell his manager about the trial by Friday at the latest. He had been putting it off for too long.

CHAPTER 31

▼

October 2nd

Tom had talked it over with his dad, Gary and Julie. He left Cindy out of the loop. He tried to call Laura, but she wasn't calling him back.

Ralph wasn't much help. He told Tom it was his decision, but five years was a lot better than life in prison. It was a sure thing. Ralph liked the sure thing.

Gary and Julie felt the same way. Gary was essentially a cop. He liked the sure thing too. Gary encouraged Tom to take the offer.

Tom met with Jamison and discussed it with him. Jamison told him anything could happen in a courtroom. While the final decision was Tom's to make alone, Jamison was in favor of accepting the plea deal. It was workable. It wouldn't ruin his life.

Bay had called Larry back on Tuesday morning and said that McNair would go along with a plea to voluntary manslaughter, but would not consider involuntary manslaughter, which carried possible parole. A man was dead. He had been beaten to death with an ax.

McNair had a reputation to uphold as a tough prosecutor. He didn't want the papers screaming about why he let an ax murderer off with probation. He didn't want his opponent in the next election accusing him of being soft on crime.

Larry called Tom to tell him that involuntary manslaughter was not an option, but voluntary was still on the table. Tom said he was thinking about it.

Larry told Tom again that he needed an answer by Thursday. Larry couldn't help but think how wonderful his life would be if the Newmans would settle, and Tom would take a plea. He would avoid the stress of two trials, he would have done a great job for both clients, and life would get back to normal, whatever that was.

The life of a trial lawyer was anything but normal. There was always an unexpected stress of some kind that would be hanging around. It didn't look like it was going to happen.

Wednesday came and went without hearing from Tom. He did get an interesting call from Mitch.

Mitch had found the smoking gun. While he was deposing the head of the recall division for Galaxy, Mitch had casually asked if any accounting analysis had been done to calculate the cost of the caliper spring repair versus a full recall. To his surprise, the answer was yes.

He followed up by asking if the deponent had any copies of the analysis. Once again the answer was yes.

Following the deposition, Mitch had sent out a Request to Produce to Galaxy. He expected them to play hide and seek for a while and object on the grounds of proprietary information, work product between counsel and client or some other lame excuse for not producing the document.

Instead, Galaxy produced it. It was a damning document. It showed some things that Mitch already knew. The full cost of the recall was calculated to be four hundred fifty million. The cost of the TSB campaign had been calculated at one hundred fifty million for a savings to Galaxy of three hundred million.

Then it went on to calculate and project the number of people who would likely die or be injured if Galaxy proceeded with the Recall or the TSB campaign.

The calculation was that many more would die, or be injured if the TSB campaign were relied on, but fewer lawsuits would be expected against Galaxy. The public would have no general knowledge of a defect. A lot of claimants would not seek representation, and Galaxy would quietly contact persons known to be injured by a caliper spring failure and negotiate a quiet settlement. The document referred to people not retaining lawyers to represent them as controlling the "penetration rate."

Then the bottom line was stated:

It is projected, based upon our computer model, which is deemed to be reliable, that the total savings to Galaxy Motor Co. in overhead costs, costs of litigation, and claims control will result in a savings to the company of seven hundred fifty million, or more if the TSB campaign is elected over the Recall campaign.

The Head of the Accounting Department signed it for Galaxy Motor Company. It showed copies forwarded to the Consumer Safety Manager, the head of the recall department, and Thomas Galaxy himself, the Chairman of the Board.

"Do you understand the importance of this document, Larry?"

Larry understood. It was the key to the Galaxy Motor Company vault. Galaxy had made a conscious, knowing decision that they could save money by using the TSB Campaign, and by doing so, many more people would die or be injured than if Galaxy used a Recall Campaign. This was corporate greed at its very worst. Larry and Mitch represented victims of that greed. Mike and Margaret Newman had lost their precious twins because Galaxy wanted its balance sheet to look better for Wall Street.

"What does Peterson have to say about this?" Larry asked.

"I don't know. I haven't talked to him about it yet. I can't believe he coughed this up. This is monumental, Larry. I have never seen anything like this. I just got it in the mail today. I called you as soon as I saw it and read through it. Money saving is one thing, but calculating human loss and plotting to control the rate that injured victims retain lawyers is something I have never seen before in all my years of doing this kind of work. I thought I had seen it all. Now, I think I have.

"I'm sure Peterson will act as if it is no big deal. He will say Galaxy, and every other manufacturer, does cost-analysis like this everyday. He will say that death and injuries are inevitable, that no one can build a completely safe car, and that Galaxy felt the TSB campaign was an adequate way to fix the problem.

"He will say there is no special relationship between Galaxy and the Newmans. Galaxy didn't sell the van to them. Galaxy could not foresee that their twins would be victims of this product failure. He will toe the company line."

"Mitch, I hope he does. I want to hear him tell that to a jury. I'll tell Mike and Margaret the good news. You know I start the Rogers Murder Trial next Tuesday. I'm sure it will last all week, and probably into Wednesday or Thursday of next week. I'm going to be hard to reach, and I don't want to be thinking about the Newmans while Rogers is going on. I need to concentrate on that. By the way, why did you ever plant the seed in their mind that this case had a value of three hundred million? Now, they will never take a penny less."

"Good luck with your trial, Larry. I'm sure Mr. Rogers will be a free man next week. Tell him to start planning a well-deserved vacation to the Bahamas or somewhere else exotic. As for Mike and Margaret, I sized them up right away."

"What does that mean?" asked Larry.

"It means I knew that money was not their motivating factor. I've seen it before. Losing a child is the worst thing that can happen to anyone. Losing two at the same time quadruples the grief. I knew they would never settle unless Galaxy admitted fault, issued an apology, and allowed unrestricted publicity on the settlement. I also knew Galaxy would never do that.

"So it didn't matter what I told them the case was worth. I could have said a billion dollars and we would still be where we are today. Galaxy could offer the money. The Newmans wouldn't take it without the apology, the admission of fault, and the opportunity to go on the talk show circuit to slam Galaxy. So what we have here is a stalemate.

"I'll take care of Newman while you are in trial. Give it your best, and think positive thoughts. You will be a better lawyer and a more confident man when these two cases are over, regardless of the outcomes."

More confident—a better lawyer! Right now he was frustrated. He wished Tom would call and take the plea. It was a good deal. He wished the Newmans would come to their senses and take the money. It was also a good deal. The life of a lawyer can be very complicated. Lawyers were out of work without a client to represent, but sometimes the clients could be so difficult!

Larry went home and went for a swim. The weather was cooling off fast, and the pool would be too cold to use without the heater in another week or so. Once the temperature started dipping below sixty degrees at night, his after-work swim would be over until late spring. He swam fifty laps before dinner. He was still frustrated after completing his swim.

CHAPTER 32

▼

October 3rd

Tom had made a decision. It didn't come easy, but he knew it was the right choice for him.

He had considered all of the advice he had sought very carefully. He thought about Laura, he thought about Cindy, he thought about Cindy's girls. He thought about his dad. He thought about Gary and Julie.

He even thought about his job. He really liked what he was doing. It was unheard of to be salesman of the month after only six weeks on the job. His sales manager had offered a new Camry demo at a mere two hundred fifty dollars per month. He told him he would wait another month and then would get back to him. His manager hated it that Tom drove a crappy old Volkswagen Rabbit. He wanted him in a new Toyota.

At ten o'clock, he decided it was time to call Larry and let him in on the decision he had made. He made the call, flirted with Cindy on the phone for a couple of minutes, and then asked if Larry was in. He was. She put him through.

"Hi Tom. Have you made a decision?"

"Hi Larry. Nothing like getting right to the point. I'm fine. How are you? And yes, I have made a decision. What do you think I've decided to do?"

"Tom, if I could read minds, I would never have to try a case. I can't read minds. That's why I try so many cases. What are you going to do?"

"If involuntary had been on the table with probation as an option, I would have taken it. You tell me that is not an option. I don't want to plead to voluntary manslaughter. What they say I did, I have no memory of, and it certainly

- 172 -

wasn't voluntary. I don't want to spend five years in prison for something I'm not guilty of. I'm going to take my chances, and go to trial."

Larry didn't know how to respond. He had expected this, but now that it was here, it was almost overwhelming. The silence continued.

"Larry? Are you there? Did you hear me?"

"I'm, here. I heard you. I think you are taking a huge risk, but it's your life. Don't get offended, but to cover my own ass from a malpractice suit if you get convicted of first-degree murder, I'm going to put all of this in writing and have you sign it. It will state that you have been given all of the options. Is that okay?"

"I'm not offended. Draft it up. I'll sign it. I expected you to cover all the bases. I wouldn't expect any less from the lawyer who has my life in his hands."

His life in his hands. He said it so casually. Larry knew full well he held Tom's life in his hands. The responsibility was magnified by those words.

"Tom, I'm going to have it ready by noon. Can you stop by before you go to work at one?"

"Sure thing."

"And Tom. Do you really know what you are doing? This is probably the biggest decision of your life."

"I'm sure. I have the best lawyer, I have the best doctors, and I won't be convicted of anything. I'm a salesman, Larry. Taking risks is what I am all about. I'm not stupid. I've thought about this long and hard. I know this is the right decision."

Larry wanted to say; yeah, and you probably thought that when you decided to go into business with Art Mendoza. Look where that got you. What he said was: "I'll see you about noon, Tom. I'll be here. I want to go over this with you personally before you sign off on it."

Tom showed up before noon. Larry spent about fifteen minutes explaining the two-page document to him. He signed it with a flourish, and Cindy notarized his signature. Larry wasn't sure why he added the notary clause. It just seemed to make it more official.

After lunch, Larry called Rick Bay to tell him that Tom had rejected the plea agreement and had decided to go to trial.

"I'm sorry to hear that, Larry. I think he is making a big mistake. You know I will do everything I can to convict him. I'm not going to ease up just because I offered him a sweet deal that he was too dumb to take."

"I know that, Rick. You have your job to do, and I have mine. Let's get the judge on the line so we can argue pre-trial motions on Monday so we can know how he stands on some of the issues before we start the trial."

"That sounds like a great idea. Hold on while I conference him in on this call."

Within a minute, Bay had Larry and Judge Donner's court clerk on the phone. Monday was law and motion day in Pima County. The judges reserved that day for pre-trial motions, sentencings, and other matters that were of a housekeeping nature. Trials were never held on Mondays.

They told her that State v. Rogers was definitely going. She reserved one thirty on Monday for pre-trial motions. She encouraged them to get their motions in writing to the judge by Friday at three P.M. at the latest, and to exchange motions with each other by fax or hand-delivery, not mail. She also told them to bring the jury instructions they would be requesting on Monday so the judge could consider them while the trial was taking place.

Larry then told Cindy to call all of the witnesses and remind them of their place in the line-up, and to tell them where to be, and when to be there. They all had subpoenas, but it was always safer to personally remind them. While she was doing that, he dictated his motions and decided which pattern jury instructions he would request.

Now he had a final decision to make. Should he call Tom as a witness; and risk letting Bay cross-examine him? What if he said something that the jury took the wrong way? What if he didn't look remorseful enough? What if he looked so remorseful he looked guilty? What if the jury didn't believe him?

The safe route was to tell Tom's story through the testimony of Ball and Jamison. Statements made to doctors for the purposes of medical or psychological diagnosis were not hearsay. Ball and Jamison could testify about what Tom told them, and the jury would learn Tom's story without subjecting him to cross-examination. That was the safe route.

It was always risky to put any defendant on the stand. Most criminal defendants weren't very smart, and would stick their foot in their mouth most of the time.

Tom was smart. He probably wouldn't stick his foot in his mouth, but he would be nervous. Even the smartest person could make a mistake when nervous and under pressure.

Bay was smart. He was experienced in the courtroom and in front of juries. Tom was a salesman, and was used to persuading an audience. This was a real dilemma.

Larry decided it would be best to promise nothing to the jury in opening statements as to whether or not Tom would or would not testify. The judge would give the preliminary instruction to the jury that all defendants had the right to testify or not testify. It was the defendant's choice. The jury would be told not to draw any inference of guilt or innocence based on whether the defendant testified or did not testify.

Larry would wait and see how the evidence developed at trial. If Ball and Jamison performed well, he would not call Tom to the stand.

If they stumbled, and things looked bad, he might call Tom to the stand. There would be no final decision on this until the very last moment before Larry would utter the words, the defense rests, Your Honor.

Cindy started working on the motions and the jury instructions by three o'clock. She had them on Larry's desk in draft form by five. He decided to leave them be until tomorrow morning. It had been a stressful day. The pool was waiting, and the weather wasn't getting any hotter.

CHAPTER 33

▼

October 7th

Larry spent the morning getting ready for the motions Judge Donner would hear at one thirty. He prepared a reply to Bay's motions, and faxed them to Bay. Bay did the same on Larry's motions.

The main bone of contention was Dr. Ball's testimony. Larry was sure it should be heard by the jury—Bay was convinced it should not. This was an area where the rules of evidence were fuzzy, and the case law was scarce. The Rules of Evidence were in conflict on the issue.

Rule 404 said:

Evidence of a person's character or a trait of character is not admissible for the purpose of proving action in conformity therewith on a particular occasion EXCEPT:

1)   Evidence of a pertinent trait of character of the victim of the crime offered by an accused, or by the prosecution to rebut the same, or evidence of a character trait of peacefulness of the victim offered by the prosecution in a homicide case to rebut the evidence that the victim was the first aggressor;

The final confusion was in Rule 406, which provided:

"Evidence of the habit of a person, whether corroborated or not, and regardless of the presence of eyewitnesses, is relevant to prove that the conduct of the person on a particular occasion was in conformity with the habit or routine practice."

What the drafters were thinking when they wrote this gobbledygook was anyone's guess. The judge had the final say.

Bay would argue that Art was not on trial; he was the victim. He would argue Art's character traits were not relevant.

Larry would argue that Tom had a right to defend himself, and the jury should hear about Art's rage disorder and the many acts of violence he had been convicted of in the past, and the acts Tom had witnessed, and even experienced himself.

Larry would argue that opinion evidence such as the opinions Dr. Ball would offer were contemplated by the rule under Rule 405. After all, Tom was on trial for first-degree murder. He should be allowed the widest latitude, and the cases interpreting these rules all said it had to be approached on a case-by-case basis and the trial judge had broad discretion in what to admit, and what to keep out.

Larry knew Donner to be fairly liberal. He was pretty sure he would rule in his favor on this issue.

Then Larry prepared his jury instructions. He included an instruction on involuntary manslaughter as a lesser-included offense of the charge of first-degree murder and set out the elements.

He prepared a form of verdict giving the jury the choice to find Tom not guilty of all counts of the indictment.

He headed over to the courthouse at about one fifteen. Bay was already there, pacing the hallway when Larry arrived. Donner took the bench at one thirty

Donner listened patiently and with amusement as the lawyers argued their respective positions. Half way into Larry's argument, which followed Bay's, Donner held up his hand as if to say: Stop! I've heard enough.

"Mr. Bay. I'm surprised to see you take this position. You know that Mr. Rogers is on trial for first-degree murder. This court is not about to risk an appeal by denying him the core of his defense, which is self-defense against a dangerous and aggressive man. I have broad discretion here, and I intend to exercise it.

"I have read Dr. Ball's report. I know Dr. Ball to be a credible and competent psychologist. I will give you wide latitude on cross examination, but, I am going to allow him to express his opinions regarding Mr. Mendoza's personality disorder which I think he labeled as Impulse Control Disorder, Diagnosis 312.34 in the D.S.M. IV manual.

"I'm also going to give Mr. Ross's requested instruction on involuntary manslaughter as a lesser-included offense. I will also give the instruction he offered on self-defense, and the jury will be given the option of finding Mr. Rogers not guilty on all counts.

"I'll be listening to the evidence very carefully, Mr. Bay. Unless I hear some compelling evidence of premeditation, I will be inclined to grant Mr. Ross's motion for directed verdict, which I am sure he will make when the state rests its case. I think your office has overcharged this case. I will keep an open mind, but I wanted you to know my thinking so that you can be prepared."

Donner continued: "I am also going to be very liberal in allowing Mr. Ross to challenge jurors for cause. If I think good cause exists to strike someone because of personal prejudice or belief, I will not hesitate to strike that person from the jury if Mr. Ross makes the proper challenge at the proper time. Do we understand one another, gentlemen?"

Bay and Larry looked at each other. They answered simultaneously.

"Yes, Your Honor."

Larry and Bay stood as Donner exited the bench. They each presented the clerk with the exhibits they had agreed upon ahead of time that could go into evidence without objection. Among them were the aerial and the floor plan that had been used at Tom's preliminary hearing. The two guns, and the ugly, bloody, ax were also marked, as were the police photos of the house.

Donner had decided earlier that the autopsy photos of Art Mendoza would stay out of evidence. The photo of him lying dead by the woodpile came in. It was pretty awful.

Larry had tried unsuccessfully to get the burglary and vandalism of the Rogers' house together with the spray-painted threats against Laura on the wall into evidence as further proof of Art's violent tendencies. As Art was dead when that happened, and the Sheriff's Office had no suspects for that crime; Donner kept it out. Larry had to agree he was probably correct on that one.

Larry went back to the office. It had been a good day. Donner had sent a clear signal that he had a chance of dodging the first-degree murder bullet. The jury would never see the horrible autopsy photos. He would not be afraid to challenge jurors for cause. Donner had even encouraged him to do it.

Dr. Ball would testify. He called Doug and asked him to stand by, ready to run down to the courthouse on thirty-minutes' notice. It was hard to predict when the state would rest. It would probably not be until Friday afternoon, and that meant Donner would probably send the jury home for the weekend early, and let the defense start its case on Tuesday morning. Larry promised to keep him informed.

He did the same with Dr. Jamison.

He called Mitch, and got an update on Newman. Not much was going on this week. Mitch told him to concentrate on Rogers and put Newman out of his mind.

He called Maggie, and asked if she and the kids could meet him at Trail Dust Town at six. He had another tie he wanted to get rid of, and wanted to have the fun of seeing the kids squeal with delight when the waitress rang the cowbell, and made a big production of cutting his tie off. By now, the kids knew he knew he should not wear a tie to that restaurant, but they liked to play along that daddy was tired and "forgot" again.

After dinner, they would watch the actors hold a "shoot-out" on "Main Street" that was staged every Friday night at Trail Dust Town at eight, and again a nine thirty. The kids loved it. He wouldn't be seeing much of them for the next two weeks or so, as he would be leaving early and getting home late. He was ready for this trial, and he wanted to spend some quality time with them tonight. He also felt like having a big steak and a baked potato piled high with sour cream and chives.

Larry put the finishing touches on his opening statement, and left the office about five thirty. Tomorrow would be one of the biggest days of his life. He would choose a jury for a first-degree murder trial, the first one he had ever done. He was up for the challenge. Tomorrow morning couldn't come soon enough for Larry.

Maria entered the courthouse for work through the judge's elevators in the underground garage at about six o'clock. She had her snub-nosed .38 revolver tucked in her purse, loaded with lethal, hollow-point bullets. She felt like all eyes were on her as she made her way on the elevator up to the fourth floor. She was sure people around her had X-ray vision, and could see the gun in her purse. A security guard nodded, and smiled at her on his way out of the elevator as she entered. She forced a smile back.

She checked the calendar for the next day on the hall bulletin board. State v. Rogers was set in Judge Donner's courtroom, which was on the fifth floor, one of her assigned floors. That was a lucky break. She could be on the fifth floor without someone wondering why she was there. Things were looking pretty good so far.

During her dinner break at ten o'clock, she made her way to Judge Donner's courtroom. She had a hard time deciding which chair to place the gun under. She wanted to be close, but she was afraid that other spectators or the press might take the front row. She had read that murder trials tended to draw a crowd. The lawyers and the law students liked to watch them to see how it was done.

She had to choose a seat that would be close, would give her a good angle to Rogers as he sat at the defense table, and would probably be available when she entered the courtroom. She didn't want to get there too early tomorrow. She was afraid she might draw suspicion to herself. The calendar said the proceedings were to start at nine. She decided to get there at nine thirty.

The defense table was on the left hand side of the courtroom, nearest the jury. She chose a seat in the middle of the third row. It would place her almost directly behind the defense table. She sat in it, and liked the angle and the distance. She took the revolver and a roll of duct-tape out of her purse, and carefully taped the loaded gun under her chair.

She made sure to count from left to right so she could remember which chair to sit in tomorrow morning. It was the sixth chair from the end. She was tempted to mark it with something like a small piece of duct-tape but decided against it. She could remember chair number six.

She left the courtroom. Task one had been accomplished in less than five minutes. She still had time to eat the sack lunch that she brought with her before her dinner break ended at ten thirty. The rest of the crew had not missed her.

As she drove home that night, she prayed to God that she would have the courage to go through with her plan. It didn't occur to her that God did not approve of what she was planning. She got home at three, and set her alarm for seven forty-five. She wanted a drink, or two, or three, but resisted the temptation. She had come this far, and didn't want to be foggy in the morning.

CHAPTER 34

▼

October 8th

On Tuesday mornings the four elevators that shuttled the public between floors were overworked. A jury trial was starting in forty-five of the forty-eight divisions of Pima County Superior Court. That was a lot of witnesses, lawyers and nervous litigants that all wanted to be in their appointed courtroom at nine

Most of the people had worried looks on their faces. Trials were the last step in a complicated process that took the civil litigants a year or more to finally get to, and represented a shot at exoneration, or a prison sentence for the criminal defendants.

Larry and Tom had gotten there early and were on the fifth floor by eight thirty.

Tom looked good in a blue blazer, red tie, and tan slacks. He looked concerned but not panicked. He certainly didn't look like an ax murderer.

Larry had on his sincere blue suit with a gold tie, and black lace-up shoes.

Bay arrived about eight forty-five. He was wearing a good-looking brown suit with a muted blue tie. Bay tried murder cases all the time. This was his third one this year, and the twenty-first in his career. Advantage: Bay.

Larry was a virgin when it came to murder trials, but he had a good track record in trial. He knew how to persuade, he knew how to be humble, and in this case he had a nice client who looked like Mr. Businessman, not Mr. Ax Murderer. Advantage: Larry.

Officer Brian Guest of the Pima County Sheriff's Office had been assigned to maintain security during the trial. It was court policy to have an armed uniformed officer in the courtroom at all times while felony trials were in progress.

Even though everyone in the courthouse had passed through the metal detector and the security guards at the front entrance before they ever got on the elevators to come upstairs, Guest still watched carefully as the players entered the courtroom. He knew the lawyers and the cops who would be testifying. It was the other witnesses he was watchful and wary of. He didn't like it that most of the men were wearing coats. He looked for the telltale bulge that could signal a concealed weapon in a shoulder holster. So far he had seen nothing to arouse his suspicions.

Detective Cotter was there early as well. Bay had decided to have Cotter sit with him through the trial as the state's designated representative. He was also the lead detective on the case, and was familiar with all of the witnesses. Bay could use him to go out to the hallway to alert a witness that he or she was up next, or inform them that they would have to wait even longer. If need be, he could place phone calls to chase down loose legal ends that always came up during a trial so that Bay could get his clerks working on a legal issue if need be while he was still in the courtroom. That way a memo would be waiting for him at the end of the day, and he could get home at a decent hour.

Larry didn't have the luxury of having a runner. It was he and Tom at the table, and no one else. Cindy had begged to come and watch the jury selection and part of the trial, but he needed her back at the office to answer the phones, and assure the public that Mr. Ross was in trial, and would return their call as soon as he could. Besides, he didn't want the jury wondering if he and this good-looking woman had something going on the side. The jury needed to concentrate on Tom's case, not Cindy's curves.

Cotter and Guest took their seats after Judge Donner entered the courtroom at ten after nine and inquired of counsel if they were ready to proceed. Bay and Larry said they were. Donner told the bailiff to bring in the thirty-six members of the prospective jury panel. None of them looked very happy to be there. Most of them were carrying a book to read during the down time that always went with jury selection.

They had been in the courthouse since seven thirty when they checked in with the jury commissioner, watched a boring video about how great it was to be a juror, and what a critical role they were going to play in the justice system. They all wore red badges that identified them as jurors. All of them were hoping they would not be called from the crowd of thirty-six to the box of twenty-six that would eventually be paired down to fourteen. Two would be chosen as alternates.

The thirty-six jurors filled all of the first three rows of the spectator section of Donner's courtroom. One by one, twenty-six names were called and twenty-six people were called to the box.

Larry watched carefully. These were the people he was counting on to bring in an acquittal. He had a bio on all of them, but it was brief: Name, age, education level, employment, and marital status, number of children. Nothing about political affiliation or religion was allowed on the bios. It was like shooting at a small target in the dark and hoping to hit a bulls-eye. The ten reserves would take the place of anyone who got disqualified for cause.

Donner somberly read the pattern preliminary instructions to all of them explaining that the lawyers would question them, and they should answer truthfully. He told the reserves to listen carefully, as they could be called up if someone were excused for cause, and they would then be asked if they had any information to share regarding the questions that had already been asked.

Larry had three strikes for cause. One had known Mendoza, one felt that anyone who killed someone deserved to be punished, no matter what the evidence showed, and a third had a religious belief that prohibited her from sitting in judgment of someone else. Bay didn't challenge anyone for cause.

With the questioning done, the jurors were excused from the room while the lawyers exercised their peremptory or "just because" strikes. When they were done, nine women and five men remained. Larry was pleased. Women were generally not as harsh as men.

The thirty-six filed back in, all hoping they would not be one of the fourteen called to the box to sit there for the next two weeks. There would be two alternates, just in case someone got sick. They wouldn't know they were alternates.

They would sit through the trial and at the end would be excused if the first twelve were alive and healthy. The lawyers and the judge knew who they were. The jurors didn't have a clue.

They would either be relieved or disappointed when told at the end of the trial that they were alternates and would not be participating in the deliberations. And for this, they were paid twelve dollars per day. It wasn't even enough to pay for parking and lunch.

Guest and Cotter noticed the woman sitting in the back of the courtroom. She had come in at about nine thirty while jury selection was in progress. Hispanic, late forties, overweight, dressed in black, with a scarf over her head. She had looked around nervously when she had entered the room.

Jury selection had consumed the morning. Donner recessed for lunch as soon as the jury was empanelled and sworn in to do their duty. He told them the lawyers would make opening statements and the state would start calling witnesses at one thirty.

He told them to reassemble in the jury room at one fifteen. He reminded them to wear their juror badges at all times, and not to discuss the case with anyone or amongst themselves, until he told them to do so. It was eleven forty five when they filed out.

The woman in black stayed behind. She left reluctantly when the bailiff told her he had to lock up the courtroom over the lunch hour. Cotter and Guest compared notes after she got on the elevator. They agreed there was something suspicious about her. If she came back for the afternoon session, they would keep an eye on her. Cotter knew she wasn't a prospective witness. She could just be a courthouse-groupie, who liked to hang out and watch trials, but he had never seen her before, and he was visually familiar with most of the groupies.

Maria left the courthouse quickly. She was shaken. She didn't know there would be cops in the courtroom. She had never considered that the jury would take up the first three rows of the spectator section. This was not going to be easy. To make matters worse, she was losing her nerve. Rogers looked like a nice young man. His lawyer did too. She wasn't sure she could go through with her plan. She decided to go home and get some sleep before she had to report for work at six. The gun would be there tomorrow.

Laura Rogers and her lawyer arrived at the courthouse at one fifteen. Her lawyer went to the file room, picked up Rogers v. Rogers, and hand carried it up to the second floor where Court Commissioner De Long would hear the default petitions at one thirty. She entered the room. It was filled with women and children and their lawyers. All of them were waiting to get a Decree of Dissolution of Marriage so they could start a new life.

Laura watched as five women went before her, and recited the magic words that her marriage was irretrievably broken with no reasonable prospect of reconciliation. Commissioner DeLong would sign the Decree of Dissolution with a flourish, hand the file back to the lawyer, and call the next case.

When she heard her name called she felt weak in the knees. She wobbled up to the clerk, raised her right hand, and took an oath to tell the truth. Her lawyer then asked her a series of about ten leading questions that all called for a simple "yes" answer. In less than two minutes, she watched as Commissioner De Long signed her Decree of Dissolution, handed the file back to her lawyer, and called the next case.

She was numb as they walked downstairs and got a certified copy of the decree from the clerk. This was her proof to the world that she was divorced, and had a new name.

She knew Tom would be upstairs on the fifth floor. She wanted to go up there to say "Hi", but decided against it.

She caught an afternoon flight out of Tucson. She would never come back.

The afternoon session went without incident. Bay's opening was his standard "listen to the evidence, don't be swayed by emotion, listen to the witnesses carefully" speech that he had given in one form or another more than one hundred times to more than one hundred juries.

Larry was on his game. He had the jury nodding and agreeing with him when he suggested that every American had the right to own a gun and defend his life with it if the need arose. He outlined what they could expect to hear from the witnesses, including Dr. Ball, and Dr. Jamison. He told them he was sure they would return a verdict of not guilty once they had heard all of the evidence.

Donner recessed for the day at four thirty after Cotter had testified. Cotter didn't say anything that came as a surprise to Larry. He agreed on cross-examination that Tom was polite, and willing to answer his questions at the scene, and had denied ever touching the ax. He also agreed that he didn't want to arrest Tom, and had only done so after conferring with Steve McNair himself. It was a good day. No surprises, no mistakes, a decent jury.

Cotter and Guest stayed behind after everyone else left. Cotter had been looking for the woman in black for the afternoon session, but she was nowhere to be seen. On a hunch, he had called the department to send a tech with a metal detector to the courtroom at the end of the day. The tech was waiting in the hall, metal detector at the ready, as everyone left the room.

On the first sweep of the spectator section the detector went off, and got very loud as the tech approached the middle seat in the third row. He bent down, and came up with a snub-nosed .38 revolver that had been taped under the seat. It was loaded with hollow-point bullets.

Cotter was relieved that his hunch had panned out. A gun with live ammunition had been planted in the courtroom, and had probably been there all day. Who did it belong to? He wrote down the serial number, and called in the number to a clerk in stolen property to see if it came up as stolen. She told him she would have an answer for him in the morning. He hoped the woman in black would be back again tomorrow.

He removed the hollow point bullets, replaced them with primer caps, dusted it for prints, and taped the .38 back under the seat, hoping that whoever had put it there would come back looking for it in the morning.

That night, Maria reported for work. As she was vacuuming Donner's courtroom, she checked under the middle seat in the third row to see if the gun was still there. It was still there, just as she had left it. She decided to think it over. Rogers had ruined her life, her boys were in prison, and she had nothing to live for. Maybe taking Rogers and his lawyer out would make her feel better.

She cleaned the courtroom for the next two nights. Each time, she checked under the seat, and each time, the .38 was still there, beckoning to her.

CHAPTER 35

▼

October 11th

The trial was moving right along. So far, there had been no surprises. Karen Hargrave had been nervous when she was called to the stand to verify that the Odyssey was not doing well, and had lost money in every month it had been in operation. In fact, the longer it stayed in business, the more money it lost.

At the time of Mendoza's death he had poured close to one hundred thousand dollars in cash into the bar's operations. Mendoza and Rogers had not taken a salary of any kind while the bar was in operation.

Bay was kind, and didn't bring up that she was also the bookkeeper for Larry's law firm, and had been friendly with Tom, and had actually referred Tom to Larry. He stuck to the relevant facts.

It was painful to suffer through Jim Weber's testimony about what he saw from his front balcony that Sunday morning.

Larry was careful with him on cross, establishing that he had lived across the street from Tom and Laura for two and one half years, and they had been decent, quiet neighbors. That was about all he could do with Weber.

The various police officers laid the groundwork for what was found, and where it was found. Mendoza's gun had been found at the end of the porch near the edge of the sidewalk, and partially covered by the oleander hedge.

The forensic expert testified about the bullet trajectories, and established that Mendoza had fired at Tom six times, all of which went wide, or high.

Parchman testified that the cause of death was not the bullet wounds, but were the blows to the head with the ax.

The best Larry could do on cross with him was to establish that Mendoza would have been dead in about forty-five minutes anyway from the chest wound if he had not received emergency medical treatment within that time period. Even though he agreed that the chest wound was potentially fatal, it just wasn't the cause of death for Arthur Mendoza. There was no way around that.

It was Friday afternoon, and time for Dr. Llewellan's performance. He took the stand, and Bay started off with the usual qualifying questions. He established that Llewellan had been in practice for over fifteen years, and was duly licensed to practice psychology in the State of Arizona, and that his privileges had never been suspended or revoked. His big claim to fame was a weekly radio show he hosted on one of the stations on Saturday morning called *Let's Get Together*. It concerned itself primarily with relationship issues between men and women.

He then walked through the interview with Tom, and Llewellan's interpretation of the standardized tests that Tom had taken.

As expected, he stated that Tom was a manipulative personality, showed aggressive tendencies, and gave answers that would make him "look good."

When Bay asked if he had an opinion as to whether or not Tom had acted with premeditation, he answered yes. When Bay asked him what his opinion was, Larry objected.

"I object, Your Honor. This testimony, if allowed, would invade the province of the jury. It asks for an opinion on the ultimate issue that this jury will be asked to decide. Dr. Llewellan may be a psychiatrist, but he is not a mind reader. There is no proper foundation for this testimony."

Donner looked at Rick Bay. "Mr. Bay, what is your position?"

"The law is clear that opinion testimony is admissible from expert witnesses, Your Honor. Dr. Llewellan's opinions are based on his interpretation of the standardized tests, and his interview with Mr. Rogers."

Donner got out the rule book and looked at Rule 404 which read:

"Although relevant, evidence may be excluded if the probative value is substantially outweighed by the danger of unfair prejudice, confusion of the issues, or misleading the jury, or by considerations of undue delay, waste of time, or needless presentation of cumulative evidence."

He then read Rule 704, which was titled: "Opinion on Ultimate Issue:"

"Testimony in the form of an opinion, or inference otherwise admissible is not objectionable because it embraces an ultimate issue to be decided by the trier of fact."

Donner called a recess, and asked that the jury be excused while he and the lawyers argued this point. He explained to the jury that a legal issue had come up that needed to be discussed out of their presence. He told them to stay close, as this would only take ten minutes or so to resolve.

"Mr. Bay, I've read the Rules of Evidence on this point, and frankly I'm troubled. The rule does say that opinion testimony on the ultimate issue, which in this case is premeditation on Mr. Rogers' part, is admissible, but it also says the evidence has to be otherwise admissible. I think that gives me discretion. Does Dr. Llewellan have any source other than his own opinions to back this up, like a statement from a witness that Mr. Rogers planned to kill Mr. Mendoza, or some admission from Mr. Rogers himself?"

"No, Your Honor. There is no other independent witness or admission from Mr. Rogers on this point."

Donner looked at Larry: "Mr. Ross, Rule 704 says what it says. I think Dr. Llewellan is entitled to give his opinion. I've given you the opportunity to call Dr. Ball on the psychiatric autopsy issue, which was also a judgment call on my part. I'm going to do the same thing here. I am going to allow the testimony, and let the jury sort it out.

"I will give you wide latitude on cross examination, and I will give your experts wide latitude in rebutting Dr. Llewellan's opinions, but I don't want to commit error. This is a close call. I'm going to err on the side of caution, and follow the rule as written. I will let Dr. Llewellan express his opinion. Mr. Ross, your objection is overruled. Bailiff, bring the jury back in."

The jury filed back in and took their seats. Donner explained that he had overruled Larry's objection, and he was going to let Dr. Llewellan express his opinion. He also told them that they would probably hear another psychologist express a different opinion later on in the trial, and that in the end, the issue of premeditation was for them to decide.

Bay asked the question again and Llewellan spouted his opinion.

"Mr. Rogers was desperate to end his relationship with Mr. Mendoza. He believed the only way to do this was to kill him. It is my opinion that Arthur Mendoza was lured to the Rogers' home the morning of June 3rd by Tom Rogers, and that Tom Rogers specifically intended to kill Mr. Mendoza that morning. As we know, he accomplished his goal."

"Thank you doctor. Your witness counselor."

Larry stood and smiled as if nothing had happened. He had learned how to deal with snakes like Llewellan before. He started a series of questions that called for yes and no answers and requested that Llewellan confine his responses to yes or no. He assured him that if Mr. Bay had any follow up, he could explain his answers further.

"Dr. Llewellan, are you Board Certified by the Board of Psychiatric Examiners?"

"No"

"Have you ever taken the written test to become Board Certified?"

"Yes."

"Did you pass it?"

"No."

"Are you scheduled to take it again?"

"No."

"Did you take the oral board exam?"

"No."

"Do you have to pass the written exam before you can take the oral exam?"

"Yes."

"And did you take the written exam as soon as you were eligible to take it?"

"Yes."

"And that was five years after you were admitted to practice?"

"Yes."

"And since you told Mr. Bay you have been in practice for over fifteen years that would mean that you took that test more than ten years ago?"

"Yes."

"And you never took it a second time?"

"No."

"Doctor, do you know Dr. Mark Jamison?"

"Yes."

"And in fact you studied under him at USC when you were doing your PhD dissertation, isn't that correct?"

"Yes."

"And doctor, didn't you petition the committee that scored your written board exam for a reconsideration, so that you would receive a passing score?"

"Yes."

"And wasn't Dr. Jamison the head of that committee that denied your request?"

"Yes."

"And in fact, Dr. Jamison has been the head of the committee that scores the written exam for board certification for over twenty years, hasn't he?"

"Yes."

"And haven't you been resentful of that decision ever since?"

"No."

"And doctor, are you aware of the DSM IV manual?"

"Yes."

"Would you agree that you find it authoritative, and useful in your practice?"

"Yes."

"And did you refer to it when reaching conclusions in this case?"

"Yes."

"And are you aware that Dr. Jamison is the author of the diagnostic criteria in the DSM IV manual for Dissociative State and Dissociative Amnesia?"

"Yes."

"And are you aware that Dr. Jamison has seven textbooks that are currently in publication?"

"Yes."

"And are you aware that Dr. Jamison has published twenty-five articles in respected psychology journals on the issue of Dissociative State and Dissociative Amnesia?"

"Yes."

"And do you have any textbooks that have ever been published?"

"No."

"And have you ever published any articles on Dissociative State and Dissociative Amnesia?"

"No."

"Have you ever published anything?"

"No."

"Have you ever made a diagnosis of Dissociative State/Dissociative Amnesia?"

"No."

"Have you ever treated a patient who was diagnosed as having experienced Dissociative State/Dissociative Amnesia?"

"No."

"Have you read Dr. Jamison's report in this case?"

"Yes."

"And are you aware that he holds the opinion that when Mr. Rogers was interacting with Mr. Mendoza on the morning of June 3rd, that after the gunshots were fired, Mr. Rogers was acting in a Dissociative State, and suffers from Dissociative Amnesia concerning those events?"

"Yes."

"And are you aware that Dr. Jamison is of the opinion that Mr. Rogers never formed any intent to harm Mr. Mendoza, but was only acting under influence of a Dissociative State, and has resulting Dissociative Amnesia?"

"Yes."

"And YOU—DOCTOR Llewellan—disagree with him?"

"Yes."

"You disagree with the man who is recognized as the world's expert on Dissociative State, and Dissociative Amnesia?"

"Yes."

"You disagree with the man who heads the committee that did not give you a passing score on your written exam for board certification?"

"Yes."

"And you believe your opinions are correct, and Dr. Jamison's are incorrect?"

"Yes."

"One last question, doctor. Don't you think that Dr. Jamison is a lot more qualified than you are to issue opinions in this case on the subject of Dissociative State and Dissociative Amnesia?"

Larry waited for the answer. This is what he called a "throw-away" question. It didn't matter if the witness said yes or no. If he said yes, he had turned his prior testimony into useless garbage. If he said no, his credibility would be torn to shreds. Llewellan squirmed in his seat. He knew he had been put in a box, and there was no way out. He tried to vary from the rules that Larry had set out when the question and answer period began. He did not give a yes or no answer.

"We each have our opinions, Mr. Ross. I happen to believe mine is correct."

Larry smiled. "Doctor, let me ask you again. Don't you think that Dr. Jamison is a lot more qualified than you are to issue opinions in this case on the subject of Dissociative State and Dissociative Amnesia? Please answer yes or no doctor."

Llewellan glared at Larry. He knew he was trapped. He looked at Bay hoping for an objection. Bay just looked back and waited for the answer. Finally, Llewellan drew a breath and gave his answer. "Yes."

"Thank you doctor, no further questions."

Judge Donner looked at Bay. "Mr. Bay, any re-direct?"

Bay knew when to stop. It could only get worse if he asked more questions. His reply was casual, as if no damage had been inflicted. "No, Your Honor, may the witness be excused?" What he really meant was: "Get him out of here before he does any more damage to my case." Instead, he stood and smiled, as Llewellan gathered his file and left the courtroom.

In less than seven minutes, Larry had completely discredited the state's witness on motive and diminished capacity. Bay was sure that the jury would be eagerly waiting to hear from the great Mark Jamison next week. They would have all weekend to think about how Llewellan was really a relationship counselor, and dared to disagree with his mentor and the man who had refused to give him a passing score on his written board exam more than ten years ago. He knew Larry would argue to the jury that Llewellan gave his opinion just to get back at Jamison for standing in the way of his board certification. It was a good argument. He looked at the clock. It was a few minutes before four.

Donner interrupted his thoughts: "Mr. Bay, please call your next witness."

"I have no further witnesses, Your Honor, the State rests."

"Very well. In light of the hour, I'm sure the jury won't mind if we recess early for the weekend. Ladies and gentlemen, please remember the admonitions you have been given. The State has rested its case. Mr. Rogers will present his defense starting Tuesday morning at nine Do not discuss the case with anyone and do not discuss it among yourselves. Do not attempt to visit the scene. Please be back in the jury room Tuesday morning at eight forty-five with your juror badges on. I would anticipate we should have this case finished, and ready for your deliberations by next Thursday afternoon or Friday morning at the latest. Have a nice weekend."

The bailiff ushered the jury out of the room. When they were gone, Donner turned to Larry: "Mr. Ross, do you have any motions to make?"

Larry stood and addressed the court: "Yes, Your Honor. Given the testimony we have heard from the State, I move for a directed verdict that the charge of first-degree murder be dismissed. There are no facts upon which reasonable men could conclude that Mr. Rogers acted with malice or with premeditation the morning of June 3rd. The state's only witness on this has been discredited completely. Mr. Bay has told you he has no other proof of premeditation other than Dr. Llewellan, and Dr. Llewellan's testimony is insufficient to meet the State's burden of proof beyond a reasonable doubt on this issue."

Donner looked at Bay. "Mr. Bay, what is your response?"

Bay stood and thought carefully before responding. "Premeditation can be as quick as successive thoughts of the mind. The case law on that is in my pre-trial memorandum I submitted to the court. It doesn't have to take a day, an hour, or even a minute for a person to plan something. It can happen in an instant.

"It is the State's position that in the time Mr. Rogers had after the shooting occurred until he bludgeoned Mr. Mendoza to death with the ax, he had time to think about what he was going to do. He had time to call Mr. Miller. He had time to talk to his wife. That is more than enough time under the case law to formulate a plan to finish what he started, and that was to kill Mr. Mendoza. The court should deny Mr. Ross's motion."

Donner looked at Larry. "Mr. Ross, I know you have an opportunity to respond, but I think I've heard enough. Do you feel the need to respond?"

Larry wasn't stupid. When a judge told you to shut up, you shut up. "No, Your Honor," was the reply.

Donner looked at Bay. "Mr. Bay, I told you I was going to be listening to the evidence very carefully on the issue of pre-meditation. I gave you the opportunity to let Dr. Llewellan express his opinions, even though I was tempted not to. I wanted to give the State the full opportunity to prove its case. Having been given that opportunity, the State failed to meet its burden of proof.

"My job is to rule on what I have before me. I agree with Mr. Ross. There is no evidence of pre-meditation. Reasonable men could not find beyond a reasonable doubt that Mr. Rogers acted with premeditation. I am going to exercise my discretion as trial judge and not let this issue go to the jury. The motion is granted. The jury will not be instructed on the charge of first-degree murder.

"Mr. Ross, I trust you will be prepared to proceed with your case first thing Tuesday morning?"

"Yes, Your Honor. I'll be calling Dr. Ball followed by Dr. Jamison. I will also call Mr. Miller back for direct examination by me on points not covered by the prosecution. I may or may not call Mr. Rogers. We may be able to rest by Tuesday afternoon depending on how quickly the testimony goes."

"Very well, court is adjourned. Have a good weekend gentlemen. I'll see you back here Tuesday morning at nine."

The bailiff intoned, "All rise!" and Donner left the bench.

Bay hustled out of the courtroom. He had to report to McNair that the first-degree charge was now history. The best they could do was a second-degree conviction, and the way the evidence stood at this point, that was doubtful.

Larry stuck out his hand, and Tom shook it vigorously.

"Does this mean what I think it means?" asked Tom.

Larry nodded. "It does. You are no longer in danger of spending your life in prison, or getting the death penalty. First-degree is off the table. Let's go celebrate!"

They left the courthouse relieved and happy. It had been a long, hard week, but knowing that first-degree murder was no longer an option for the jury was a huge relief for both of them. They walked down the street to the Cushing Street Bar to have a beer and wind down a bit.

Cotter got back to the office about four thirty. There was a report from the stolen property section on his e-mail that the .38 found in Donner's courtroom had in fact been reported as stolen over three years earlier in a home burglary on the south side. He e-mailed the technician back, and asked her to send the prints lifted from the gun to forensics on Monday to check against known fingerprints. Who knows? He might get lucky, and find prints that were actually on file. If he did, he would have a good lead on who actually placed the gun in the courtroom. In the meantime, he left it taped to the chair he had found it under.

Maria Mendoza went to work that night unaware that Tom Rogers had gotten a lucky break from Judge Donner earlier in the day. She was still considering whether she should carry out her plan.

She had completely forgotten about the fact that when she had applied for her license from the State Banking Department to be a registered Collection Agent so she could do car repo work, she had to be fingerprinted. Her fingerprints were on file with all of the law enforcement agencies, including the F.B.I., and would prove to be a match to the .38 she had placed in Donner's courtroom Monday night.

Cotter matched her prints to her name, and discovered she worked for the courthouse janitorial service. He decided not to pick her up right away. He continued to watch to see if she would come back to watch the trial. Cotter wanted to arrest her for attempted murder if he could. She would not know the gun was filled with blanks.

CHAPTER 36

▼

October 14th

Larry spent Monday trying to catch up on phone calls and mail. It was a thrill to be in trial, but the world didn't stop while he was over at the courthouse. The mail still came, and the phone still rang. Clients and other lawyers were impatient. Deadlines had to be met. A missed deadline meant a malpractice claim.

He set aside the afternoon to meet with Dr. Ball and Dr. Jamison. He filled them in on the destruction of Dr. Llewellan on cross-examination. Dr. Jamison had provided Larry with the information to get that job done in short order.

Ball and Jamison were ready. They were firm in their opinions, and would not budge on cross-examination from Bay. Larry had his outline ready so he wouldn't forget to lay out all of the elements of Dissociative State/Dissociative Amnesia and Impulse Control Disorder. He had the CV's for Ball and Jamison handy, and planned to have Dr. Jamison testify at length about his qualifications and publications.

Since Bay had stipulated to let the Cinco de Mayo videotape into evidence, there was no need to call Ed Carlson, the DJ, or Sandy Rathman, the reporter, as witnesses.

Bay had also stipulated to copies of Mendoza's criminal convictions including the five aggravated assault convictions, and the marijuana conviction that he had done time for. The convictions would come in one way or the other, and rather than make a fuss, he was hoping that just referring to them would draw less attention to Mendoza's evil ways than objecting to them in open court, and then have Donner rule against him. That would make it look like he was trying to hide the ball, and juries never liked that from prosecutors. Prosecutors always had to look as if they were only interested in fairness and justice, not winning at any cost.

Larry also prepped Gary Miller. He would testify right after Ball. Ball would set the stage that Mendoza was a dangerous, multi-convicted violent felon. Miller would testify that Tom was a hard working, creative, gentle soul who didn't even want a lesson on how to shoot the gun Gary had given him.

Jamison would then follow with his opinion on diminished capacity as Tom was operating under a Dissociative State when Mendoza was hit with the ax, and had Dissociative Amnesia of the event because violence was so foreign to him.

He would also testify that the manipulative and aggressive tendencies that Tom exhibited in the standardized tests were not bad things. It was just a personality trait that made him successful as a salesman, and made him a good mediator and problem solver. It was a trait shared by diplomats and negotiators who handled delicate affairs on a national level.

It would be Jamison's final opinion that Tom was a negotiator, not a violent person, and had only acted as he had been shot at first. When he went out to the porch to check on Mendoza, and he was not where Tom had left him, he went into protective mode, and automatic pilot from that point forward.

The end result would be that Tom was not capable of forming any criminal intent at the time Mendoza was struck with the ax. He would agree that Tom could not distinguish right from wrong at that point, so the defense could fit the definition of temporary insanity. He would also agree that this was an isolated event that would not repeat itself, that Tom posed no threat to society, and was not in need of any psychiatric counseling or confinement to a mental institution.

The final decision was whether Tom should take the stand or not. Larry was not in favor of it. He thought it would be much safer to tell Tom's story through Dr. Ball and Dr. Jamison.

Tom was being difficult, and pouting like a child about wanting to testify. The super-ego of the salesman in him told him he couldn't "close" this deal without testifying. It was a huge risk, and Larry decided to make the final decision himself.

Tom would stay at counsel table. He would not take the oath, he would not testify. He wasn't happy about it but there wasn't any choice in the matter. He wasn't going to stand up in court, defy his lawyer, and beg to testify.

Saturday's mail had brought Tom a copy of the Decree of Dissolution that Laura had obtained on Tuesday. He felt a sense of sadness, and a sense of relief at the same time. He tried to call her, but her cell phone had been disconnected, her mother said she wasn't in, and was non-committal about passing on the message that he had called.

He and Cindy spent their Sunday afternoon together out by the heated pool at the apartment complex discussing their future together. They were both afraid to make any commitment to one another, but each could sense an undercurrent of anticipation that things could get permanent between them if the trial went in Tom's favor.

Cindy was relieved to hear that Tom and Laura were now divorced. She didn't have to feel like the "other woman" any longer and Tom didn't have to feel like he was cheating on his wife.

The sex they enjoyed was fantastic. They were truly compatible in bed as well as other aspects of their lives. Both had been raised Catholic, so religion was not an issue between them. Both had a failed marriage behind them, and were anxious to make the next one work. Cindy wanted a father figure for her girls. Billy had moved to Tennessee to work for his brother shortly after the divorce, and because of distance, time, and money constraints, summer was really the only time he had with the girls. They were growing up so fast, and needed a male role model. They liked Tom, and constantly asked Cindy if he was going to be their new daddy. She would reply, "No, you have a daddy. He lives in Tennessee. You only have one daddy."

The girls would giggle and say, "Mom! You know what we mean. Are you and Tom getting married so he can live with us everyday?"

Everything was so simple in the minds of young children. Her reply was the standard: "We'll see," which meant nothing, but appeased the girls somewhat. At least it wasn't a "No."

Tom loved the girls. They were adorable. He realized that the more he was around, the harder it would be on them if he and Cindy didn't work out together. So much was riding on this trial. He wished he could read the minds of the jurors. He would watch them carefully, without seeming to stare. They were a serious bunch. There weren't many smiles, and there was very little interaction between one another. He was good at reading people, but he couldn't read this bunch. Maybe he was too close to the situation.

CHAPTER 37

▼

October 15th

Cotter was secretly pleased that Llewellan had been destroyed on cross-examination. He liked Tom, and had never agreed with McNair's decision to have him arrested and charged with first-degree murder. He didn't like Llewellan. He thought he was an asshole know-it-all.

He was also glad that Donner had the balls to dismiss the first-degree charge. It was the right thing to do. Most judges were wimps, and would defer to the jury. Donner was a take-charge guy who was not afraid to call them as he saw them.

He even hoped the jury would find Tom not guilty on all charges. He and Bay were buddies, to be sure, but Tom didn't deserve to be convicted. Cotter knew Mendoza was a violent scumbag who was guilty of a whole lot more than he had ever been convicted of. Tom had done a service to the community by taking him out of circulation for good.

Cotter also liked Larry. A big win in a murder case would boost his career. Sometimes, it was hard to keep a perspective on whom he was working for, and who he was rooting for. He was looking forward to hearing the testimony from Dr. Ball and Dr. Jamison. He had seen Ball in action before. He was good. He was sure Jamison would be better.

Cotter arrived in Donner's courtroom at eight fifty. Larry, Bay, Tom and Dr. Ball were all there. The fun was about to begin.

Donner took the bench right at nine, and asked the lawyers if they had any preliminary matters that needed to be discussed before he called the jury in.

They both answered, "No."

Donner turned to George: "Bailiff, please bring in the jury."

The jury filed in. They wore the same stone-faced expressions they had worn all last week.

Donner addressed them. "Welcome back ladies and gentlemen. I trust you had a restful weekend. Thank you for being here on time this morning. After you left last Friday the lawyers argued some legal matters and I issued some rulings.

"I have dismissed the charge of first-degree murder. You will no longer be asked to consider that charge. The charge of second-degree murder, and the lesser-included offenses of voluntary and involuntary manslaughter remain at this time.

"Mr. Ross tells me he has three witnesses to call. You will hear from Dr. Ball, Gary Miller, and Dr. Jamison. Depending on how quickly things go, we may finish testimony today. The lawyers and I still need to settle the final jury instructions that you will be given. There is a good chance you will hear final arguments tomorrow and your deliberations will begin tomorrow.

"Please continue to remember the admonitions I have given you. Do not discuss this case among yourselves, or with anyone else until your deliberations begin. Do not form any final opinions until you have heard all of the testimony, and I have read the final instructions to you. Mr. Ross, call your first witness."

"The defense calls Dr. Douglas Ball."

As Ball was walking to the clerk to take the oath, Cotter noticed the woman dressed in black enter the courtroom, and take the very seat the .38 was still taped under. Cotter quietly took the seat directly behind her.

The clerk swore in Dr. Ball, and he took the stand with the authority of someone who had been there many times before, and felt comfortable about being in a courtroom. After the preliminary questions about who he was, what his qualifications were, and when he conducted his interview with Tom, Larry got down to the meat of the testimony. Cotter tuned everything out, and focused on the woman in black who he now knew to be Maria Mendoza.

"Dr. Ball, did you do a psychological autopsy on Mr. Mendoza at my request?"

"I did."

"Would you please tell the jury what a psychological autopsy is?"

"A psychological autopsy is done when the person being analyzed is deceased. We gather up as much information as possible on the person's life to determine personality characteristics and determine how a person would most probably react to certain situations."

"What did you find in reviewing Mr. Mendoza's history?"

"I found that he was a sociopathic personality. He routinely operated outside the boundaries of the law. He was used to getting his way through the use of force, threats and intimidation. He was not well educated. He had no respect for authority.

"I also determined that he suffered from a severe case of Impulse Control Disorder that would cause him to fly into a rage if provoked. The man had five convictions for aggravated assault.

"I also reviewed a videotape taken May 5 of this year that shows Mr. Mendoza engaged in a brawl. He started the brawl, and several persons, including Mr. Rogers and two large young men were unsuccessful in stopping him. He only stopped when sirens could be heard in the distance, and he knew the police were on the way."

"Doctor. Did you bring that videotape with you today?"

"I did."

"Your Honor, I would request the court's permission at this time to show the tape to the jury before we continue with Dr. Ball's testimony. We have the video machine set up and the tape is in the deck."

Donner nodded to George and George rolled out the TV and video machine to the center of the courtroom, plugged it in, dimmed the lights, and turned on the tape.

Tom looked at the jury. They looked very interested. Tom had seen this tape several times before. It was a good representation of Art's temper and almost superhuman strength when he was angry.

The members of the jury watched with interest as a drunk Art Mendoza approached Sandy Rathman and essentially tumbled to the ground with her as she tried to break free of his grasp. It was one thing to hear about something being described. It was another to actually watch it.

The jury saw Tom Rogers approach Mendoza and try to pull him off Sandy. He was elbowed to the stomach and swatted away like a fly.

Then two large young men approached. They were successful in getting Mendoza away from Sandy, and he seemingly gave up the struggle. As soon as they backed away, he got up, roared, and charged at them again. The fight was on, and Mendoza had restarted it.

When sirens could be heard in the background on the audio portion of the tape, Mendoza stopped fighting, straightened up, and tried to smooth out his clothing. At this point, Larry turned off the tape. George brought the lights back up, and Larry resumed his questioning.

"Dr. Ball, do you have a psychiatric diagnosis for what we just witnessed?"

"I do."

"Please tell us what it is."

"Arthur Mendoza acted in rage as an inability to control his impulses. It is coded in the DSM IV manual as Intermittent Explosive Disorder. The diagnostic criteria for this disorder are several discrete episodes of failure to resist aggressive impulses that result in serious acts of assault or destruction of property. The degree of aggressiveness expressed during the episodes is grossly out of proportion to any precipitating psychosocial stressors.

"This is totally in keeping with Mr. Mendoza's five aggravated assault convictions. He does not learn from prior bad behavior that it is unacceptable to act aggressively towards others.

"As we could see in this tape, once the young woman resisted his advances, he became very aggressive. When Mr. Rogers attempted to stop his inappropriate behavior, he reacted angrily with a violent outburst.

"When he was finally subdued by the large young men, it is evident the crowd thought the scuffle was over. However, Mr. Mendoza charged back explosively, and started the whole fight over again, and he did so without any provocation from anyone.

"He literally exploded, much like a volcano. As you could see, he was out of control, and would hurt anyone who tried to get in his way. It wasn't until he heard the sirens, and knew the police would be there soon that he stopped fighting."

"Doctor. Are you aware that Mr. Rogers takes the position that Mr. Mendoza fired at him first, after going out to his car, getting a gun, and walking back to the house?"

"That is what he has consistently told everyone from the police on the scene to myself, Dr. Jamison, and Dr. Llewellan."

"Do you have an opinion of how Mr. Mendoza would have reacted to Mr. Rogers shooting back at him and actually wounding him?"

"I do."

"Please tell us what that opinion is."

"I believe Mr. Mendoza would have been extremely surprised, and enraged that Mr. Rogers would not only stand up to him, but shoot back. He would have exploded and become enraged. His goal at that time would have become "seek and destroy." He would not have hesitated to kill Mr. Rogers if he had further opportunity to do so. Even in his wounded state, Mr. Mendoza would be extremely dangerous, much like a wounded animal is dangerous."

Larry asked the next question: "At what point in time, doctor, do you believe Mr. Rogers entered the accepted definition of a Dissociative State?"

Ball paused, considered the question, and then answered: "In my opinion, once Mr. Rogers went back to the porch to lend assistance to Mr. Mendoza, and Mendoza was missing, Mr. Rogers entered the state known as Dissociative State.

"He had been subjected to a tremendously stressful situation. A man with very little experience with guns had been shot at, and had been forced to shoot back in defense of his own life.

"He looked, but could not find Mendoza's gun. This meant to him that Mendoza was still out there, still armed, and still dangerous.

"It was at this point that he reached Temporary Insanity, as the courts like to call it. He was no longer in control of his faculties. He no longer had any concept of right from wrong.

"He switched to automatic pilot, so to speak, without realizing it. He sought out Mendoza as an act of self-preservation. When he found him, Mendoza acted towards him in a threatening manner again, by standing and raising his right hand towards Mr. Rogers. The last time Mendoza had done that movement a few minutes earlier, bullets had come flying in Mr. Rogers' direction. His uncontrollable reaction was to protect himself."

"Doctor, how do you explain that Mr. Rogers has no memory of the events out in the driveway?"

"He might as well have been in another universe when this was happening. These events were so foreign to Mr. Rogers' life experience that his brain could not comprehend what had happened. Because it could not comprehend it, the brain put up a barrier, and blocked out the event entirely. It is as if it never happened as far as Mr. Rogers is concerned.

"He has developed what we call Dissociative Amnesia of the events that took place during the Dissociative State. Amnesia means absence of memory. Rather than being erased from the mind, which is how we usually think of Amnesia, this memory was never imprinted. Having never been imprinted, he will never remember it."

"Are you telling this jury that Mr. Rogers has no memory of the events in the driveway that led to Mr. Mendoza's death?"

"That is exactly what I am telling this jury."

"Is it your position that he will never have any memory of this event, no matter how much time goes by?"

"It is not only my position, it is a fact. He will never have any recall of these horrible events because his mind never recorded them in the first place. In many ways, the mind is very much like a tape recorder. The events in the driveway were never recorded. The recorder was turned off. Something never recorded, can never be played back."

"Doctor, does Mr. Rogers need any psychiatric rehabilitation?"

"He does not. This was an isolated instance. He will likely never be faced with a situation like this again in his life. Most of us live our complete lives without even coming close to experiencing what Mr. Rogers experienced that morning."

"Doctor, does Mr. Rogers pose any threat to the general public at this time?"

"He does not. He is a remarkably well-adjusted individual. In the face of over-whelming adversity, he has continued to carry on with his life. He found employment, and was successful at it. He sold his home. He has continued to function quite well. Many people would have slipped into a deep depression, and their world would have crumbled around them.

"Mr. Rogers is a very mentally healthy individual. He shows no evidence of any psychosis that is in need of treatment. I'm confident he poses no threat to anyone at this time. I can foresee no circumstances other than something similar to what happened on June 3rdrd that could ever cause him to act in that manner again. It was an isolated occurrence."

"Thank you doctor. I have no further questions."

Bay stood and approached the witness stand. He stood about five feet from Ball, and rocked on his heels, his forefinger on his right hand held to his lips. "Doctor, let me see if I understand your testimony. Is it your position that Mr. Mendoza reacted like *The Incredible Hulk* and developed superhuman strength when someone made him angry?"

A few members of the jury chuckled and looked at one another.

"No. That is not my position. It is my position that Mr. Mendoza suffered from Intermittent Explosive Disorder. It is a recognized diagnosis from the DSM IV manual, and is based on my psychological autopsy performed on Mr. Mendoza."

Bay had already violated the first rule of cross-examination. Never lose control of the witness. Don't let the witness give answers that amount to explanations. Keep a tight leash on the witness at all times and limit the witness to Yes or No answers when possible. Bay went on to violate the rule.

"And is it your position that when Mr. Rogers beat Arthur Mendoza to death with this ax, (holding it up for emphasis), that he was in *The Twilight Zone*, and didn't know what he was doing?"

"No, Mr. Bay. As I said, he was operating in a Dissociative State at that time. He was not in *The Twilight Zone*, as you called it."

"So he knew what he was doing?"

Larry stood: "Your Honor, I object. Dr. Ball is here as an expert on the issue of Psychological Autopsy, not Dissociative State. This is irrelevant."

Bay replied, "He opened the door, Your Honor. He asked questions about Dissociative State. I should be allowed to cross-examine on the issue."

Donner looked annoyed. "He's right, Mr. Ross. You went off in left field. You asked the questions. Mr. Bay has the right to cross-examine. Your objection is overruled. Dr. Ball, please answer the question."

Ball realized where this was going. He was surprised that Larry had asked questions on Dissociative State, but he was the lawyer, Ball was only the witness. He needed time to think.

"Mr. Bay, would you please repeat the question?"

Bay turned to the court stenographer and asked him to read the question back.

The stenographer fumbled with his machine for what seemed like forever. This gave Ball more time to think. Finally the stenographer held up the tape that looked like it came out of a cash register, and was filled with funny symbols. He read: "So he knew what he was doing?"

Ball cleared his throat. "Mr. Bay. I defer to Dr. Jamison on the issue of Dissociative State/Dissociative Amnesia. He is much more qualified than I am to give opinions on that diagnosis." There! That would do it! Bay would back off! He didn't.

"Doctor, you weren't shy about telling this jury about your opinions on Dissociative State a few minutes ago. Are you telling this jury you won't answer my questions because you don't know anything about Dissociative State?"

Bay had really stumbled this time. He had given Ball an excellent opportunity to educate the jury even more on how expert he was on the issue of Dissociative State/Dissociative Amnesia.

OK. He wanted to play rough. Ball looked at Larry. Larry acted as if he couldn't see him. He didn't want the jury to think that there was any non-verbal communication between he and Ball while Ball was being cross-examined. Ball decided to let Bay have it.

"Mr. Bay, I know a lot about Dissociative State/Dissociative Amnesia. I have written an article on it that was published in a respected scientific journal. I presented that article at a psychiatric convention attended by hundreds of psychologists from all over the country. I have treated at least a dozen patients, or more, who have suffered from the condition.

"I am the psychologist of choice in the community when fellow psychologists have a question on the subject, or want to refer a patient suffering from the condition. I have had great success in the area.

"And to answer your question specifically, No, Mr. Rogers did not know what he was doing when he hit Mr. Mendoza with the ax. He was totally out of control as he knew it, and was in a self-preservation mode. He did not know the difference between right and wrong at that point, and he fit the legal definition of legal insanity. This was so outside the realm of Mr. Rogers' experience, that his mind chose not to record what happened, hence, he has no memory of it."

Bay continued to rock back and forth on his heels. "I see, doctor, and please tell us how many of the dozen or so patients you have treated with this mysterious disorder that you are so expert on killed someone with an ax?"

"None."

"Have any of them killed anyone?"

"No."

"So this case is a first for you?"

"It is the first time I have treated someone suffering from this disorder who killed someone, yes."

"And in the studies of this disorder that you are aware of, violent behavior is a rarity isn't it?"

"You are correct that the violence is usually directed towards the person who develops the condition. That happened here. Violent behavior is not a rarity when it comes to this condition. What is unique about this case is that the stressful situation went on for a long period of time, and can be divided up into three distinct segments.

"Segment one is the argument that occurred on the back porch. Segment two is the gunshots that were fired at Mr. Rogers. Segment three is when Mr. Mendoza seemingly disappeared, and Mr. Rogers believed he was still armed and dangerous. It was the third segment that pushed Mr. Rogers into the State, and took over his persona. It was at that point that he was no longer in control.

"You see, Mr. Bay, self-preservation is the most basic of instincts. Just as Mr. Mendoza was engaging in an act of self-preservation by leaving the spot where he had been wounded to get to a place of perceived safety, Mr. Rogers acted in self-preservation when Mendoza raised his hand towards Mr. Rogers a second time.

"Having been faced with dodging bullets, literally, back on the porch, Mr. Rogers' brain went into automatic self-preservation mode at that point in time."

Bay didn't like this answer. He should have stopped right there, but he continued, thinking he could get a concession from Ball. Ball was not about to give him one.

"And doctor, was his mind in self-preservation mode when he picked up this ax from the wood pile, and went searching for Mr. Mendoza out in the driveway?"

"No."

"Then why did he pick it up and go looking for him?"

Ball was becoming annoyed. "His perception was that Mr. Mendoza was still alive, armed, and dangerous. His gun had no more bullets. He grabbed the first object he saw that could be used as a weapon."

"So he was in control when he picked up the ax?"

"He was."

"But he was out of control, and not responsible for his actions when he killed Mendoza with this ax?"

"That is correct."

"And you really believe this crazy theory?"

"I do, Mr. Bay, and it is not a crazy theory. It is scientific fact, backed up by research by psychologists that goes back for more than one hundred years. Dr. Jamison was the first one to codify it in the DSM IV manual and give it its own code. That was close to thirty-five years ago. It is a recognized diagnosis, and is a correct diagnosis in this case."

Bay could see he was getting nowhere with Ball. The more he asked, the deeper the hole got. His problem was, *he* didn't believe it, and he couldn't see how a jury could believe it. He decided to stop. "Thank you doctor, I have no further questions."

Donner looked at the clock, and then looked at Larry. "Mr. Ross, do you have any redirect?"

Knowing he was way ahead, Larry took the safe route: "No Your Honor. May the witness be excused?"

"He may. Ladies and gentlemen of the jury, we will take our morning recess. Please be back in the jury room in fifteen minutes."

As Donner got up to leave the bench, Maria Mendoza rose up. Cotter could see the .38 in her right hand. "My brother was a wonderful man! Why do you tell these lies to protect the coward who shot him like a dog?"

Cotter was leaping over the seats as she raised and pointed the .38 at Tom Rogers.

The jury began to react.

Cotter yelled: "GUN! GET DOWN!"

Before anyone could get down, a huge boom echoed through the courtroom. The .38 was pointed directly at Tom Rogers. Cotter tackled Maria, taking her to the ground.

Tom was looking straight at the barrel of the .38 when Maria pulled the trigger. He watched as the smoke curled out of the barrel. He watched as Cotter tackled Maria.

Tom expected to feel pain. He looked down at his chest expecting to see blood. He saw only his sport coat, undisturbed by any penetration. Tom slumped to his chair and hung his head between his knees. His chest heaved up and down. He fought back the urge to throw up. Could this really be happening?

The courtroom was in chaos. Everyone was yelling, and trying to get out of the room.

When the smoke and noise had cleared, Maria was in handcuffs.

In plain view, the jury had witnessed an attempt on Tom Rogers' life by someone claiming to be Art Mendoza's sister.

At Bay and Larry's urging, the trial was recessed for the day so everyone could collect their thoughts, and decide where to go from here.

The next morning Bay made a motion for a mistrial.

"Your Honor, given what happened yesterday in this courtroom, the State requests that the court grant a mistrial. The State's case has been prejudiced by the attempt on Mr. Rogers' life in full view of the jury. We believe this jury can no longer be fair, or impartial."

Donner looked at Larry. "Mr. Ross, what is your position?"

Larry rose. He had expected this from Bay, and had even considered making the motion himself. The more he thought about it, the more he thought that Maria's attempt on Tom's life was probably the best thing that could have happened in this trial to prove that the Mendoza clan was violent, dangerous, and to be feared. It was better than the photos of the house that had been trashed.

"Your Honor, we oppose Mr. Bay's motion. There is no prejudice to the State that cannot be overcome by a jury instruction. A jury has been empanelled. Jeopardy has attached. This trial should go forward. If a mistrial is granted, it should be with prejudice to the State, and the charges against Mr. Rogers should be dismissed with prejudice so that Mr. Rogers won't have to stand trial again." Larry felt he had said enough. He sat down.

Donner looked at Bay. "Mr. Bay, do you have a reply?"

Bay stood nervously. "Your Honor, to let this trial proceed in light of what happened yesterday would be a sure acquittal for Mr. Rogers. I beseech you to grant a mistrial without prejudice."

Donner rocked back and forth in his chair. "Mr. Bay. I had a talk with Detective Cotter last night after the confusion had died down. I learned that he knew the gun was in the courthouse since last week. I learned that he had loaded it with primer caps in the hope that the person who planted it would return and try something, so he or she could be arrested for attempted murder.

"I learned that he knew the identity of the person who had placed the gun in my courtroom as early as last Friday. I also learned that he didn't tell me about his plan, nor did he tell you.

"I am very disappointed in Detective Cotter's judgment. He put all of us at risk with his behavior.

"At the very least, he should have informed me of his plan. Had he done so, I never would have allowed the plan to be carried out. Law enforcement is an arm of the State, and the State is vicariously liable for the actions of all of its agents and employees, even if they work for separate arms of the same government. Detective Cotter was your choice to have with you at counsel table. As such, your office is vicariously liable for his ill-advised actions. I cannot grant a mistrial without prejudice. In essence, the State created the situation it now wants me to correct with a mistrial.

"If I grant a mistrial, it will be with prejudice to the State, meaning the charges against Mr. Rogers will be dismissed, and the State will not have leave to re-file. He will be a free man.

"What is your pleasure? Should we proceed with the trial, or should I send Mr. Rogers home a free man?"

Bay was shaken. This wasn't much of a choice. By proceeding, there was at least a chance that Rogers would be convicted. A mistrial with prejudice to the State would mean it was over for good.

Bay rose again and addressed the court. "Your Honor, I'm glad to hear you acknowledge that I had no knowledge of Detective Cotter's plan, nor would I have allowed it had I known about it. The State is willing to proceed."

Donner looked pleased. "Very well. Mr. Ross, please call your next witness."

Gary was next up. His testimony was anticlimactic after yesterday's events. He told about how long he had known Tom, how he had given Tom the .44 Bulldog for protection, and how confused Tom had been the morning of June 3rdrd. Bay didn't even bother to cross-examine.

During the morning recess Larry called Jamison, and asked him to meet him at the Ramada coffee shop over the lunch hour so they could finalize everything and Larry could brief Jamison on Ball's testimony.

Tom still wanted to testify. Larry told him no. There was no way Larry was going to let Tom take the witness stand now, and possibly screw up what was looking more and more like an unconditional acquittal.

CHAPTER 38

$$\blacktriangledown$$

October 15th, afternoon session

Donner recessed for lunch early, and told the jury to be back at one thirty.

Larry went over to the Ramada and met Jamison for lunch. He told him all about Ball's testimony, and told him to expect similar questioning from Bay on how many of his patients had committed murder.

Jamison smiled and said, "Actually, quite a few. Let me think about it, and I'll give you an answer to that question on direct. That will take the wind out of his sails."

When you are ready to go, and anxious to put on your best witness, the lunch break can seem like an eternity. When you are desperate to find the answer to a legal question that needs an answer right away, and you have to skip lunch and hit the library, the lunch break is over in a flash. This lunch break took forever.

At one thirty, the jury took their seats, and George rapped the gavel and intoned, "Alllll Riiissse," as Donner took the bench.

Donner played the part of judge so well. Even though he was young, he looked regal in his black robe. He welcomed the jury back, and turned to Larry as if he didn't have a clue what was coming next. "Mr. Ross, do you have anymore witnesses?"

"Yes, Your Honor, the defense calls Dr. Mark Jamison."

Jamison stood when he heard his name, and made his way to the court clerk who took his name and swore him in.

He looked the part of the all-knowing doctor. He had traded in his well-worn tweed jacket for a subdued dark-blue suit, which fit well. It was accentuated with a red power-tie and gold cufflinks. The black Ferragamo loafers completed the ensemble. Jamison's white hair was well groomed. He was the picture of sartorial splendor.

Larry spent a lot of time on Jamison's career, including his numerous publications, his appointment as Head of the Psychology Department at USC and the number of weeks he spent on the lecture circuit every year.

It was established that Jamison had first written the diagnostic criteria that had later become the standard in the DSM IV manual in 1975. He estimated that he had treated over one hundred twenty patients who had suffered from the condition, and readily agreed that he was regarded as the world's expert on Dissociative State/Dissociative Amnesia. He was the professional the other professionals looked to for advice when they were stuck, or needed assistance with a diagnosis or a treatment plan.

Larry spent some time establishing that Dr. Llewellan had been a student of Jamison's, and that he was not a stand out by any means. He defended his decision not to reconsider Llewellan's score on his written exam for board certification and estimated that about forty percent of those who took the test did not pass it the first time. Most of them took it a second time, and received a passing score.

Llewellan had never reapplied. Jamison had been the head of the certification committee for almost twenty years and had designed and written many of the questions that made up the test.

Larry couldn't help but notice that the jury was listening intently. They had a superstar in their midst, and were definitely paying attention. Some of them were wondering where Tom Rogers got the money for such a well-qualified witness when Larry asked Dr. Jamison: "Dr. Jamison, what is your agreed upon hourly rate for the work you have performed on this case?"

"My agreed upon hourly rate is zero."

"And why is that, doctor?"

"I am a visiting professor here at the UofA this semester. I only have one class to teach. I learned about this case through a phone call from my colleague Dr. Ball. I was interested. I needed something else to do. I wanted to help, and I offered my services. At this point in my career, money is not a motivating factor in my decisions on what to do with my time. I am glad to do this for no fee."

The jury looked impressed. Here was a world-renowned expert in psychology working for free for Tom Rogers and Larry Ross in little Tucson, Arizona.

"Have you reviewed the standardized tests that Dr. Ball administered to Mr. Rogers?"

"I have."

"Do you agree with his assessment that while Mr. Rogers shows tendencies of aggression, manipulative behavior, and wanting to look good, that those are not necessarily bad character traits?"

"I do. They are not bad at all. Many successful people, among them General Eisenhower, and President Roosevelt were very aggressive and manipulative personalities who were obsessed with looking good. They were also very successful negotiators. They got this country through a period of crisis by knowing how to manipulate, and knowing how and when to be aggressive. Mr. Rogers has a similar personality. He knows when to be manipulative, and when to be aggressive. He, too, is a good negotiator. That is why he has been successful."

Larry was very happy. Tom had just been compared favorably to Eisenhower and Roosevelt. He snuck a peek at the jury. They were looking interested. Some were even leaning forward in their seats. He continued: "Doctor, did you conduct a personal interview with Mr. Rogers?"

"I did."

"Did that assist you in forming opinions and conclusions in this case?"

"It did."

"What did you learn in the personal interview concerning the relationship between Mr. Rogers and Mr. Mendoza?"

"I learned that Mr. Mendoza was a terrible partner who was obsessed with self-gratification, and was sabotaging the business by his behavior. I learned that he had threatened Mr. Rogers at least once when he told him he would kill him if he interfered in his affairs again.

"I learned that Mr. Mendoza regarded Mr. Rogers as physically and emotionally weak, someone that he could push around physically, as well as monetarily. It was not a good partnership."

"Did Mr. Rogers describe the events of June 3rdrd to the best of his ability and memory?"

"He did."

"What was the significance of his description?"

"Mr. Rogers was faced with a situation he had never been faced with before, and in all likelihood will never be faced with again. His life was in danger. As Dr. Ball has told you, Mr. Mendoza suffered from Intermittent Explosive Disorder. He would literally explode into a rage if he didn't get his way. He wanted Mr. Rogers to step away from the partnership without any kind of compensation. Mr. Rogers declined. Mendoza exploded, and went to get a gun. He returned with a gun, and fired it at Mr. Rogers. This presented Mr. Rogers with a choice. Take a hit, or fire back. He did the instinctual thing, and fired back."

"Did he have any memory of hitting Mr. Mendoza with the ax?"

"He did not."

"Why not?"

Bay stood: "I object, Your Honor. Rule 26 states that presumptively a party is only entitled to one expert witness per issue. Dr. Ball has already testified on Dissociative State. I expect that to be the next line of questions and answers from this witness. Mr. Ross should not be allowed two bites at the apple."

Donner considered excusing the jury for a sidebar, and then decided against it. He wanted to rule decisively from the bench in full view of the jury, and not have to explain to them later what had happened out of their presence. "Mr. Bay, your objection is overruled. The rule does say "presumptively." It also says that for good cause, the court can allow more than one witness per issue.

"When Mr. Ross started asking Dr. Ball questions on Dissociative State, I expected an objection from you, as you knew there were two witnesses on the two psychological issues in this case. All of this had been discussed prior to trial.

"Had you made that objection, I would have sustained it. You chose not to make an objection, so the jury heard the testimony.

"I then allowed you to cross-examine Dr. Ball over objection from Mr. Ross. Your objection is untimely. I gave you your bite at the apple. Now Mr. Ross will have his. You may proceed, Mr. Ross."

Bay looked pissed. Larry looked pleased. Bay had tried to set him up, and it didn't work. It might have worked with another judge, but it didn't work with Donner. Bay had just shot himself in the foot with his little trick. Now the jury was going to get to hear about Dissociative State/Dissociative Amnesia not once, but twice. It was hard not to gloat in victory, but Larry overcame his thoughts and pressed on.

"Doctor, the question was, why doesn't Mr. Rogers remember hitting Mr. Mendoza with the ax?"

"He doesn't remember it because his brain never recorded it. It is as if it never happened. A memory once imprinted generally will stay with us. A memory never imprinted is never a memory, and there is no way to access it again."

"And why did his brain not record the event?"

"These events were so far out of Mr. Rogers' realm of experience and comprehension that his brain just shut down and did not record the events. This is why we label the behavior Dissociative. The person is disassociated from reality at this point in time. Amnesia means absence of memory. As the brain never recorded the event, there can be no memory of it. No matter what happens, Mr. Rogers will never remember this event."

"Did Mr. Rogers know right from wrong at the time he struck Mr. Mendoza with the ax?"

"He did not. He was on automatic pilot, and the pilot was set on a course of self-preservation. Self-preservation is one of man's most basic instincts. It is the primary reason we have survived as a species despite overwhelming odds against our survival.

"We aren't particularly strong, agile, or able to survive adverse weather conditions without the help of artificial clothing, yet survive we have for hundreds of thousands, if not millions of years.

"But our brains are advanced. The brain is so advanced, it can even shut down if it needs to, so the inhabitant of the body that houses the brain can do what is necessary to survive, and then continue to survive by not having to remember the horrible events that necessitated the survival.

"Would this fit the definition of Temporary Insanity?"

"Yes. We psychologists don't like to use the term, but yes. It means not understanding right from wrong, which is exactly what happened to Mr. Rogers when Mendoza raised his hand towards him in the driveway.

"Mr. Rogers had instant recall of what happened the last time Mendoza raised his hand towards him. A gun had been fired at him. He wasn't going to let that happen again. It was at that point that the recorder got turned off, and the automatic pilot switch got turned on. He no longer had any control of his mind, or his body at that point in time."

"Has this condition continued in Mr. Rogers?"

"Absolutely not. He had a brief State, followed by a brief period of amnesia of the horrible events. He has good recall of everything else. There is no underlying mental disease process here. Mr. Rogers is a very mentally healthy individual."

"Is this behavior likely to be repeated?"

"Not unless Mr. Rogers is faced with a similar situation which is highly unlikely. We most often see this behavior in wartime situations. Many soldiers are considered to be heroes, and are told of heroic acts performed under combat situations, and are even given medals for them, yet they have no memory of the events."

"How many persons have you treated with a similar condition that have been in situations where they actually killed someone and had no memory of it?"

"Many—at least a dozen or more. As I said, it is usually the combat veteran who comes to me with a guilty feeling of being hailed as a hero, and told of the enemy that he killed single handedly, yet has no memory of it. He doesn't feel like a hero, and is ashamed to be honored as one. My most recent experience with this was after the first Gulf War. I suspect when this Gulf War is over, I will have others come to me and have the same complaint."

"Have you ever had patients regain their memory of the horrible event?"

"No. As I said before, the brain can't recall what it does not record. No record, no memory. Forever."

"Is Mr. Rogers responsible for the behavior that led to Mr. Mendoza's death on June 3rd?"

"He is not. That responsibility lies with Mr. Mendoza. He exploded irrationally because of his impulse control disorder, which I understand you have already questioned Dr. Ball about. Had that not occurred, he would be alive today. Mr. Rogers is a victim of Mr. Mendoza's psychological pathology, which was deep, severe, and long standing. Mr. Rogers has no psychological pathology."

"Are you telling us that Mr. Rogers needs treatment?"

"No. I'm telling you he is perfectly healthy from a psychological standpoint. He needs no treatment. He needs no confinement. He needs no rehabilitation. He needs no counseling. He has coped well with this situation. He presents no threat to society as a whole, or anyone in particular at this point in time."

Larry turned and looked at the jury as he began to take his seat. They were all nodding in approval.

"Thank you doctor. Your witness, Mr. Bay."

Bay stood. He wasn't sure what he was going to do so he stuck to the tried and true. Control the witness. Limit him to yes and no answers. Bay wasn't going to give the world's expert on Dissociative State/Dissociative Amnesia a chance to educate this jury on his theory any more than he already had.

"Doctor. You agree that Mr. Rogers killed Mr. Mendoza in a very violent fashion?"

"Yes."

"And the instrument of murder, this ax, belonged to Mr. Rogers?"

"Yes."

"And this perfectly mentally healthy man, Tom Rogers, brutally murdered another human being and he has no memory of it?"

Jamison could see what was coming. He hated being limited to yes and no answers. In the last three questions, Bay had used the words "killed," "murder," and "violent." Jamison was sure more emotional words would be used in the questions to come. He decided to play along for a while. "Yes."

"And prior to that, Mr. Rogers had shot and wounded Mr. Mendoza twice, isn't that correct?"

"Yes."

"And after he did that, rather than call 9-1-1, he called his best friend to ask for advice?"

"Yes."

"And Mr. Miller told him to check on Mr. Mendoza's welfare, and call 9-1-1. Isn't that correct?"

"That is my understanding of the testimony, yes."

"And rather than check on Mr. Mendoza's welfare or call 911 as he had been told to do, Mr. Rogers hunted down Mr. Mendoza and killed him with this ax?"

Here was an opening. Jamison seized it. "I disagree with your characterization of 'hunting Mr. Mendoza down' like he was some animal. Your phrase "killed him with this ax" implies that Mr. Rogers knew what he was doing at the time. He did not know what he was doing at the time. This was totally involuntary on his part."

"I think, doctor, you have already told us that. Please answer my questions."

Jamison and Larry looked at the jury. The members looked annoyed that Bay was treating this great man with disrespect.

Bay continued. "And was Mr. Rogers acting involuntarily when he dragged Mr. Mendoza's lifeless body over one hundred fifty feet to hide it by the garage out of the sight of his neighbors?"

"Yes, he was."

"Doctor, aren't you doing this case for free because it will be the subject matter of your next book on Dissociative State/Dissociative Amnesia?"

"Absolutely not. I'm doing it for free because this diagnosis is so often overlooked, and when it is properly made, as it was in this case, law enforcement disbelieves it, and ridicules the defense, much as you are doing now with these questions."

That was it. Bay had lost control of the witness. The jury was smirking as if to say "Good job doctor! Let him have it!" Bay might as well have been standing in front of the jury with a pie in his face. Bay shut down his cross quickly.

"Doctor, in your opinion, is there room for doubt in your diagnosis?"

"Mr. Bay, there is always room for doubt. However, there is no reasonable doubt. I am certain, to an overwhelming degree of psychiatric probability, that my diagnosis is correct."

Jamison had just nailed the lid shut. He had used the term "reasonable doubt," in a favorable context for the defense. Put another way, Tom Rogers was an innocent man. Bay knew he had been defeated.

"Thank you doctor. I have no further questions."

Judge Donner looked up from his notes, surprised that Bay had finished so soon. "Mr. Ross, please call your next witness."

Larry stood and addressed the court. "The defense rests, Your Honor."

"Very well. Ladies and gentlemen, the evidence portion of this trial has been concluded. You are excused for the day. The lawyers and I have to settle some legal issues. Please be back here for final arguments at nine A.M. At that time, the lawyers will argue the case to you, and I will read you instructions. You will then begin your deliberations. Counsel; please meet me in chambers to work on the legal matters. Court is adjourned."

George banged his gavel, everyone stood, and Donner left the bench. The finish line was looming. The members of the jury were pleased they got to go home early.

CHAPTER 39

▼

October 16th

Arguing instructions the night before had been easy. The judge gave the standard pattern instructions on second-degree murder and the lesser-included offenses of voluntary and involuntary manslaughter. He told the jury to disregard the incident with the gun that had happened in open court, as it had nothing to do with Mr. Rogers' guilt or innocence. That was probably about as effective as telling a lottery winner to forget about the money he had just won and go on with his life as if nothing had changed.

He gave four forms of verdict. Guilty of Second-Degree; Guilty of Voluntary; Guilty of Involuntary; and Not Guilty. He told Larry and Bay he expected them to take no more than forty-five minutes in their respective closing arguments. He warned them he would not tolerate any mischaracterization of any of the evidence or misstatements of a witness's testimony. He also let it be known he didn't want any sarcasm or theatrics from either of them. They were forbidden to mention the outburst from Maria. Everyone was to act as if it had never happened.

Larry got home early for a change, and took a swim. The pool was cooling off pretty fast, but it was still pleasant once he dove in and got used to it. Swim season would be over by the end of the month at the latest.

He worked on his closing outline for about an hour after dinner, and then watched *Law and Order*. He was impressed with how well the writers could compress a final argument into about two minutes of airtime. With Tom's life on the line, he would take longer than two minutes, but he didn't want to take too long.

He was sure members of the jury were watching the show too. It worried him a little that the prosecution got a conviction every week, even if the evidence was only circumstantial. The evidence was more than circumstantial in this case. He was sure Bay would be parading that damned bloody ax all over the courtroom in the morning.

Larry got to the office about seven forty five, asked Cindy to type up his final outline just as soon as she came in, and headed out the door by eight forty five. Tom met him outside the courtroom. Not a word was spoken between them. They entered the courtroom somberly, and with the knowledge that the next few hours would make all the difference in the rest of Tom's life.

The jury filed in at nine, and the Judge took the bench. He turned to Rick Bay. "Mr. Bay, do you have any closing remarks for the jury?"

Bay stood. "I do, Your Honor."

"Please proceed."

As expected, Bay walked over to the clerk and picked up the bloody ax. He walked to the front of the jury box and began his opening statement.

"On June 3rd, Tom Rogers ended Art Mendoza's life with three vicious blows from this ax. We brought you an eyewitness who saw him do it. He doesn't deny doing it. He is guilty of second-degree murder, and you should return a verdict of guilty on that charge."

The jury looked uninterested.

Bay babbled on about the sanctity of life and how no man has the right to take the life of another. The longer he talked, the less the jury seemed to listen. Maybe they had already made up their minds to convict. Maybe they thought Bay was full of shit. Who the hell knew what they thought? The whole exercise was nerve-wracking and mind numbing.

Tom had been instructed to sit and listen politely, and not show emotion. That was hard to do when Rick Bay was trying to persuade fourteen people that he should be convicted of second-degree murder. He did his best not to show emotion by pretending to take notes. In reality he was writing over and over again: Bay is full of shit. Don't believe a word he says ... He couldn't help but think of Jack Nicholson's character in *The Shining* who wrote over and over and over: "All work and no play makes Jack a dull boy."

Nicholson had gone insane in the movie, and had killed Scatman Cruthers with an ax to the chest, and had tried to kill his wife and child with the ax as well. After a few minutes, Tom stopped writing and just listened. He didn't want to be like Jack Nicholson's character who ended up dead. The similarity of the ax was too close to home.

After a while, he couldn't hear a word Bay was saying. The words just didn't make any sense any more. Tom was afraid he was going insane. How ironic would it be if he lost it again, went into a State, picked up the ax, and beat Bay to death with it? That would make the headlines.

Come on, Tom, snap out of it! Sticks and stones can break your bones but words can never hurt you! Well, words *could* hurt a lot. At least Bay wasn't shooting at him.

All of sudden, he was aware of the fact that Larry was in front of the jury and he was talking. Bay must be finished. He decided to give Larry his attention.

Larry was good. He went over the evidence witness by witness. He reminded the jury of all of the good things Tom had done in his short life. He reminded the jury of all the bad things Art Mendoza had done in his fifty-nine years on this earth. He asked the jury not to let the actions of Art Mendoza ruin yet one more life, Tom's.

Larry summed up by telling the jury, "The law does not hold people who do not know right from wrong criminally responsible for their actions. We have shown you beyond a reasonable doubt that Tom Rogers was not responsible for his actions on June 3rd when he hit Arthur Mendoza with this ax. He did so to protect his own life. A life, which just minutes before, had almost been taken from him by Mr. Mendoza.

"We ask that you find Tom Rogers not guilty of the charges the State has brought against him, and return a verdict of Not Guilty. End this nightmare he has been living for the last four and one-half months today. Set Tom Rogers free!"

Bay had one more chance. He only took a few minutes. He basically told the jury that if they believed the story the defense had given them, then God help us all, society will crumble, and the world as we know it will end.

He reminded the jury that Tom was a salesman, and while he might have sold his lawyer and his psychologists on his story, he was sure the jury wasn't buying what Tom was trying to sell them. A man was dead, and Tom Rogers needed to be punished for his death.

The jury was stone-faced. This bunch was impossible to read.

Bay sat down, and the judge read the instructions. Before eleven o'clock, the jury had the case, and was in the jury room deliberating Tom's fate. The next few hours would be what Larry called Ulcer Time. Juror number thirteen looked a bit surprised when his name was called and he was told he was an alternate and would not participate in the deliberations.

CHAPTER 40

▼

October 16th

Tom and Larry headed over to Café Poca Cosa in the old Santa Rita hotel. The food was delicious, and the restaurant had a delightful patio. It was a beautiful fall day. The jury would be out for a while. Larry left his cell phone number with George so he could be reached if necessary. It rang before the meal came to the table.

It was George. The jury wanted a video player and a TV set so they could watch the Cinco de Mayo tape again. George had already talked to Bay. The tape was in evidence. Watching it again was not any different than looking at scene photos or the aerial view of the house. Bay told George he had no objection. Larry had no objection. The more they watched that tape, the more they would see that Art had caused his own death by being unable to control his impulses and his rage.

The cell phone rang again at one o'clock. It was George again. The jury decided to take a lunch break, and would be back to work at two thirty. Larry resisted the temptation to order a pitcher of margaritas, and decided to go back to the office instead. Showing up drunk to take a verdict would probably not go down well with Judge Donner.

After assuring Tom that juries did in fact eat lunch and that going to lunch was not a bad sign, they walked back to Larry's office together.

Larry went into his office and closed the door. Tom and Cindy talked for a while, and then ran out of things to say. The tension was unbearable. Tom went into the conference room and jumped on the Internet just to bounce around and waste some time until the jury came back. It didn't take long to catch up on the news of world events and the latest stock market rally.

Four o'clock came and went. Bored with the Internet, Tom turned on the conference room television. He caught *Dr. Phil* counseling a couple about their mutual infidelity and ways to break their bad habits of cheating on one another.

They were ugly people. Tom couldn't imagine why anyone would want to have an affair with either one of them. They were probably in the perfect marriage, for them. Mutual cheating—lots of risk and excitement; but the stability of marriage and a place to call home.

At five on the nose, Larry's cell phone rang again. The jury was making progress. They wanted to work another hour or so before calling it quits for the day. Larry again assured Tom that the longer the jury was out, the better it looked for him. Someone had reasonable doubt, and it took a unanimous verdict for a conviction.

Larry called Maggie, and told her he wouldn't be home for dinner. He promised to call as soon as he knew more.

Cindy decided to stick around. She called her mother, and asked her to keep the kids for dinner and for the night. She had to see what was going to happen. Her mom understood. She knew that Cindy and Tom were more than just friends.

It was after five o'clock. Larry returned a few client calls, but his heart wasn't in it. At five thirty he decided to bag it, and just hang out in the conference room with Tom and Cindy.

At six, he was hungry and wondered if they should go over to El Minuto for dinner. It was a close walk to the courthouse if the phone rang. The jury had eaten a late lunch so their stomachs were not on the same clock as his. They decided to wait a while longer.

The cell phone rang again at six thirty. It was George. The jury had a verdict. Judge Donner was still in the building, and wanted to know if Larry could come over to take the verdict, or if he wanted to wait until morning. Bay had been notified and would do whatever Larry and Tom wanted to do. They decided to take the verdict tonight. They couldn't wait another minute.

The three of them hurried over to the courthouse. They met Bay at the after-hours entrance where George met all of them to let them in. No one spoke a word.

George brought them upstairs on the judges' elevator. Donner was on the bench when they entered the courtroom. Officer Guest was present. If the verdict was guilty, he would take Tom into custody and place him in handcuffs. Cotter was there too. He wanted to see the show for himself. He didn't care that Donner was pissed at him for the Maria incident. He didn't work for Donner, and Donner couldn't do anything to him. Donner told George to bring in the jury.

The stone-faced twelve filed in one-by-one. They looked at no one, and offered no outward sign of what their verdict was. Tom thought he would pass out when Donner asked the jury if they had reached a verdict and the forewoman stood and said: "Yes, we have, Your Honor." She handed the verdict to George. George handed it to Donner. Donner opened it, read it without expression, and handed it to the court clerk. Donner then uttered the famous phrase that all judges say when the defendant is about to hear his or her fate:

"Will the defendant please rise? Madam Clerk, please read the verdict."

Tom and Larry stood together. They looked at the jury. There was still no expression from anyone. They would have to wait to hear the words. Then the words came:

"We, the jury, being duly empanelled, and after due deliberation do find the defendant, Thomas Wayne Rogers—NOT GUILTY."

Tom looked at Larry as if he couldn't believe what he had heard.

Suddenly Judge Donner was speaking again. "Ladies and gentlemen of the jury, is this your verdict?"

The forewoman answered: "It is, Your Honor."

Donner turned his attention to Bay. Mr. Bay, would you like to poll the jury?"

Bay looked at the forewoman. "No, Your Honor."

Donner looked at Larry. "Mr. Ross, would you like to poll the jury?"

Was he crazy? There was no way Larry was going to question each individual juror if this was his or her verdict. One of them might change his or her mind. "No, Your Honor," was the reply.

Donner turned to the jury. "Ladies and gentlemen, thank you very much for your service, and your willingness to work a little longer today to reach a verdict. Your service is very much appreciated by all of us. You are now free to discuss the case with anyone, including the media or the lawyers, but you are not obligated to do so. Your service is complete. George will escort you down and let you out of the building. Good night."

The jury filed out, and it was over.

Donner addressed Tom: "Mr. Rogers, you are free to go. The charges against you are dismissed. I will sign an order exonerating your bond as soon as Mr. Ross prepares one and presents it to me. Congratulations, Mr. Rogers, and good luck to you."

Donner left the bench. George wasn't even in the room to utter his famous "Alllll Riiissse." He was downstairs letting the jury out.

Bay came over and offered his hand to Larry. "Good job, Larry. You tried a helluva case, and did everything just right."

He then extended his hand to Tom. "Tom, I wish you well. Whatever you paid Larry for this miracle, it wasn't enough. He did a great job for you."

Cindy came up and gave Tom a big hug and a kiss on the cheek. They were still trying to be discreet in front of Larry.

Tom pumped Larry's hand until Larry asked him if he could have his hand back so he could go home. Cotter came over and offered congratulations, and told Tom he never wanted to arrest him in the first place. Guest escorted them down the elevator where George was waiting at the after-hours entrance to let them all out. The courthouse was closed. They would have to celebrate elsewhere.

Larry left Tom and Cindy in the office parking lot as he drove home. He called Maggie to tell her the good news. She was thrilled to hear him say Tom had been found not guilty.

He turned to the Oldies Station. Kool and the Gang were just starting to sing "Celebration." Larry cranked up the volume and sang along at the top of his lungs.

Tom and Cindy went to Cindy's apartment and enjoyed each other's bodies until they were both exhausted. Then they showered and curled up in each other's arms. At ten thirty they finally remembered to call Cindy's mom and give her the good news.

She told them to sleep in, as she would take the kids to school in the morning. They had extra clothes at grandma's just for such an occasion. They took her up on her offer, and didn't get up until ten the next morning. By four o'clock the next afternoon, they had had sex three more times. Then it was time to get back to reality.

CHAPTER 41

▼

Eight Months Later

Tom was brushing his teeth when he looked into the mirror and watched Cindy as she got out of the shower. God! Her breasts were huge! Her nipples were starting to turn dark brown. Her areolas were as big as saucers. Her hips were getting wider. Her tummy was getting rounder too. She had gained fifteen pounds since March. Pregnancy will do that to a woman.

Tom got an erection just looking at her as she toweled herself off. She saw it, and was glad he didn't have to report to the sales floor until ten o'clock. It was mid-June. The girls were in Tennessee with Billy for the summer, and Tom and Cindy had the house to themselves. In two months, when the girls returned, Cindy knew she would be huge. Time for sex would be difficult to find with the kids back in the house, and her pregnant belly would get in the way of the vigorous sex that she and Tom enjoyed almost daily. There was no time like the present.

She dropped her towel and pressed her body into his. He could feel her full breasts pressing on his chest. They stood in front of the sinks kissing passionately for several minutes. They then moved from the bathroom to the bedroom and used every square inch of the king-size bed they had bought as a wedding gift to themselves. Tom was a few minutes late for work. No one challenged his late arrival. He was the King of Sales. At the dealership, he could do no wrong.

Since getting married last Valentine's day, life had been a whirlwind for them. Tom went back to work at the Toyota dealership and was now assistant sales manager. He set a new sales record every month. The sales manager was beginning to worry that his job was in jeopardy. Toyota USA was talking about grooming him to be the dealer at a new dealership that would be opening in Albuquerque.

They bought a five-bedroom house in Cimarron, a non-gated community in the Foothills at Wilmot Road and Sunrise Drive. The house came complete with a swimming pool, spa, and a three-car garage. It had a big back yard, and Tom's two Old English Sheep Dogs had rejoined the family. The girls loved them.

The girls, now eight, nine, and ten, were enrolled at Sunrise Elementary, located in the prestigious Foothills School District. They were taking piano lessons, and dance lessons. They were flourishing. They were excited about their new brother who would arrive in late October. They each had their own room and no longer had to share anything.

Cindy gave her old Mustang to her younger brother. Tom got her a new Toyota Sienna van to haul the girls and their friends around in. Cindy had quit working in January, just before the wedding. Karen Hargrave had given up her free-lance bookkeeping work to work full-time for Larry. It was a good arrangement for everyone.

The wedding had been held at The Manning House, an old mansion located in Downtown Tucson that was rented out for private parties. Judge Donner had performed the wedding ceremony. Larry had been the best man, and Karen had been the maid of honor.

About seventy guests attended. The cover band, "Ron's Garage," came from San Diego to perform. It was a blowout affair. Nobody left until one A.M., when the band quit playing, and the bar closed down.

Julio and Oscar Mendoza had been convicted on multiple counts of grand theft auto, conspiracy to conduct an illegal enterprise, and unlawful trafficking in cocaine and marijuana. They were serving twenty-five years without possibility of parole, and were housed at the Wilmot Prison on the southeast side of town out by the Pima County Fairgrounds. They were currently busy organizing a Chicano gang to do their bidding in prison. Crime was all they knew. It was all they would ever know. Now they had a captive population they could control.

Maria had been convicted of possession of stolen property, unlawfully bringing a firearm into a public building, and attempted murder. She had pled guilty to all of it. She had no defense. She was sentenced to five years in prison and did her time at the Wilmot Prison where Julio and Oscar were housed. They never saw each other as the woman's unit and the men's unit were completely separate.

Maria was put on cleaning detail. Cleaning shitty toilets just seemed to keep coming back to her. At least in prison, she knew where her next meal was coming from; she had a safe place to sleep, and she couldn't drink.

Larry and Mitch had been working hard on the Newman case. Mitch had gotten a favorable verdict against Galaxy in the Texas case he had pursued primarily as a discovery tool.

Five million dollars in punitive damages. Galaxy had filed a motion for new trial, and a motion to reduce the punitive damages award.

The media had taken an interest in the story, and Galaxy was feeling the pressure.

Larry had picked up another Arizona case. A van owned by a summer-camp in Prescott had rolled while southbound on Interstate 17. Thankfully, the children had been delivered to their destination safely before the accident occurred. The van driver had been alone at the time.

The driver was a twenty two-year-old college Senior from Arizona State University in Tempe. His name was Walter Simmons. Walter had been a counselor at the camp from the summer following his eighteenth birthday. He was a wonderful young man. He had a 3.75 GPA in Mechanical Engineering, and was scheduled to graduate the following December. He would never realize his dream of becoming an engineer.

While he had serious orthopedic injuries, he also had a severe closed-head injury that had left him severely brain damaged. He would require nursing care for the rest of his life. His case was worth millions.

Mitch agreed to help Larry with this case, too. This one was taken on a forty percent contingent fee, the standard fee in products liability cases. A guardian had to be appointed by the court to monitor Walter's case, as he was incapable of handling his own affairs. The court would have to approve any settlement, and would also have to approve the attorney's fees and costs.

Another flaw had been found in the Galaxy van. The roof was weak. Because of the van's high center of gravity, this model was prone to rollovers when accidents occurred. The Simmons van had rolled over, just as the Newman van had rolled over.

Because of a structural design flaw in the roof system, the roof would collapse on rollover when it came into contact with the road or the ground. A seat-belted driver or passenger in the front seat would be subjected to a crushed roof impacting the skull, and causing serious brain damage. This one had rolled over to the left, and Walter's head had been right in the path of the collapsing roof. The roof caved in like an aluminum beer can. Walter's skull didn't fare much better.

Mitch had done many rollover cases before, and had the engineers all lined up who would provide the testimony that such an accident was foreseeable, and that Galaxy could have prevented the crush by a simple re-design of the roof that would have added only minimal cost to the van as a whole. Galaxy was looking bad on two counts on the Simmons case, and for any other cases that would come along involving a head injury to a driver or passenger of one of these vans.

Walter's case was filed, and benefited from the discovery Mitch had done in the Texas case, and the Newman case.

Because of the publicity the Texas case had received in the media, other cases started being filed in other states, mostly by prominent law firms that had the money to go the distance against Galaxy. By this time, Galaxy had thirty-two cases pending on the caliper spring issue. The cases were spread out across twenty states, which kept the Galaxy defense team of lawyers hopping from place-to-place, and making sure their discovery responses were consistent. It was becoming a management headache for Galaxy.

Conner Peterson had suggested mediation to Larry and Mitch. Galaxy would come to Tucson. Mitch and Larry could choose the mediator. Tom Galaxy, the Chairman of the Board, and the great-grandson of George Galaxy, founder of the company, would attend the mediation.

The Newmans agreed, and the mediation was set for October 3rd.

In the meantime, Larry and Mitch kept up the pressure by taking depositions and sending out requests for document production. They were hoping to score big at the mediation and set the stage for the cases yet to come. Even if the case didn't get resolved, the Newmans would get a chance to meet Tom Galaxy in person and hear what he had to say.

Laura Rogers was enrolled at Ohio State University for the fall semester. She was determined to finish her degree in Art History. She was dating a young architect who was just getting his private practice started after having worked for a large architectural firm for about four years.

Angie Mendoza was also enrolled for the fall semester at the UofA. She wanted to finish her degree in Art History as well. She and Laura had lost touch.

Angie's aunt and her cousins were behind bars, and her father was dead. Unlike her greedy cousins, and her stupid, drunken aunt, she had saved a lot of the ill-gotten gains from Maria's Auto Salvage, and was living quite well. She hoped to become a teacher of Art History at the Jr. College level once she completed all of her degree requirements.

Bay had tried four more first-degree murder cases since Tom's acquittal, and had gotten four convictions. He was back in favor with County Attorney Steve McNair. As time went on, he came to believe that the jury came to the right conclusion in Tom's case.

McNair was up for re-election in November. His only opposition was a perennial Libertarian candidate who didn't stand a chance of being elected. McNair could be Pima County Attorney as long as he wanted the job. He was doing a good job, he looked good on TV at the press conferences, and no serious candidate would challenge him.

CHAPTER 42

▼

October 3rd

Retired Judge Sam Langer sat in his conference room and looked out to the parking lot at his vintage 1968 Oldsmobile Delta 88 convertible. He could afford to drive anything he wanted to, but the Olds was a status symbol with him. It was the first new car he had purchased after graduation from law school, and it was a stretch purchase for him then.

Brand new, it cost less than a junker used car would cost now. He kept it as a reminder of inflation, and the process of the dues he had paid while coming up through the ranks.

Along the way, he had used his cars as achievement-symbols to let the legal community, and his clients know how well he was doing in his practice.

The Oldsmobiles became Cadillacs, the Cadillacs became Mercedes', the Mercedes' became Jaguars, the Jaguars became BMWs, and that was where it stopped. He realized no one cared about what he drove, and didn't pay any attention to the new achievement symbol he would show up in.

All anyone cared about was how effective he was. He was very effective: First as a lawyer, then as a judge, and now as a private mediator.

When he drove the Olds, the older it got, the more of a conversation piece it became. People, young and old, would approach and ask what it was, or tell a story about a similar car that had been in the family, or the glory days of G.M., when every model they offered had a convertible in the line-up.

The Olds was pretty cool. It had power windows, power steering and brakes, an electric top, and factory-spoked wheels. His only modification to it had been replacement of the factory radio with a Bose/F.M. radio with a built-in CD player and installation of a Sirius Satellite radio system.

Now, he drove it full time. It was getting harder to maintain and find parts for, but it was a kick to put the top down and cruise the Speedway Boulevard corridor to the head turners and the thumbs up signs the car would inspire. He was thinking it could use some new tires when he realized it was almost nine A.M.

The crowd would be arriving soon for the mediation in Newman v. Galaxy. His secretary pulled up and parked her new Tahoe next to the Olds. He watched carefully to make sure she didn't bump his passenger door as she got out of the huge SUV. He had just had the Olds repainted less than three months ago, and so far had not picked up any new door dings.

Langer had spent twenty years in practice, and fifteen years on the bench, before resigning his judgeship to become a private mediator. He had a knack for resolving disputes, and negotiating contracts. As a mediator, he got to do both, and got paid handsomely for it.

Within a year of starting his private mediation practice, he had successfully negotiated several multi-million-dollar contracts for UofA athletes drafted by the NFL, or the NBA. He was paid for those negotiations on a percentage of what he was able to negotiate the contract for. His piece of that pie earned him more in a year than he had earned the entire time he had been on the bench.

He also did private mediations for lawyers who had high profile and high dollar cases that needed a helping hand to get resolved. Nobody would talk to one another anymore. They needed a neutral third-party to get the job done for them. He was glad to be of assistance.

Sam would do those on an hourly-fee basis. His fee was a hefty five hundred dollars per hour, with a three-hour minimum. He charged the same rate to review the material submitted to him ahead of time. He already had a two thousand dollar bill racked up in this one before the mediation had even started.

Sam was looking forward to this day. He would get to meet the great S. Conner Peterson, Tom Galaxy himself, and the legendary Mitch Branch. He was impressed that the young, but up and coming, Larry Ross was in on this one. This could be a career maker for Larry. Larry had been quite the talk of the Tucson legal community since getting an acquittal against the great Rick Bay in State v. Rogers.

Langer had three conference rooms set up. The large conference room would be where they started. He would introduce everyone; explain the process to the clients, and the rules of mediation to the lawyers. They would then split out.

Each side would have their own conference room to hang out in. Langer would shuttle from room-to-room, acting as a messenger and a negotiator.

Galaxy and its crowd of lawyers and number crunchers would stay in the large conference room.

The Newmans, Larry, and Branch would take the second conference room.

Alan Gimble and his client, Ed Allison, would take the third conference room. Allison and the Newmans had competing interests. Galaxy wasn't going to let Allison know what they were offering the Newmans. Allison only got to come to this party because the cases were consolidated and Gimble had filed a motion to consolidate the settlement conferences as well. The judge had granted his motion, and ordered all of the parties to include him in the process.

The office was arranged to keep people away from each other, but allow Langer easy access from room-to-room. The walls were filled with soundproofing material, and the doors were thick and tight, so confidentiality would be maintained.

The coffee was ready, the doughnuts were on the kitchen table, and the order-out lunch menus were on the conference tables, as they were sure to work through lunch. Langer had learned that it was never wise to take a lunch-break in the middle of mediation. It broke the momentum of the negotiations. It gave people too much time to reflect, and think about what was going on, and it gave them an opportunity to talk to each other without using Langer as the communication conduit. He didn't use bright lights and rubber hoses, but he had his methods down to a science. He was confident this case would settle today.

The parties would share his five hundred dollar-per-hour fee equally. There would be no favoritism. His one goal was to get the job done. If Galaxy walked out thinking it had paid too much, and the Newmans and Allison walked out thinking Galaxy had not paid enough, then it would have been a successful day.

Larry, Branch, and the Newmans were the first to arrive. They came in separate cars. The Newmans arrived in their Buick; Larry and Branch pulled up in Larry's Camry. Gimble and his client were next. They arrived in Gimble's stupid "Bathtub-Porsche" replicar. The Galaxy entourage was fashionably late. They arrived in a new, black Commander. It was the only Galaxy product seen in the parking lot that morning. Langer had to smile at that one.

Being late was a power statement. Being early signaled anxiousness. Galaxy was signaling power by showing up late, and making everyone wonder if they were going to show up at all. Langer's secretary ushered everyone into the large conference room as they arrived. Langer made sure to time his entrance after everyone had been assembled into the conference room. He was sure Peterson and Galaxy would be seated at the end of the large table with Tom Galaxy at the head of the table, and Peterson beside him. This was another power statement. He was right. Peterson and Galaxy occupied the exact spots Sam had imagined they would.

Langer established his power by taking the seat at the other end of the table. He welcomed everyone, and asked each of them to go around the table and introduce themselves to each other. He purposely looked at Larry first and signaled him to start the process. Based on the seating arrangement, that would put Tom Galaxy in the middle of everyone else in the room. Everyone would be on equal ground. Once that was done, he took over by making a preliminary statement.

"Good morning. My name is Sam Langer. I will be your mediator today. We have gathered here because all of you have expressed an interest in resolving this case short of a trial.

"I have read your position statements including the portions of depositions you have supplied me. I assure you I am thoroughly familiar with your respective positions.

"Mr. and Mrs. Newman, I am sure I speak for all of us here when I offer condolences on the death of your children. It is a tragedy of immense proportions. Mr. Allison, all of us regret that you were injured as well.

"I am a retired Superior Court Judge. I spent fifteen years on the bench, and during that time, I watched a lot of surprising jury verdicts come in. I watched people lose who should have won. I watched people win who should have lost. I saw people awarded a lot of money for fairly trivial claims, and I saw others with significant claims be awarded very little. The one thing I never saw was somebody lose a negotiated settlement.

"As of today, you still have control of how this case can be resolved. Once you walk into a courtroom and choose a jury, you trust the outcome of the case to eight people you know very little about. In Arizona, only eight, not twelve jurors decide civil cases. Only six of the eight jurors have to agree to reach a verdict. I encourage you to be flexible today. I encourage you to reflect on what could happen if we are not successful today, and this case goes to trial. In that event, someone will probably be very disappointed with the result.

"We will split into three rooms. The defendant can remain in this room. Mr. Gimble, you and Mr. Allison can take the room down the hall marked conference room two. Mr. Ross, you and your clients, and Mr. Branch, can take the conference room to my right near the front door.

"Mr. Gimble, and Mr. Ross, please be prepared to give me an opening number in a few minutes. I want to spend some time with the group from Galaxy. I intend to get an opening number from them for both cases.

"We will negotiate until we run out of room to negotiate. I want to emphasize that we are here to resolve this case. I expect everyone to act in good faith to accomplish that goal.

"We have coffee and doughnuts in the kitchen. There are soft drinks in the refrigerator. Please make yourselves at home. The bathrooms are at the end of the hall to my left. If we need to, we can order in lunch from the menus I have on the table. Are there any questions?"

Everyone looked around the room at each other and shook their heads no.

"Very well, then. Let's get started. Mr. Ross, Mr. Gimble, please escort your clients to your assigned conference room. I'll be with you in fifteen minutes or so."

The chairs squeaked, and the papers shuffled as the two plaintiff parties prepared to leave the room. The Galaxy people stayed behind. After the door was closed, Langer addressed Tom Galaxy directly.

"Mr. Galaxy, welcome to Tucson. I am pleased that you have chosen to participate personally in this process. I have been following the caliper spring issue in the news. I have read the plaintiffs' material. I am sure you are aware that Mr. Branch is a very worthy adversary. Do you have an opening number to take to the plaintiffs?"

Galaxy looked uncomfortable being addressed personally by this man that he had just met. Lawyers were a presumptuous lot. Personally, he didn't care for them as a group, but relied on Peterson and his firm heavily to pull the strings necessary to minimize the damage in situations like this. He had expected Peterson to do the talking, but since he had been addressed personally, he answered personally. He was used to being in charge.

"I am confident in our ability to defend these cases. As you know, the verdict from Texas is being appealed. Galaxy Motor Company prides itself on its record of consumer safety. We recognize that publicity on this issue is not good for the company, and we are anxious to settle this case. We will make no admission of wrongdoing, and we will not issue an apology to the Newmans, or anyone else. That part is non-negotiable. We have already offered the Newmans thirty million dollars to settle this claim by way of an offer of judgment. We did this early on. You need to advise them of their exposure to costs should they lose this case."

Langer considered these comments before he replied. Galaxy had come out roaring, defending his company, and establishing an inflexible position on two points that the plaintiffs were adamant about: an admission of wrongdoing, and an apology.

He looked at Peterson. "Mr. Peterson, I'm sure you have advised Mr. Galaxy that the plaintiffs are very interested in an admission of wrongdoing, and an apology from Mr. Galaxy, himself. If these issues are truly non-negotiable, I'm wondering why we are even here. You have known this since taking the plaintiffs' depositions, and since they turned down your thirty-million-dollar offer. Some things are more important to people than money. I would suggest you take a few minutes to discuss this further with Mr. Galaxy."

Peterson took the lead. "I respect Mr. Galaxy's position. However, all things are negotiable. We would like to start by offering the Newmans fifty million dollars. As an incentive, we will also set up an endowed scholarship fund at the St. James School in the sum of two million dollars to offer tuition scholarships to underprivileged children who have the academic ability, but lack the financial resources to attend St. James. This will be a perpetual way of memorializing the Newman children. The fund will be called the Thomas and Timothy Newman Scholarship Endowment Fund. Galaxy Motor Company will expect no recognition from anyone for this gift to the school."

Galaxy smiled. Peterson looked pleased with himself for tossing out another carrot and at the same time backing up his employer. The Galaxy account was vital to Peterson's law firm. He certainly didn't want to piss off the boss.

Langer replied, "Let's not forget Mr. Allison. What is your position on his claim?"

Galaxy started to reply.

Peterson nudged his foot from under the table as a signal to shut up. He might be the chairman of the board, but he could be a stubborn, stupid son of bitch at times. His comments had already caused a problem.

Peterson and Galaxy had agreed before entering the room that Peterson would do the talking, and Galaxy would do the listening. This wasn't a board of directors meeting for Christ's sake! These people weren't here to listen to Tom Galaxy's words of wisdom, and to kiss his ass because his last name was Galaxy.

Peterson spoke up: "We don't regard Allison's claim as having much value. He has recovered well from his injuries. We are prepared to offer him one hundred twenty-five thousand dollars."

Langer thought that was interesting. One hundred twenty-five thousand dollars for a man who was injured badly in the same accident, and had close to sixty-five thousand dollars in medical bills and an ugly scar on his shoulder that he would have for the rest of his life. Langer suspected that Peterson and Galaxy weren't concerned with Gimble's ability to carry the day by himself; they were hopeful that settling out with the Newmans, would force Gimble to take the bone that was offered, or face the prospect of going to trial by himself without Branch and Ross to help out with the experts and the costs.

If Gimble lost, Galaxy would have a caliper spring win to crow about. That would scare off a lot of new cases. Of course that was the plan. Galaxy was pretty transparent about it. This was not a new or novel strategy. Langer had seen it used many times before. Divide and conquer was a tried-and-true negotiating tool.

"Mr. Peterson, are you sure the Company is inflexible on the apology and admission of fault issue? You know that is important to the Newmans."

Peterson replied, "As I said, all things are negotiable. Let's see what the response is to our offer. It is a long time to the end of the day. We are just getting started."

"Okay. I'll go talk to the plaintiffs. I'll be back in a few minutes."

Langer left the large conference room thinking that Galaxy was going to have to do better than this. Just last summer they had been hit with a verdict for three hundred fifty nine million for a rollover accident involving a Galaxy Starflight. Of course, it was on appeal, and yes, a large portion of the verdict had been for punitive damages, which were not favored by the Federal Appeals Courts and the Supreme Court specifically.

It didn't do a plaintiff any good to have a verdict that wouldn't hold up on appeal, or might get sent back to the lower court for another trial. That verdict didn't mean a whole lot until all of the appeals were exhausted. This was going to be a day in which he would have to use all of his negotiation skills and talents to get the parties to see eye-to-eye.

He started with Gimble first. Gimble's opening offer for Allison was twenty-five million. Langer told him the opening offer from Galaxy was one hundred twenty-five thousand. Gimble was, of course, outraged. Unspoken was the fact that a fee, plus cost recovery sounded pretty good to a lawyer who had grossed less than one hundred thousand dollars from his practice in each of the last three years, and had netted less than the fee that was on the table at the moment.

Langer told him that his opening offer was too high and that Galaxy had already telegraphed a divide-and-conquer strategy. He reminded Gimble that if the Newmans settled out, Gimble and Allison would be stuck going to trial by themselves. He would have to foot the bill for all the expert witnesses, and he wouldn't have Mitch Branch's ten percent of where Gimble had started.

He moved down the hall to the Newmans.

Mike and Margaret Newman looked very distraught when he entered the room. He gave them the good news first. The offer was fifty million plus another two million for an endowed scholarship fund at St. James in Tom and Tim's names.

Mike spoke first: "Are they going to admit fault and apologize to us publicly?"

Langer looked at Larry. He then looked at Branch. They were both looking at Mike.

Langer spoke slowly: "I'm told that all things are negotiable. I'm also told that Galaxy is not willing to admit fault, or issue an apology, either public, or private, at this time."

Mike spoke again: "Then tell them we have nothing to talk about. If they won't admit fault, and won't apologize, we won't settle. It is that simple."

Larry felt sick to his stomach. How could Mike and Margaret be so inflexible? The only answer was that just as Mitch had assessed when he met them, the money was not the issue to them.

Mitch looked annoyed. He spoke next.

"Mr. Langer, we came here in good faith. Galaxy knows how important an apology and an admission of fault are to Mike and Margaret. Tell Galaxy our offer is five hundred million, two hundred fifty million less than the money they saved by trying to cure this problem with TSBs rather than a recall. Tell them we insist on an apology from Mr. Galaxy himself, in person, and in writing. Tell him we expect an admission of fault. Tell him we expect to be able to publicize this settlement. Tell him these three items are not negotiable with us."

Langer was impressed. Branch was persuasive. He stuck up for his clients. He held his ground. He was confident. He wasn't afraid to fight Galaxy in the courtroom. He had never lost a case against Galaxy, and this wouldn't be his first loss. Cases didn't come any better than this one. He had the perfect clients, the perfect facts, and the perfect emotional pull to make a jury want to punish Galaxy for its outrageous behavior. He had Galaxy on the ropes, and he knew it. Langer thanked them, and said he would convey the offer to Galaxy.

Peterson, Galaxy, and the number crunchers didn't like what they heard. How could these strictly middle-class people from Tucson, Arizona say no to fifty million dollars so easily? That was more money than Galaxy used to net in a year back in the sixty's when the Lightening was introduced.

Peterson had already told Galaxy and his board of directors that these people were trouble. Money was not their motivator. Branch didn't need any more money. The combination could be lethal if put in the hands of the right jury for the Newmans, and the wrong jury for Galaxy. Peterson asked Langer for a few minutes to discuss the offer from the Newmans with his clients.

He agreed and left the room. Langer couldn't hear what was going on in the conference room, but he could hear it was getting loud and angry. A few minutes turned into more than thirty.

Finally, Peterson stuck his head out the door and signaled that they were ready to proceed.

When Langer entered the room, Tom Galaxy looked red-faced, and pissed-off. If he was a poker player, he didn't win very often. Langer could only surmise that Peterson had told Galaxy he needed to reconsider his position on fault and apology.

The number crunchers were sitting with their arms folded across their chests; a typical, "go to hell" body language signal. Peterson was the only one who still looked to be in control. Langer could feel the tension in the room. He broke the ice by speaking first.

"Gentlemen, have you come to an agreement on a response?"

Peterson took the lead: "Please tell the Newmans Mr. Galaxy is prepared to issue a personal apology today. We are working on a written apology and should have the language worked out within the next half hour or so.

"We will also admit to errors in judgment that led to the crash that killed the Newman children. The money offer remains at fifty million.

"Tell Mr. Gimble our offer for Mr. Allison is increased to one hundred seventy-five thousand, and we are quickly running out of room on that claim."

Langer was pleased. Peterson had convinced Mr. Galaxy that he was going to have to swallow his pride and eat a little crow on this one.

It was already after eleven o'clock. Time flew when negotiations were in progress. Langer took a bathroom break and helped himself to a fresh cup of coffee before conveying the next offers to the plaintiffs. He was sure the Newmans would be glad that Galaxy had made a concession on the apology part of the negotiations.

CHAPTER 43

▼

Well, the Newmans weren't pleased.

Mike Newman spoke first after he listened to the latest offer from Galaxy. He was emotional, but effective. "Mr. Langer. We have had a lot of time to think about this. Not just today, but ever since it happened.

"We lost our only children in a crash that never should have happened. It happened because Mr. Galaxy and his corporation were more concerned with the bottom line than they were about our children's lives. They knew people would die because they wouldn't do a recall. Well, two of those people were our only children. This is just unacceptable.

"We are well aware that nothing done here today will bring the children back. They are gone forever. All we can do now is to make sure they will not be forgotten, and to do our best to make sure that the Galaxy Motor Company realizes it can't play with people's lives.

"You tell them our offer stands. We aren't budging."

Langer had a hard time digesting that one. No movement at all? How could that be? Galaxy had just made a huge concession. This was bad. He spoke to Branch.

"Mr. Branch, I understand your clients' passion regarding this case. However, Galaxy has made a huge concession. Surely you have some room for movement."

Branch looked at Langer and said in even tones: "You tell Galaxy that until we see their written apology, and until they are ready to admit fault, not admit to "errors in judgment," there will be no movement from us on any issue."

Langer left the room and went in to see Gimble and Allison. Gimble came down to two million.

Langer went back to the large conference room. Tom Galaxy still looked pissed. He wouldn't like what he was about to hear. Peterson handed him a letter hand-written in draft form.

Dear Mr. and Mrs. Newman:

All of us at Galaxy Motor Company deeply regret the loss of your children. Galaxy Motor Company accepts complete responsibility for this tragic accident. As you are aware, a full recall is in progress to correct the problem that remains in the products still on the road that have not yet been refitted with new parts.

Galaxy Motor Company now realizes that this mechanical problem should have been handled by a full recall, rather than through technical service bulletins to our dealers. Had we realized the magnitude of the potential losses to you, and others, a recall would have been implemented.

Please accept my sincerest apology for your loss.

Sincerely,

Thomas C. Galaxy

Chairman, Board of Directors,

Galaxy Motor Company

Langer raised his eyebrows and looked over at Tom Galaxy. Galaxy had gotten up to look out the window at the parking lot. He was trying to act like he didn't care. Langer was sure he cared deeply.

He started by telling Peterson that Gimble and Allison had come down to two million. He then told Peterson that he was sure that the Newmans would negotiate on the money now that Galaxy had made the apology and admission of fault concessions.

The number crunchers had brought Galaxy Motor Company letterhead. Langer gave it to his secretary, and she began preparing the letter. She came in and presented it to him. He looked it over. It was perfectly done. There were no misspellings, and the spacing was good. He handed it to Peterson. Peterson looked it over, and handed it to Galaxy.

Galaxy didn't even read it. He produced a Mont Blanc pen from his coat, signed it, handed it to Langer and said, "We'll need at least two copies of this. You cannot give possession of this to the Newmans until we have a deal. The final point is the money. We are prepared to pay three hundred million. We will still fund the endowed scholarship. The Newmans can have their publicity. We won't try to control it; we will not participate in it, or try to refute it in any way. That is where we stop. Even Galaxy has its limits. There will be no further offers."

Langer spoke to Peterson: "And what do I tell Mr. Gimble and Mr. Allison?"

"You tell him our final offer on his claim is three hundred thousand. It is a fair amount for the injury his client suffered, and I'm sure he can figure out that it divides easily by three. Tell them that is our final offer."

Langer was smart. He knew how to present offers. He had his secretary prepare a written settlement agreement that set out all of the specifics and included that the settlement would be funded within thirty days. He had one prepared for Gimble and Allison, and one for the Newmans. He made sure to add a signature line for all the lawyers, all the clients and Tom Galaxy.

Gimble and Allison didn't hesitate. They signed, and were out the door before Galaxy could change its mind. Gimble was already doing mental calculations on which credit card bills he would pay off first, and if he would have enough money left over to buy a real car. He was pretty weary of his topless replicar. The novelty was long gone.

Langer entered the conference room where the Newmans were staring out the window at the Catalina Mountains. Without saying a word, he first handed the letter of apology to Mitch. When Mitch had finished reading it, he handed him the settlement agreement. Peterson and Galaxy had already signed it. When Mitch had finished reading the settlement agreement, Langer spoke.

"I have just handed Mr. Branch a letter of apology that I watched Mr. Galaxy sign. I have also handed him a settlement agreement that Mr. Peterson and Mr. Galaxy have also signed. I am told this is their final offer. I am also told that if you accept this offer, Mr. Galaxy is prepared to come into this room and issue a personal apology to Mike and Margaret, if they are still interested in that. I cannot let you have possession of the letter of apology until the settlement agreement is signed.

"You will notice that there is nothing in the settlement agreement about confidentiality. That means the settlement is not confidential. There is no restriction of any kind on reporting this settlement to the media, or going on the talk-show circuit, if that is what Mr. and Mrs. Newman want to do.

"Galaxy has accepted full responsibility for the series of events that led to Tom and Tim's death. They have apologized in writing. Mr. Galaxy will apologize in person. They have agreed to pay three hundred million to settle the claim, and they have agreed to set up the endowment fund at St. James in Tom and Tim's name as previously offered. Galaxy expects to receive no recognition of any kind for establishing this fund.

"This is a good settlement. It gives you the admission of fault and the apology you have been seeking, it is a huge sum of money, and there will be an endowment fund established at St. James that will carry your children's names in perpetuity. I highly recommend you accept this offer. I believe they are serious when they say this is the final offer they will make on this case."

Mike and Margaret looked stunned. They had wanted this so bad for so long, they couldn't believe what they were hearing. Mike walked over to Mitch and took the apology letter and the settlement agreement from him. He and Margaret sat down at the conference table and began reading it. When they were done, Mike asked Mitch, "Does this mean what it says? Can we count on this?"

Mitch nodded his head. "Yes, you can count on this. It is an enforceable contract. There are no contingencies. It is everything you have asked for and more. The endowment fund is a bonus."

Larry was in a daze. Three hundred million dollars was almost too much money to comprehend. The Newmans would have to say "yes" to this one. They did. They also wanted Tom Galaxy to come in and apologize.

Galaxy entered the room hesitantly. He issued a sincere, heart-felt apology. He told Mike and Margaret that he had children, couldn't imagine what it would be like to lose one of them, and certainly couldn't imagine what it would be like to lose two of them. He even said he was sorry that he let a business decision get in the way of good sense. He said this had been a learning experience, and that he would make sure Galaxy never repeated its behavior by making a similar mistake in the future.

Mike and Margaret were satisfied with the apology.

Langer made copies of the apology letter for Galaxy and copies of the settlement agreement for them as well. He let the Newmans keep the originals, and kept a copy for his own files as well. He planned to frame his copy of the settlement agreement to use as a display to his effectiveness as a mediator. This was by far the largest settlement he had ever negotiated. It truly had been a good day.

Galaxy left feeling it had paid too much, and had made concessions it didn't want to make. The Newmans had gotten everything they had asked for, and more. Even Allison's settlement had been a fair one. Days like this didn't come along too often. He planned to savor the moment.

Mike and Margaret couldn't stop hugging Larry and Mitch and thanking them for the wonderful job they had done. They kept reading the apology letter over and over. The words never changed. It was a full apology and a full acceptance of responsibility. The letter meant more to them than the three hundred million. Finally, they ran out of "Thank You's" and left to go home.

Larry and Mitch called the local TV stations to report the settlement. Mitch called his office and had his media advisor start arranging for Mike and Margaret to make appearances on *Today* and *Good Morning America*. They faxed a copy of the settlement agreement to the local newspaper and left numbers for the reporter to call them. This was big.

Mike and Margaret would also need a financial advisor. Mitch started getting that set up as well.

He then turned to Larry. "Larry, last week Brad King told me he plans to retire next April when he turns seventy. His corner office will be available. I would like to save it for you. You have impressed me every step of the way. From the first phone call we had until just a few minutes ago, you played every card in your hand just right. Please consider bringing your family to Texas. I promise to make it worth your while."

Larry hadn't seen this one coming. He would have to talk to Maggie about this. They loved Tucson. Leaving would be hard on everyone. Yet the opportunity was great. Larry was being offered a partnership with Mitchell Branch, one of America's premier lawyers. The best he could stammer out was, "Thanks, Mitch, that's very generous of you. I'm flattered. I'll talk to Maggie about it. That would be a big move for us. Can I have some time to think about it?"

Mitch hadn't expected an answer on the spot. "Larry, you take all the time you need. It's a long time between now and April. I know this is a big decision. Talk to me again after Thanksgiving, unless you make up your mind sooner. In the meantime, we still have the Simmons case to work on. We'll be seeing each other pretty regular."

As he was taking Mitch to the airport later that afternoon, Larry felt like he was in a fog. After he dropped Mitch off, he called Maggie on the cell phone and told her the unbelievable good news of the settlement. He decided to tell her about Mitch's offer in person when he got home.

James Brown started singing, "I Feel Good" just as Larry pulled into his garage. Larry let James finish the song before he turned the car off and went into the house. Larry felt good too. Days like today didn't happen very often in a person's life—if ever.

Epilogue

▼

Unlike most couples that lose their children, the Newmans stayed together. They donated another ten million dollars to the scholarship fund in their children's name that Galaxy had created.

Margaret took a job at St. James as the Director of Development and Scholarships. She managed the money in the scholarship fund, and had a great deal to do with choosing the scholarship recipients.

Mike quit his job at Raytheon Missile Systems and started a foundation to aid research into helping make cars safer for children. All of the major manufacturers contributed to it.

They realized that safer cars meant fewer lawsuits and fewer claims to pay out. He soon had full-time engineers working on better door latches, better centers of gravity, recessed handles and knobs that would minimize injuries, and had the satisfaction of knowing he was doing something positive.

They had been guests on all of the talk shows and news magazines. They had been featured on the cover of *Newsweek*. As time went on, the wounds began to heal.

Tom, Cindy, and the kids moved to Albuquerque. Tom became a Toyota dealer in a major market. His success continued.

Cindy reveled in being a stay at home mom and became involved in all of the kids' school and after-school events. Tom became president of the Albuquerque New Car Dealer's Association and set new standards for dealer ethics, and customer service. The Rogers family became well known in the Albuquerque business and social circles.

Larry and Maggie stayed in Tucson. Maggie's extended family was there and they didn't want the kids to be away from their cousins, aunts, uncles, and grandparents. They did buy a beach house in La Jolla, and a new home in La Paloma, Tucson's premier gated foothills community. Larry Jr. and Leann were enrolled in the best private school Tucson had to offer.

Larry and Mitch settled the Simmons case for another three hundred million. The court approved the settlement, and approved the one hundred twenty million dollar legal fee. The settlement was structured over time, and provided an annuity for Walter that he could never outlive. He would have the best of care and his life would be as comfortable as possible.

Larry bought the office that he had rented for years. It was ideally located, and suited his purposes well. He took in Bill Wilson as a partner so he would have some coverage while he was in La Jolla for weeks at a time during the summer.

He and Bill took the cases they wanted, and sent out the rest. Personal injury, medical malpractice, and products liability were all they handled. Mitch would still help out from time-to-time on the cases they felt they couldn't or shouldn't be doing alone. Mitch was disappointed Larry had declined to come to Dallas, but he understood the decision.

Julio and Oscar continued to control the prison drug trade. They were feared and respected by all of the inmates. In the prison hierarchy, they were the top dogs. They dreamed of escaping one day and setting up shop in Mexico. The money in their Mexican bank accounts would be waiting for them.

Maria continued to scrub toilets.

Gimble developed a gambling problem, and spent way too much time in the Indian Casinos. Soon, he was "borrowing" money from his client trust fund.

He was charged with and convicted of embezzlement, was disbarred, and filed for bankruptcy. He spent a year in the Pima County Jail on a work release program, and was on supervised probation for two years after that. He planned to reapply for admission to the State Bar once he "rehabilitated" himself. Alan wasn't one to go away quietly.

Life went on in Tucson. It was still too hot in the summer, it never rained often enough, the streets were rough, and the traffic was congested.

There were still about eighty homicides a year. It kept Rick Bay and Steve McNair very busy.